HER DYING SECRET

BOOKS BY LISA REGAN

HER DYING SECRET

LISA REGAN

bookouture

Published by Bookouture in 2024

An imprint of Storyfire Ltd.
Carmelite House
50 Victoria Embankment
London EC4Y 0DZ

www.bookouture.com

ISBN: 978-1-83525-472-1
eBook ISBN: 978-1-83525-471-4

For Marilyn House, who showed me what fierce, unapologetic independence looks like.

ONE

When he comes back, he is covered in blood. I try not to act scared because he always says there's nothing to be afraid of as long as we're together. But he lies. He still treats me like a baby, like I don't know what he did. Like I don't know what anything means. His hands shake as he washes away the blood. So much blood. I don't ask whose blood because I am afraid of the answer. My heart feels heavy and sad.

"It's okay," he tells me.

"No, it's not. What did you do?"

He doesn't answer. There's blood on his shirt, too. His pants.

"You ruin everything!" I yell at him.

He keeps rinsing and rinsing. The water turns light red like the crayon I use to draw my flower.

"I hate you!"

With a sigh, he stops washing. "I know you don't understand but I did what had to be done. To protect us. If they find you, they'll take you. They'll kill me."

I almost shout that I wish they would kill him. He always says he'll protect me. He'll do anything to protect me.

But who will protect me from him?

TWO

Josie Quinn's kitchen looked like the scene of a massacre. Thick red liquid oozed into the grout between the kitchen tiles. Splatters had formed an intricate pattern across her kitchen cabinets. Scarlet fluid dripped from the knobs of the drawers and slashed across the white door of the refrigerator. Something wet landed in Josie's hair. She reached up, using an index finger to probe her black locks. It came away red.

"You've got to be kidding me," she muttered to herself.

How had it gotten onto the ceiling?

Scratching sounded at the back door.

"Just a minute," she called.

Her Boston terrier, Trout, whined when she didn't open the door for him precisely two seconds after his first scratch. She ignored his plea. The last thing she needed was the dog tracking the red mess all over the house. Another droplet splashed onto her forehead. This time, a stream of expletives left her mouth, rising in volume as she moved out of dripping range. Outside, Trout started barking. From elsewhere in the house, she could hear her husband, Noah Fraley, moving around. He'd taken charge of cleaning the living room.

There would be no time to clean up the mess before he came into the kitchen. The thought had barely crossed her mind when she heard his footsteps approaching, likely drawn by Trout's increasingly agitated barks.

Noah appeared in the doorway. "What's going— Holy shi—"

Josie turned to face him, grimacing. "I'm sorry."

Noah took in the room, his eyes widening as he noticed the spatter on the ceiling. "Is that—"

"Yes." Josie sighed. "It's spaghetti sauce. No, it's not hot. I never even made it to the stove. I opened the jar and dumped it into the pot. I was on my way to the stove and the pot just..."

"You dropped it."

"It slipped out of my hand!"

Noah looked toward the back door where Trout now stood, his paws pressed against the screen, watching them with the kind of intensity that he normally only reserved for treats. "Just a minute, buddy," Noah said.

With a sigh, Trout spun three times and lay down on the doormat.

"How come he always listens to you but not me?" Josie complained.

Noah grinned. "Don't change the subject. Heating up the sauce is like the easiest part of making spaghetti."

Josie put a hand on her hip. "Oh really? Did you or did you not overcook pasta just last week?"

He shrugged. "Well, yeah, but it didn't go quite..." his eyes panned the room again, "this badly."

Josie tried to tamp down her annoyance. A corner of Noah's mouth twitched, and she knew he was about to laugh.

She held up a hand. "Don't. Don't even think about laughing at this."

Carefully, he stepped over a particularly elaborate splatter along the floor and walked over to her. He touched her hair and came away with a smudge of sauce on his index finger, which he licked clean. "It's not that bad."

Josie swatted his arm. "It is that bad! Look at this place."

"I've seen worse at crime scenes." He leaned closer, one hand pushing her hair from her shoulder. "You have a little bit..." She felt his mouth against her neck. In spite of herself, a shiver of delight ran down her spine. She braced her hands against his chest. "Noah."

His arms snaked around her waist, pulling her closer to him. As always, her body responded instantly to him. The kitchen suddenly felt extremely hot. He trailed kisses from under her ear to where her collarbone met her throat. "I prefer whipped cream," he said against her skin. "But I can make spaghetti sauce work."

Heat rose to her cheeks. "Don't make this sexy. This isn't sexy."

His hands roamed up and down her back. Now his mouth was at the hollow of her throat. "Just give me a chance."

Gently, Josie pushed against him. He lifted his head to meet her gaze. His hazel eyes flickered with playfulness, and again she had to remind her traitorous body that they had things to do —other than what her mind was already envisioning. "I'm serious. We need to get this cleaned up. This will set us behind."

He kept her body flush against his but used one hand to brush a stray hair behind her ear. His expression turned serious. "The case manager won't be here until tomorrow at ten. We have plenty of time. Besides, the main criteria is that the house is safe for a baby. It's okay if it looks lived-in, remember?"

He was right, of course. Josie was confident about their safety measures, and the house was relatively clean to begin with since they were hardly ever home. They both worked for their local police department. Noah was a lieutenant and Josie was a detective. Both of them were part of the four-person investigative team. The city of Denton was not a major metropolitan area, ensconced as it was in a valley bisected by a branch of the Susquehanna River and nestled among some of Central Pennsylvania's most beautiful mountains. Still, it saw its fair share of crime. Its population had been steadily rising in the last several years so their department was busier than ever.

Josie felt a stab of worry at the thought of their schedules. If they ever hoped to adopt a child, they'd have to be home to do it. Assuming that the case manager from the adoption agency they'd chosen would approve them to do so. They'd decided to try to have a baby last year but when they couldn't conceive, Josie underwent extensive testing only to find out that her chances of having a baby were slim to none. Her fertility issues were not easily remedied and even if she endured surgery and fertility treatment, she still might never conceive. They'd decided instead to look into adoption.

They'd done weeks of extensive research into the process and vetted licensed adoption agencies until they found one they'd felt comfortable with. Then they had gone through a lengthy intake process, which included a head-spinning amount of paperwork. Financial information, proof of insurance, medical records, even their dog's medical records—and that was just the tip of the iceberg. Josie had had to disclose the child-hood abuse she had endured at the hands of a woman who'd posed as her mother as well as the details of her ongoing mental health treatment.

They'd had to complete the requisite hours of training and take classes on multiple topics like how to talk to your child about adoption; how to talk with birth parents; how to care for a baby; and more. Josie had felt overwhelmed at first but the classes were a blessing, putting her more at ease and helping her feel more prepared for what was to come. For her, more infor-mation was always better. It always helped alleviate anxiety. The next step in the application process was a home study by their case manager at the agency. The very thought of it had

Josie's nerves frayed. It had taken months just to get to this point and it was the culmination of all their efforts thus far. The home study was crucial to getting approved to adopt.

"Hey." Noah brushed his fingers through her hair, looking for more sauce, no doubt. "What is it?"

"No one is ever going to give us a child if we can't even cook a meal."

Their lack of culinary skills was legendary among their friends. Noah was passable but Josie was downright terrible. The sauce massacre was tame compared to her usual kitchen catastrophes. They relied heavily on takeout and the kindness of their best friend, Misty DeRossi, who was a masterful cook. She brought them meals two or three times a week. It was her way of thanking them for being such a huge part of her son's life. Harris was almost eight now. Josie's late first husband Ray had become involved with Misty after he and Josie separated. After Ray's death, Misty gave birth to Harris. Josie had initially detested Misty, letting her jealousy get the best of her. Then she held Harris for the first time and felt a surge of love so strong, she knew she'd do anything to protect him and be part of his life. Misty had extended Josie the grace that Josie had been too emotionally insecure to give her, and now they were close friends. Found family.

"We already had to disclose that our culinary skills need work," Noah said, breaking through her thoughts. "It's not like we have to cook a meal for our case manager tomorrow. At least, I don't think so."

Josie took a step back from him. "But we *can't* cook! How are we supposed to feed a child when we can't even cook for ourselves? I mean sure, there's formula and baby food when they're infants, but what happens when they get older?"

"We'll ask Misty to teach us," Noah said easily. "If she gets too frustrated with us, then we'll take a cooking class together."

"With our schedules?" Josie demanded. Part of the home

study involved in-depth interviews with the case manager.
Their crazy work schedules would come up and neither of them
was about to lie as to just how much time they devoted to work.

Josie could feel her face burning but not with desire this
time. She threw her hands in the air and let them fall back to
her sides. Trout must have heard her voice go up an octave
because he was standing with his paws pressed into the screen
again, watching her closely. He whimpered this time, the sound
mournful instead of demanding. He had always been uncannily
in tune with her feelings, and he didn't like it when she was
upset.

"You're worried about how our work schedules will affect
our application for adoption again?"

"Of course I am!"

Noah snagged one of her hands and held it tightly. His skin
was warm and dry. This time, his touch sent a wave of comfort
through her. Gone was his earlier playfulness. Now his eyes
were filled with compassion and sympathy. "Josie, we talked
about all of this. We will work it out. We managed to make time
for all the classes, didn't we? Maybe we'll need to make adjustments. Sacrifices. Plenty of couples both work full-time and
manage to raise families."

"But—"

He squeezed her hand. "But we won't know until we try.
Come on, I'll help you clean this up and then we'll get the rest
of the house ready. Also, let's just order pizza."

Josie felt some of her anxiety ebb. Smiling, she said, "That
sounds good."

From the door, Trout barked. He loved pizza crust.

An hour later, little remained of the pizza, and they were
still working on the kitchen. Noah stood on a ladder, using a
cloth to wipe at the spots on the ceiling. Trout sniffed every
square inch of the room, occasionally licking a speck on the floor
that Josie had missed.

Her cell phone rang. She walked over to the kitchen table and glanced down at the screen. Discomfort turned the slice of pizza she'd just eaten into a stone, heavy in her stomach. A generic outline of a man showed up where the contact's photo was supposed to be. Josie hadn't added a photo for their newest team member because she didn't want to see his face any more than she absolutely had to. But she knew it was him because the word *Douchebag* appeared over the top of the non-photo. One day, after a particularly irritating shift with him, she'd saved him in her contacts under that name.

"Who is it?" said Noah.

Josie sighed. She swiped the red icon to decline the call. "It's Turner."

"Great." Noah sounded anything but thrilled.

Over a year ago, they'd lost a beloved member of their investigative team, Detective Finn Mettner. He'd been shot and killed in the line of duty. Josie had held his hand while he bled out. She had been so deeply affected by Mettner's death that she'd even gone on a retreat to help deal with some of her trauma. That hadn't gone as expected at all. Then, upon her return, she met the department's new hire, Detective Kyle Turner.

He wasn't a good fit.

He was arrogant and rude. He took forever to finish reports and he frequently passed off more difficult cases to the rest of them instead of handling them himself. He also disappeared for hours at a time during his shifts with little or no explanation as to where he went or what he was doing. Their other detective, Gretchen Palmer, who had more experience than Josie and Noah combined, detested him the most. She frequently called him lazy, and Josie couldn't disagree. She still wasn't sure why he'd been hired in the first place. Their Chief had had nearly a hundred applicants for the position.

Her phone rang a second time, the word *Douchebag* floating across the screen once more.

Noah said, "Don't answer it."

"But why is he trying to get in touch with me? I'm not on call."

Noah dabbed at what remained of the spaghetti sauce stain on their white ceiling. "Maybe he has a question about something."

Josie sent the call to voicemail again, irritation rising in her throat like acid reflux. "Then he can send a text message like a normal person."

She went back to scrubbing the cabinets. A moment later, her phone chirped.

"There's your text," Noah muttered.

With a groan, Josie walked back to the table and picked up her phone. Turner had texted two words in all caps: *PICK UP*.

He wasn't going to stop until she spoke to him. With another sigh, she stabbed the call button under his name. The phone rang eight times. A headache started to pulse in her temples. She was about to hang up when he finally answered. "Quinn, I need your help."

"Gretchen's on call today."

"I know. She's busy with a shooting. I've got a bank robbery in the shithole part of town. There's some big accident out on Prout Road. The middle of damn nowhere according to Google Maps. Dispatch asked for a detective but I'm fresh out. Can you come in?"

She felt Noah's presence behind her. He'd come down from the ladder and now leaned in toward her shoulder, listening to the conversation.

There was only one reason the uniformed officers would need a detective at a motor vehicle accident. Josie said, "There was a fatality?"

"That's what I heard."

Noah groaned softly and Josie knew what he was thinking. Beyond the sad reality that someone had lost their life, the paperwork would take hours.

"Did the Chief authorize me to come in? Have you talked with him about this?"

Having served as interim chief at one point, Josie knew that one of the most pressing things about the job was the constant worry about going over budget.

"He's MIA. Look, it's not like this will cost the department extra. You come in and he'll give you your paid time off another day. Easy-peasy."

He was so cavalier about everything, although he had a point. They could cover all the bases without pissing off Chief Chitwood, which Josie was all for.

"Have you called anyone from the Fatal Accident Reconstruction Team? You'll need one of their officers. They're in the station directory. Labenberg is probably on. She works afternoons."

Turner snickered. "You want me to call the FART?"

How old was this guy?

Ignoring him, Josie asked, "Can't you go over to the scene once you're finished with your bank robbery?"

"Is Fraley there? Maybe he can come in."

Noah blew out a breath, sending a lock of her hair fluttering. "I'll go in."

"No," Josie said. "You're much faster at housework than me. I've done a lot of MVAs with fatalities. It's only noon. I'll be home before you go to bed."

"Quinn?" said Turner. "What did you say?"

Noah laughed. "You just don't want to clean up anymore spaghetti sauce."

"Text me the precise location," Josie said into the phone. "I'll be there in twenty."

THREE

A tight knot of anxiety twisted in Josie's stomach as she drove to the location Turner had texted her. She knew the road. It was a two-lane strip of asphalt that spider-legged into the mountains northwest of Denton. As it wound out of the more densely populated part of the city, foliage closed in on either side. April had brought lots of rain and now, in May, the trees were lush and wild, branches forming a canopy over the road. Josie put down her window to take in some of the fresh air. She hated fatalities of any kind, and she was not looking forward to notifying the family of the accident victim. She'd have to shatter someone's entire life today and then smile and be genial tomorrow morning when the case manager came to their house for the home study. As usual, the only way to get through a tough shift on this job was to compartmentalize like it was an Olympic sport.

The road slowly inclined and the shade of the trees fell away. On either side, untouched tracts of grass and brush spread, pushing the forest back. She passed a small farm, black cows lumbering across a green field. The smell of manure suffused the air. Putting the window back up, Josie punched her gas pedal, speeding away. There was an occasional residence sitting a few acres back from the road but for the most part there wasn't much out this way, not for miles. As she crested a hill, she saw emergency lights strobing red and blue. The road had been closed except for where patrol officers stood alongside the southbound shoulder, ready to guide any vehicles past the cluster of police cars and ambulances should anyone happen to be driving along. A fire truck slanted across both lanes. Josie had to pull around it to get the full picture of what had happened.

On the northbound side of the road, heading out of Denton, stood a souped-up Ford F-150 pickup truck. Its back was angled toward the shoulder. The driver's side door hung open. Yellow caution tape formed a perimeter around it. Two uniformed officers stood sentry along the border of the scene, ensuring no one crossed the tape without authorization. As Josie parked her vehicle and got out, a prickle of apprehension crawled up the back of her neck. The Denton police Evidence Response Team's SUV was parked nearby, its hatch open. Beside that was the small white pickup truck that belonged to their county medical examiner, Dr. Anya Feist.

The uniformed officers nodded at Josie in greeting as she moved past them. The front end of the Ford had turned a tiny blue Hyundai sedan into a facsimile of a crushed soda can. Josie tried not to visibly wince at the destruction. Officer Hummel and his ERT techs moved methodically through the scene, dressed in white Tyvek suits, complete with skull caps and booties. Hummel, the head of their ERT, stood near the passenger's seat of the sedan, scribbling on a clipboard. Dr. Feist, also garbed in a Tyvek suit, lingered behind him, her crime scene bag in hand.

One of the uniformed officers, Brennan, beckoned Josie. He, too, had a clipboard in hand to record every person who entered and left the scene. "Thought Turner and Palmer were on today," he said.

Josie sighed. "So did I." She gestured toward the sedan. "The car crossed the lines directly into the path of the F-150. The truck couldn't stop in time. What else do you have?"

Brennan quirked a brow. "How can you tell all that?"

"The truck is on the northbound side. It was headed away from Denton. Skid marks behind it where it tried to stop abruptly. The sedan was headed back to the city and crossed over. That's why it's facing south but not in the southbound lane. The truck is bigger, taller. The crash probably had little impact on its cab. Truck driver is fine?"

"He's upset but yeah, physically he's fine."

"What's his name?"

"Nolan Waters. Forty-seven. No warrants and no priors. Lives in Denton. Breathalyzer test was clean. He passed the field sobriety test with flying colors, and he's agreed to be transported to the hospital to have his blood tested for illegal substances." Brennan used his pen to point toward a cruiser parked in the southbound lane. "He said he was driving along, saw the car coming toward him. There were no other vehicles on the road in either direction. Everything seemed fine and then at the last minute, the car swerved directly in front of him. Bam!"

"No sign of a struggle inside the car before it crossed in front of him?" Josie asked.

"Not that he could see. He has no idea what happened or why the car came into his lane of traffic. Said it happened in a millisecond."

The things that changed lives irrevocably often did happen in milliseconds. Blink and you'd miss it. "The fatality was someone in the car, then."

"Yeah. The sedan is registered to a woman called Mira Summers. Thirty-seven. She also lives in Denton. No warrants, no priors. Her purse was in the car. ID matches up, so we know that she was driving."

"How many people were in the car?"

"Two adult females."

Josie saw the deflated driver's side airbag peeking out from the destroyed windshield of the sedan. Behind it was an empty seat. Scanning the scene, she saw two ambulances. One for Mira Summers and one to transport the fatality to the morgue. "Is Summers badly injured?"

"She was disoriented when we arrived and quickly lapsed into unconsciousness," said Brennan. "EMTs have been trying to rouse her. They're going to take her to the hospital now, I think. I had Dougherty go to her residence to see if anyone else lives with her—family or partner—just in case things go south for her."

"That's good." Josie glanced over at the ambulances again, noticing activity in the back of one of them. "I'll check with the EMTs before they take her. The passenger is deceased?"

"Yeah." Brennan used the tip of his pen to scratch at the bridge of his nose. Josie could tell by the way he grimaced that there was something she hadn't deduced. "But not from the car accident."

The knot of anxiety in Josie's stomach tightened. "Are you saying we've got a homicide?"

"See for yourself."

FOUR

Josie wanted to make a beeline for the wreckage but knew that the ambulance carrying Mira Summers would not be there much longer. She wanted to get eyes on the driver before she was transported to the hospital. Mira Summers was strapped to a gurney, a cervical collar stabilizing her neck and head. Her feet came almost to the edge, which meant she was nearly six feet tall. Mud crusted along the bottoms of her knee-high black boots. Two EMTs, one on each side, leaned over her upper body. One of them started an IV in her hand while the other adjusted the oxygen mask covering her mouth. A blue emesis bag sat in her lap, the odor of vomit wafting from it.

Dark splotches were scattered across her purple T-shirt. Blood? Both her arms were wrapped in gauze from wrist to elbow. Another square peeked from under her collar. Wounds from the glass of the windshield, maybe. From what Josie could see of Mira's pale face, it was covered in freckles. Her hair was dyed a deep burgundy and cut into a short bob. A long, angry bruise stretched across her forehead. Two smudges of dried blood the size of fingerprints marred her jawline. Her eyes were closed, body still.

Josie rapped her fist against one of the doors. The EMT who had just inserted the IV turned. His eyes darkened at the sight of her. "Josie," he said. There was no warmth in his greeting, in spite of Josie's past efforts to bring him into her life.

"Sawyer," she said, smiling tightly.

At three weeks old, Josie had been kidnapped by a woman who cleaned her parents' household. That same woman, Lila Jensen, had set their house on fire, causing the authorities to believe that tiny Josie had perished. Meanwhile, Lila had spirited Josie away to Denton where her ex-boyfriend, Eli Matson, lived. Eli had dumped Lila. In an effort to get him back, Lila passed Josie off as his daughter. Back then, there was no mail-in DNA testing. Eli Matson had accepted Lila's assertions that Josie was his and raised her as his own, loving her fiercely until the day he died. What no one had known was that during the time Lila and Eli were broken up, Eli had become involved with another woman. Unbeknown to him, that woman had given birth to Sawyer and kept him away from his paternal family to avoid Lila's wrath.

The other EMT didn't spare Josie a glance as he began jotting down Summers's vital signs on a clipboard.

"You caught this case?" Sawyer said. With quick, efficient movements, he flushed Mira Summers's IV with saline and then started a bag of fluids. A lock of his dark hair fell across his forehead.

Josie had had the benefit of knowing and being loved by Eli until she was six years old. She'd also been partially raised by his mother, the woman she had thought was her real grandmother, Lisette Matson, who had saved Josie's life and salvaged what she could of Josie's tumultuous childhood. It was only a couple of years before Lisette's death that Sawyer had connected with her and proven his blood relation.

"Yeah," Josie said. "I just wanted to check in on the driver before you transport her."

Sawyer deposited the tube from the saline flush into a nearby garbage bin. "I don't think she's up to talking right now."

The other EMT pressed some buttons on the monitor and then scribbled something else in his notes. "She's unconscious, but her Glasgow score was within normal range. Pupils equal and reactive."

Which meant that she was neither comatose nor on death's door. Yet. Josie knew head trauma could sometimes lead to serious complications hours or even days after the initial injury.

Sawyer checked the pulse oximeter on Mira's index finger, studying it extra closely. "She was sensitive to light and vomited twice so she's probably concussed, at the very least. You'll have better luck later on, at the hospital, after she's been evaluated."

"Right," Josie murmured.

She wished he would look at her. Were they really back here in the land of awkwardness? He hadn't liked her from the start, and then later blamed her for Lisette's death. There had been a brief period of time when Josie thought he had finally come around, joining her and Noah whenever invited and slowly becoming part of their group of found family, but then he'd disappeared again. She had no idea how he felt about her now but given his demeanor, she was back on his shit list.

His partner finally turned long enough to nod a greeting at Josie and then climbed into the driver's seat, snatching up the radio to communicate with Denton Memorial Hospital.

"Was she awake or lucid at any point after you arrived?" Josie asked Sawyer.

His icy blue eyes locked on her again. A jolt went through her. Sometimes he looked so much like her father—no, *his* father —that it took her breath away. "Are you asking me if she said anything that would help you figure out what happened here?"

Josie sighed. "Yes."

Sawyer bent his head as he double-checked the straps over

Mira's thighs. "No. She was already unconscious when we got here."

"Thanks."

"You see the passenger yet?" Sawyer said.

"That's where I'm headed now."

He gave a slow nod and then motioned toward Mira. "She's got defensive wounds."

Josie stepped closer, her legs brushing the bumper. "What do you mean?"

Gently, he lifted Mira Summers's right arm and indicated the edge of her forearm. "I know I'm no detective or forensic expert, but I've been doing this long enough to know what defensive wounds look like. She has them here. Same place on the other arm. She's got a more superficial wound along her chest. Her jacket was shredded. We had to stop the bleeding and clean her wounds, but I took photos just in case you needed to see how she looked before that."

"Oh," said Josie. That kind of documentation wasn't really necessary in this situation, but she appreciated his effort. Not knowing exactly how to respond, she added, "That was... thoughtful."

He nodded and took his phone out of his pants pocket. Another lock of his dark hair fell across his forehead. The lines of his face tensed as he punched in his passcode. As she watched him, Josie realized that the difference between him and Eli Matson was that Sawyer looked broody even when he wasn't.

"Here," Sawyer said, flashing the phone screen toward her. A freckled forearm filled the screen, covered in what looked like a half dozen puncture marks and jagged gashes of varying sizes. Blood congealed around the wounds. Some were shallow while others gaped open. Yellow fatty tissue bulged from a gouge in the meatiest part of her arm while another showed what Josie thought might be bone.

"That's not from a car accident," she said.

"Didn't think so," Sawyer said with a sigh. He swiped to a second photo which showed Mira's other forearm. Fewer wounds but similar to the first set he'd shown Josie. "I saved her jacket, too," he added.

Sawyer's partner banged a fist against the dash, calling for them to move.

"Thank you. Someone from the ERT will collect all her clothes and boots at the hospital," Josie said. "To process them."

"I'll send you these pictures," Sawyer said.

She watched the ambulance pull away, trying to ignore the dread building inside her at the thought of what she was going to find at the accident scene.

FIVE

Ten minutes later, Josie was dressed in her own Tyvek suit. She pushed the last of her black locks under the elastic of the skull cap as Brennan lifted the crime scene tape for her to slip beneath it. She dodged evidence markers and did her best to avoid the broken glass scattered over the road as she approached the passenger's side of the sedan. Up close, she could see that its hood was crushed accordion-style. Somehow, the damage hadn't deformed so much of the car's frame that the doors couldn't be opened. Both of them stood ajar. Dr. Anya Feist knelt at the opening to the passenger's seat, taking photos with her own camera. She glanced up when she heard Josie approach. As she always did when they met at crime scenes, she offered Josie a pained smile.

"Thought you were off today."

"I am." Josie moved in closer, getting her first look at the passenger. Her breath caught in her throat.

Studying her, Anya said, "It's disturbing, I know."

Josie's heart fluttered. She'd seen some horrific things on the job. Bodies so destroyed from accidents and murders that she would have been nauseated for days if she hadn't learned to deal with carnage early on in her career and become so good at squashing her visceral reactions in favor of getting her job done. This certainly wasn't the goriest thing she'd ever seen, but something about it set off her inner alarm bells. "It's not what I expected."

Anya snapped another photo of the woman. Her skull rested against the headrest, looking too big for her frail body but that was only because she was emaciated. The pale skin of her face was taut against her bony cheeks. Even her teeth seemed to protrude, as though her lips had started to shrink back—or maybe it was that her gums had swollen. A stained T-shirt, that might have been white at some point but was now yellow and gray with grime and age, hung on her shoulders. At the neck, the ends of her collarbones jutted out. Her short brown hair was dull. Josie could see the places where it had been unevenly cut. Not cut, she realized. Hacked away. In some places, the hair had been shorn so close to her scalp that only skin remained.

Someone had done this to her—not by her choice.

Josie's stomach turned. Anya stepped to the side, snapping photos from a different angle. "Don't ask me what happened to her. You know I can't tell you that until I get her on the table."

"Brennan said this was a homicide. Sawyer just showed me defensive wounds on the driver's forearms. Most of them look like puncture wounds although not any type of bite mark. What's going on here?"

Anya beckoned her closer to the car. Careful not to touch anything, Josie poked her head inside. There was a distinctive odor emanating from the passenger. It was a putrid mixture of body odor, human waste, and something else—something earthy. Trying her best to ignore it, she scanned the woman, immediately zeroing in on what the rest of the team had already seen. "Well, shit."

Behind her, Anya said, "Doesn't get much more obvious than that."

Through a pair of threadbare gray sweatpants, the shape of the woman's knobby knees was visible. They kissed the dashboard, the impact having lodged them in place so that her bare feet dangled over the floor. One of her thin hands rested in her lap in a tight fist. The other curled around a small, oddly shaped wooden handle protruding from her abdomen. A knife? No part of the blade was visible. Blood, still fresh and red, bloomed all around the hilt.

That was why Sawyer had mentioned the wounds on Mira Summers's forearms. But what kind of knife left puncture marks? Unless it wasn't a knife. Josie craned her neck, trying to get a better look, but the woman's fist covered most of the handle. They'd have to wait for it to be removed from the body in order to confirm that it was a knife.

"They were both stabbed with something. Do you think the passenger died in this car?" asked Josie.

Anya shrugged. "It's possible. Either that or she died shortly before she got into it. Her death was in the last two hours. She hasn't gone into rigor yet."

Josie's eyes were drawn to the tan seat belt strapped across her chest, above the hilt of the knife. "She'd already been stabbed when she got in here. Even if the dashboard was where it should be, there wouldn't be enough room for someone to drive this thing into her abdomen straight on like that from inside the car—even if the blade was relatively short. Whatever happened, it didn't happen inside this car."

"Agree."

The car's interior upholstery was tan, now smeared and splattered with blood. Glass sparkled in the crevices of the driver's seat. Blood dried on the center console and the driver's side door. It was smeared across the steering wheel. The back seat was empty. Backing up slightly, Josie studied the bottom of the passenger's side doorframe and saw more blood droplets.

Glancing over her shoulder at Anya, she said, "Either these two managed to get away from whoever attacked them before he could finish the job, or her killer left the knife in her body."

"We don't actually know if the stab wound is what caused this woman's death," Anya pointed out. "She could have died from injuries sustained in the accident. I won't know until I do the autopsy."

Josie knew Anya was right, but she also knew enough about anatomy to have already made the leap from motor vehicle accident fatality to murder. "What's your educated guess? MVA fatality or homicide?"

Anya sighed. "Given the location of the knife and assuming the blade is three to four inches long, my educated guess is that this is a homicide. Murderers don't usually leave the weapons behind. I haven't seen that many retained knives as medical examiner. Only once. It was a domestic. Messy. Multiple stab wounds. The husband left it in her on purpose. He was making a statement." Anya shuddered, and Josie knew she was thinking of her own abusive ex-husband. He was now in prison for multiple crimes, not least of which was murdering Josie's former colleague, Detective Finn Mettner. Josie's palms tingled. Whenever she thought of Finn, her body remembered the feel of his hand in hers as he bled out. Sometimes it felt like she'd never really let go. She quickly found the box in her mental vault where she kept her most traumatic memories and stuffed the thought back inside.

"What a bastard," Josie said.

"Yeah." Anya studied the victim, head tilting in thought. "In my experience, though, stabbing deaths resulting from domestic violence are usually much worse than this. These men—they never stab just once."

But someone had tried to stab Mira Summers multiple

times. Had she been trying to defend the passenger? Had she been stabbed with the same weapon that now protruded from the victim's stomach?

Josie's eyes were drawn to the woman's hollow cheeks again. "If we're looking at a domestic, maybe the stabbing wasn't the worst of what he did to her."

"Or maybe you're not looking at a domestic. Maybe the killer is someone other than a partner. Maybe she was trying to get away. Could be the driver was trying to help her. In my ER rotation, I saw a few retained knives from stabbing incidents. It was usually because the person was too afraid to pull the knife out. In at least two of the cases, the patient thought that somehow the knife was holding all the vessels and tissue in place and preventing them from bleeding out."

Under her cap, sweat beaded at Josie's hairline, making her scalp itch. "Were they right?"

"One of them was, yes. Sort of. He would have bled out anyway—the damage was done—but leaving the knife in did slow the bleeding long enough for him to get the medical care that saved his life."

"You think she was trying to keep the knife where it was until she got help?" Josie asked, gaze flitting to the woman's skeletal fingers curled around the knife handle.

"I don't know. Maybe she was too weak to pull it out, or maybe the driver was afraid to pull it out," Anya said.

"Mira Summers put a seat belt on this woman. She was driving her somewhere. Maybe to the hospital?"

"Why not call 911?" Anya asked.

Josie looked toward the north where the road stretched on until the horizon, nothing ahead, and then south, where it rolled down a long hill leading into the city. "If they were fleeing someone, she might not have had time. If they were attacked somewhere out here, it would probably take 911 too long to get to wherever they were." She pointed to the northbound side of the road. "This goes on for at least fifteen miles before it reaches another town. There might be a few residences in between, but this is a fairly deserted stretch of road."

She'd have to find out where the driver was coming from and at what point and under what circumstances the passenger got inside the car. According to what Brennan had read off from Mira Summers's driver's license, she lived in Denton, which meant she must have traveled this road and then turned back toward the city.

Anya said, "That's your department. I'll do what I can on exam and autopsy to give you something to work with in terms of the actual homicide."

Josie stepped back so that Anya could continue her examination. She snapped a few more photos before returning her camera to its case. Then she leaned inside the car, arching her back so she didn't disturb the handle of the weapon, and used her gloved hands to probe the pockets of the woman's sweatpants. Josie couldn't help but notice that those, too, looked old and dirty. Mud streaked down their front.

"Nothing in the pockets," Anya muttered.

Josie hadn't expected anything. The woman didn't even have shoes on. It appeared the only thing in her possession was the weapon that had killed her.

"Almost done," Anya said. "I just want to check her other hand."

Josie watched as Anya pried the woman's fist open. Flakes of dried blood fell from her fingers. In the center of her palm was a folded piece of white paper.

"What do we have here?" Anya said, her voice tinged with excitement.

"Hummel!" Josie called. "We've got something."

A moment later, he was at her side, his clipboard tucked under his arm. Josie stepped back several feet and Anya joined her as they let the ERT document and photograph the paper before it was removed.

Finally, they gathered near the open door again as Hummel unfolded the page with care. It looked like regular copy paper they used in the office. "It's damp," he said. The ends of it hung limply from his hands. Smears of blood marred the edges.

Anya said, "Is that—"

"A child's drawing," Josie said.

SIX

Hummel held up the picture so that all of them could see it. Drawn in crayon, its center showed a thick black ring with a larger dark brown ring around it. In the very center of both rings was what appeared to be a flower. At the top of a straight green stem was what looked like a red cup. A tulip, maybe? A rose? Above and below the rings, darker, wavy brown lines ran the length of the page. Crossing one section of those lines was a straight gray one that started at the rings and ended near the edge of the page, its tail forming a small rectangle. Next to that were several tiny circles drawn in a lighter brown. Josie was pretty sure the crayon color was called Desert Sand. She could identify most of the crayon colors just by sight after spending so much time watching Harris—her best friend Misty's son—use them. All in all, the drawing was messy, like the kinds of pictures Harris used to draw when he was in kindergarten. The thought made Josie's heart flutter wildly, like a trapped hummingbird. There was a child connected to this woman. Where were they, and more importantly, were they safe?

"What is that?" asked Anya.

Hummel rotated it. "I don't know."

"Maybe an eye?" Josie suggested.

"Because of the way the black circle is inside the brown circle?" Hummel said. "Maybe. The gray could be a teardrop, I guess, although it's kind of square. Then you've got the flower in the center. Maybe the person is looking at the flower?"

Anya pointed to the brown wavy lines. "Those are horizontal. Wouldn't the lines be shorter and vertical if they were meant to be eyelashes? Also, what are those small circles?"

Hummel said, "You can analyze its meaning later. Let me get this into an evidence bag and log it in."

"Turn it over," Josie said.

"Right. Hang on." Gingerly, so it didn't fall apart in his hands, he flipped the page. Along one edge was the same flower and below that, large, awkward letters, scrawled in the crayon color Josie recognized as Screamin' Green.

HELP

The hummingbird in Josie's chest beat so hard against her rib cage, it was painful. She tried to say something, anything, but no words came.

Anya did it for her. "Oh God."

"Fuck," said Hummel.

Josie took a deep breath and stowed the secret panic she felt at the prospect of a child being in the hands of whoever had stabbed Mira Summers and her passenger. There was a job to be done, and that child's life might depend on how well Josie and her team performed it. Steadying her nerves, she took out her phone and snapped a photo of each side of the paper. Hummel carried it away. Josie and Anya exchanged a look. Anya let out a shaky breath and turned back toward the passenger, searching on and around her body. "No identification."

"Of course not," Josie mumbled. The child's drawing was already taking up permanent residence in her mind. Did the woman have a child? The knife in her abdomen notwithstanding, she didn't look healthy enough to take care of herself, let alone anyone else. Was her child being held somewhere, or had they already perished? Or were they dealing with some other, unimaginable scenario?

HELP

"Here," Anya said, pointing at something stuck to the woman's shirt, near her waist. "Give me my camera."

Josie retrieved it from its case and handed it over.

Anya snapped several more photos of what looked like a thick clump of short white hair. "Is that from an animal?" Josie asked.

"I don't know." Anya probed the back of the woman's head. "There's more on her collar here." Careful to avoid the knife handle, she knelt to get a look at the woman's legs and feet. "Here, too. It's very short. A cat, maybe? Call Hummel back over. It might be of use to you later."

Josie went to find him. Her mind formed a preliminary picture of this woman's home life. Child. Cat. She'd clearly been in poor health for a long time. It could have been from a prolonged illness but from the way her hair had been shorn, Josie's gut told her that her condition wasn't from illness at all and that if it was a cat that had left the clumps of fur on her, it didn't belong to the woman but to the person who'd killed her—and who might this very minute have her child. A child who needed help.

SEVEN

He won't tell me what he did. It's been hours and he says we can't leave which is weird because we're always leaving. That's all we do is leave places. He has always said that we have to keep moving so that the bad people don't come.

"They'll take you away and we'll never see each other again," he always says.

I used to be terrified of never seeing him again but now all I want to do is get away from him.

He walks up behind me and clamps a hand down on my shoulder. Dark red flaky stuff covers his fingernails. He didn't rinse away all the blood.

Whose blood?

The words are like a whisper inside my brain that won't go away.

I should say something. Make him rinse again. But I don't. Maybe if he goes out where all the people are someone will see it and tell on him.

"Get away from there," he says.

I shrug his heavy hand away and fold my arms across my body. "No one can see me."

"You don't know that. You have to listen to me. It's the only way to stay safe."

But I'm beginning to think the only way for me to stay safe is if the bad people take *him* away.

EIGHT

Leaving Hummel and Dr. Feist to their work, Josie went back to her car. She texted Noah to let him know that she'd be a lot longer than expected. Even though the attack on Mira Summers and the murder of Jane Doe—as well as the probability that a child was in danger—horrified her, it felt good to work on what was potentially a complex case again. For the first time in a month, she wasn't consumed with anxiety about the home study or their adoption journey. She'd often been accused by her colleagues and her therapist of hiding behind her work—throwing herself into it so she didn't have to deal with her emotions—but her job was always where things made sense. It was the one place she could always be of use, where there was always a clear path forward. Procedure could sometimes seem limiting, but in fact it was a guide that always helped her know what to do next, especially in more serious and challenging cases. Her phone chirped, drawing her out of her thoughts.

No worries. Trout and I have everything under control. We've officially got a sauceless kitchen. All smoke and carbon monoxide detectors are in working order. We're going to be a hit with the case manager. I love you.

He'd followed it with several heart emojis. Josie couldn't help but smile.

She put her phone away. From where she was parked, she could see the other set of EMTs rolling their gurney toward the car in order to remove the passenger. Hummel and Dr. Feist stood nearby. In her rearview mirror, a flatbed tow truck lumbered into view. About a minute later, Labenberg, the officer from the Fatal Accident Reconstruction Team pulled up behind it. There were still hours of work to be done at the scene, but Josie had gathered what information she could for her own purposes for now. Still, it was going to be a long afternoon, followed by a very long evening. The sight of the passenger's gaunt, sallow face was burned into Josie's mind. It was one of the things on the job you could never unsee. The more she turned things over in her head, the more she thought that the woman hadn't been sick at all. Although neither she nor Anya would say it out loud until they had concrete evidence, Josie's instincts told her the woman had been tortured for some length of time before she was stabbed.

HELP

Josie's gut also told her that this case was going to be a lot bigger than it appeared. She would need help. Voices sailed through the air, reaching her inside her car. The Fatal Accident Reconstruction officer and the tow truck driver were arguing over when the sedan could be removed from the scene. Josie put her window up and took out her phone again, searching until she found Douchebag in her contacts.

Kyle Turner didn't answer.

She tried again. He still didn't answer. She sent him the same text he had sent her earlier: *PICK UP*.

She waited a minute and then called him again. He

sounded out of breath. "Sweetheart, what's got your panties in a knot?"

"Are you finished with the bank robbery or what?"

"No. Why? What's up?"

"The fatality is a homicide," she told him. "The driver was also stabbed. Several times. There appears to be a child involved somehow. They may be in danger."

"No shit." She couldn't tell if he was faking his surprise or not.

A thought occurred to her. It didn't really matter but she asked anyway. "Did you know this involved a homicide when you called me?"

There was a beat of silence. Then he said, "No, no. Dispatch just said MVA. One fatality."

"When will you be finished at the bank?" she asked.

His tone remained unbothered, half joking, but he said, "Why are you so far up my ass?"

"Because this case just got a lot more complicated than a simple motor vehicle accident, and I have a ho—" She stopped short of telling him why she needed to be home in the morning. Her Chief knew and so did Gretchen, but she didn't want to tell Turner about the home study or the fact that she and Noah were trying to adopt a child. He hadn't earned access to her personal life, and she didn't owe him an explanation at all.

"You have a what?" Turner said.

"Listen," she said. "I don't want to lose any steam on this case. If there is a child in danger, then we need to move as quickly as possible. But I have an appointment in the morning that I have to keep."

"No one's stopping you."

She suppressed a sigh and pinched the bridge of her nose with her thumb and forefinger. He was right. There was no reason that she would miss the home study in the morning except that she didn't trust him to take up the slack. She had a sinking feeling that somehow—even with Gretchen on—Turner would be missing in action the next morning. A new thought made her stomach acids roil. What if the child was in the same shape as Jane Doe? Automatically, Josie dropped into her box breathing.

Turner said, "Are you doing that weird breathing shit you learned at that fucked-up retreat last year?"

"I'm— Turner, I'm going to the hospital to see what I can find out from this driver. Hopefully she's lucid. I could use your help with this. We're going to need warrants for the vehicle, the vehicle's GPS system, and depending on the state of the driver and if she is not yet alert enough to give us any information, we may need warrants to search her phone as well. Then, depending on where she traveled today or what she tells us, if she's able, we'll need to look at property records or possibly retrace her route to find out where she's been."

Turner chuckled. "You're really catching on to how this procedure thing works, aren't you?"

Josie bit back a stinging reply. "Never mind. I'll call Gretchen."

She hung up. Maybe it was a blessing that she wouldn't have to deal with him. She missed Mettner. When he was alive, the team worked like a well-oiled machine. Everyone pitched in. They all got along. They prioritized their cases and took care of one another. Josie felt a momentary stab of grief in the center of her chest and quickly squashed it. There was no time to sit with her feelings now.

NINE

Denton Memorial Hospital was a large brick building located on the top of one of the city's highest hills. Josie parked in the visitors' lot near the ER trauma bays and snuck inside, flashing her credentials at the security guard as she went. For a Wednesday afternoon, the place was crowded. Nurses strode along the row of curtained-off treatment areas, shouting to one another. A baby wailed from behind one of them. Several machines beeped throughout, indicating changes in vital signs. Josie went weak with relief when she saw Detective Gretchen Palmer standing by the nurses' station, her hand inside a brown bag from their favorite coffee shop, Kommorah's Koffee. On the counter next to her was a carrier with two cups of coffee. She looked up as Josie approached. Smiling, she removed a pecan croissant from the bag.

"Is that a pastry?" Josie said, giving Gretchen a mock-stern look.

Gretchen bit off half of it and chewed. After gulping it down, she said, "You saw nothing."

Josie laughed. Then, feigning seriousness, she said, "It doesn't feel right to keep secrets from Paula."

Gretchen, now in her late forties, had had her twins in her early twenties and then given them up for adoption. At the time, she'd been caught up in a bad situation and felt it was the only way to keep them safe. Years later, both children had come back into her life. Her adult daughter now lived with her and had talked her into following a strict diet and exercise routine. Paula wanted her mother around as long as possible, and Gretchen didn't have the heart to tell her no. Plus, as a detective, her schedule wasn't always conducive to healthy habits. Still, Josie knew Komorrah's pecan croissants were Gretchen's weakness.

In fact, Gretchen stared at the rest of the croissant like it was her lover. "It's bad enough she's still got me jogging every damn day." With one hand she pinched the skin at her waist. There was considerably less now than in all the years Josie had known her. "Look at this. I'm wasting away to nothing. She's slowly cutting back on our sugar intake. Soon I won't even be able to put sugar in my coffee. She's been tracking my A1C like a bookie at the racetrack."

Josie laughed. "I thought grad school was time-consuming."

"Not enough that it keeps her from being my in-house nutritionist." Gretchen popped the rest of the croissant into her mouth, chewing more slowly this time. Her eyes fluttered closed as she savored the pastry.

"You couldn't talk her out of criminology, I guess."

Gretchen opened her eyes, swatted some crumbs from her chest, and grabbed one of the coffee cups, handing it to Josie. "I'm just glad she didn't want to join a police department. I'm not thrilled about criminology, but at least she'll be behind a desk. Better to be an analyst than to be in the field. I never want her to see the things we've seen—not up close."

Josie opened the lid of the paper cup, letting the steam waft up over her face. "Is this a flat white latte?"

Gretchen arched a brow. "I'm insulted you'd even ask. How many years have we been working together?"

"Almost eight." Josie took a long sip, feeling a wave of anticipation as she waited for the caffeine to hit her system. "Don't ever leave me."

Gretchen chuckled. "I promise." She pointed at one of the glass-fronted trauma rooms directly across from the nurses' station. "My shooting victim is in there. He'll be fine. Already got the shooter. It was a neighbor. Dispute over a tree. I wish you had called me as soon as Turner asked you to come in. I could have saved you all this trouble. I know you've got the home study tomorrow."

"I can still make the home study," Josie said.

"Tell me about this one and I'll take it from here."

Josie took another long sip of her latte. "I can take the lead."

"It's not a problem for me," Gretchen said. "Do what you need to do at home."

She thought about what Noah had said about making adjustments in their lives if they were to adopt a child—that couples with full-time jobs raised kids all the time. "Thanks, but I can do it. I can handle this and things at home."

Gretchen narrowed her eyes. "Is this about the woman you think you lost at the retreat last year?"

Josie lowered her voice to a whisper. "I don't *think* I lost her. I did. If I had chosen differently, she'd still be alive. But it's not that. Not entirely."

For a moment, Gretchen looked like she was going to argue with Josie. Again. But she let it go. "You have a bad feeling about this one."

"I have a bad feeling about all of them."

"You know what I mean."

As they waited for someone on the staff to update them on Mira Summers, Josie filled Gretchen in on the details of the case and finished by showing her the photos she'd taken at the scene. Gretchen did a far better job than Josie had at hiding her emotion when she saw the message asking for help and the condition of the passenger. "Jane Doe should be in the morgue now," said Josie. "But Anya probably won't have the results of the autopsy until tomorrow."

"Where is the child who drew the picture?" Gretchen asked, immediately zeroing in on the most alarming detail, the thing that was currently burning a hole right through the lining of Josie's stomach.

"Exactly," Josie said. "Jane Doe wanted someone to find that drawing. Even with a weapon still inside her body, she held onto that picture."

"In a literal death grip," Gretchen muttered. "What can we tell about this kid from the drawing? Anything? There's a flower. I don't want to stereotype or be sexist but that could be an indicator that we're looking for a little girl."

"It could, but we shouldn't rule anything out. Honestly, the drawing raises more questions than it answers." Josie slugged down the rest of her latte and tossed the empty cup into a trash bin nearby. "I also think, based on Jane Doe's appearance, that she was held somewhere and possibly tortured before being stabbed."

"Well, that's terrifying," Gretchen muttered, sipping her coffee. "But the 'help' makes a lot more sense in that context."

Josie heard footsteps behind her and turned to see the emergency department's attending physician, Dr. Ahmed Nashat, walking toward them. He smiled. "Detectives, a pleasure, as always, though I do hate meeting under such distressing circumstances."

"You're in a good mood," Gretchen said.

Dr. Nashat's smile loosened. He looked behind them as if he expected to see someone else. "Truth be told, I'm glad to see you two and not your new colleague."

"You're not the only one," Gretchen grumbled. "What's he

done now?"

"Let's just say he doesn't have the same finesse with witnesses or the medical staff as the rest of you."

"He doesn't have it with anyone," Josie muttered. "What can you tell us about Mira Summers?"

"When she was brought in, she had regained consciousness. She has a very large bruise on her forehead. She responded appropriately to verbal commands. I noted several signs of a concussion. She was immediately sent for a CT scan of her head. Don't worry, one of your officers already came and took possession of her clothes and boots. One of the residents will get her arms sewn up as soon as possible, but the head injury took precedent. Anyway, Ms. Summers's CT doesn't show any visible injury, but I've diagnosed her with a concussion based on her other symptoms. For now, we will admit her for observation and continue to monitor her symptoms."

"She's awake?" Josie asked. "Lucid?"

Dr. Nashat frowned. "She is awake. She's in a great deal of pain although the medication we've given her will help with that. She appears to have some memory loss."

Gretchen narrowed her eyes. "What kind of memory loss?"

A nurse strode past them, pushing a man in a wheelchair. He held an ice pack against his nose. Dr. Nashat stepped out of the way. Josie and Gretchen followed suit. "She doesn't remember much about the accident or the events leading up to it."

Gretchen said, "Is that normal?"

"What we normally see in patients who have sustained concussions is short-term memory loss such as not remembering people's names or forgetting where they put their keys, that sort of thing. It's usually temporary and will resolve over the course of weeks or months. Miss Summers may very well present with that type of short-term memory loss in the coming weeks. In terms of her not remembering the accident? It can happen but it's not common. There have been cases of patients not having any memory of the event that caused the concussion, so it's not out of the realm of possibility. That said, it is also possible that she'll recover those memories at some point. She doesn't have complete memory loss. She knew she'd been in an accident when I spoke with her. She even knew which road she'd been on."

It was selective, then. Josie looked at Gretchen and then back at Dr. Nashat. "Don't take this the wrong way, but is there any possibility that Mira Summers is... faking it?"

He raised an eyebrow at her. "Faking her memory loss?"

Gretchen said, "We had a case, several years back, where a woman faked her memory loss. Surely you understand how we'd be concerned about that happening again."

He brought his hands together at his waist. "It's difficult to say. Concussions present differently for every patient. Whether Mira Summers's memory loss surrounding what led to her accident is real or whether she is"—here he used air quotes—"'faking it,' is not something I am in a position to comment on."

"But she could be faking it," Josie pressed.

Dr. Nashat pursed his lips. They were well out of medical territory now and Josie knew exactly why he didn't want to answer. "Your personal opinion. Between us. Nothing you'll have to testify to in court should the need arise."

"We have experts for that," Gretchen noted.

He rubbed his fingers across his forehead. "There is no measurable test by which we could determine that."

That was a non-answer if Josie ever heard one. She genuinely liked Dr. Nashat, but she knew that was as much as he was willing to say on the matter.

"If you don't mind," he said. "I have patients."

They thanked him for his time. As he walked off, Gretchen drained the rest of her coffee. "What do you want to do?"

Josie caught a flash of blue behind Gretchen. Officer

Dougherty strode in their direction. Josie gestured toward him. "Talk to him first."

A notepad appeared in Dougherty's hands as he reached them. He flipped a page. "Quinn," he said. "Brennan told me you'd be here."

"What did you find at Mira Summers's residence?" Josie asked.

Dougherty flipped another page. "She resides in a town house. A rental. One of those developments with dozens of identical town houses. I knocked and rang the bell. No response. One of her neighbors was home. He said she left in her car around eight this morning—by herself. She did not appear to be injured. He said she lives alone. Landlord confirmed. No one else is on the lease."

"No children?" asked Josie.

Dougherty glanced at his notes. "No children on the lease, and the neighbor said he's never seen any children coming or going."

"Any pets?" asked Josie.

He looked up at her, as if surprised at the question. "Neighbor says she's got a cat. You counting cats as roommates now?"

Gretchen raised a brow. "Cats are smarter than most people, Dougherty."

"If you say so," he muttered.

"What kind?" asked Josie.

"Are you serious with this?" he replied.

Josie and Gretchen stared at him intently. He gave a heavy sigh. "I didn't ask." When neither of them responded, he added, "I can try to find out."

"It's fine," Josie said, flashing him a quick grin. "We'll ask Summers."

"She should remember her cat," Gretchen added, drawing a confused look from Dougherty.

TEN

Once Dougherty left, Josie and Gretchen walked down the hall to Curtain 12, which had been left partially open. Mira Summers lay on the gurney, now clothed in a hospital gown, her eyes closed. Her arms were still wrapped in gauze although it was considerably looser than it had been in the ambulance. Under the stark fluorescent lights of the hospital, she looked deathly pale, her freckles more pronounced. The angry bruise across her forehead looked even darker than when Josie had seen her in the back of the ambulance. Beside her, a portable monitor tracked her vital signs. On the other side, a bag of fluids hung, slowly dripping into the IV in her hand. Her eyes fluttered open as Gretchen pulled the curtain all the way around the track, giving them some privacy.

"Mira Summers?" Josie asked softly.

She lifted a hand, shading her eyes. "Who is it?"

Josie and Gretchen introduced themselves, offering credentials. She glanced blankly at them from under her arm. "The police?"

"Yes," Josie said. "We'd like to ask you some questions, if you're up to it. If not, we can come back another time."

She squinted at them. "About the accident."

"Yes," Gretchen said. "What do you remember about it?"

Next to the bed, the monitor beeped, indicating that Mira's heart rate had increased. Josie waited for a nurse to come in but none did. Mira covered her eyes with her arm now. Both Sawyer and Dr. Nashat had said she was sensitive to light due to the concussion, yet no one had dimmed the lights in her treatment area. "Not much. I just remember waking up in my car, this big bag in my face—the airbag. Then this man was there asking me if I was okay. He was on the other side of the car. I think there was someone else there, too. In my car."

Josie noticed that in addition to the blinding overhead light, there was a smaller one on the wall over the gurney. "That's right. There was a woman in your passenger's seat. You don't remember her?"

Mira shifted her arm so it wasn't putting pressure on her forehead but kept her eyes covered. "No. I don't even know who she is or how she got there. I was alone in my car when I left the stables."

Gretchen's notepad was in her hands. She flipped a page and grabbed the pen behind her ear. "What stables?"

"Tranquil Trails. I ride there every Sunday. Horseback riding. I'm in their therapeutic riding program, um, for my anxiety. I finished up, got into my car, and the next thing I know, there's an airbag in my face and..." Her chest rose and fell rapidly. On the monitor, her respiration count was high. "Do you know what happened to me? Where that woman came from?"

Josie found the light switches along the wall and flipped them until the overhead light was off and the one on the wall was on. "We're working to figure that out," she told Mira. "See if this is better. I turned the overhead light off. Miss Summers, you have wounds on your forearms. Do you remember how you got those?"

Mira slowly lowered her arm. Fresh blood bloomed in irregular patterns through the gauze. She blinked several times. "I don't remember. I'm sorry. I told you. I got into my car to leave the stables and the next thing I know, I wake up in a wreck. My head hurts and my arms—" She lifted the other one, staring at the gauze. "They feel like they're on fire."

"You've been stabbed multiple times," Gretchen said. "Is there anything at all you can tell us about your attacker?"

Mira slowly shook her head. Her eyes narrowed against the light, although she did look more comfortable.

"Could it have been someone from Tranquil Trails?" Josie asked.

Her pulse shot up again, sounding another alarm. Still, no nurse arrived. "No. No. The people there are so nice, and Rebecca and Jon would never do anything like that. They're good people. They help me."

Josie said, "Are Rebecca and Jon the owners?"

Mira nodded. Her pulse was still racing.

"What about one of the other clients?" asked Gretchen. "Is it possible that someone else who was there today attacked you?"

"I don't know. I just don't know."

The alarm on the vital signs machine continued to squawk. If a staff member did come in here, they'd be asked to leave. In an effort to calm Mira down, Josie turned the questions toward more mundane matters. She didn't want Mira having a cardiac event when she asked her about the child. "Let's talk about things you do remember. Have you lived in Denton long?"

It didn't bring her pulse or respirations down, but she answered. "Three years. I moved from Bucks County. Got a job here working for an insurance firm. I just answer phones and do some intake but the money is good."

Josie flipped the switch to turn off the wall light. The area inside the curtain was dim but not so much that they couldn't see one another. "Do you live alone?"

Mira's body visibly relaxed. "Oh. Yes. Just me and my cat."

"What kind of cat do you have?" asked Gretchen.

Her heart rate slowed, the alarm cutting off. "The all-black kind? I don't know. I got her at a rescue. Is that—is that important?"

Gretchen shook her head. "I'm just a cat person. Do you have children, Miss Summers?"

Her pulse spiked but not enough to set the alarm back off. More blood oozed from under the gauze pads, staining the sheet that covered her body. "No. I never had kids."

Gretchen said, "Do you ever come into contact with any children at Tranquil Trails?"

"I mean, I've seen kids there but I don't talk with them or anything."

Josie took out her phone and pulled up the child's drawing found at the scene. "Does this look familiar to you?"

Mira stared blankly at the picture until the silence became awkward. Then, licking her lips, she answered, "No. What is that supposed to be? Did a child draw that?"

"We believe so," Josie swiped to the photo of the back, where the green letters jumped off the page.

Mira stared at the message, her pulse suddenly jumping all over the place from the low fifties to over one hundred ten and everywhere in between. The alarm started to blare, cut off, and then began again. Josie wondered if it would short-circuit at the rate that Mira's heart rate was changing. "I don't know what to say," she whispered.

Josie kept the photo in view. "This was found in the hand of your passenger. We have reason to believe that whoever drew it and wrote this message on the back is in danger. I know you've just been injured, but please think carefully. Can you think of any child who might have drawn this?"

The alarm bellowed again for three beats before going silent. "No," Mira said. "I'm sorry. I have no idea."

Gretchen tapped her pen against her notepad. "You don't have children, but are there any in your life who might have drawn this?"

"No, no."

"Nieces, nephews?"

"I don't— I have no siblings."

"Do any of your friends have children?" asked Gretchen.

"I've only got one good friend here and she doesn't have any kids. Wait. You said the passenger in my car was holding that. Can't you just ask her?"

"I'm afraid not," Josie said. "The passenger is deceased."

Shock slackened the features of Mira's face. "Oh God. Did I kill her? In the accident?"

Did she really not remember anything that came before the accident? The handle sticking out of Jane Doe's abdomen? Josie looked for any telltale signs that she was lying, but in her current state, it was difficult to decipher what might indicate a lie and what was simply shock and pain from the accident.

"The medical examiner will have to perform an autopsy to determine her cause of death, but it appears as though she was in very bad shape before she got into your car."

Josie heard a click and then a loud whir. The blood pressure cuff around Mira's upper arm inflated.

Gretchen flipped another page in her notebook. "The passenger didn't have any identification. Do you have any idea who the woman in your car might be?"

Mira had already told them that she didn't know the passenger, but Josie knew Gretchen was testing for consistency by making her answer the question, especially given that she was claiming memory loss.

Mira shook her head. A grimace stretched across her face. She lifted one of her forearms again. Blood dripped down to her elbow and onto her hospital gown. The alarm on the vital signs machine shrieked again. Her blood pressure was high.

Josie searched a nearby rolling cabinet, coming up with a handful of gauze and handing it to Mira. "Can you see which wound is bleeding? Put pressure on it. The doctor said someone will be in to stitch you up soon."

Mira did as she was told.

Gretchen said, "We're going to show you a picture of the passenger."

Josie really didn't want to show anyone a photo of Jane Doe. She barely looked human. Part of Josie felt as though using the photo was an affront to her dignity, but not trying to identify her and find justice for her would be worse. Reluctantly, Josie held the picture up to Mira's face. The gauze fell from her fingers. A strangled gasp wrenched itself from her throat.

"Do you recognize her?" asked Josie.

Would anyone recognize her in the state she'd been in?

The alarm kept going. Why did they even have these things if the staff didn't respond to them? Again, Mira shook her head. Tears rolled down her face. "What do you think happened to her? She doesn't look... My God."

There were no tissues in the curtained area, so Josie grabbed another fistful of gauze for Mira. "We'll know more after her autopsy. Is there someone we can call for you while you're here in the hospital?"

Mira used a gauze pad to dab at her cheeks. "The nurse already did. My friend from work. Bobbi Ann Thomas. She's all I have around here."

"No parents?" Gretchen asked.

She found the place on her forearm that seemed to be the source of the ongoing bleeding and pressed the rest of the fresh gauze against it. "I haven't spoken with my parents in years. We don't get along."

"How about romantic partners?" Josie asked. "Are you seeing anyone?"

The alarm cut off abruptly but only because the blood pressure cuff was swelling again.

Mira said, "No. I haven't dated in years. There's no one."

"How about former partners?" asked Gretchen.

Josie held her breath as the blood pressure cuff slowly deflated, waiting for the shrill bark of the alarm to begin again. If Mira's blood pressure didn't set it off, then her heart rate would very soon. Everything was climbing again.

"What do you mean?" asked Mira.

Josie said, "Do you have any exes who were bothering you?"

As predicted, the vital signs machine began its discordant symphony once more.

"No," said Mira.

"Do any of your exes have children?"

"Um, I don't know? I told you, I haven't dated anyone in ages."

"Is there anyone else who was giving you a hard time lately?" Gretchen kept scribbling in her notebook. "Someone hanging around? Making you uncomfortable? Anything like that? Neighbor, coworker, anyone at all."

"No, nothing like that. Really, I live a quiet life. Go to work. Hang out with Bobbi sometimes. Go to the stables. That is it."

The curtain flew open, light from outside slashing across Mira's face. Her eyes snapped shut and she turned her head to the side. A nurse strode in and punched a series of buttons on the machine, quieting it. Next, a young doctor stepped into the space. "Miss Summers, I'm here to do your sutures."

Josie laid one of her business cards on the tray table next to Mira's bed. "We'll go now, but if you remember anything, anything at all, about what happened to you today, the woman in your car, or who might have made the drawing we showed you, please give us a call. Our colleague took your phone into evidence. We'll try to get it back to you as soon as possible. Until then, someone on the staff can help you get in touch with us."

ELEVEN

The Fatal Accident Reconstruction officer was still working the scene when Josie drove back up Prout Road. Three other officers from the team had joined her, taking photos and making sketches. Two cruisers remained to protect the scene and direct traffic. The tow truck was also there, the driver asleep in the cab. Josie waved to Officer Brennan as they rolled past. Gretchen sipped at the new coffee they'd stopped for and studied the wreckage. As they climbed the hill, the fields spread on either side of them, nothing but high grass and an occasional patch of wildflowers with the forest in the distance. They crested the hill and the road flattened out. A mile passed and then another, and there were no driveways or buildings in sight.

"You were right," Gretchen said. "There is literally nothing out here."

"We should still take a look at the aerial maps when we get back to the station. I'm not sure how far these fields go or what's on the other side of these trees. What did you think of Summers?"

"You mean, do I think she's lying about not remembering anything about Jane Doe or who stabbed them or what happened before the accident? Or, most importantly, if she knows anything about the drawing? I have no idea. I can't see what reason she would have to lie and yet, she only forgot the exact things we need to know. I get what Nashat was saying about concussions, and I've even seen people block out traumatic events—like being stabbed—so who knows? We should talk to her again when she's stitched up and has had some rest. We might get a better read on her then."

Josie calculated they'd driven almost five miles by the time the Tranquil Trails Equestrian Academy came into view. Paint peeled off the small sign at the edge of a gravel driveway. Josie turned onto it and drove past trees along one side and a large field on the other. She braked when the gravel expanded along her left side into a grove of maple trees thirty yards away. A wooden produce stand, painted a faded red, nestled in the clearing beneath them but nothing sat on its shelves except a wooden box that said, LEAVE SOMETHING, TAKE SOME-THING. She continued on. The driveway wound to the right. Finally, they came to a large two-story building behind a split rail fence. The structure appeared to be a former barn that had been partially converted into a house. Its wooden siding was old, its brown fading to gray in places. The driveway continued to curve around the house, out of their line of sight, but just past a massive pine tree, there was a dirt parking lot to her left, so Josie pulled in there. Gretchen said, "I think 'academy' is a bit of a stretch."

Josie got out and stretched her arms over her head, noting two other vehicles in the lot, one a sedan and the other a pickup truck. "Maybe the inside is nicer?"

From across the car roof, Gretchen scoffed. As she closed the door, she said, "Are we even still in Denton?"

Josie looked in the direction of the road. "Believe it or not, yes. The city limit goes a few more miles north of here."

As they walked toward the house, Gretchen shook her head,

laughing softly. "The city limits. This place is a far cry from the concrete jungle of Philadelphia. I'll never get used to it."

They walked through the split rail fence and followed a stone walkway to the front of the house. An unwelcoming white door greeted them. There were no signs. Not even a doorbell.

"It doesn't even look like this place is in operation," said Gretchen.

They hadn't had time to properly research the place, having come directly from the hospital. Normally, Josie would have done a deep dive on Tranquil Trails Equestrian Academy before arriving, but if this was the last place that Mira Summers had been before the accident, she wanted to check it out right away. If there was any evidence or witnesses who could help them figure out who their Jane Doe was or what had happened before Mira Summers crashed, and most importantly, whether or not a child was at risk, Josie wanted to get to it immediately.

"There are cars in the lot," Josie said, rapping on the door.

Gretchen was already on her cell phone, tapping the name of the place into her internet browser.

No one answered. Josie knocked again with the same result.

Gretchen said, "It's got good reviews. Doesn't look like it does a ton of business."

"Do they have their own website?" Josie stepped back from the door and scanned the front of the building. It didn't even have windows on the first level.

"Yes." Gretchen kept scrolling. "Family-owned. Passed down three generations. Now owned by a granddaughter of the original owners and her husband, Rebecca and Jonathan Lee. Here we go. It says to park in the lot and walk around the back."

They followed the curve in the driveway, avoiding puddles and muddy spots as they went. It widened as they passed the back of the house, leading to a stable which was painted white and appeared far more modern than the house. Two large trucks sat nearby, one with an open bay that held bales of hay, the other partially open with stacks of lumber protruding from the back door. The smell of mud and animal waste combined with that of straw and horse feed coalesced into a vaguely unpleasant odor, and yet it wasn't the earthy scent that Josie had encountered when she was leaning over Jane Doe's body. The doors to the stable stood open. The brown head of a horse poked from one of the stalls. It huffed. From somewhere beyond it came the sound of a man humming.

"Hello?" Josie called. "Mr. Lee? Jonathan Lee?"

"Just a minute now," came a man's voice. As promised, a moment later, a man in his fifties appeared in the center of the stable. He closed a stall, reached in to give a white-faced horse a pet, and then wiped his hands on his flannel shirt. As he came closer, a welcoming smile died on his ruddy, stubbled face. "Police?"

Josie and Gretchen presented their credentials. He read their names out loud and then his eyes narrowed on Josie's face. "You're the one on TV all the time. Don't you have a show?"

"That's my sister," Josie explained. Her twin, Trinity Payne, was an accomplished journalist who now had her own show about unsolved crimes. "Though I am on local television some-times to address cases that occur here in Denton."

This seemed to ease some of the tension in his face. Trinity had always told Josie that being on television made people feel like they knew her and that was part of why she got so much information out of them. In Josie's experience, being a police officer, it often had the opposite effect.

"My wife just went into the house," said the man.

Josie glanced at Gretchen for only a second, but she could hear Gretchen's unspoken comment: the police show up, and his first thought is to take them to his wife?

Before either of them could respond, a woman's voice behind them called out, "I'm right here, Jon." A woman in a fitted white T-shirt, jeans, and riding boots strode toward them. Her long gray-brown hair lay in a thick braid over her shoulder, bouncing against her chest as she walked. When she reached them, she extended a hand. "Rebecca Lee. This is my husband Jon."

Josie and Gretchen both shook her hand. Her grip was firm. She exuded a confidence that Josie felt immediately drawn to and a warmth that would put anyone at ease. The tension in Jon's shoulders drained as Rebecca took charge.

Gretchen took out her notebook and pen. "We're here to talk to you about Mira Summers. We understand she's a client here."

Jon crossed his arms over his chest. Rebecca's smile faltered, concern flaring in her wide, brown eyes. "Is Mira okay? Did something happen?"

"She was in a motor vehicle accident today," Josie said, giving them the approximate time. "She's being treated at Denton Memorial. She has a head injury. In addition, when she was removed from the car, the EMTs noticed that she had defensive stab wounds on her forearms."

Rebecca gasped. "Someone stabbed Mira?"

"It appears so," Gretchen answered. "That's all we know right now. We're trying to piece together what happened. The accident occurred on Prout Road. Mira doesn't remember much about it, but she said that she was on her way back from here."

Jon said, "That sounds right. She was here this morning. She comes every Sunday at the same time and rides Petunia."

"Was anyone with her?" asked Gretchen.

Rebecca slowly shook her head. "No. Why?"

"She had a passenger in the car with her," said Josie.

Jon and Rebecca exchanged a puzzled look. Jon said, "She always comes alone. Do you think—do you think maybe this passenger was the one who stabbed her?"

Rebecca said, "Where would she have picked up a passenger?"

"Was there anyone else here this morning?" asked Josie. "Other clients?"

"Sure," said Rebecca. "Sunday mornings tend to be busy. Most of those clients are gone now but we've still got two riders out. I didn't see Mira talking with any of them, though. Nobody left at or near the time she did. She was alone. She keeps to herself."

"She's very quiet," Jon added.

From the stables, a horse nickered. Josie said, "Does Mira come into contact with any children here?"

"I don't think so," Rebecca replied. "We have children's programs, but Mira isn't usually here during those hours. I've never seen her interacting with any of the children here."

Jon pushed a hand through his hair. "Me either."

"Do you two have children?" asked Josie.

"No," Rebecca said with a strained smile. "It wasn't in the cards for us."

"Nieces? Nephews?" Gretchen pressed.

"None, I'm afraid," Rebecca answered.

Josie pulled up the photo of the child's drawing. Before leaving the hospital, she'd cropped out the smears of blood. She showed it to Rebecca. "Does this look familiar?"

She studied it. "Is that an eye?"

Jon sidled up to her so that he could see it as well. There was no recognition in either of their faces.

"We're not sure," Gretchen said. "Are there any children who are here regularly who might have drawn that?"

"No," Jon said. "We don't really do that sort of thing. Heck, we don't even have crayons in the house."

"I honestly have no idea," Rebecca answered. "When they're here, they work with the horses. I have no idea what they do when they leave here. I'm sure all of them draw pictures, but if you're asking me if this drawing looks like something I would recognize as belonging to a specific child, the answer is no."

Another nicker came from the stables, followed by a banging sound. Jon sighed. "That will be Nutmeg wanting attention."

"She can wait," Rebecca said. "Why are you asking us about children?"

Josie pocketed her phone. "We believe that Mira or her passenger might have had contact with a child prior to the incident today. How about the produce stand alongside the driveway? Is that in use?"

"Not currently," Rebecca replied. "Next month, I expect we'll begin stocking it. We've got a garden on one of our lower fields and in the summer, if we've got surplus, we put it out there. Depending on the kind of year we're having and the weather, sometimes that thing is empty all year round."

"It's mostly clients who use it when it's stocked," said Jon. "They take what they need and leave a few dollars—or sometimes they leave other things in exchange, like firewood or hay. People are pretty good about it."

Rebecca smiled. "It's the faith system. We put good faith in people. We haven't been disappointed yet."

Josie had seen these types of stands in many places in rural Pennsylvania. She'd even seen some of them that had minifridges stocked with eggs. Those were usually close enough to the residence to be plugged in. Just as Jon said, she'd seen stands stocked exclusively with excess firewood bearing signs that told people to take what they needed and leave what they could afford.

Gretchen said, "We're going to need a list of all the other clients who were here this morning, if you don't mind."

Josie braced herself, waiting for the inevitable question about a warrant, which was well within the Lees' rights, but which would slow down the investigation, but Rebecca only shrugged. "Sure. That's not a problem, but shouldn't you be more concerned with this passenger?"

"The passenger was deceased at the scene," Josie explained. "With no identification."

Rebecca sucked in a sharp breath. "I'm so sorry to hear that."

"If you have a photo of this passenger, we could probably tell you if they were here this morning or if they're a client," Jon offered.

Rebecca shook her head, giving him a dark look. "Jon, please. I don't want to see a picture of a dead person."

He pushed a hand through his dark hair again. "Right, right. Of course." He smiled tightly and started walking toward the house. "I'll get that list for you."

Rebecca said, "But maybe you could describe the passenger? I might be able to tell you something from that, although..." She drifted off, looking down the driveway to where it turned toward the front of the house. "I just can't imagine where Mira would have picked up a passenger. Were there any vehicles broken down along the road?"

"No," Gretchen answered.

Josie took out her phone once more. "We have a photo."

Rebecca held up a hand, as if to ward her off. "Please. I'm sorry. I really don't want to see it."

Josie put her phone back into her pocket. "Female, Caucasian, short brown hair. Undernourished. Very thin. Wearing a white T-shirt and gray sweatpants."

"That doesn't sound like a client." She panned their surroundings. "It's so strange. All of our clients drive here. We're pretty far out of the city. Not in walking distance of anything, really. Right now there are three cars in the parking lot—I looked before I came out because I thought I heard Jon talking with someone out here. Two of them belong to our clients, who are out riding, and the other is yours, I assume."

"Yes," Josie confirmed.

"Everyone is accounted for. Well, I don't know where Mira would have picked up a passenger, but it wasn't here," Rebecca concluded.

"Do you always hear when cars pull up?"

Rebecca waved a hand. "If I'm in the house. I was down here with Jon and the other clients all day. I only went back to the house about a minute before you arrived."

Which meant that the passenger was probably not a Tranquil Trails client, but that someone could have brought Jane Doe with them to the stable and whatever happened could have transpired in the parking lot.

Probably thinking along the same lines, Gretchen asked, "Do you have cameras in the parking lot, or anywhere on the property?"

Rebecca laughed. "Goodness, no. What for? It's not like we've got thoroughbreds, and none of our horses participate in racing."

If Mira and Jane Doe had been stabbed in the parking lot or even in the driveway, she would have been close enough to the stables to come to the Lees for help. Which meant that it was possible she hadn't come into contact with the killer here—or Jane Doe.

"Standard procedure to ask," Gretchen explained. "Mrs. Lee, we understand that Mira is in your therapeutic riding program."

"Yes." Rebecca's eyes lit up. "It's a program for people who want to improve their mental and physical health. It's beneficial for people struggling with emotional issues, like past trauma, whether it arises from childhood problems or domestic violence. It also helps with processing grief. The reasons that clients come to us are many and often complex. Or sometimes they're not. We have a teenage boy who was routinely bullied at school. This program has helped him build confidence and self-esteem.

For some people, just being on horseback, enjoying the peace-fulness of the outdoors and nature can be very healing."

She beckoned them to walk with her through the stable to the opening on the other side. Spread before them was a huge expanse of rolling green pastures, punctuated with dirt riding trails, that went on for what looked like a couple of miles before terminating at a line of trees. Several of the paths continued into the tree line. Josie wondered what was beyond those trees. She tried scanning her mental map of Denton but came up empty. Denton PD rarely got called out this far.

Gretchen nodded. "It sure is beautiful."

Rebecca beamed. "Yes. Clients love it. I've always wanted to do this. I was a licensed psychologist before I quit my practice to take over this business for my parents. The results I've seen with our clients have been really rewarding."

"So you're actually Dr. Lee," asked Gretchen.

Rebecca rolled her eyes. "No one's called me that in ten years. It's just Rebecca." She sighed contentedly, surveying her domain. "This is so much better than sitting in a stuffy office all day."

Josie glanced over her shoulder where a couple of the horses huffed and nudged against their enclosures. "It definitely is," she agreed. "Do you keep records?"

Rebecca folded her arms over her chest, keeping her eyes straight ahead on the fields. A horse and rider emerged from the tree line, slowly climbing one of the trails back toward the stable. Finally, she said, "Yes, but they're confidential. I'm sure you're aware of what would be required if you wanted access to records pertaining to our clients' mental health."

"Of course," Gretchen said. "While we're here, would you mind if we looked around?"

Rebecca glanced back toward the house. "Sure, why not? Let's go to the house first. Jon should have that list for you by now."

TWELVE

He's sleeping now. We're still here. All alone. Of all the places we've been, I hate this one the most. I don't know time, but it feels like the forever-est place we've ever stayed. I sneak away from him and find my backpack. It's the one thing that is mine and only mine. I have all kinds of things in it. I'm not supposed to take things from other people in case the bad people put a camera in them or a microphone or something, but at the very bottom of the bag I hid some things that I got when I was in the normal world. A doll. A teddy bear. A Lego set of women who went into space.

I wish I could go to space. There wouldn't be any bad people and I would be far, far away from him and from being lonely and being careful all the time and hungry.

I don't get any of my secret things out. Instead, I find my big box of crayons and the coloring book that he gave me. It was one of the best special treats he ever bought me. I've colored all the pictures already and now I'm filling in all the places where there is no color, drawing my favorite things. My red crayon is just a small thing now. Even the wrapper is gone. Today I don't want to use it anymore because it reminds me of the blood.

Whose blood?
The whisper is back.

THIRTEEN

"Did you see the cats hanging around the stable?" asked Gretchen as they took a slow walk around the parking lot. The pickup truck that was parked there when they arrived had gone, leaving only the sedan, which they'd looked beneath using a flashlight.

"Yeah." Josie kept her eyes on her side of the lot. "But their fur colors don't match what we found on Jane Doe's body."

There was no way that someone had stabbed two women without leaving some kind of blood evidence behind. If the altercation happened in the Tranquil Trails lot, Josie would expect to find something.

Gretchen didn't take her eyes from her portion of the lot. "Doesn't mean there aren't more cats. Those are just the ones we saw."

Without a warrant, Josie and Gretchen had only been able to look around the portions of the Lees' premises that they'd been given permission to view. Although the house was unremarkable, together, Josie and Gretchen had only seen the first floor. Josie had been able to sneak upstairs, feigning the need to use the restroom, to do a plain-view search of the second floor.

Only one of the doors had been closed, but Josie hadn't heard anything from behind it. She still wasn't convinced they didn't have some sort of torture chamber that held a child in their basement. But if they wanted a look, they'd need a warrant, and to get a warrant, they'd need to prove that the crime happened on the property.

Which was why they were now searching for evidence that the stabbings happened in the parking lot. That was still within plain-view parameters.

Once they reached the end of the lot, they turned again, going back over ground they'd already covered twice. "We should get a geofence warrant," Josie said. "To extend from the accident site to here, since this is Mira Summers's last known whereabouts prior to the accident. If the attack happened within those parameters and the killer left with a child in his custody, we might be able to locate him that way."

A geofence was a virtual perimeter around a specific geographic area that enabled police to track which smart devices like cell phones were inside that area during a certain time period. Law enforcement had first started using geofence warrants in 2016. There were people who felt they were a massive invasion of privacy and in fact, in response to them, Google had recently changed the way it treated users' location history, which would now make it more difficult for law enforcement to effectively use geofence warrants, but it was worth a try. Presently the practice was still legal in Pennsylvania.

"Good idea," Gretchen agreed.

They took another pass through the parking lot. At this point, Josie wasn't sure why they were still looking. Although a great deal of blood had been found in Mira Summers's car, Josie would still have expected to find a significant amount wherever the actual stabbing had occurred. If it happened in this lot, it should have been immediately obvious.

A man appeared from behind the house, headed toward

them. As he got closer, Josie could see he was likely in his late twenties or early thirties. A drawstring bag swung from one of his thick hands. He was short and stocky with a mop of blond curls tumbling into his eyes. Like Mira's had been, his black riding boots were covered in mud. Thick thighs strained against his jeans. Red print across a black T-shirt proclaimed: *I Ride Horses Because Punching People is Frowned Upon.*

A fob appeared in his free hand as he approached the sedan. Squinting against the sun, he took in their Denton PD polo shirts and the guns at their waists. "You with the police? What's going on? I don't have no parking tickets due."

Josie and Gretchen walked over and presented their credentials. Josie said, "One of the other Tranquil Trails clients, Mira Summers, was involved in an incident today. We're trying to piece together her movements starting from this morning."

Gretchen added, "We know she was here until about eleven, eleven thirty. Do you remember seeing her?"

"Mira?" he said. "Sure. She's here every Sunday."

Gretchen's notebook was in her hand. "What's your name, sir?"

He clicked the key fob to unlock his doors but made no move to get inside the car. "Todd Stapleton."

"Are you in the therapeutic program?" asked Gretchen.

Todd tossed his bag onto the roof of the car. It landed with a clunk. Josie could see the outline of his riding helmet. "Nah," he said. "Not me. I just like to ride."

"Really?" Gretchen said, eyeing his shirt.

He leaned a hip against the driver's side door and smirked at Gretchen as he folded his powerful arms across his chest. "Really."

Josie said, "Do you know Mira Summers?"

Todd shook his head. "No. Don't know her other than to say hi, and that's all I've ever gotten out of her. She's real quiet. I know that what happened is probably none of my business, but is she under arrest or something?"

Gretchen shook her head. "No, the opposite, in fact. She was stabbed this morning. Her and another woman."

Todd's mouth dropped open. He pushed off the car and looked around, as if the person who'd attacked Mira and Jane Doe might still be lurking nearby. Then he pointed toward the ground at his feet. "Here?"

"That's what we're trying to figure out," Josie said. "Rebecca and Jon didn't see or hear anything."

"Damn." He scanned the trees edging the parking lot. "That don't make a damn bit of sense. I've been coming here five years. It's peaceful, and the people here are great—even the quiet ones like Mira. Who in the hell would do such a thing? You sure it was here?"

"This is the last place that Mira was seen," Gretchen said. "We know she left the stables to come here to the parking lot."

"Did you see anything unusual while you were here today?" asked Josie. "Anyone hanging around that you didn't recognize?"

He scratched the back of his neck. "No, but I was out on the trails."

"How about the other times you've been here?" Gretchen said. "Ever see anything or anyone who seems out of place?"

"I'm not sure. A lot of people come and go from here."

"Have you ever seen Mira Summers with any children?" asked Josie.

"No. Never saw her with any kids."

"How about adults?" Gretchen asked. "Ever see her with any adults?"

His lips pressed together while he considered her question. "Maybe? I don't know if it counts as 'with her.' I guess it does."

"What's that?" Josie said.

"I'm talking last year though," Todd added.

Gretchen's pen hovered above her notepad. "That's okay."

He pointed in the direction of Prout Road. "A few times I was leaving—I usually leave after Mira—and I saw her car parked at the produce stand. There was a guy there, too. He had a white box truck."

A frisson of excitement streaked up Josie's spine. "You saw them together more than once?"

He nodded. "Yeah, that's why I remember it."

"How many, precisely?" Gretchen asked.

Again, he scratched the back of his neck. "Don't know. At least three, maybe. Spring and summer. In the warm weather."

It was warm now. Just from walking around the property, a sheen of sweat covered Josie's skin and dampened her hair. "Was there any writing or anything on the side of the truck? Anything identifying?"

"No. It was just white."

Unlike most witnesses they spoke with, Todd Stapleton was not one to elaborate or bombard them with superfluous details. "What about the man you saw?" Josie asked. "Can you describe him?"

"Didn't get a real good look at him. I was just driving past. The produce stand sits back from the driveway a bit. He was older than me, maybe Jon's age? Maybe younger. Hard to say."

They waited for him to say more. Instead, he turned to the bag resting on top of his car and rifled through it until he came up with a plastic water bottle. Josie waited as he took a long swig and then squirted some down the back of his neck. When he still didn't speak, she said, "Did you see what he was wearing any of the times he was at the produce stand? His hair color? Anything like that?"

"Where's my manners?" He held out the water bottle to Gretchen, who refused, and then to Josie. She felt like she could down an entire gallon of water at the moment, but she wasn't comfortable drinking from Todd Stapleton's bottle.

"No thanks," she told him.

Gretchen said, "Mr. Stapleton. The man you saw—"

He tossed the bottle back into his bag. "Right, right. He wore a hat, like a baseball cap, but I didn't see what kind. Brownish-gray hair, I think. It was a little long and curly coming out from under the back of the hat. Looked like he had a beard. That's all I could see."

Gretchen scribbled in her notebook. "Tall? Short? Fat? Thin?"

"Average, I guess. Oh wait, you know what I remember? The one time I saw him, he had on a white T-shirt with cut-off sleeves and his arm had like this thick, gnarly scar on it. Right here." He pointed to the outside of his upper left arm, a couple of inches below the shoulder.

Gretchen flipped another page in her notebook and thrust it at Todd, along with her pen. "Could you draw it?"

Todd stared at her offering. His meaty palm rubbed at the back of his neck, fingers digging into the muscle. "I'm not real good at drawing, and like I said, he wasn't that close."

The scar that ran down the side of Josie's face from just below her ear to the center of her chin tingled. "But he was close enough for you to notice his scar, so it must have been pretty big."

"Yeah, I guess." With a sigh, he took Gretchen's notebook and pen and slowly began to draw, speaking as he went. "I'm pretty sure it was on his left arm, but not positive. It was kind of like, diamond-shaped, sort of? Except it didn't have straight lines. It was thick and white. He was real tan, that's why the scar stood out so much. Also, it was really lumpy..." He paused.

Josie tried not to grimace when she saw what he'd drawn. It was just a diamond with a thick border. He started to draw small half-crescents in the middle of it to represent the lumpiness, she guessed. "See? It's hard to show it but the scar looked raised. Like I said, it was gnarly."

The white told Josie that the scar was old but the thickness and raised skin indicated that perhaps it had needed to be stitched but hadn't been.

Gretchen took her notebook back, not doing much to hide her disappointment.

Todd chuckled. "Hey, I told you I couldn't draw."

"It's fine," Josie said. "Thanks for trying. Did you see this man speaking with Mira or interacting with her in any way?"

Todd opened his driver's side door and tossed his bag inside the car, clearly done with this conversation. "Never saw 'em talking. Just saw her car and him and his truck there at the same time. At first I thought he was just dropping stuff off at the stand and she was picking up some things on her way home, but then after I saw them together a few times, I thought they must know one another, or if they didn't before, they ought to by the third time they saw each other there."

"Did you see any children with him?" Josie asked.

A line creased his forehead. "No. None that I could see. Hey, we about done yet? I gotta get home. I really need a shower."

Gretchen took down his personal information and then gave him a business card before they watched him drive off. The second he was out of sight, they began to walk, following the curve in the driveway until the faded produce stand came into view. Driving past it earlier, Josie hadn't paid too much attention but now, as they stood along the edge of the driveway, she could make out where faint tracks had tamped down the grass between the driveway and the stand. Two of the tracks were thin and came from the direction of the stables. The other two were much wider and came from the direction of the road.

Josie's heart picked up its pace, hammering out a rapid beat. This had to be their crime scene.

Using her phone, she started taking photos. She and Gretchen took a wide berth, coming at the stand from an angle that avoided both sets of tracks. Josie was relieved that the rain they'd had in the last month had made parts of the terrain soft and muddy so that the wider tracks were sunk deep enough to make impressions. Hummel could make casts of the tire treads.

Up close, the stand was sturdier than it appeared from the road. The wood, though faded, was in good condition. Here, the mud and grass gave way to gravel. A breeze sighed through the tree branches overhead. For just a moment, Josie had a sense of the quiet and peace all around them. Away from the road, the house, and the parking lot, it felt private, even a bit secluded. The shade offered a cool refuge.

Then she rounded the other side of the stand, and the copious amounts of blood splattered and congealing across the small stones before her told a different story.

FOURTEEN

Gretchen waited near the produce stand, guarding the scene while Josie informed the Lees what they had found. They seemed shaken but had no objections to the police processing the scene and searching the premises. Despite that, Josie drove back to the stationhouse to prepare a warrant. It was still necessary in case the couple had a change of heart. Josie had seen that sort of thing happen before. Once she had the warrant, she contacted the ERT and called in a few more units to help with the search. By the time things were underway at Tranquil Trails, Josie estimated they had about two hours of daylight left.

While Hummel and his crew processed the crime scene, everyone else fanned out for a thorough search of the premises. Josie had checked the property records before returning. The place was far larger than they initially thought, extending south along Prout Road almost to the scene of the car accident. Their land included large tracts on the other side of Prout Road as well. It was a lot of ground to cover, but Josie didn't want to risk missing anything—especially if there was a child at risk.

She and Gretchen started at the house. Both Lees were in the kitchen. Jon paced back and forth in front of the long, rectangular oak table that spanned nearly the length of the entire room. His movements were frenetic. The wooden floorboards creaked beneath his boots. His mouth moved, as if he was mumbling, but no words came out. Rebecca sat calmly at one end of the table, sipping tea. The only sign of strain was a tightness at the corners of her eyes. She said, "How long will this take?"

Josie's gaze caught on the warrant spread out in front of Rebecca. "Probably several hours."

"Do you think you'll be finished by tomorrow?" Rebecca pressed. "I'm concerned that our clients will get upset if they see all this."

Gretchen tracked Jon's movements. "We'll be finished by tomorrow. There are a few more things we're hoping you can help with."

Rebecca wrapped her hands around her teacup and took a small sip. "Anything."

Jon paused to stare at his wife. Josie waited for him to speak, to object, as he seemed to grow more agitated the longer they were there, but he said nothing. It was almost like he was waiting for Rebecca to do it. However, she didn't even glance his way. With a huff, he stomped out of the room. Rebecca didn't acknowledge this either.

"We'll need to take a more thorough look around the house," Gretchen said.

"Of course," Rebecca agreed.

Josie inched away from the table and toward the doorway that connected the kitchen to the living room. Jon sat in a rocking chair in front of a dormant fireplace, pushing the chair to its limits until the floor groaned.

Gretchen continued, "Mrs. Lee, we're going to need a list of all commercial trucks that come and go from here regularly, their reason for being here, and their owners."

"Commercial trucks?" Rebecca echoed.

Hummel had taken one look at the larger tracks leading to the produce stand and declared that the treads definitely belonged to a commercial vehicle. Casts of the tracks would have to confirm it but Josie would bet a month's pay that Hummel was right. "We found tire tracks near the produce stand," she explained. "We believe that they're from a commercial truck. Our team will compare them to the trucks that you and your husband own, but we'll still need a list of any commercial vehicles that regularly come and go from here and that may have been here today."

Rebecca's brow furrowed. "There were no trucks here today —other than our own."

"We'll still need that list," Gretchen pressed.

"I'm happy to provide it," Rebecca answered. "Though I'm not sure what help it will be."

Josie asked, "Is there a man who drives a white box truck who delivers or picks up supplies here? Or who regularly visits the produce stand?"

She relayed the description they'd gotten from Todd Stapleton, including the diamond-shaped scar. Gretchen found the drawing Todd made in her notebook and showed it to Rebecca.

Rebecca's hands clenched the teacup until her knuckles went white. "I've never seen anyone like that here. Are you saying this man was there today? That he was driving a white box truck? The produce stand isn't even stocked right now. Why would anyone be there?"

From her peripheral vision, Josie noted that Jon had stopped rocking. "We have reason to believe that Mira had been meeting a man in a white box truck at the produce stand. We don't know for sure, but given their past meetings, it's possible they met there today."

Heavy feet trudged back into the kitchen. Jon stood in the doorway, looking stricken as he stared at his wife. Some silent communication raged between them. Rebecca's eyes narrowed until she was glowering at her husband. "Jon," she said. His name was a question that only he understood.

Clearing his throat, he said, "Can I see the drawing of the scar?"

Gretchen walked over and showed it to him.

Rebecca watched him carefully. "Jon?"

Looking up from Gretchen's notebook, he held his arms out, palms up, as if to show her they were empty. "I don't know for sure."

"Don't know what for sure?" Josie asked.

Rebecca pushed her teacup away so violently that it flipped onto its side, spilling what was left of its contents across the search warrant. Her tone was razor-sharp. "You promised, Jon."

Gretchen arched a brow. "It would be really helpful if you could tell us what's going on. We've already had two stabbing victims today, one of whom did not make it, and we're concerned there could be a child at risk."

Rebecca's rancor faded a bit, her face softening. "It can't be Seth then. He doesn't have children. I don't even think he knows anyone with children."

Jon didn't look quite as relieved, but he nodded.

Josie said, "Who is Seth?"

"My brother," Jon answered.

FIFTEEN

"Rebecca's right, though," Jon added. "He doesn't have children, but he does have a scar just like you described on his upper arm. It was from when he—"

Jon broke off mid-sentence, looking at his wife, as if waiting for her to throw some sort of lifeline. She offered none. He opened his mouth as if he was about to continue but then clamped it shut again.

"Mr. Lee?" Josie prompted.

With a sigh, Rebecca stood up and went to the counter for some paper towels. "Really, Jon. Just tell them."

Still, he said nothing. Finally, Gretchen said, "Let's just get some basic information for now. You two have the same last name?"

Jon nodded.

Gretchen jotted the name down. They'd look Seth up on one of the mobile data terminals as soon as they left the house. "Seth Lee. How old is he?"

"Younger than me. Forty-eight this year, I believe."

Jumping in, Josie asked, "Is he violent?"

Jon stole another glance at his wife. "No, nothing like that."

Rebecca sopped up her spilled tea with the paper towels. "Seth has some issues. He's always struggled."

Josie retrieved more paper towels, handing them to Rebecca so that she could blot the warrant. "Struggled with what?"

"Mental health." Rebecca worked at the pages of the warrant, but the ink had already blurred in most places. "You have to understand that what I say here is my personal opinion. I've never treated Seth. He's never been a patient. I would never see him—not that he would agree to any type of mental health treatment—because it's a conflict of interest."

"But you *are* a psychologist," Josie said. "Kind of like a doctor is always a doctor even if they're not seeing patients."

Rebecca smiled tightly. "Yes. If I was a dermatologist, I might see someone in the grocery store with a rash on their hands and have a strong suspicion of what it was because that's my field."

"But you can't say for sure..." Jon began but trailed off when Rebecca scowled at him.

"I know he's your baby brother, Jon, but this needs to stop."

He stepped toward her, his tone pleading. "You don't understand what he went through, Bec. In the army—"

Rebecca threw down a sopping wet handful of paper towels, wetting the warrant all over again. "Nothing happened to him in the army, Jon! That's a fiction that his brain created. It's all part of his disorder."

"He said that things happened to him while he was in that made him the way he is."

"No, Jon. That is coming from his disorder. Even if he'd never joined the army, he would still be like this! Don't you get it?"

"How do you know that?" Jon pushed. "How can you know that?"

Rebecca's voice rose to a shout, causing all three of them to jump. "Because it's my goddamn job, Jon! Do we have to have this same fight again? I thought we settled this years ago."

Jon pointed a trembling finger at her. "You decided this."

Rebecca rushed around the table. For a moment, Josie wondered if they were going to have to break up a physical altercation between the spouses. "You want to point fingers?" Rebecca spat. "You lied to me. Again. Like the time you rented him that apartment without telling me—without even consulting me! How long has he been coming here? How long have you been helping him?"

Jon lowered his arm, suddenly not able to meet his wife's eyes.

With a huff, Rebecca threw her arms in the air and let them fall to her sides. "Unbelievable. Since we took over this place, then. Absolutely unbelievable."

"I told him he couldn't come any further onto the property," Jon said quietly. "He agreed to only come when he was in dire need of food. There is no harm in letting him access the produce stand."

Rebecca strode back to the table and fisted a page of the warrant, shaking it. Pieces of moist paper broke off and fell to the floor. "No harm, Jon? No harm? One of our clients was stabbed today! At the produce stand! Tell me it wasn't him? It's the same damn scar!"

"He wouldn't be meeting Mira!" Jon roared, whatever was left of his self-control slipping. "They don't even know one another. If you would stop being such a fucking bitch for five seconds—"

Gretchen was in front of Jon before Josie even saw her move, making him back up into the other room with her proximity. "That's enough. Mr. Lee, I'd like you to step outside with me for a few minutes."

When he didn't move, Gretchen used her notebook to

gesture toward the door and said in her most stern, no-nonsense voice, "Now, Mr. Lee."

This seemed to get through to him. "I'm sorry," he said. "I got angry. I'm sorry."

"We'll talk outside," Gretchen told him. "There's a uniformed officer out there I'd like you to meet. He'll keep you company while we finish speaking with your wife. You'll calm down and then she'll join you while we search the house. Let's go."

Once the door slammed, Rebecca sank back into her chair and put her face in her hands. Josie walked over and took the seat closest to her. "Should I be worried about leaving you alone with your husband when we finish what we're doing here?"

Rebecca lifted her head and gave Josie a tired smile. "No. Jon won't hurt me, and I can handle myself. It's certainly not the first time we've resorted to name-calling in our marriage."

Noah had never resorted to name-calling in their marriage, but Josie's first husband, Ray, had—when he was drunk. Josie had never imagined he would hit her until he did. Then again, name-calling didn't always escalate to physical abuse.

As if she could see Josie trying to work something out in her mind, Rebecca said, "Really, Detective. I'll be fine. Jon just gets very worked up when it comes to Seth. He's very protective."

The back door slammed again. A moment later, Gretchen appeared. She pulled out the chair opposite Josie and sat. "Mr. Lee has declined to discuss his brother at this time."

"I'm sure," Rebecca said.

"Do you mind telling us what you can about Seth?" asked Josie.

Rebecca gave them a sad smile. "Would you like some tea before we begin?"

SIXTEEN

Josie and Gretchen declined tea but Rebecca prepared some anyway. While the kettle heated, she cleaned up the rest of the mess on the table, transferring what was left of the warrant onto the counter and speaking as she worked. "I suppose you should know about his disorder first since all things flow from there. Again, I can only tell you what I suspect, and I would never testify to it in court."

"Of course," said Josie. "We understand."

"If I had to guess, he's got delusional disorder. The average age of onset is forty but that's not written in stone. It can start manifesting as early as eighteen, or much later than forty. I think he's been struggling with it since his early twenties. He was in the army then. He enlisted at eighteen. He was discharged at twenty-two. A general discharge, so not honorable but not dishonorable. I don't know the details but I'm quite certain, based on what I knew of him at that time, that his disorder started to manifest while he was in the service and eventually led to his discharge."

Gretchen scratched her temple with the cap of her pen.

"Delusional disorder. What exactly does that mean? I've met people in this line of work with a pretty wide range of delusions. Everything from thinking a celebrity is in love with them to believing that aliens abducted them."

The tea kettle whistled. Rebecca turned down the heat and then began pouring hot water into three teacups. "The alien thing is not delusional disorder. That's something else. Bizarre delusions. Those are delusions that certain things are happening that have no basis in reality. They could never happen. Delusional disorder is typically characterized by non-bizarre delusions which are scenarios that could happen in real life, like being followed or that your spouse is being unfaithful despite all evidence to the contrary. The delusions may be unlikely but they could technically happen. There are various types of non-bizarre delusions: grandiose, somatic, jealous, persecutory, erotomania. However, I have always believed that Seth presented with mixed delusions."

Josie accepted the teacup. "What makes you say that?"

Rebecca set a cup in front of Gretchen and then offered them a box with various types of tea. "For most of his life he's thought that people were out to get him, whether it was a boss or a neighbor or the guy who sold him his car. He often expressed fears that he was being spied on. He believed that his superiors from when he served in the army were after him. He used to say that they thought he saw something that he wasn't supposed to see and wouldn't believe him if he said he'd seen nothing. He thought they were going to take him away and kill him and no one would know what happened to him."

Josie chose Earl Grey. "Do you think there was any truth at all to his suspicions? Maybe something did happen while he was in the army?"

Rebecca left the table to retrieve milk, sugar, and spoons. "And that he blew it out of proportion? No. I don't think so.

Like I told Jon, if he had been doing something else at that time in his life, his delusions would have to do with that. He's always been suspicious of everything and everyone. Even beyond the army thing. He's never had a cell phone—because of the spying thing. In the past, Jon never had a way to reach him. He just had to wait for Seth to show up."

Gretchen stirred milk and sugar into her own tea. "All that paranoia must make it hard for him to lead a normal life."

Rebecca prepared her own tea slowly and carefully. "It does. He's never been able to hold a job for any significant length of time—not because he is unable to behave normally but because he would get too wrapped up in his delusions that coworkers were trying to get him fired, or that his employer was somehow monitoring him even after he left work."

"What kind of work does he do?" Josie asked.

"Odd jobs. Handyman stuff. He's worked on farms. He generally takes jobs that are under the table. Cash only, so it's untraceable. He doesn't like there being records of anything. For a time, he worked in a factory but that didn't last. The scar on his arm? He thought his employer at the time had planted a microchip inside him, almost like the kinds that people have put into their dogs, except he became convinced that it could track his movements. Evidently, he became aware that the FDA had approved an implantable chip for humans in 2004. They were supposed to be for holding a person's medical data so that in an emergency, doctors or hospitals could scan the chips and have the patient's history instantly available. The practice never caught on, but Seth believed that one had been implanted in him and he was trying to cut it out."

"That's..." Josie trailed off. What kind of damage could that kind of person do to others if he were violent? Was the fact that his delusions led him to inflict bodily harm on himself any indicator that he might be violent toward others?

"Disturbing," Gretchen filled in.

"Yes," Rebecca agreed. "That's the worst he's ever been, as far as I know. His other behaviors can be odd but not necessarily harmful. For example, he's never stayed in one place very long. He's kind of a nomad. Likes to stay outdoors if he can, and I mean sleep outdoors. State gameland. Campsites. There were a few times he set up camp on private property and got kicked out. I think he was charged with trespassing a few times, but nothing ever came of any of it."

"Why isn't he welcome here?" asked Josie.

Rebecca grimaced. "Listen, Seth presents quite normally most of the time. He's quiet, polite, pleasant. He's not a monster. It's the longer-term that becomes an issue. The more time you spend around him, you begin to see how his delusions manifest and honestly, he gets to be disruptive. I can't have him thinking that the food we're eating has been tampered with or that our water supply has been poisoned. Or that our clients are out to get him. Over time, his delusions take over every aspect of life. Having him around would not be good for our business. We do need income to survive. It's as simple as that, and in spite of Jon's behavior today, he knows that."

Gretchen sipped her tea. "Your husband said Seth isn't violent, but could someone with delusional disorder be violent?"

Rebecca shrugged. "Anyone can be violent. The vast majority of people suffering from any particular mental illness never become violent, but it's not outside the realm of possibility."

"Have you ever known Seth to be violent?"

"No, but I haven't seen him in years. Jon deals with him."

"How about girlfriends? A wife?" Josie asked. "Has he been able to maintain any relationships?"

Rebecca smiled weakly. "My mother always said, 'there's a lid for every pot,' so who knows. He brought a woman to our wedding. That was decades ago. I think her name was Debbie or maybe Deirdre. I'm not sure how long they were together, but we never saw her again and he only talked about her once after that. He told Jon he didn't think it would work out between them because she wanted children and he didn't. I do remember that he accused her of cheating on him with someone at our wedding even though she never left his side except to use the ladies' room. One of Jon's friends made him leave the moment he started causing a scene. It could have been so much worse."

Josie let her tea steep, stomach turning. "You're absolutely sure that Seth had no children and no access to children?"

"As sure as I can be," Rebecca said. "I haven't seen him since we moved here and took over the business. He used to come by our apartment in Denton's central district back when we lived there, and I had an office. He never gave any indication that he had had children or had any cause to be around them. Like I said, he didn't want them. Maybe he had a girlfriend who had children of her own? But he never talked about having a girlfriend and he was always alone. That said, he didn't engage much with me. Jon would probably know more."

Gretchen tapped her pen against her notepad. "I asked him while we were outside. He said the same. No kids, no girl-friends. Do you think there is any possibility that Seth would abduct a child? One that is not known to him?"

A look of horror flashed across Rebecca's face. "No, no. Despite all of his issues, I can't see Seth ever doing something like that."

Yet, if Seth was the one who had attacked Mira Summers and Jane Doe earlier in the day, that meant he was capable of murder. In that case, it wasn't a stretch to think him capable of kidnapping.

Josie said, "We can run an address search on Seth, but given what you've told us about his lifestyle, I'm guessing he might not be found at his address of record. Do you have any idea where we might find him?"

"I'm sorry, but no. Jon might—"

"He doesn't," Gretchen said.

"Right," Rebecca said. "We've never known where to find him. We've always just waited for him to show up and wreak havoc."

SEVENTEEN

Josie dropped the receiver of her desk phone back into its cradle. Her chair creaked as she stood and massaged the stiff, aching muscles of her lower back. Three empty Komorrah's cups were lined up on her desk. Despite the mass quantities of caffeine she'd ingested upon their return from Tranquil Trails, she still felt exhausted. Immediately after speaking with Rebecca, Josie and Gretchen had pulled up a copy of Seth Lee's driver's license on one of the mobile data terminals and found his address listed in a small town in Bucks County, about two hours east of Denton. Josie had called the local PD there and asked them to make contact with Seth.

"That was Officer Renee Simmons of the Doylestown Police Department. Seth Lee is not at his last known address, and the landlord says he hasn't lived there for over three years. He never forwarded his mail, so they've got three years' worth of it. Doesn't remember Seth that well—if he ever had kids with him or anything—but said he was the only person on the lease."

Across the room, Gretchen affixed a copy of the child's drawing they'd found clutched in Jane Doe's hand to the huge rolling corkboard the Chief had purchased the year before. She

turned toward Josie, brushing the remnants of two pecan croissants from her chest. "Why doesn't that surprise me? How
about the sedan registered in his name?"

"It wasn't there either," Josie answered. "And we can't put
out a BOLO for the car or for Seth Lee unless we can connect
him to the crime scene. Just because he was at that produce
stand last year doesn't mean he was there today."

"True." Gretchen picked up a copy of the back of the
drawing and hung it.

HELP

The letters were a taunt and a challenge, and eerily at odds
with the cheery flower above them. Gretchen sifted through the
documents on her desk and came up with another piece of
paper which she pinned to the corkboard. This was an enlarged
copy of Seth Lee's driver's license. It hadn't been lost on either
one of them that he had a commercial driver's license, which
meant that he could legally drive a box truck or any other
commercial vehicle.

Piercing blue eyes stared at them from the photo, which,
according to DMV records, was three years old. The resemblance to his brother was there but it was minimal. Seth had a
stronger, sharper jawline. His dark hair was thick and wavy
with fewer gray hairs than Jon. He was definitely more striking
than his older brother. Except for the hint of menace in the flat
line of his mouth, he was attractive. It wasn't a stretch to think
that as a younger man he might have caught the eye of many
women. The question was whether or not those women had
stuck around once his disorder became obvious to them—and
had any of them had children? Or had he kidnapped a child
who had no relation to him at all? Although they could check
for any missing children in the state, without more information
on the child with Seth, they wouldn't be able to determine
whether or not he'd abducted someone.

"We could try the hospital again," Josie suggested.

They'd gone there once after leaving Tranquil Trails to ask Mira about Seth Lee, but she'd been sleeping and the medical staff were adamant about them leaving her alone until morning. Apparently, she had become hysterical after being admitted to the ward, and it had taken them hours to get her to calm down.

Instead, Josie and Gretchen returned to the stationhouse to finish their reports and prepare additional warrants; one for the geofence and two for Mira Summers's phone. The first warrant was a 'power up' warrant that gave them permission to plug the phone into their GrayKey device in order to access its contents. Law enforcement used GrayKey to unlock cell phones even if they were password-protected or turned off. The second warrant allowed them to search the contents they downloaded. Since Summers had a concussion, Josie wasn't comfortable getting her consent to search her phone. It would take longer to access it with warrants, but if it held critical information, there would be no questions about how that evidence was obtained.

Gretchen started hanging up printouts from Google Maps, slowly forming a picture of the area between the expansive Tranquil Trails property and the scene of the accident. "I know it's after midnight, but I'm pretty sure when the nurse said tomorrow, she meant the part of the morning with daylight. Besides, it might be better to gather more information about this guy before we talk with Mira."

Josie picked up the nearest coffee cup and took the lid off, hoping for some dregs. There was nothing. "Seth's prints are in AFIS from his various felony trespassing arrests." The charges from all of which had been dismissed. Josie wondered if Jon Lee had footed the bill for Seth to have good attorneys—and whether Rebecca was aware. "If Hummel can match any of the prints he pulls from the murder weapon to Seth, we won't need confirmation from Mira that he was at the scene."

"Exactly," Gretchen agreed. "Although if Seth is our

suspect, we'll still need to figure out the connection between him and Mira and him and Jane Doe. For that, we'd have to start with Mira."

"One thing at a time," Josie murmured. She reached past the coffee cups and picked up a small sheaf of copy paper. "By the way, I ran both the Lees' names. Rebecca's got no priors and no warrants. Jon Lee was convicted of simple assault eleven years ago. He spent nine months in prison before being released for good behavior. He was on probation for two years after that. There were a slew of other misdemeanor charges, but they were dropped."

"Really?" Gretchen turned away from the board to gawk at Josie. "Were you able to get any details?"

Josie edged around her desk, moving toward the corkboard. She was momentarily distracted by the drawing. What was the drawing supposed to be? Was it really an eye? Where was the child now?

"Josie?" Gretchen prompted.

"I did get some information. Jon Lee punched a woman in the parking lot of a department store."

Gretchen gave a low whistle. She picked up a Sharpie and used it to mark the boundaries of Tranquil Trails—from the bank of the Susquehanna River on one side, across Prout Road, to a strip of forest on the other. "Well, well, well, that is certainly interesting."

Josie wondered if Rebecca had told the truth when she said Jon was not a threat. She glanced at the clock on the wall. Now half past midnight. She had been so absorbed in the case that she hadn't paid attention to the time. It was late, but she would still make the home study and that was all that mattered.

The door to the stairwell whooshed open and Chief Chitwood strode in. His acne-pitted face was red, which usually meant he was unhappy about something. Although, to be fair, that did seem to be his natural state. He was also dressed in jeans and a long-sleeved cotton shirt rather than the more formal suits he usually wore to work. "Detectives!" he barked. "What in the hell is going on around here?"

Gretchen looked over at him, unimpressed. She hung another piece of the map. "What are you doing here after midnight?"

He advanced on them. "I was on a college visit with Daisy today. God, not that I want this kid to go to college hours away from me. Never mind that. The point is that I had my phone turned off. I had told Sergeant Lamay to give me any important updates. When I got home and turned it on, guess what?" He held up two fists and then made a noise that sounded like an explosion as he splayed his fingers outward. "It blew up."

Gretchen shrugged. "You should have waited till morning to check your phone."

He pointed a long finger at her. "Don't be a smart-ass. No one likes a smart-ass."

Josie tossed the report on Jon Lee onto her desk. "Actually," she said. "That's not true."

It was an exchange they had often. As usual, he had no patience for the argument. He whirled on her. "Don't you start, too. Wait. What are you doing here? It's your day off."

"No shit." Josie made a fist and used her knuckles to knead the muscles in her lower back.

"What happened to Turner?" he asked.

Gretchen shot him a look so caustic, Josie half expected him to drop where he stood. "Good question."

"Not sure," said Josie. "He was on a bank robbery that evidently took all day and most of the evening. Maybe he came in after, but we were out in the field, so we didn't see him."

The Chief's bluster dissipated. His gaze swept toward his office door. Quietly, he said, "I'll talk to him. I'm sure you just missed each other."

"Did you lose a bet?" Gretchen called after him. "Is that why we're stuck with him?"

"Shut it, Palmer," the Chief hollered back.

"You owed someone a favor?" she pressed.

Josie mouthed 'stop' at Gretchen. Then she covered her mouth to quiet her laughter.

Undeterred, Gretchen stepped toward the Chief's office. "I'm just saying, all those applicants, and he was the best we could do?"

"Seriously," Josie hissed. "Stop!"

But she could hear the Chief's frenetic steps as he burst back into the great room. He glared at Gretchen. "One more word, Palmer, and it's your ass. Not that you're owed any explanation, because you're not, but Turner's got experience. He's just as qualified as any of you. He worked at a similarly sized department north of Philadelphia. He's been at this for a long time."

"I know that," Gretchen shot back. "I checked. He was profiled in their city paper for taking the lead on the escort serial killer case, which I'm surprised he was even able to solve, given his work ethic."

"Palmer!" he started to yell, but changed his mind when she turned her back on him, walking over to Turner's desk—Mettner's old desk. She placed both hands on the back of the chair and squeezed. She kept her head down and breathed deeply, as though trying to shore herself up. The Chief locked eyes with Josie, asking her an unspoken question, to which she nodded. This wasn't just about Turner.

The Chief sighed and dragged a hand over his face. His voice softened to its gentlest tone, one that he normally only used with two people: his much younger sister, Daisy, whom he'd adopted, and Josie. He'd become a lot less prickly with her, at least, since she'd helped him solve the murder of his other sister. "Palmer," he said. "No one is going to be Mett. There is no one I could bring in here who would be satisfactory to all of you. You don't have to get along. You just have to do the job. You got problems with Turner? Be adults. Figure it out. Now, tell me what the hell's going on around here."

EIGHTEEN

Josie arrived home before two a.m. She took a brief tour of the house, astounded by how neat and clean it looked. Turned out Noah was a hell of a cleaner. In the bedroom, she let her eyes adjust to the darkness. They'd put a nightlight in the hallway for when Harris slept over and with their bedroom door open, it gave off just enough light for Josie to make out Trout lifting his sleepy head from the foot of the bed. Josie pet him and kissed the top of his head. He made a snuffling sound and burrowed his face under the covers. Once he was asleep, he rarely woke. As guard dogs went, he was pretty useless, but he made up for it in cuteness. Josie stripped her clothes off and deposited them into the hamper. Then she slid into bed behind Noah, pressing her chest against his back, happy to find him shirtless. She snaked an arm around his waist, her fingers moving slowly upward as she traced the lines of his torso.

"Welcome home," he said, his voice foggy with sleep.

His skin against hers sent her pulse into overdrive, in spite of the late hour and the exhaustion that tugged at every muscle in her body. She snuggled closer, fitting her legs against the backs of his as she trailed light kisses over his shoulder. He caught the hand lazily tracing the ridges of his abdomen and held it against his chest. His heartbeat thudded beneath it, strong and steady.

"Want to talk about the case?" he asked.

HELP

She tried to put the drawing and the idea of a child suffering somewhere as well as the image of Jane Doe into her mental vault for the night. She'd never sleep if she didn't. "No," she said.

Even half-asleep, Noah was attuned to the tone of her voice. He rolled toward her, bringing a hand to her cheek. "You sure about that?"

At their feet, Trout stirred. He made a noise like a huff and then jumped down from the bed and flopped onto the carpet. Seconds later, he was snoring.

"I'm sure," Josie told Noah. She pressed the full length of her body against his and took his hand from her face, sliding it down her body until it rested against the bare skin of her hip. She smiled when he pulled her closer. He sounded fully awake when he asked, "You want me to clear your head?"

She pulled him in for a kiss. "What do you think?"

Josie woke before their alarm went off. The bed was empty. She listened to the sounds of Noah and Trout moving around downstairs, cycling through the stages of their morning routine. Would that routine one day involve a child? Today would go a long way toward determining the answer to that very question. Immediately, she squashed the anxiety that bubbled in the pit of her stomach. She hadn't even had coffee yet. There would be time for worry later. She turned her head toward the sunlight streaming through the miniblinds. Noah had opened them before he went downstairs. He knew she liked the light. He knew everything that she liked. A smile curved her lips as she thought about the night before. Gone was the muscle pain and fatigue in her body. Even her mind felt quieter. It had become a joke between them that sex cleared her head, but in fact, it had always been true. Lucky for her, Noah was more than willing to oblige.

She found him downstairs in the kitchen, pouring himself a cup of coffee. The back door stood open. Through the screen she could see Trout selecting the perfect place to do his business. On the kitchen table was a basket of muffins. Josie knew just by the sight and smell of them that Misty had baked them. She must have dropped them off that morning. Next to the basket was a drawing from Harris. In it, Josie and Noah stood next to what looked like a crib. Inside rested a bundle that represented a baby. Along the top of the page, in big, awkward letters he'd written: "Good Luck" and at the bottom of the page, simply: "Harris."

The quality was far more advanced than the drawing they'd found in Jane Doe's hand but the writing looked about the same in terms of the accuracy and spacing of all the letters.

HELP

"Josie," Noah said, his tone so serious that her hand froze over the page. When she looked up at him, he gave her a tight smile. "The case manager called about ten minutes ago. She's sick. We have to postpone."

Josie picked up Harris's drawing, clutching it against her chest as she plopped into the nearest chair. She knew she shouldn't feel defeated. The entire process was fraught with setbacks and lots of waiting, but she couldn't stop the disappointment from rolling over her like some kind of emotional rogue wave.

Noah walked over and squeezed her shoulder. "I'm sorry."

She shook her head. "It's not a big deal. We'll still have the home study, just not today."

He laughed. "Yeah, now we get to be anxious for another week or two or three. Good times."

From beyond the screen door, Trout whined. Noah let him in. He made a beeline for Josie, his nails click-clicking on the tile. With her free hand, she scratched behind his ears and assured him that he was the best boy in the entire world. Satisfied, he curled up on top of her feet.

Josie turned her attention back to Harris's drawing.

Noah's gaze followed hers. "Harris might be more disappointed than us about this postponement."

For a seven-year-old, he was strangely invested in the idea of Josie and Noah "getting a baby" so he could have a "cousin" to play with. Josie's heart clenched. She put the drawing back on the table, face down. As he often did when Misty took him to work with her, Harris had used the back of her office letterhead as his canvas. His art teacher this year had ignited his new love for drawing. Josie was pretty sure it rivaled his love for T-ball at this point. He drew on any piece of paper he could get his hands on, and sometimes napkins.

Did the child responsible for the drawing in Jane Doe's death grip like to draw as much as Harris did? Who had given them the paper and crayons? She hoped that Hummel would be able to get prints from it that might help lead them to the child.

Trout shifted on top of her feet and let out a small whimper.

"Hey," Noah said, brow furrowing. "What's going on?"

Josie traced her fingers over the embossed letterhead. Denton Women's Center. "It's this case I caught yesterday. I think there's a child involved."

Noah leaned down and gave Trout a reassuring pet. "Work is always a good distraction. Tell me."

He poured her a coffee and they sat at the kitchen table. Josie walked him through the case in detail. When she'd finished, Noah laced his hands behind his head and leaned back in his chair. "Do you have a picture of the drawing?"

Josie found the photo on her phone and showed it to Noah.

"It looks like... an eye, maybe?" he said, taking the phone from her hands so he could better study it. Then he swiped to the photo of the plea for help.

"Yeah," she agreed. With a sigh, she pulled the basket of muffins closer. Blueberry, and chocolate chip with banana. Their favorites. "That was my first thought, but look closer. It makes kind of a weird eye."

"At this point," Noah said, "I'm not sure it matters what this is supposed to be. What we really need to do is work with what we already know. Two women were in the car. So far you can't connect any children to Mira."

Josie broke off a chunk of one of the chocolate chip banana muffins and stuffed it into her mouth. There was nothing that Misty made that didn't make her eyes roll into the back of her head. She wondered if there was some kind of cooking gene, and she just hadn't gotten it. Turning her attention back to the case, she said, "You're right, and since Jane Doe was holding the drawing, she should be the focus now. I've got to talk to Anya. Get the autopsy results and see if she had any luck getting an ID. I'm sure we can get the Chief to approve you to come in today and take your PTO when the home study is rescheduled. I'll call Anya now to see if she's ready for us."

Ten minutes later, Josie hung up with Dr. Feist. "Ten a.m.," she told Noah.

"Perfect," he said. "We just had an opening on our calendar."

NINETEEN

"Put that away!"

He stands over me. I didn't hear him coming because he is so quiet when he moves. He says it's from so much time avoiding the bad people.

"I'm coloring," I say. He slept all night and all morning and didn't give me any food and I'm so bored and sad.

I'm using my blue crayon now. The one called Robin Egg Blue.

He yanks the book out of my hands, tearing the cover. I jump up. "Stop!" Tears sting my eyes and my face.

He looks all around us and then his voice gets soft, like he's trying to be nice. "I'm sorry, but you know that you can't be seen with this stuff."

"Tell me what you did, and I'll put it away." I'm trying hard not to be afraid of him but there are two dried reddish drops on his left boot and I'm worried.

"I told you," he says. "I did what was necessary to protect us. You're too young to know the details."

Who did you hurt? Who did you hurt? Who did you hurt?

I want to ask but the drops on his boot must be blood and I want to know whose blood but if he tells me, I might die, too.

He gives me the book and I hide it inside my bag with my crayons. Tears roll down my cheeks. I can't stop them. I think it's because I know who he hurt and I wish I didn't.

TWENTY

The morgue was located in the basement of Denton Memorial Hospital. Fittingly, it was in one of the most depressing areas of the building. Yellowed tile cracked beneath their feet as Josie and Noah walked the long hall leading to the suite that comprised Anya's domain. Every other room in this section of the basement was unused, giving the space a creepy, abandoned feeling. The walls, once white but now gray from a thick coating of grime, didn't help. Neither did the putrid odor of stringent chemicals and decomposing bodies that hung heavy in the air.

Kyle Turner stood outside the doors to the exam room, leaning against the wall with one heel tucked up behind him. His head was bent to his phone. Thick brown curls, shot through with gray, fell across his forehead. In his other hand he held a can of the energy drink he always consumed in lieu of coffee. Hearing their footsteps over the tile, he turned his deep-set blue eyes toward them. He pushed himself off the wall, coming to his full height. He towered over Josie but only had a few inches on Noah. Pocketing his phone, he stroked his thumb and index finger over his beard.

"If it isn't the lovebirds," he said, the snark in his tone grating on Josie's nerves.

"Don't start, Turner," Noah said.

He raised a brow. "Someone's grumpy this morning. What? You two having trouble in the bedroom?"

Josie looked up to see a muscle in Noah's jaw tick. "Turner, keep it professional or I'm writing you up. In case you've forgotten, I'm your lieutenant."

Turner eyed Noah with a wicked glint in his eye. For a second, Josie was certain that he was going to keep pushing. It certainly wasn't the first time he'd remarked on the fact that Josie and Noah were married, but he'd never been so crass before. Josie could tell by the tension rolling off Noah's body that he was near his breaking point with Turner.

Lucky for him, Turner didn't press. Lowering his eyes, he mumbled a sorry.

Josie said, "What are you doing here?"

He slugged down the rest of his drink, crumpled the can and walked across the hall to throw it into a trash bin. "Apparently, I'm not working hard enough."

"Did you come to that conclusion on your own?" Noah asked. "It's very insightful."

Turner kept his eyes locked on Josie. "Thanks, Lieutenant, but no, I did not. I was out doing my job yesterday and I guess someone wasn't happy with my performance."

"I'm not even going to dignify that with a response," Josie said. "No one tattled on you, Turner. Your 'work' stands for itself."

Gretchen had given the Chief a hard time for having hired him, but she hadn't come right out and talked about his shoddy work, which meant that the Chief must have checked the files and seen that Turner had either not completed the paperwork on the bank robbery or had only partially completed it. The fact that Turner hadn't even made an appearance at the stationhouse while Josie and Gretchen were there, in spite of still being on shift, was also obvious. The Chief had noticed without either of them pointing it out.

Noah said, "That's between you and the Chief. We've got work to do."

"I'm here to help with your Jane Doe." Turner drummed his fingers against his thigh. "I read all the reports. I'm up to speed."

"Fine," said Noah. "But if you want to help, your time would be better spent on other things while we talk to Dr. Feist about the autopsy. Go upstairs and interview Mira Summers. Find out what she was doing meeting Seth Lee at the Tranquil Trails produce stand last year. We need to know the connection between them and whatever she knows about him, like where we can find him and whether he's got a kid with him. Also see if she remembers anything about the attack now that she's had some rest. Then go back to the stationhouse and check on the warrants that are outstanding. Mira Summers's phone records and the GPS report for her vehicle as well as the results of the geofence warrant. Our priority is finding the child who made the drawing as soon as possible."

Turner didn't respond right away, giving Noah an assessing look. For a long moment, the only sound in the hallway was the tap-tap-tap of Turner's fingers against his suit pants. Again, Josie wondered if he would push back. He never liked being told what to do, and he enjoyed provoking people just for the sake of it. As though he liked to see just how angry he could make all of them.

Noah said, "I'll expect a briefing when we get back to the stationhouse."

With that, he pushed open the door to the morgue and ushered Josie through, leaving Turner alone in the hallway.

Josie took a deep breath in and out. Noah touched her lower back briefly, easing some of her agitation. Just being in the same vicinity as Turner made her irritable, which made her feel idiotic. This wasn't middle school, and he wasn't some asshole bully on the playground. She didn't even let criminals get under her skin this much. Why did he raise every hackle she had? Thinking about what the Chief had said the night before, she wondered if it was because of Mett. Was Turner really that irritating, or was it simply that he wasn't Mett? Or a bit of both?

"Focus on Jane Doe," Noah said softly.

Nodding, Josie walked over to the stainless-steel autopsy table that held a shrouded body. A moment later, Anya walked in from her office, which adjoined the exam room. She wore her customary dark blue scrubs with her silver-blonde hair tucked beneath a matching skull cap. Her laptop was tucked under her arm. She flashed them a smile as she set it onto the metal countertop lining the back of the room.

"Sorry to hear about the home study." She opened the computer and punched in an access code.

"It's not a big deal," Noah said.

"It will just get rescheduled," Josie added.

Anya looked over her shoulder, gazing at them with skepticism. It hadn't been a secret to any of their friends how nervous they'd been about this part of the application process.

"We're fine," Josie assured her.

Anya turned back to the laptop, where a set of X-rays filled the screen. "Distracting yourself with work. I can relate. Before I give you my findings, good news. Hummel just called. He took Jane Doe's prints last night. He finally had a chance to run them through AFIS this morning and got a hit."

A buzz of excitement spread through Josie's limbs. "Who is she?"

With a few clicks, Anya brought up a page on NamUS, the National Missing and Unidentified Persons System, a public database utilized by law enforcement, medical examiners and families of missing people to resolve missing persons cases. Often that involved matching a missing person to unidentified deceased persons or remains. Someone had obviously uploaded all of Jane Doe's information into NamUS.

"April Carlson," Anya announced, pointing to a photo of a woman with long, shiny brown hair and a wide smile. It wasn't her driver's license photo. This looked as though it was taken by a professional photographer. April wore a long, flowing blue skirt and a short-sleeved white blouse. She sat on the steps of a gazebo near a lake with the sun setting in the background. Her legs were drawn up and she leaned forward. One of her arms hugged her waist and the other was bent, elbow on her knee. Her hand curled loosely into a fist that supported her chin. A gold scarab bracelet circled her thin wrist, the stones shimmering in the soft light. Josie hadn't seen one of those in ages. It was probably vintage. Beautiful. But nothing compared to April's radiant brown eyes. The very sight of this effervescent woman made Josie's heart sink. April Carlson didn't deserve what had happened to her—wasting away to nothing and then being impaled. No one deserved that.

Noah read the details out loud. "Forty years old. Single, no children. Family contact is listed as her mother, Teresa Carlson. She was an elementary school teacher."

Which meant even though she had no children of her own, she had had access to them.

"Went missing from her home in Newsham just over a year ago. That's, what? A half hour from here? Forty-five minutes, maybe. Heather Loughlin is the lead."

Detective Heather Loughlin was an investigator for the Pennsylvania state police. In areas of the Commonwealth where local police departments were not equipped to handle major crimes like homicides or missing persons, the state police took over. Josie had worked with Heather on multiple cases. She was no-nonsense, efficient, and never made them wait on the results of an inquiry.

Anya said, "I already called her. With there being a child

involved, I figured you'd want to speed things up. She sent over Carlson's dental records right away. They're a match. She's a couple of hours away on another case but said she can be in Newsham in an hour to brief you, if you can meet her there."

"We can," Josie said, unable to tear her eyes from April Carlson's vibrant smile. "I'll text her and get an exact meeting spot before we leave here."

"Thank you," said Noah. "In the meantime, why don't you take us through the results of the autopsy."

TWENTY-ONE

Anya walked over to the table, flipped on the hanging light above the body, and then gently turned the sheet down, folding it across April Carlson's shoulders.

"Wow," Noah said.

On the exam table, under fluorescent lights, April looked twice as disturbing as when Josie had seen her. Sallow, gaunt cheeks. Teeth that seemed to be trying to climb out of her mouth. Bruised circles under her eyes. Hacked hair, showing pieces of her scalp. Her collarbones looked ready to poke right through her delicate skin.

Anya winced. "Yeah. Sometimes gory is easier to take, especially if you know the person went quickly. This woman—she was dying long before she was stabbed."

"She was tortured?" asked Josie.

Anya nodded. "Deprivation is a form of torture, yes, although her cause of death is a penetrating stab wound to her small bowel. As you know, the weapon was retained. Hummel was here earlier to take it into custody. He's going to try to get prints and DNA from the handle. It wasn't a knife though."

Josie tried to think of a weapon with a handle similar to that of a knife that could stab through human skin and sinew to its hilt, but came up blank. "What the hell was it?"

Anya beckoned them back toward the laptop. With a few clicks, April's smiling face disappeared and a series of photos replaced it. "It was an awl."

Noah's arm brushed Josie's as he leaned in to study the pictures. Now that April's hand wasn't wrapped around it, Josie could see that the handle didn't look as close to that of a knife at all. In fact, it was shorter and rounded, similar to the shape of a light bulb. The blade was not a blade but a spear, no thicker than a pen with a sharp, pointed end.

Anya reached past them and enlarged one of the photos. She pointed to the bloodied shaft. "This part is made of steel. Three and a half inches."

It explained why Mira's wounds had been mostly punctures and gouges. Josie said, "I know that an awl is a tool, but what is it used for?"

Noah said, "The most simplistic answer is that awls are used to poke holes. I've seen guys use them in woodworking projects. They use the point to make a hole where they want to drill. I'm pretty sure they're also used in upholstery repair and for stitching leather—anything where you have heavyweight fabric or material that standard sewing implements won't penetrate. There are different kinds, different sizes."

Anya led them back to April Carlson. "I had to look it up. They're also used in shoe repair and bookbinding. Lots and lots of uses for them, and unfortunately, they're effective murder weapons. I've seen a lot in this job, but this is my first awl. No hesitation marks. Given the injuries inside her small bowel, it appears that it had been jostled quite a bit. It's difficult to tell the angle of the original wound but everything I saw is consistent with someone standing in front of her and stabbing on a very slight angle upward."

She pulled Josie toward her with her left hand and used her

right hand to drive an imaginary awl into Josie's stomach, swinging the weapon low before bringing it up into Josie's abdomen. "The hilt left an imprint on the skin of her abdomen which is consistent with what we know about the car accident."

Noah said, "But she would have died regardless of the stabbing?"

Anya sighed, looking at April Carlson's face. "Eventually, yes, if she didn't get medical attention. It's impossible for me to say how long she would have had without knowing the exact conditions of where she was before Mira Summers's car, but wherever it was, she wasn't getting enough food or sun."

"Walk us through your findings," Josie said. "From the beginning."

Anya nodded. "April Carlson is an extremely malnourished adult female. External exam showed several characteristics consistent with long-term starvation: sunken eyes and abdomen, bony protuberances, cracked lips, dental erosion, purpura—" She moved to April's feet and lifted the sheet, folding it up to her knees. Skeletal legs set Josie's stomach roiling. Anya pointed to a smattering of dark pink, almost purple, patches across April's shins. "This is often due to deficiencies of Vitamin C and K in cases of starvation." She pushed the sheet up, revealing thigh bones just as thin as the lower legs. More of the pink-purple spots dotted April's skin. Anya pointed out a few other places where the skin looked like April had a permanent case of gooseflesh. "This indicates a deficiency in Vitamin A."

Josie moved from one side of the table to the other, noting a tattoo on the outside of April's right ankle. Three pink flowers along a green stem, their petals almost like fans.

"A sweet pea," Josie said, almost to herself.

"What?" Anya said.

Josie gestured toward the tattoo. "The flower. It's called a sweet pea. It's one of the birth flowers for the month of April."

Both Noah and Anya joined her near April's right ankle. "How do you know that?" Anya asked.

"Her father," Noah said. "Well, Eli Matson. He used to take her hunting for wildflowers. But sweet peas aren't wildflowers, are they?"

"I'm not sure if they're officially considered wildflowers," Josie said, staring at the tattoo. "But Dad and I—Eli and I—often found them on our travels." Her heart clenched at the memory of Eli, his eyes that deep, deep blue like Sawyer's, smiling at her, and holding the flower out to her. "A sweet pea for my sweet pea," he used to say, making her giggle. Making her feel loved—such a stark difference to what waited for them at home with Lila. At least she had that memory. Poor Sawyer had nothing of his father. Josie sucked in a breath, trying to shove the memory and all thoughts of Sawyer back inside their boxes.

"Sorry," Noah said softly. "I know even the good memories can be painful."

"Isn't that the truth," Anya sighed.

"It's fine," Josie said, steadying herself mentally.

Anya pulled the sheet back down, leaving April's feet exposed from the ankles. "In addition to my other findings on external exam, I noted abrasions of the ankles and feet, consistent with her walking barefoot over rough surfaces and perhaps through brush."

Noah rounded the table to get a better look at the slashes along Jane Doe's ankles and the scrapes on the soles of her feet.

Anya continued. "Internal exam showed no signs of sexual assault. Several of her organs were underweight. Her intra-abdominal and abdominal wall fat were severely decreased compared to what I would expect to find in a healthy woman of her age. Her pancreas showed signs of atrophy. The left ventricle of her heart showed a loss of mass and volume—again, compared to what I would expect to find in someone her age in reasonably good health. All of these things together are consistent with starvation that took place over a long period of time."

"Is it consistent with how long she's been missing?" asked Josie.

"I believe so. Other findings support that she may have been deprived of food and sunlight for up to a year." She waved them over to the laptop, closing out photos of the awl in favor of X-rays. "She showed the beginnings of osteomalacia."

"What's that?" asked Noah.

"Softening of the bones," Anya said. "It's from a lack of Vitamin D. Now, that can be from starvation as well, but it is also consistent with not getting enough sunlight over a long period of time."

"Like a year," Josie said.

"Exactly." Anya pulled up X-rays of April's right shoulder and collarbone. "Could be more or slightly less. If it had gone on much longer, I'm not sure she would have survived. Here." She pointed to where the ball of the shoulder met the collarbone. A portion of April's ribs was also visible. Between them and the humerus, the edge of the scapula could be seen. Just below the shoulder joint was a thick, dark line that otherwise marred the hazy whiteness of the bones. Anya pulled up a view of the left scapula, showing a mirror image.

Noah said, "Are those fractures?"

"Pseudofractures," Anya answered. "Also called 'Milkman lines' after an American radiologist who presented his findings on them all the way back in the 1930s. Also sometimes called 'Looser's zones' after a Swiss doctor named Emil Looser. These are incomplete fractures. They never heal properly or completely because, since the bone is demineralized, new bone never strengthens. A pseudofracture alone is not enough to diagnose osteomalacia unless they are bilateral and symmetrical and found in what are considered classic locations like this or the ribs or ulna."

"Would it have been painful?" asked Josie.

"Yes," said Anya. "Although April was probably in agony from her body slowly wasting away and shutting down as well."

Noah's eyes flared with anger. "Imagine stabbing someone in this condition."

Josie sidled over to him and discreetly touched his hand. Looking back at Anya, she asked, "Would April have been able to walk? Before or after she was stabbed?"

Anya shook her head and snapped her laptop closed. "That is impossible to say. If she was able to walk, it would not have been very far. Once she was stabbed, I doubt she would have been able to walk at all."

"Was there anything in her stomach?" asked Josie.

Anya winced. "Mud. Some grass."

Josie said, "Which means that, at least recently, she'd been kept somewhere that she could access mud and grass."

"Right," said Anya.

Josie could feel Noah getting more agitated, rage rolling off him in waves. He took a step away from them and pushed his fingers through his thick brown locks.

"We'll find the person who did this," Josie promised him.

"Then we'll make him pay," Noah added.

TWENTY-TWO

The heady smell of roses invaded Josie's senses. It was welcome after their visit to the morgue. She counted a half dozen red rose bushes along the walk to the quaint, white two-story house where Heather had asked to meet. It had Josie thinking of the flower on the child's drawing while she and Noah waited on the sidewalk. Was it a rose? What was the significance of it?

"This place is so quiet," Noah muttered, looking up and down the street. He was right. The only noise was the sound of birds chattering in the branches of maple trees that lined the street. Josie hadn't been to Newsham many times but to her, it always looked like one of those cute, sleepy towns from a rom-com where the heroine retreats after a big breakup to put her life back together.

Is that what April Carlson was doing here? According to what Josie gleaned from various sources on the way here, while Noah drove, she'd spent her entire life in a small town called Hillcrest which was in Bucks County. It wasn't lost on Josie that Mira Summers also hailed from Bucks County, and Seth Lee's last known address was in Doylestown—the county seat. It was a loose connection among the three of them, but it was worth looking into if other leads didn't pan out. Seth's brother lived in Denton but what had brought Mira and April out here?

"This is April's last known address," Noah said, interrupting Josie's thoughts. "That's why Heather wanted to meet here."

She took another look at the large porch with its black roof, white pillars, and painted green decking. There was no outdoor furniture but a security camera had been installed over the door. Someone was definitely maintaining the rose garden. Was it a coincidence that this place had a rose garden and that a red flower had been in the drawing?

"We really must stop meeting this way." Detective Heather Loughlin strode down the pavement toward them, a grim smile on her face.

"I wish we could," Josie said.

Heather's eyes were drawn to the roses. "They're beautiful, aren't they? I only like the other colors now, though. The red reminds me too much of blood. Dr. Feist told me April was a match for her Jane Doe and that it was a homicide, but didn't say much else. I knew the outcome wouldn't be good, but I hoped that April might still be alive."

It was the outcome they all wished for—every time—but it rarely happened.

Heather let out a long breath, lifting her face to the sky. Her blonde ponytail swished along her upper back. "Sometimes I really hate this job."

Noah jammed his hands into his pants pockets. "Same."

The sound of a doorbell had Josie looking toward the house.

"That's me." Heather took her phone from her back pocket and replied to a text. "Funny, right? I always know it's my phone though. Anyway, Dr. Feist will call the Bucks County coroner and they'll give April's parents the death notification. You mind telling me what she found on the autopsy?"

Although Heather had been working April Carlson's disappearance, since her body was found in their jurisdiction, the homicide case was theirs. "You'll wish we hadn't," Noah grumbled. "But of course."

A woman walking a corgi approached. Instead of crossing the street to avoid them, she walked right into their path, her curious gaze sweeping over the insignias on their shirts and the firearms on their waists. Josie made a point not to smile. She didn't want to invite conversation. The dog, at least, was too busy chasing a scent to even notice them.

Once she was out of earshot, Heather said, "Just give me the highlights."

Josie took her through everything Anya had told them earlier that day, drawing uncharacteristic gasps from Heather. "Now," Josie said. "We need to know everything you know."

"Come on. No one is living here right now. Landlord gave me the keys so we can have a look around." Heather started up the walk, waving for them to follow her. "Quinn, remember when you and I met at the truck stop last year?"

Josie said, "About the Woodsman case? Yes. You were looking for a woman. That was April Carlson?"

Heather nodded as they took the steps onto the porch. "Yes. April was an elementary school teacher at a school a few blocks from here. Single, no kids. Her parents and siblings live in Hillcrest in Bucks County, which is where she took her first teaching job. They were pretty sad when she moved here but understood that she was after better pay—except that when I was digging up everything I could about her, I found out that she actually took a pay cut to teach in Newsham."

Even up on the porch, the smell of roses was overwhelming. Josie still didn't mind. "Why would she lie to her family about that?"

Heather fished a set of keys from one of her pockets. "I don't know, but that wasn't the only thing that she didn't tell them. She had only been living here for about a year before she went

missing. She hadn't made any connections. Had some drinks
with a couple of coworkers now and then but no new friends.
However, she was being stalked by someone."

Noah held open the screen door while Heather fit the key
into the lock on the front entry door. "After she moved here? Or
in Bucks County as well?"

After a brief struggle, the lock gave way and Heather
pushed the door open. "It started after she moved. I talked with
Hillcrest PD. They had no record of any harassment or stalking
so it started here. She rented this house and about a month after
she moved in, she started having issues. First, it was break-ins.
Nothing would be taken but something would always be
destroyed."

Josie followed Heather across the threshold with Noah in
tow. A musty smell greeted them. "Like what?"

Heather shrugged, glancing around the empty living room.
"I'll send you the file but from what I remember, her couch was
slashed. Her dishes were destroyed. Her mattress was knifed.
Her clothing was shredded. Her, uh, feminine hygiene products
were jammed down her toilet, causing a clog that cost the landlord thousands of dollars."

Noah walked the perimeter of the room, testing the
windows. "All this went on and nobody saw anything?"

Heather led them deeper into the house, into another
empty room that, given the chandelier in the center of the ceiling, was probably a dining room. "April and her closest neighbors worked days and that's when these things happened.
Eventually she decided to put cameras out front and back and
then the stalker just came in the side windows." She pointed to
the two windows along the wall. Josie joined Noah, noting that
they overlooked a sizable side yard with a high privacy fence
that would have prevented the next-door neighbor from seeing
someone break in.

Noah said, "I don't see any pry marks outside. These locks are intact."

"Right," Heather said. "He tore the screens and broke the glass every time. The landlord gave her additional cameras for all angles on the exterior of her building. They did catch a man climbing in here, but they had no luck identifying him."

"Fingerprints?" Noah suggested.

"Too smart for that. In the video we have, he wore gloves. He was covered head to toe. Hoodie, jeans, even a gaiter up to his eyes. No way to identify him. The local PD wasn't equipped to pull DNA, not that there would have been any, I'm sure."

"They didn't call you guys in? Sounds like it was escalating," Noah said.

Heather led them into the kitchen. This room, at least, had a table and chairs. From the back windows, Josie saw a yard with more roses and behind that, an empty driveway. A dirt path, rutted by tire tracks, separated the row of houses on April's street from the backs of houses on the next street over. It was secluded.

"It was escalating," Heather answered, leaning her hip against the countertop. "And no, local PD didn't ask us for assistance. It only got worse. April's tires were destroyed so many times that she could no longer afford to replace them. She started using a rideshare. The guy was caught twice on surveillance slashing her tires out back. Once while she was at work, he walked right onto the faculty lot and did it, and once while she was at Walmart. Problem was that he kept covered up. He knew where the cameras were, never looked toward them, but we think he was a white male, about five foot ten to six foot. Maybe one hundred eighty pounds. Couldn't tell much other than that, unfortunately. Followed the cameras but were never able to link him to a vehicle."

"Geofence?" asked Josie.

Before Heather could answer, Noah said, "Let me guess: local PD didn't do it."

"You'd think so—they're small and not used to crimes that go beyond a stolen car or shoplifting—but no, they did the geofences. Nothing came of them."

The description, vague as it was, matched Seth Lee, and the fact that the vandal either hadn't been carrying a device of any kind or that he'd turned off any devices on his person sounded like the type of behavior Rebecca Lee had described when talking about her brother-in-law. Josie said, "Anything else?"

Heather motioned for them to follow her. "He left her a message."

TWENTY-THREE

They took the steps to the second floor, this time Noah directly behind Heather. "What kind of message?" he asked.

Heather didn't answer until they were inside the barren master bedroom. Ghostly imprints of the message were still visible along one of the white walls where the letters had been spackled and painted over. "He used some kind of knife or other sharp object to carve it into the drywall of her bedroom."

Josie stared at the words. A peculiar fluttering filled her stomach.

STAY AWAY

"But why write 'stay away?'" Noah said. "Stalkers usually want the opposite. Domestic abusers, as well. A lot of what you described sounds like something an intimate partner would do —the feminine hygiene products, destroying her clothes, her mattress, the message being in the bedroom."

"True," said Heather. "But I think this guy was trying to get her to leave Newsham. I just don't know why, or who this guy could possibly be."

Josie found a photo of Seth Lee on her phone and showed it to Heather. "Did the name Seth Lee ever come up in your investigation?"

Heather took a good, long look at Seth's face before shaking her head. "I stopped at my office on the way here and reviewed the file again. I don't recall coming across that name, but I can double-check. I'll send you a copy of my file as well."

Although Seth Lee was a person of interest in April's murder and the attack on Mira, he wasn't a suspect until they could put him at the murder scene. They had to keep all avenues of investigation open and not try to make what they learned fit the narrative that Seth was the perpetrator.

Heather continued, "The local PD asked April several times if she had any idea who might be behind the stalking, and she swore that she had no idea. Once, she suggested it was a case of mistaken identity."

"How about former partners?" asked Noah.

"None recent or significant," Heather said.

"What about her family?" Josie asked. "Did they have any idea who might have targeted her?"

Heather shook her head. "None. According to them, April was well-liked by everyone she knew and hadn't had any conflicts with anyone."

"It sounds like even if she had, she wouldn't have told them," Josie said.

"I agree," said Heather. "Listen, I turned over every possible stone here. I even found this weird connection between her and another missing person in her hometown—Hillcrest—but nothing came of it."

Noah arched a brow. "What kind of connection?"

"You might remember this guy's name—Shane Foster? He was a police officer on the Hillcrest PD. He went missing about three years ago. I actually assisted on that case."

The state police were always brought in when a local law

enforcement officer was reported missing, although it was a rare occurrence. Josie did remember his name precisely because she couldn't remember the last time an officer had gone missing in Pennsylvania.

Heather continued, "He was late thirties, divorced. No kids. Veteran on the force. One day he drove to Nockamixon State Park, parked his car near the lake, and was never seen again. We searched the lake for days but turned up nothing. He left his wallet and phone inside the car. No sign of any kind of struggle or violence. A lot of people speculated he died by suicide but if that were the case, I would have expected to find his body. We chased leads until our feet were ready to fall off and got nothing."

"What was the connection to April?" asked Josie.

"They went to the same gym. Met there. Went on a couple of dates right before he disappeared. I actually interviewed her. She was devastated. Guess they hit it off really well. Then two years later I'm out here in Newsham, investigating her disappearance. I'm not big on coincidences but I couldn't find anything at all linking the two cases."

"Sometimes that's how it goes," said Noah.

"April's case was as frustrating as Shane Foster's. I interviewed all of her friends in Bucks County as well as most of her former coworkers and the principal at the school she taught at before she moved here. No one had anything of use to tell me. They were all just as baffled as her family that she'd decided to pull up stakes and move here."

Noah stared at the faded message on the wall. "You don't take a pay cut, leave everyone you know and love behind, and endure months of harassment without a reason."

"That's what I think." Heather's doorbell notification sounded again. She took her phone back out and tapped in a response to a message at warp speed. "I just don't know what that reason was. Her phone records, emails, all that stuff checked out. I went back as far as the phone companies and the judge signing the search warrants would let me, which was two years. Her social media was practically non-existent but apparently many teachers either don't have social media accounts or if they do, they don't post. Privacy issues. Students and parents can get intrusive, I guess. Whatever her reasoning, whatever she might have known about the stalker, she didn't put it in writing anywhere."

Josie said, "What about parents or students? Were there any issues while she was at her old school?"

Heather gestured for them to follow her back downstairs. "None that stood out to the staff or principal."

Back on the porch, Josie sucked in the rose-scented air. A cool breeze lifted the ends of her hair. The thought of April Carlson going from living in this quaint little house to being cut off from sunlight for almost a year sickened Josie and made her even more grateful than usual to be standing outdoors. Once Heather locked the door, Josie pulled up the photo of the child's drawing on her phone. "We also found this in April's hand." She swiped to the child's message.

"Oh shit," Heather said.

Noah waved to a couple pushing a stroller down the street, as though it was perfectly normal for three detectives to be hanging out on the front porch of a vacant house. The man waved back. The woman looked away, hurrying their pace. "Yeah," he said. "Somewhere, there's a child who drew that. We need to find them. Yesterday."

"As you know, April didn't have kids. Other than her students, there weren't any young children in her life," Heather said. "Her youngest brother and his wife were about to have their first child when April disappeared."

Josie said, "Did you talk to anyone at the school here where April taught?"

"Of course. She hadn't been there that long, so there wasn't much to find out. Talking to the teachers she had the most contact with, it was clear that she missed her family terribly. After the harassment reached the point that she could no longer hide it from them, her principal asked why she didn't just go back to Bucks County, and all she would say was that she couldn't."

"Couldn't?" Noah echoed.

What would make April Carlson believe that she couldn't return to her family and the place she had called home her entire life? The fluttering in Josie's belly intensified.

Noah eyed a jogger passing on the street. The man never even glanced at them. "Did Mira Summers's name ever come up during your investigation?"

"Not that I recall," Heather said. "But again, I can double-check and you can triple-check when you get the file."

"When we met last year," Josie said. "You were showing April's photo at truck stops. Why?"

"She was last seen at a truck stop between Hillcrest and here. She parked her vehicle in the lot. Went inside the stop and bought a soda and a chocolate bar, waited outside the entrance for ten minutes, just looking around, and then she walked back to her car. She used her phone to take one call from a burner phone. We never could track anyone down using the number. After that call, she drove twenty-three miles west on Route 80."

Josie's stomach turned at the thought that the chocolate bar would be one of the few things April ate for the next year of her life. "Not a lot of cameras on 80."

Heather sighed and reached back, smoothing her ponytail. "Exactly. She pulled onto a wide part of the shoulder. Then poof! she's gone. Left her car, phone, purse. Everything. The burner phone only turned on long enough to make that call and it didn't show up in the geofence. It bounced off a tower a few miles from where April pulled over, but it wasn't on long enough for us to pinpoint it in any location where we might catch the user on camera. Dead end. The only other thing we found where her car was left was a set of tire tracks that belonged to a commercial vehicle. A truck, probably, but not a semi."

Josie glanced over at Noah. He was thinking the same thing. "Maybe a box truck," he suggested.

Heather shrugged. "Sure, but good luck finding it."

They could at least try to match the photos and casts the state police had taken near April's car to the ones found at Tranquil Trails.

Josie's phone rang. "It's Hummel."

Heather descended the porch steps. "On that note, I'll leave you to it. As soon as I get back to my office, I'll send over the Carlson file."

Josie swiped answer and put him on speaker so Noah could hear. "Tell me you have something."

Hummel laughed. "Oh, I've got a bunch of somethings. One of them's pretty big, too."

Noah said, "We love it when you talk dirty to us, Hummel. Where are you?"

More laughter. "I'm at the impound lot."

"We'll be right over."

TWENTY-FOUR

The Denton police impound lot was in an area of North Denton only slightly more populated than Prout Road. It was surrounded by a tall chain-link fence. A small booth at its entrance was occupied by an officer who let Josie and Noah through to the parking lot. They rolled past two rows of cars that had been impounded for various reasons until they came to the rear of the lot. The ERT's unofficial headquarters was located in a squat cinderblock building with a single navy-blue door. Attached to the building was a garage with two bays, their windows covered with white laminate for the sake of privacy. Josie and Noah went through the blue door, then through the small office at the front, and into a larger room of white cinderblock. Aluminum shelving lined one wall, filled with supplies for processing evidence. Hummel sat at a large stainless-steel table in the center of the room, typing on a laptop.

He greeted them with a smile and gestured for them to sit at the table. Once Josie and Noah were seated across from him, he spun the laptop around, revealing a fingerprint report. "Your suspect is Seth Lee."

Excitement sent a surge of energy through Josie's veins.

Noah pulled the computer closer, reading the report. "I can't remember the last time it was this easy."

Josie's shoulder bumped his as she leaned in to view the findings. "Oh, it's not easy. We still have to find him."

Hummel turned the laptop back toward him. "Dr. Feist told you about the awl?"

"Yes," said Josie.

"Never saw that before. First time for everything, I guess," he muttered as his fingers swiped over the touchpad. "This thing was a bitch to process. I had to collect the prints before I swabbed for DNA. Got a bunch of them by fuming it. Since the wood was varnished, non-porous."

He angled the screen so they could all see it. The awl appeared, its wooden handle covered in white fingerprints. Fuming involved placing the item into an airtight cyanoacrylate fuming chamber. Once locked inside, the item was exposed to what were essentially superglue vapors, which reacted to the traces of fatty and amino acids, sweat, and proteins in the prints. The chemical reaction caused the sticky white substance to appear along the ridges of the prints.

"I pulled three sets of prints from the awl handle. One is an unknown. No hits in AFIS. I also checked the NCMEC database. No matches there."

Josie hated to think that the child who had drawn the picture and plea for help might have handled the awl. Not every missing or abducted child has prints on file at the National Center for Missing and Exploited Children database.

"One matched to April Carlson and the last matched to Seth Lee. From where the Carlson's prints were found, it appears that she was holding the awl in place with her palm supporting it from underneath and her thumb and fingers wrapped around the handle. The unknown prints are on the underside and Seth Lee's prints are pretty much everywhere."

Josie suppressed a shiver, thinking of poor emaciated April

Carlson, wasted down to nothing and still being stabbed so coldly and cruelly. This job involved an endless parade of the worst human depravity imaginable—and some unimaginable— but Josie never got used to the brutality or the savage cruelty some people inflicted on others. She just got better at stowing her feelings and moving forward with purpose.

Under the table, Noah's knee brushed against hers. As always, he could practically read her thoughts. "Enough for an arrest warrant."

"Circumstantially, sure," Josie said. "We can draw one up but for charges to hold we'd need more. Even if his DNA is found on the murder weapon, a good defense attorney can say it's because the awl was his and he used it for awl-related things. What we really need is to be able to put him at the scene. If we can find him and arrest him, we can try to get a statement from him that puts him there."

"Then we'll work on that. What else do you have for us, Hummel?"

Hummel clicked to a close-up of the awl's blood-soaked shaft, similar to the one Dr. Feist had shown them. "I was able to type some of the blood found on the blade. I wanted to try to confirm that April Carlson and Mira Summers were both stabbed with it. It gets a little complicated when you're dealing with a weapon that has the blood of two victims on it. Even though there are two of them, you only get one result. In this case, I would have expected the result to come out as Type AB —a combination of both their blood types—and it did. Getting you anything more than that in terms of typing would be too complicated for me but I sent the DNA swabs to the state lab for analysis, which should definitively confirm that both of them were stabbed by the same blade. But more importantly give us the DNA profile of Seth Lee."

He closed out the picture of the awl and brought up photos of Mira Summers's sedan, clicking through them quickly. Each one was a new tableau of blood spatter. Droplets on the floor and console. Smears on the sides of the seat. A partial handprint on the passenger's side seat belt. "As expected, I got two different blood types from the car. One a match to April Carlson, the other to Mira Summers. No surprises there."

"What was the killer doing while she was buckling April Carlson into the passenger's seat?" Josie mumbled.

Noah said, "Maybe he had already gone."

What kind of killer stabbed two women and then left them behind—one of them still alive—with the murder weapon? It made no sense. Unless, as Josie suspected, the killer was Seth Lee. Had his delusions caused him to flee for some reason?

Hummel turned the laptop screen back. "We collected tissue from beneath April's nails. We also took into evidence the clothes of both victims. April Carlson didn't have any shoes, but we took Mira Summers's boots into evidence. Everything has been swabbed and sent to the state lab for testing, but the results could take weeks."

Josie asked, "How about the clumps of hair found on April Carlson's clothes?"

Hummel closed his laptop. "Had to send those out, but I should hear something soon."

Noah leaned back in his chair, draping one arm across the back of Josie's, his fingers lightly grazing her shoulder. Even though his touch was light, it still eased some of her burgeoning anxiety. Sure, they could get an arrest warrant out on Seth Lee now while they continued to build their case, but they had to locate him.

They still had to find the child.

HELP

"The drawing," said Josie, the words coming out raspy. Noah's fingertips skimmed her shoulder again in reassurance.

Hummel nodded. "I was able to get a few sets of prints from that, most of them unknown. Nothing in the NCMEC database. It's a piece of paper, so who knows how many people have touched it. However, I was able to match one set—only one— and that was to Mira Summers."

Josie felt a jolt of surprise.

Noah turned to her. "Wasn't that drawing found in April Carlson's hand?"

Hummel answered before Josie could. "Yes, folded up in her fist. But her prints aren't on it. However, Mira Summers's prints are on every fold."

The fluttering was back, filling her stomach with an unsettling feeling. "She folded it up," Josie said. "And put it into April's fist."

Hummel shrugged. "I don't think we can prove that but it's certainly a possibility. A probability."

"That's interesting," said Josie. "Because when Gretchen and I interviewed Mira Summers, she told us there were no children in her life."

TWENTY-FIVE

He goes away and comes back. We're still all alone in the forever-est place and I hate it more than ever. I've tried everything not to be bored and not to think about blood. I don't look at him because I hate him. Even when he sits next to me, I act like he's not there. Then a shiny wrapper appears in front of my nose.

"Here," he says.

My stomach cramps and growls. I wish it would shut up so he didn't know how much I want the candy.

"It's a protein bar," he adds. "Your favorite flavor. Birthday cake."

Spit fills my whole entire mouth. "We're not supposed to eat those."

"I checked this one. Just like the others. It's okay to eat. I wouldn't offer it to you if it wasn't."

I make my hand go slow when I take it from him and also when I open it. The smell is so delicious that a weird feeling goes through my whole body. I think it's called anticipation. I might not be a regular, normal person who goes to school but I know some big words. It tastes so good, I want to cry again. I don't understand my brain sometimes.

"Remember to bury the wrapper when you're finished," he says. "Things will be very bad if it's found."

This is one of the most special-est treats that he brings me, and the rarest. I know he is trying to make things nice between us again. I know he won't tell me about the blood, but this is a good time to ask questions.

"Did you give her back? Like you promised?"

He stands up and sighs. "I'll get you a new coloring book, okay? Maybe a book to read."

I hate the way my heart soars when he says these things because I know he's trying to distract me from the fact that the only bad person here right now is him.

TWENTY-SIX

Josie and Noah drove to the stationhouse. The arrest warrant for Seth Lee was their top priority for the moment. Turner sat at his desk, throwing his tiny foam basketball over and over again into the small net next to his blotter. He didn't look up when they walked in and waited until they were seated to speak. "Let me guess. Jane Doe died from a stab wound."

"You're so smart," Josie said, intentionally keeping the sarcasm from her tone.

Turner's gaze snapped toward her, confusion creasing his forehead. Josie liked it when he didn't know what to make of her, or when he wasn't sure if she was insulting him or not. Let him wonder.

Noah said, "Her name is April Carlson. We've got a lot to catch you up on."

Josie started preparing the arrest warrant while Noah brought Turner up to speed. She kept glancing over at him while Noah spoke. It was difficult to tell if he was listening. Most of the time he wasn't even looking at Noah, his gaze wandering around the room. Using his feet, he rocked the seat of his chair back and forth. His long fingers drummed against his desk, unless they were throwing his tiny basketball at its tiny hoop. If Noah noticed any of this, he didn't let on. When he finished, he asked, "What did Mira Summers say when you asked her about Seth Lee?"

Turner leaned forward and dribbled the foam ball along the surface of his desk. "She didn't say anything. By the time I got up there, she'd already been discharged. Some work friend came and picked her up. Bobbi Ann Thomas. Summers is staying at Thomas's house, which is good since Stabby Stabberson is still out there."

Noah said, "Did you try to follow up with Mira Summers at her friend's residence?"

Turner pushed his chair away from the desk and tried to make a basket from three feet away. As usual, he missed. "This isn't my first day, LT. Thomas said she was resting. Refused to wake her up. Told me to come back later."

Josie stopped typing. It had been hours since they saw him outside the morgue. "Did you go back later?"

Turner reached for the ball again. Threw it. Missed. "No, because the LT wanted me to do a bunch of other shit. Speaking of which..."

He picked up a stack of papers from his desk. They were clipped together in a thick pile. He tossed the packet across to Noah and resumed playing desk basketball. "Summers's phone? A whole lot of nothing. She didn't make any calls on Sunday morning and didn't get any. No text messages either."

"What about Friday and Saturday?" asked Josie.

"She texted back and forth with Bobbi. They talked about work and yoga class. On Saturday, Summers had a reminder text about her stable session on Sunday and some dentist appointment coming up next week. That's it. Pretty sad for a woman her age. Lonely spinster with a cat by the looks of it."

"So every woman who lives independently is sad?" Josie said, immediately regretting taking the bait.

A smirk lifted one side of Turner's mouth. "Come on, sweetheart. There's gotta be something wrong with her if she doesn't have someone in her life, don't you think?"

Bastard.

"Or she keeps meeting people like you and decided it was far better to be alone, champ," Josie shot back.

She glanced at Noah, who was flipping through the reports. To anyone else, he'd look stone-faced, but she knew him well enough to know that the purse of his lips was him holding back laughter. Before Turner could respond, Noah asked, "Social media?"

"She's got Instagram and TikTok accounts. Looks like she uses both to view other people's shit but not post anything of her own. Probably because her life is so damn boring."

This time Josie ignored his comment.

Noah handed the pages back to him. "Now that we know the identity of Jane Doe, and Detective Loughlin has sent over a copy of her file on April Carlson's disappearance, you can familiarize yourself with that and see if you can find any connection to Seth Lee or Mira Summers."

Turner took the stack of pages back with a long sigh. "Don't you think I'd be better used in the field? I could go back to Bobbi Ann Thomas's house. See if Mira's awake yet and ask her about Seth Lee."

Noah gave him the look Josie thought of as his 'take precisely no bullshit' look which she hardly ever got to see and had to admit was pretty damn sexy. Turner had a way of bringing it out in him. "You can do that, too, after you review the Carlson file. Right now, I think you'd be most useful doing what I tell you to do, Turner. Did you have a chance to check out the GPS from Summers's car?"

Turner fished out another sheaf of papers and threw them onto Noah's desk. "No surprises there. Sunday, she left her house and went directly to Tranquil Trails without stopping.

She was there for three hours and seventeen minutes and then she got into her car, drove to the produce stand, and stopped there for thirteen minutes."

Thirteen minutes. That was all it took for Seth Lee to stab two women and leave them bleeding. Then again, Josie knew from personal experience that it only took seconds for an entire life to be shattered by violence. "Then she left the produce stand and got into the accident."

Turner waggled his brows and grinned. "Not so fast, sweetheart. She stopped along the road. Before the accident. For twenty-two minutes."

Noah said, "What?"

Josie said, "Where?"

Turner stood up and walked over to the corkboard map, pointing to a red pushpin that hadn't been there the night before. Pointing to it, he said, "According to the report, my best guess is right here."

Josie momentarily abandoned the arrest warrant and joined him, studying the map. The pin was about a mile and a half from the accident.

Noah stood beside her. "I don't see anything anywhere near where she stopped."

"Because there's nothing," Josie said. "Absolutely nothing. Why would she stop?"

"Why would she stop but not call 911?" said Turner.

It was a valid question. Mira had been stabbed. She was bleeding profusely. Had she felt so faint that she pulled over? Had she lost consciousness for twenty-two minutes, then wakened only to get back on the road? That was the only thing that made sense.

Josie said, "Turner, what about the geofence results? Did those come in?"

He rolled his eyes. "What do you think? I've been stuck here all morning buried in reports."

Josie folded her arms over her chest, ignoring his dig. "Just tell us about the results."

He walked back over to his desk, pulling another document out from under his tiny basketball. He thrust it at her as he came back to the map. She skimmed the results, Noah following along over her shoulder. Turner pointed to the map. "It tagged a bunch of devices in the area between the horse place and the accident. Now look, you know we just get a list of devices with no names attached first. Then we have to try to match those devices to a pattern of movement that's consistent with the crime. Like if a guy goes into a corner store and robs it and then an eyewitness puts him at the bus stop down the street, and the geofence shows a device leaving the corner store and going to the bus stop, we can ask for the personal identifying information from that device—because it follows a pattern that matches what we know about the perpetrator's movements."

Josie smiled at him. "You're really getting the hang of this procedure thing, aren't you?"

Turner's mouth hung open.

With a frustrated sigh, Noah said, "We know how it works, Turner. We need to know if there's anything we can use to put Seth Lee at the crime scene."

Turner turned back to the map, stroking his beard. "No."

"No?" said Josie.

Turner dropped his hand to his side and shrugged. "Hey, I'm just telling you what this shit says, honey. No devices stopped at the produce stand other than Mira Summers's phone. Listen, you were the one who said this guy is some kind of off-the-grid-survivalist-tech-is-the-devil lunatic. I don't know why you're surprised."

The stairwell door whooshed open, and the Chief stalked in, pulling up short to peer at the three of them, suspicion deepening every line in his craggy face. One bushy eyebrow kinked. "You three getting along, or what?"

Gretchen would have said, "Or what."

Josie said nothing.

Turner slung one arm across Josie's shoulders and the other across Noah's and pulled them into his sides, like they were old friends. "One big happy family, Chief."

Chief Chitwood didn't look convinced. Josie stepped out from under Turner's arm, putting a foot between them.

"Fraley," the Chief snapped, striding toward his office. "Meet me in my office in five minutes. You'll brief me on the Summers case and then I need about an hour of your time. The DA wants to have a conference call about that double murder you caught last year. The one over the drug dispute. It's going to trial soon."

He slammed the door behind him. Turner left Noah standing by the corkboard while he scooped up his car keys and phone from his desk. "Looks like we've all got our assignments. I'll be at Bobbi Thomas's house to talk to Mira Summers about our big suspect. Who knows? Maybe once I tell her Lee's prints are all over the murder weapon, she'll conveniently remember that he stabbed her."

Josie thought about offering to do the interview instead or at least to go with him, but then decided against it. The sooner they got the arrest warrant signed for Seth Lee, the better. What if he had the child who drew the picture? What if the child had witnessed the attack? Would Seth let them live? Or was the child in some dank, sunless hole starving to death like April Carlson had? Josie needed to stay put and finish her paperwork.

She didn't entirely trust Turner to do anything, really, but it made sense for them to split the workload.

Turner winked at her. "You don't need to come with me, honey. I'm a big boy. I've done this before. You stay here with your hubby and your little keyboard."

Josie glared as she watched him walk out the door. She glanced up at Noah. Annoyance was etched into every line of his face. She nudged him with her elbow. "Are you going to say anything?"

His eyes remained on the door. "My mother always said that if you don't have anything nice to say, don't say anything at all."

TWENTY-SEVEN

A couple of hours later, Josie watched the evening news from her desk in the great room. The television that hung on the wall in the corner wasn't the best quality, nor was it very large, but it would do. The top story was Seth Lee with the chyron reading: *Murder Suspect Sought in Case of Missing Teacher*. It wasn't the best caption but both murder and missing persons usually caught people's attention.

Once the arrest warrant was ready, Josie had uploaded it to NCIC and updated the information in the BOLO they'd put out earlier on Seth Lee. It wasn't often that Chief Chitwood encouraged using the press, but in this case, since there could be a child at risk, he'd told Josie to get them involved. She had contacted their press liaison, Amber Watts, who'd been working from home as much as possible now that Turner had taken over Mettner's position and his desk. They hadn't held a press conference, but together they'd drafted something to send out to the local media.

Now Seth Lee's driver's license photo stared back at Josie. She was only half listening as she picked at the dinner Noah had gotten for her at a nearby takeout place before he went home. Josie planned to join him soon. Turner hadn't responded to any of her texts or calls yet regarding making contact with Mira Summers. She had a sneaking suspicion he'd gone home early, in which case, Josie would wait until Gretchen arrived and then she'd go over to Bobbi Ann Thomas's house herself to talk to Mira.

Beside Seth's photo, bullet points began to appear. Diamond-shaped scar upper arm. May be driving a white box truck. May have a young child with him. May be camping outdoors. Possibly armed and dangerous. If you see him, do not approach. Call 911 immediately.

Next, the photo of April at the gazebo flashed onto the screen except that it had been cropped so that only her face and the wrist with her scarab bracelet showed. The chyron now read: *Teacher Missing for a Year Found Murdered.* Before releasing any details to the press, Josie and Amber had made sure that the death notification for April had been made by the Bucks County coroner. Josie spoke briefly with April's mother, Teresa, to prepare her for the fact that they were about to release information regarding the suspect in April's murder to the press. They'd only notified Denton news outlets, but Josie had little doubt the story would get picked up in April's hometown as well.

Josie's cell phone buzzed. Fishing it out from under a mound of paperwork on her desk, she saw Douchebag calling. She swiped answer. "Where have you been? Did you make contact with Mira Summers?"

Turner chuckled. "What? No foreplay? Come on, sweetheart. The least you could do is give me a, 'Hey, Kyle, how's your day going?'"

Josie rolled her eyes. Why couldn't he just talk? Like a normal person? Why did everything out of his mouth make her eye twitch? She didn't have time for his weird banter, but she played along anyway. "Okay. Hey, tiger. How is your day? Do you need a nap? Maybe a juice box?"

"Come on, Quinn. Play nice."

"Oh, so you do know my name."

Ignoring that comment, he finally answered her questions. "I had some things to take care of this afternoon, but then I tried to make contact with Summers. Went to Thomas's house again. She said after Mira went to sleep this morning, she went to work."

Josie was stuck on what things he could possibly have to take care of other than this case, but Turner just kept talking.

"Bobbi came home about two hours ago and Mira was gone. Mira left her a note saying she was walking to the store to get a temporary cell phone. You know, since we still have her phone? She didn't say what store but there's a pharmacy a couple of blocks away that has those shoddy pay-as-you-go phones. I walked over there, poked around. No one remembers seeing her. No sign of her on their surveillance footage."

Frustration bubbled in Josie's stomach, her dinner no longer feeling as settled as it had before this call. "Did you pull what-ever surveillance was available between Bobbi's home and the store?"

"I was getting to that. Got a home doorbell camera from across the street that shows her coming out of Bobbi's house and heading in the opposite direction. There's a couple of stores in that direction that also have those phones. She went into one and bought a phone but when she came out, she didn't head back in the direction of Bobbi's house. She went the other way. I lost her on the cameras, though. There's a lot of houses over here that don't have any security cameras."

"What's in that direction that a woman with a head injury and stab wounds who was just discharged from the hospital would walk to besides a place to get a new phone?"

There were a few beats of silence and then a muffled

conversation before Turner came back on the line. "Mira's place. Bobbi said maybe she was going to check on the cat."

Josie had a sinking feeling that Mira hadn't made it to her house or to wherever she'd been headed. Seth Lee could have lurked somewhere around the hospital, waiting for her to be discharged, and followed her back to Bobbi's house. He could easily have abducted her somewhere between Bobbi's house and her own without getting caught on any cameras. But Josie's hope was that they'd find Mira in her own home.

"Great," Josie said. "Find out if Bobbi Thomas has a key to Mira's house. Regardless, I'll meet you there in ten minutes for a welfare check."

TWENTY-EIGHT

Streetlights cast a golden glow over the sidewalk in front of Mira Summers's town house. No lights came from inside the house. Turner stood near Mira's front stoop, his eyes locked on an attractive brunette about his age. For once his phone wasn't in his hand, although one of his brown loafers tapped against the pavement. Josie parked behind his car. The cluster of town houses had only street parking, no driveways. They were relatively new, built about five years earlier in an area surrounded by some of the city's oldest and most historic residences. The city council had tried repeatedly to kill the project since the townhomes, although not ugly, just didn't fit the aesthetic of all the other homes around them.

"You made it," Turner said as Josie approached. As if he'd been waiting hours. The police station was less than ten minutes away.

It doesn't matter, Josie reminded herself. She ignored him and introduced herself to Bobbi. Up close, Josie could see why she'd been able to hold Turner's attention for more than five seconds. Black yoga pants and a tank top highlighted the toned muscles of her arms and legs. Her brown hair was pulled back and twisted into a bun that only served to accentuate her high cheekbones and sharp jawline. "We tried knocking a few times," she said. "No answer."

"She probably decided to rest after her walk and fell asleep," Turner reassured her. "I'm sure she's fine. Go ahead. Open the door. We'll get her up and give her and her cat a ride back to your house."

Worry pooled in Bobbi's dark eyes as she walked up the three steps to the front door and put the key in the lock.

"I told Mira I would come with her after work to get the cat and bring it back to my place," Bobbie said. "But she loves that ornery thing."

Bobbie pushed the door open and reached a hand inside, feeling along the wall until she found the light switch. A dim overhead glow illuminated the living room.

Josie stepped inside. The space was only large enough to accommodate a couch, one end table, a coffee table and a television console. On the other side of the television, near one of the front windows, a cat tree nearly larger than Josie hulked over everything else.

"Mira?" Josie called. "It's Detective Quinn from the Denton PD. I'm just here to check on you."

On the coffee table were two mugs. One had a quarter of what looked like black coffee left in it. The other was empty, a light brown film coating its bottom the only evidence of what had been in it. Next to it was a napkin, the handle of a spoon peeking from between its folds.

Someone had been here with Mira. Not Bobbi, but someone that Mira had welcomed with coffee.

Josie turned to say something to Turner, but he was still on the steps, captivated by Bobbi, making noises of reassurance. Shameless.

"Don't let the cat out," Josie said. He didn't even look at her. The only sign that he'd heard her was a weak wave.

"Mira?" Josie called again as she made her way into the kitchen. There was enough light from the living room to find the switch just inside the door. Bright light flooded the room. It, too, was small but clean. A pile of mail sat unopened on the table. An unopened pay-as-you-go cell phone sat beside it. In the center of the table was a large glass vase filled with a dozen red roses. They weren't as fragrant as the ones at April's rental house in Newsham, but they were every bit as beautiful —and fresh—though it was hard to say just how fresh. It was possible that Mira had received them over the weekend, before the attack at Tranquil Trails. Josie walked closer to the table, her gaze catching on a small white card tucked among the buds. A piece of it had been torn away and the back of it wasn't visible. On what was left of the card was one hand-written word: SORRY. A small knot of anxiety formed in Josie's stomach. Was it a coincidence? The rose from the child's drawing and these roses on Mira's kitchen table with a note saying SORRY? Sorry for what? Who would have brought her flowers? According to Mira, there was no one in her life besides Bobbi.

Seth?

Knowing what she did about him from Rebecca and Jon, and from what he had done to April and Mira, Josie couldn't see him as a flowers-and-apology type of guy.

It was a mystery she could ponder later. For now, she had to check the house to make sure that Mira wasn't lying on the floor in one of these rooms, incapacitated from her head injury having worsened. Josie scanned the kitchen one more time. A hiss sounded from one of the lower cabinets. The door was ajar. Pale yellow eyes stared at her from inside. Behind the cat was a mess of torn bags—dry food and treats. Josie didn't even try to disturb that scene. She looked out the back door. There was nothing but grass leading to another sidewalk. None of the yards behind the townhomes were divided in any way. A few neighbors had lawn furniture or children's toys scattered near the backs of their homes. Mira had nothing.

From the front, she heard Turner laugh at something Bobbi said. As Josie passed through the living room again to get to the stairs to the second floor, she said, "Turner, Mira's not on the first floor, if you care. The cat is, though, so don't let it out."

He didn't spare her a glance, slowly pulling the front door closed, leaving him alone on the steps with Bobbi. "At least the cat won't get out," Josie mumbled to herself as she flicked on the light switch at the bottom of the steps and trudged up to the second floor, calling Mira's name again.

The overhead light in the upstairs hallway revealed three open doors. Closest to the top of the steps was the bathroom. Josie turned on the light. It was empty.

"Mira? Detective Quinn. Just here to check on you."

Josie reached inside the doorway to the second room, her fingers searching for a light switch. She flicked it on. No Mira. Just a neatly made twin bed with a matching nightstand. Nothing in the closet but a litter box.

"Mira? It's fine if you don't want to talk. Bobbi's downstairs. We're just making sure you're okay."

No answer. From her position in the hall, Josie could see a portion of the master bedroom. A nightstand. Lamp on top. A portion of Mira's bed was visible, the maroon sheets and comforter rumpled. The door stood mostly open, giving Josie a view of the entire room once she reached inside the threshold to flip the light switch. The icy fingers of trepidation trailed up the back of her neck. Her heart flapped. She had a flash of Mira's lifeless body waiting on the floor in the only part of the room she couldn't yet see.

But when she crossed the room, rounding the bed to check the floor on that side, there was nothing. No Mira. One of the sliding doors of the closet was open, clothes hanging; shoes lined up on the floor. Josie was struck by how few personal touches the place had even though Mira had lived here for a few years. No photos. No trinkets. There was only a small jewelry box on top of the dresser that sat across from the foot of the bed. From downstairs came the muffled sound of Turner's laughter again.

"That son of a bitch," Josie said under her breath.

She was only a step away from the threshold when she smelled it. The same rank, acrid, almost earthy odor she'd encountered leaning over April Carlson's body at the scene of the accident. Adrenaline surged through her veins like wildfire. Her heart seemed to stop for a long, slow beat and then it exploded back to life, pumping at a speed that felt unsustainable. Her hand went to her holster. Everything felt like it was happening in slow motion and yet it was all happening at the same time, in the same second.

Her mouth said, "Turner!"

Her brain said, *Behind the door*.

Her head swiveled toward the crack where the inside edge of the partially open door met the frame. Through it, a single blue eye stared at her.

TWENTY-NINE

There was no time to unsnap her holster, much less draw her weapon. There was no time to yell again for Turner. No time to identify herself properly, to tell him to freeze or stop or put his hands up. There was no time. Seth Lee pushed the door into her at the same time that Josie tried to kick it into him. He won. Her kick slowed his efforts but only a fraction. The door slammed into her with all of Seth's one hundred eighty pounds behind it. Her body snapped to the right, her head, shoulder, and hip smacking into the other side of the doorframe. Her fingers, scrabbling for her weapon, caught between the wood and her pistol grip. The pain was sharp and immediate, blotting out all other sensation in her body. Like a pinball, she bounced off the frame and back into the door.

Seth drew it back and pushed it into her again. This time her body was turned, and her spine met the edge of the frame and then careened back into the door. The impact of her forehead against it made a loud crack. Some frantic part of her brain screamed at her to try to do something besides getting tossed back and forth like a rag doll. She gripped the doorknob, the pain in her injured knuckles like shards of glass piercing her to the bone. Certain that Seth would expect her to push or kick the door back into him, she instead yanked it away. It felt light in her hands, almost weightless, and that was how she knew he was no longer holding it.

He stepped out from behind it, glaring down at her. Josie took note of his faded flannel shirt and dirty, torn jeans. No weapon in his hands but he'd already assaulted her with the door.

"Stop," she said, the word coming out breathless.

Had Turner really heard nothing from downstairs?

Josie's hand still throbbed mercilessly as she unsnapped her holster. Seth lunged for her. She threw her arms up, sure he was going to punch her or try to choke her, but his palms caught her shoulders, pushing forcefully, sending her into the hallway flat on her back. For a split second, he loomed over her. She bent her knees, using her feet to push her back, away from him. Her abs held her shoulders off the carpet as she went for her pistol again. But Seth kept coming, falling toward her, his hands outstretched like he was going to choke her. Josie rolled to the side, hitting the wall, but staying out of his grip. Her pistol, still in the holster, was under her hip.

Losing his balance, he fell forward, using his hands to break his fall. Josie rolled back, throwing an elbow into his kidney, eliciting a grunt. She speared him twice more in the same place but without the momentum of the roll, her strikes weren't as effective. Seth was breathing heavily as one of his hands clamped down on her shoulder and whipped her onto her back. He slid over her like a snake, straddling her and pinning her upper body to the floor with one forearm pressed against her chest. She tried to reach her pistol, but it was trapped between her hip and his inner thigh. He rose up and lifted his arm from her chest, taking away the pressure. A second later, the same arm was drawn back, and a fist flew at Josie's face. She got her forearms up but not in enough time to take the full brunt of the

strike. Seth still managed to make contact with her cheek. Her
head whipped to the side. Her teeth sliced into the inside of her
cheek. Blood filled her mouth.

It disoriented her long enough for him to slip his large hands
between her forearms and wrap them around her throat. His
thumbs pressed into her windpipe. Panic numbed every feeling
in her body. Her vision narrowed to Seth's face—bearded now—
blue eyes flashing with fury. Spittle gathered on his bottom lip
as he squeezed harder. Josie's good hand slid along one of his
forearms, up his wrist to his fingers until it found his pinky
finger. Finding the tip of it, she peeled it away from her skin
until there was enough room for her to grasp the first knuckle.
Her vision grayed. Fire erupted in her lungs. She yanked the
pinky all the way back as hard as she could, feeling a perverse
satisfaction at the sound of bone cracking.

Seth roared, raining saliva onto her face. His grip loosened.
Josie folded both of her arms over his forearms and pressed
down. It brought his face closer to hers, which turned her stomach, but it broke his hold on her throat. While she had his forearms pinned against her chest, she bent her knees until they
touched his rear and then pushed with her feet, rolling her hips
toward the side. She bucked him off fast and hard enough that
the drywall caved in.

She shimmied away from him, trying to put as much space
between their bodies as possible—which was pretty much
impossible given the narrow hallway—and lurched to her feet.

He was on his knees already and as she drew her weapon,
one of his strong arms shot out, sweeping her ankles out from
under her. She landed on her back. Her fingers still throbbed
from earlier. The pistol flew out of her hand, toward the master
bedroom.

"Stop," she said, gasping for air.

Before she could say another word, Seth jumped to his feet
and sprinted for the stairs. Josie scrambled upright, searching

the floor of Mira's bedroom until she found her pistol. Retrieving her weapon cost her precious seconds. Seth was gone. She bolted after him, taking the steps two at a time.

"Turner!" Josie tried to shriek as she reached the landing, but her voice came out a rasp. When she swallowed, it felt like there were razor blades in her throat. She banged a fist against the front door. Seth wasn't in the living room. Something crashed in the kitchen. Wood splintered. Glass shattered. As she ran toward the noise, she finally heard Turner's voice but decided she must be having an auditory hallucination because he used her actual name.

The kitchen table and chairs were on their sides. The roses were scattered across the tile. Pieces of the glass vase sparkled. The back door hung open and Josie ran through it into the unending green of the communal yard. A shadow darted to her left, heading toward the edge of the development. There was no time to go to her vehicle and grab her flashlight. Josie veered in the direction of the movement, legs pumping. The shadow resolved into Seth Lee, running toward the trees that separated the town houses from the backs of a row of large Victorian homes on Denton's historic register. Misty and Harris lived only two blocks away.

"Quinn!" Turner was behind her.

"It's him!" she said over her shoulder. Again, her voice came out much quieter and raspier than she intended. "It's Lee! Call for backup!"

Seth Lee disappeared into the tree line. Josie plunged in after him. Low-hanging branches whipped at her, snagging on her clothes and scraping against her forearms. She heard Turner crashing through the brush behind her.

"Turner! Call for backup!"

She emerged from the wooded area and onto a thin strip of grass, no more than three feet wide, that separated the trees from the yards of the city's oldest houses. Most yards were hidden by wooden or vinyl privacy fences anywhere from six to eight feet high. A few were hemmed in by old stone walls. Wide alleys stretched between each house. No Seth. An exterior light glowed two doors down and rear windows in many of the houses were lit up. Still, where she stood it was almost total darkness. To her left, dogs started barking. Huffing, Turner drew up beside her.

"This way," she said, turning toward the noise. Keeping her pistol up and at the ready, she ran, stopping at the end of the first fence where an alley opened up. She didn't want to cross the alley blindly without ensuring that Seth Lee wasn't waiting there to attack. She didn't think he would be—her money was on him running as far and as fast as he could away from them—but she didn't want to be surprised by him twice in one night. "Turner!" she hissed, pain burning her throat.

Staying close to the fence, he crouched so his height didn't give him away and drew his weapon. With one hand, he squeezed her shoulder, signaling for her to go first. Josie led with the barrel of her gun, moving into the mouth of the alley, scanning it for threats while Turner ran past her to the next section of fencing. Methodically, they continued past the backs of the houses in that fashion. The barking dogs ahead grew more frenzied. At least one of them snarled. More exterior lights from the houses snapped on but it was still quite dark where she and Turner raced along in pursuit of Seth Lee.

From somewhere in front of them a creak sounded. Then wood slammed against wood. Josie only had seconds to register that someone was opening a gate. From the blackness of an alley two houses ahead, a shadowy form about waist-high charged at them. It crossed a patch of light coming from the back of the next house.

"Oh fuck," said Turner.

Teeth bared, a hulking German shepherd ate up the space between them. Josie felt a squeezing in the center of her chest, almost painful. They couldn't outrun it. Turner aimed his pistol at it.

"No!" Josie said. "Don't shoot it."

It went against every survival instinct she had but she didn't want to see a dog shot, even one that might tear the two of them limb from limb. It was only protecting its home from strangers skulking around near its territory.

Turner hesitated.

There was nowhere to go.

Spinning, he holstered his pistol and with lightning-quick motions, positioned himself behind her. For a fleeting moment, she wondered if he was going to use her as a human shield but instead, his large hands clamped around her hips, and he lifted her as if she weighed nothing at all. The privacy fence beside her was vinyl and on the shorter side but still, only Turner's height enabled him to toss her over it like a sack of potatoes.

With a yelp, Josie hurtled through the air. Her pistol flew out of her hand again. She landed on her right side, pain streaking into her shoulder. Something soft brushed her face and arms. A myriad of floral scents invaded her nostrils. She'd landed in someone's garden bed. Hopefully there were no dogs in this yard. Rolling onto her back, she saw the fence shake violently and then Turner's body flew over it. There was no time to move so she curled into a fetal position and hoped he didn't land directly on top of her. It was the only bit of luck she'd had so far that he landed inches away from her and on his feet, no less. The German shepherd threw itself against the other side of the fence, still barking and snarling ferociously.

Josie heaved a sigh of relief. Light washed over the yard. The back door opened and a woman appeared. She took one look at them and screamed over her shoulder, "Someone's in the yard! Call the police!" Then she slammed the door closed. Josie heard a lock click into place.

Great.

Another voice cut through the night, from where the dog had appeared. "Kiki! Kiki! Come!"

Suddenly, the onslaught against the fence ceased. The owner's voice carried again. "Kiki! Get over here!"

"That monster's name is Kiki?" Turner mumbled, brushing at his pants. "I hope you're happy, sweetheart. I didn't shoot the dog, but these pants are torn."

Hauling herself to her feet, Josie said, "Thank you."

"I think I messed up my knee again," he said, by way of answer.

Josie searched around for her pistol, finally finding it under a lawn chair. "Did you call in more units?"

From his jacket pocket, he pulled his cell phone. "I'm doing it now. Not that I need to 'cause Mrs. Better Homes and Gardens in there will probably have a SWAT team here before I get through to dispatch."

Josie pointed in the direction of Mira's development, voice rising to a shout dimmed by the feeling of gravel in her throat. "I told you to call back there!"

Turner put the phone to his ear. "I was backing you up. What do you call what I just did? By the way, you've got dirt in your hair."

THIRTY

The moment Josie stopped moving, pain flooded her system, aches erupting in almost every single part of her body. The fingers and knuckles of her right hand, her forehead, her cheek, her back, her shoulder. The scrapes along her forearms burned. The skin of her throat was tender and bruised and every time she spoke or swallowed, an unpleasant stinging sensation assailed her. Everything hurt. It had been hours. Every available resource on Denton's police force had been called in to search for Seth Lee. Officers had canvassed blocks and blocks of residences, interviewing people and requesting their surveillance footage. Patrol units prowled the streets. After being safely escorted out of the yard she and Turner had landed in during their escape from Kiki the menace, they'd apologized to the owners and joined the search.

Seth Lee was gone, and Josie was thoroughly exhausted.

She'd made her way back to her vehicle, which was parked in front of Mira's house. A couple of members of the ERT were still inside, documenting where Josie had been attacked. She noted that Turner's vehicle was still there although she had no idea where he'd gone. As usual.

"I've been looking for you." She was so tired, she hadn't even heard Noah pull up behind her car. He walked over, brows furrowed. She didn't realize just how tense she was until he gently lifted her chin to study the bruising on her cheek and then her neck. The moment he touched her, the tightness in her jaw, neck, and shoulders started to drain away.

"Heard you got banged up pretty good," he said.

On her scale of having her ass kicked, this night was fairly low. "I'm sore, but I'll survive. I know I have to go to the hospital later to document these injuries and make sure there's no permanent damage to my vocal cords, but tell me, did you get anything? Anything at all?"

He dropped his hand and reached into a pocket for his phone. "We found Mira Summers on camera several times. At the end of this street a neighbor has a security camera. It shows her headed toward her home in the afternoon while Bobbi Thomas was at work. On foot, walking slowly. About two hours later, she appears on a residential camera moving in the other direction, about two blocks from here."

Josie ran her tongue along the shredded portion of the inside of her cheek. "She came home. She was here for two hours." She'd come home and had coffee with someone in her living room. "There were flowers in her kitchen. What was left of the note said, 'sorry.' I don't know when she received them, but—"

"Roses?" Noah asked.

The coppery taste of blood still clung faintly to the inside of her mouth. She kept her voice at a near whisper to avoid more pain. "Yeah."

Noah pointed toward the end of the block in the direction Mira had come when she arrived at her house. "We got a guy carrying a bouquet of roses on that camera there about forty, forty-five minutes after Mira passed by. Figured he was delivering for a florist."

"What did he look like?"

"Hard to tell because the camera only caught his profile. He was wearing a hat. Possibly late teens or early twenties. The quality of the footage isn't great."

Not Seth Lee then.

"We'll get someone to start calling florists though," Noah added. "See if we can track him down and find out who sent the flowers and whether he saw anything or anyone else when he delivered them."

"I don't know that it's important," Josie said. "But it's odd."

Noah smiled. "Everything is important until we know it's not. We'll run it down."

Josie rubbed her shoulder. She was going to need a very hot, very long bath when she finally got home. "Were you able to follow Mira on cameras from here?"

Noah took out his phone. His index finger flew across the screen. "Yes. About five blocks west of here. Not sure where she was headed but she kept looking around like she thought someone might be following her and then..." He turned the screen toward her where black and white footage showed a large front yard with a picket fence. Beyond that, cars whizzed by along the street. On the opposite sidewalk, a tall, loping figure appeared. It was difficult to make out but there were white wraps around her forearms. Mira Summers. She kept looking behind her. Then a white box truck entered the frame, only its cab and half of the cargo area visible. From the distance of the camera, it was impossible to make out the driver. The truck jolted to a stop, eclipsing the view of Mira. Josie watched the timestamp at the bottom right of the screen as the seconds ticked by. Fifteen seconds. Sixteen, seventeen. The truck pulled away. Mira was gone.

"He took her," Josie said, stomach churning. "He could have thrown her into the back of the truck. You can't see it from this angle. Any witnesses?"

"Unfortunately, no. We pulled footage from as many cameras as we could—residential and commercial—trying to follow the truck, maybe get a plate number from it. He avoided all the traffic cams. We caught him on a couple of other residential cameras but with the shitty angles and the distance, we were only able to capture a single number from the license plate—a 7. That's it. We lost him somewhere near North Denton."

"Even fewer cameras up there." Josie pointed at the screen. "But this was fairly early in the afternoon. He took her but then he came back."

"Yeah," Noah said, putting his phone away. "Our canvasses of this area didn't turn up any mention or footage of a white box truck in the hours before or after you encountered Seth Lee in Mira's home, so he must have parked it pretty far from here and then walked. But, with WYEP all over this now, I don't think he can drive a white box truck anywhere in the city without someone calling 911."

If what Rebecca Lee had told them was true, then Seth Lee wouldn't have known about the warrant or the press coverage. Living outdoors didn't give him much access to a television. Unless he heard about it on the radio in the truck.

Josie glanced at the house. "He was looking for something."

But what? There was hardly anything in the place. He already had Mira. What could possibly be inside her home that was worth the risk of returning to a populated area? Or was he operating under some sort of delusion? Did he think there were cameras inside? Was he the person Mira had coffee with after leaving Bobbi's house? Josie frowned. That was a pretty civilized thing to do with someone who had stabbed you only a day ago. Or had Mira been so frightened of him that she'd tried to placate him? Had she convinced him that she wouldn't turn him in so he would leave? Then, when she tried to return to Bobbi's house, he'd followed her and abducted her? Maybe he thought she'd had cameras installed in her house. Based on what

Rebecca had told them, it seemed like something he might suspect. He hadn't destroyed the place. Barely anything was out of place. Only the cabinet with the cat food in it, which was being guarded by said cat.

But how had Seth known when and where to find her in the first place? Had he been following her from the hospital?

Noah interrupted her thoughts. "We've already got Mira's name and photo out to every law enforcement agency and press outlet. Amber's working on blasting it across social media."

It should have made Josie feel better, but instead her stomach felt like someone had lit it on fire. Obviously, Mira had already had some kind of connection with Seth if they'd been meeting at the produce stand for at least a year. Josie entertained the idea that they might even have been dating but only seeing a guy at a produce stand, in secret, a handful of times out of the year, when he deigned to appear, didn't seem like an ideal relationship for any person. He had kept April Carlson for over a year. Josie shuddered thinking about whether or not he was going to do that to Mira Summers. Or would he just kill her? Whatever had happened at the produce stand on Sunday, Josie knew one thing: Mira had put herself between Seth and April, risking her own life to save a woman who had little chance of survival to begin with and receiving horrific wounds for her trouble. Would Seth want to punish her for that, or would he just want to quickly tie up a loose end?

Noah touched her back again. "You okay?"

"Look at this! The lovebirds, reunited." Turner appeared from down the street, swinging a cat carrier in his hand.

Neither Josie nor Noah bothered to respond to his comment, but Josie must have scowled because Turner laughed and said, "What's the matter, sweetheart? You don't have a smile for me? I saved your life tonight, remember?"

If he'd been in the house with her when she encountered Lee, there would have been no chase and no need to save her life. But she didn't feel like arguing with him. "I'm tired, Turner."

He stopped in front of them, peering down at her. "You look like hell. Sound like it, too. You should get checked out and then go home. Get some rest. Maybe brush your hair."

"Turner," Noah snapped.

Ignoring him, Turner held out the cat carrier to Josie. "After you get Mira's cat. Bobbi said she'll keep it until we find Mira. Assuming Mira is still alive. But I didn't mention that. She's already pretty upset."

That's where he was—flirting with a witness, again. Josie didn't take the carrier. "What's wrong with you? You can't get the cat and take it back to her?"

"She's coming on a little strong. Not sure I should be the one to take the cat back there."

Anger sent a flush from Josie's collar to the roots of her hair. "Are you kidding me? You were the one flirting with her earlier while Seth Lee tried to kill me!"

Turner put the carrier on the ground between them. His fingers drummed against his thigh. His phone appeared in his other hand, and he used his thumb to enter a passcode. Whatever was on the screen was far more important than the conversation they were having. As usual. Josie edged closer, trying to see what it was, but Turner kept the phone out of their view. "That's not how it went down," he said. "I was interviewing a witness, on the premises, I might add, while you checked the house. It was a welfare check on a woman who lives alone and had just sustained a head injury. There weren't any lights on. Pretty low-risk. Neither one of us could have reasonably predicted that a murder suspect was hiding inside."

Josie opened her mouth to argue but Turner kept talking. "Besides, I saved you from getting mauled without shooting the dog, so I'd say we're even. You get the cat, okay?"

Noah's hand against her lower back kept her from saying

anything else. "We've got an animal control officer for that sort of thing."

Turner shrugged. "Then call them."

"No," Noah said through clenched teeth. "You call them."

"What's the number?" Turner asked. "And the name? Also, you mind waiting here for them? The Chief wants to talk to me."

Josie didn't want to wait for their animal control officer to arrive—not when she and Noah were right here. This day had already been long enough. "Forget it," she said. "I'll do it. This time. Then Noah can take the cat to Bobbi while I go to the hospital."

Noah looked as though he might object but one look at Josie and he kept quiet. "I can meet you at the hospital after."

Turner looked up from his phone long enough to grin at Noah. "Hey, LT. Did she tell you I threw her over a fence? Like a paper airplane. She took out a shit-ton of geraniums though. For a little thing, she sure caused a lot of damage."

"That's enough, Turner," Noah said, annoyance edging into his normally even voice. "Go see the Chief."

Eyes back on his phone, Turner walked away. Josie pinched the bridge of her nose between her thumb and forefinger. Just talking to him for a few minutes made her head pound. Somehow, every word out of his mouth managed to grate on her. Noah ran his hand up and down her back. "I already talked with the Chief about the welfare check."

"He wasn't interviewing a witness," she said. "He was flirting!"

"I believe you," Noah said. "I'll conduct a thorough investigation into his conduct and discuss it with the Chief. It will get handled. Just put it out of your mind for now."

She snatched up the cat carrier. "Noah, Turner is not just a shitty coworker."

He waited for her to say more, as if sensing she wanted to

unload. She hesitated. Yes, Seth Lee could have killed her while Turner stood on the front steps of Mira's house laughing at everything Bobbi Thomas said, but Josie also bore some responsibility. She, too, had let her judgment lapse when she decided to search the house herself. She could have insisted that Turner accompany her and not moved until he joined her. Yet, she shouldn't have to insist that he follow basic procedure.

Noah said, "Say what you need to say."

Josie sighed. Every word hurt coming from her tender throat, but she had to get it out. "I don't want to be a tattletale so I'm going to talk to you as my husband right now, okay? Not as my superior officer."

He smiled that smile he reserved just for her, and the mere sight of it eased her headache a bit. "I don't think you've ever called me that."

She arched a brow. "I'm your wife right now, remember?"

"Right. Okay. Go on."

"Tonight was bad. Yes, Turner did save me from being attacked by a German shepherd but most of the time, he isn't even around. He rarely even answers his phone when he's on shift—despite the fact that he's glued to it ninety percent of the time—and don't get me started on his paperwork. He's messy and disorganized and I don't know how the hell he even keeps track of anything."

Noah's voice dropped, his tone gentler. "If he wants to keep this job, he'll make sure he doesn't put a fellow officer at risk the way he did tonight. As your husband? I want to kick his ass, but we all have jobs to do and as long as the Chief intends to keep Turner around, we have to live with it. Also, not everyone works the way Mett did with his desk organized to within an inch of its life and his reports so thorough and timely that it made the rest of us look lazy."

Josie couldn't help but laugh.

He brushed an errant lock of hair from her face, his

knuckles gently grazing her jaw in one of the few places she didn't hurt. "We just need to be more careful when working with Turner, and as long as he's here, we have to get used to him because we have no other choice."

She didn't point out that it had already been nearly five months, and that the only person in Denton who had gotten used to him was the kid at the corner store near the stationhouse that sold him energy drinks. And she was pretty sure even that guy didn't like him.

"Now can I be your superior officer again?" Noah grinned.

Josie laughed again, ignoring the way it made her throat burn. "Are you trying to make that sexy? Don't try to make that sexy."

He looked around. "Well, not here."

"Good choice."

"We'll talk later at home."

Barely able to conceal her smile, she swung the cat carrier. "Come on, help me catch this cat. I want it to be in good hands when we find Mira and bring her back."

She hoped saying it would make it true.

Noah followed her inside. The two ERT officers dispatched to Mira's home were working in the upstairs hall, likely taking photos of the damaged drywall and the blood Josie had gotten on the carpet after Seth punched her. In the kitchen, the table and chairs remained on their sides. They edged around the scattered roses, avoiding the shards of broken glass from the vase and the water that had splashed everywhere when it broke. The lower cabinet door was still open but now the cat stretched out across the space, lazily licking one of its paws. Josie set the carrier down nearby and opened its door. Then she knelt in front of the cabinet. Noah waited behind her, ready to pounce if the cat decided to dart. It stopped licking when Josie reached for it. As her hands brushed its fur, it hissed and sprang up, batting at her with its paws. After a brief struggle that resulted in several slashes across her hands and wrists, she got it into the carrier. Noah latched the door closed.

"Should I try to salvage some of this food?" Josie asked, grabbing the torn food bag.

As she pulled it toward her, something fluttered from the bottom of the drawer over the top of the cabinet. An envelope. As it fell, its contents tumbled out, landing on the food scattered across the cabinet floor. Josie blinked to make sure she wasn't imagining things.

"Josie?" said Noah.

Mira's name was handwritten across the front of the envelope. Tape surrounded its edges. A shiny, colorful brochure for Tranquil Trails Equestrian Academy had come partially unfolded, one flap standing straight. Inside the brochure, affixed to a photo of the rolling hills and horse trails, was a Post-it note.

"Get one of the ERT officers," Josie said.

THIRTY-ONE

I wish I knew how to count hours because then I would know how long I've been all alone, and also how long since the last time I had a visit. I love visits most of all. They remind me of the fun before-time when I pretended to be a normal girl and had all the things normal girls have. Before we had to run and hide from the bad people, never stopping, always moving until I felt so tired.

Before all the blood.

No.

I can't think about that. I will be too sad and I'm already sad enough with nobody here. I play with all my treasures, put them back, play again, put them back. I eat what food was left for me. I don't like it but it's important to only eat things that haven't been tampered with or poisoned by the people who want to take us away. My belly still wants more. I fall asleep thinking about protein bars.

One day you'll have all the protein bars and food and special treats that you could ever want.

I hear her voice in a dream. She was the one who told me

about promises. When I wake up, I think about all the promises she made, but then the whisper comes back.

Whose blood?

By the time I hear the noises that mean he's back, I almost can't wait to see him. I run to greet him but when I get there, my feet get frozen to the ground. I don't understand what's happening.

"Not now," he snaps.

But I can't help the question that falls out of my mouth. "What did you do this time?"

THIRTY-TWO

Josie stared at the photos of the envelope, Tranquil Trails brochure, and Post-it note now arrayed on the corkboard. After sending Noah to Bobbi's to drop off the cat, Josie had gotten checked out at the hospital. No permanent damage to her vocal cords, luckily. Then she went home with Noah to their sweet, cuddly dog. She got lots of Trout snuggles, took the longest bubble bath of her life, and got a full night's sleep. As refreshed as she felt, with lots of ibuprofen on board to dull the pain all over her body, she still couldn't figure out the significance of the note or why Mira Summers had taped it to the underside of a kitchen drawer. Josie had even had two cups of coffee to jump-start her day and she was still stumped. The handwriting on the Post-it was the same as on the outside of the envelope. It said: *He's here. We have to tell.* It was unsigned.

"He" had to be Seth. Who else? They didn't know who had given Mira the envelope, but Hummel was trying to pull prints from it as well as from the Tranquil Trails brochure and Post-it which might shed some light on that. Still, the message "we have to tell" was bothering Josie. Tell what and to who? Tell the authorities about the child in his custody? For all they knew, the child was Seth's. Or did the "we have to tell" refer to April? But April had been kept without sunlight for the better part of a year, so if Seth had been camped out on the Lees' property with her, that didn't make much sense. Also, Denton PD had searched the property extensively and hadn't found any evidence that April had been kept there.

Josie was guessing that if Seth was, in fact, driving a box truck, he'd probably locked her in the back most of the time. A white box truck on the Tranquil Trails property would have drawn Rebecca's attention for sure. Then again, they had no way of knowing how old the note was or when Mira had received it. She'd become a client at Tranquil Trails three years ago. Had she received it before then? Before moving to Denton? Or after? Had she received the brochure with the Post-it note affixed to it stating 'He's here,' and then decided to become a client at Tranquil Trails? She'd been meeting secretly with Seth at the produce stand, so she had clearly known he was there. Was this how she'd found out?

The stairwell door whooshed open, and a gust of hot air rushed over her. The edges of the pages that weren't completely secured fluttered briefly. Footsteps trudged behind her. Then came the creak of Gretchen's desk chair. Josie knew it by heart. No matter how much WD-40 Noah sprayed on it, it always creaked.

"Stop obsessing," Gretchen told her.

Without tearing her eyes from the pages, Josie said, "I can't help it."

"Try."

Gretchen was right. The note wasn't going to help them find Seth Lee or the child in his custody or, now, Mira Summers. All it did was raise more questions than it answered. But why hide it in a place nobody would ever look? It hardly seemed worth hiding at all. Was she missing something? It had to have some meaning to Mira that Josie couldn't yet see.

"Seriously," Gretchen said. "Stop."

It still hurt to talk but the painkillers helped. "I can't help it."

The door opened again and this time, Noah strode through it, his phone and a notepad in hand. As he walked past her, he said, "Stop obsessing."

Gretchen said, "She can't help it."

"Try," said Noah.

Josie turned and put her hands on her hips, the motion only setting off a dull ache in her shoulder and hand. "You two should be life coaches."

Gretchen snorted.

The door to the great room opened for the third time in less than twenty minutes. Hummel this time. A folder was tucked under his arm. Josie was struck at how different he looked in his regular uniform and not a Tyvek suit. "You're all here," he said, striding toward their desks. He looked at Mettner's old desk—no, Turner's desk—and his expression darkened. "Almost all of you."

"Do you have something that is going to break the Summers/Carlson case wide open?" Gretchen asked.

"I wish." Hummel sighed and took out his phone. "Shit. I should have brought coffee to soften this blow."

"Surely it's not that bad," Josie said. "Unless you couldn't get prints from the envelope and its contents that we found at Mira's house last night?"

"Um, I did," Hummel said. "But I don't think it's really helpful. Probably just confuses things more. Unfortunately, nothing I have for you today is going to locate Seth Lee, the child in question, or Mira Summers."

Josie tried not to let her disappointment show.

Noah leaned back in his desk chair and folded his arms over his chest. "What do you have?"

"The only set of prints from the envelope found in Mira's

house—with brochure and Post-it—that I got hits on were Mira Summers's—"

"To be expected," said Josie.

"—and April Carlson."

"What?" said Josie.

Gretchen's chair creaked again. "April Carlson gave that brochure to Mira?"

Hummel shrugged. "Listen, I just process the evidence. I can't tell you who did what, but both women's prints were on those items."

He's here. We have to tell.

They had no way to know how old that message was, but Josie was certain that April had delivered it to Mira. But why? How did April know Seth? Or that he had a child? The most obvious answer was that April had encountered them both as a teacher and yet, Heather's extensive investigation into April's disappearance hadn't turned up any connection to Seth Lee—or even Mira Summers. Neither of their names appeared anywhere in Heather's file. Josie had checked twice.

"Also this." Hummel took the folder from beneath his arm and put it on Noah's desk, opening it to reveal several photos which he spread before them. "I took a close look at the tire tracks from the crime scene at Tranquil Trails. I have a buddy at the state lab who is an expert in tire tracks. I asked him to confirm my findings, which he did." He pointed at the first photo. "The tracks are consistent with a type of tire called an XDA5, distributed by a tire company based in New York. They're made specifically for box trucks. None of the vehicles registered to the Lees or to Tranquil Trails use this particular tire. However, the tracks are a match to the kind the state police found near April Carlson's car after she disappeared from Route 80." Here, he indicated a different set of photos. "I'm not saying they're the same tires, just that they're the same kind of tire at both scenes."

"Which means that there is a possibility that the same guy was at both scenes," Gretchen said.

"Yes," Hummel answered. "But lots of box trucks use this kind of tire, so there's no way to prove that it was the same truck."

"You were right," Noah said. "This is good stuff, but it doesn't point us in a direction and right now we've got three people we need to find."

Hummel sighed. "I told you so."

"What else do you have?" Josie asked, sensing there was more. Hummel was never one to linger.

He pulled up a photo on his phone and turned it toward them. Josie crowded next to Noah to see it. "That's one of the clumps of hair we found on April Carlson's clothes at the scene of the accident," she explained to Noah.

"It's not hair," Hummel said, swinging the phone so Gretchen could see. "The lab doesn't know what it is, but it's not hair. Not human or animal."

"Then it's some kind of fiber," Gretchen said.

Hummel shook his head. "Nope. It's not synthetic."

"Then what the hell is it?" asked Noah.

"Your guess is as good as mine," Hummel said.

"Send me that photo," Josie told him.

He took out his phone and texted it to her. "The lab will do more analysis to try and figure out what it is, but that will take a while."

Staring at the photo on her own phone, Josie said, "If it's not synthetic and it's not hair, it has to be from a tree or a plant."

"That makes sense," Gretchen said. "But what? Dandelion fluff?"

Josie shook her head. "No. Way too thick for that."

"It really does look like hair," Noah said. "Very short, coarse hair. Remember when Dougherty had that Siberian husky and used to brush her out every day? Big clumps of her hair would fall out and end up all over his uniform. Looked just like that only the hair was longer." He reached up and rested his hand on Josie's hip. "Our resident amateur botanist doesn't know what it is?"

She smiled at him. "Out of my area of expertise."

Gretchen said, "If it's some kind of plant or something, what's the quickest way to find out what it is?"

"Find an actual botanist," Josie suggested.

Hummel said, "Let me know what you find out. It would be good information to have for future cases. I'm out."

After he left, Gretchen stood up and stretched her arms over her head. "Our only witness has been abducted. Our suspect is still at large. None of the clues we have so far give us any direction as to where to find them. We still have no idea who drew the picture or how Seth Lee came to have a child with him. His last known address was a bust. We know that he was meeting Mira at the produce stand pretty regularly, but we have no idea what his connection is to April Carlson, why he took her or why he held her for a year."

Josie looked at the corkboard again. The drawings. Seth's face. The map of Tranquil Trails Gretchen had formed using Google Maps printouts. The cryptic note. Gretchen was right. Everything about this case seemed disjointed, out of whack. They were missing something. Some glue that held all the ill-fitting pieces together. "Seriously," she said. "Life coaching. Or maybe a motivational speaker."

Noah didn't look up from his computer, but he snickered.

Gretchen said, "I'm asking you where we should go from here."

Josie spun away from the board. "Where all of this started."

THIRTY-THREE

Two and a half hours later, Josie was in the passenger's seat of Gretchen's car, watching the scenery flash past as they arrived in a small town in Bucks County called Riddick. It was on the outskirts of Doylestown, which was where Seth Lee's last known address had turned up nothing. It was also less than a half hour from April Carlson's hometown of Hillcrest. Gretchen turned onto what looked like Riddick's main street. Storefronts in old brick buildings lined both sides. Potted flowers, outdoor benches, and black metal lampposts appeared at regular intervals.

"This is a lot nicer than the three strip malls and the shopping center we passed on the way in," Gretchen remarked.

"Yeah," Josie said softly. She was trying to save her voice for the interviews to come.

From each lamppost hung the same flyers that they'd already seen taped to the windows of various businesses. The photo showed the face of a uniformed officer, his hat positioned just right, smiling stiffly for his official department photo. Josie didn't need to read his name to know he was the officer Heather Loughlin had told them about. The one April Carlson had gone

on a couple of dates with before he disappeared. Shane Foster.
Above his head the word MISSING shouted in huge capital
letters. Below his face was a date almost three years ago to the
day with the words *Never Forgotten* and under that, *Hillcrest
PD* with a contact number.

"I think this is it," said Gretchen as she turned onto a residential street.

Five minutes later, they stood in front of a tiny, one-story
home. Grime clung to its formerly white siding. The strip of
grass that served as a front yard was high and unruly. Other
than the single pot of colorful spring flowers on the front stoop,
it looked like no one lived there. But this was the address they'd
found for Mira Summers's parents. Josie had confirmed it with
Carol Summers when she'd called to set up this meeting.
They'd decided to start here and then work their way over to
Hillcrest to speak with April's parents. Josie wasn't even sure
what they hoped to find out besides anything that connected
Mira, April and Seth Lee. Something that might lead them to
the identity of the child whose plea for help had ended up in
the hand of a dead woman.

Josie wiped at the sweat dampening the back of her neck
and then knocked on the door. She heard movement inside and
then the door swung open, revealing a small woman in her
seventies. Brittle white hair framed her weathered face. "You
the police that called earlier?"

"Yes," said Gretchen.

They presented their credentials. Carol gave them a cursory
look and then waved them both inside. The odor of stale cigarettes hit Josie like a slap. On the coffee table sat a blue ceramic
ashtray filled with butts. A single lit cigarette still burned, the
smoke curling upward. Carol shuffled over to the sagging gray
couch and picked it up, taking a long drag. "Sit. Wherever."

The only other furniture in the cramped living room was a
brown armchair that looked even older than the couch. Its seat

was crooked. Josie wasn't sure it was sturdy enough to hold a human being. Gretchen seemed to have the same idea, standing on the other side of the coffee table, but leaving Carol with a view of the television across the room currently playing a game show. Josie maintained her position a few feet away from Gretchen.

Carol sighed. "Fine. Don't sit. Whatever. So, you're here about Mira?"

"Yes," said Josie. She looked around the space. Only a half-wall separated the living room from the kitchen. It was empty. "You might have seen on the news—"

"Don't watch the news," Carol interrupted. "Too depressing. Haven't watched the news in ten years."

"Then you might have seen on social media—" Gretchen began.

Carol cut her off again. "Don't spend much time on there either."

Josie was going to suggest that she might have gotten wind of Mira's abduction from friends, assuming the coverage had reached Bucks County, but Carol Summers didn't strike her as the kind of person who had a lot of friends. "Is Mr. Summers here?"

Carol gave a harsh laugh. "Mr. Summers is dead. May God deliver his soul to the gates of hell." Using the two fingers cradling her cigarette, she made the sign of the cross. Then she laughed again.

Josie didn't need to look at Gretchen to know that she, too, had no idea how to respond to that. But Gretchen made an attempt. "I'm... sorry for your loss?" It came out as a question more than a condolence.

Carol waved the cigarette, sending the smoke trail into a zigzag. "Don't be. Gordon was a bastard. A mean old bastard. Mira probably told you he used to beat the shit out of me. Never laid a hand on her. Still can't figure out why but that bitch stood by and watched him hit me till I was black and blue and never lifted a damn finger."

Josie couldn't help but feel a twinge of sympathy for Mira. No wonder she didn't speak to her parents. The dysfunction in the household was distressing. Had Carol really expected Mira to try to stop her father's violent assaults as a child? Or did she mean when Mira was an adult?

"When did your husband die?" Josie tugged the collar of her polo shirt up, making sure it covered the bruises Seth Lee had left behind.

"Five years ago. May he rot in eternal hell."

That was well before Mira had left Bucks County to move to Denton.

"When is the last time you spoke with Mira?" Gretchen asked.

"Don't know. Four years ago? She don't talk to me no more, and that's just fine by me. I'm not surprised you're here. What's she done?"

Gretchen said, "She hasn't done anything. On Sunday, she had a car accident after being stabbed. Yesterday she was abducted by the man we believe stabbed her. We think that she knew him. There is a warrant out for his arrest, but we haven't been able to locate him."

While Gretchen spoke, Josie took out her phone and pulled up a photo of Seth, turning the screen toward Carol so she could see it. "Seth," she said immediately. Shaking her head, she turned her attention to the television. "Fucking crazy bastard. I'm not surprised. It was only a matter of time before he tried to kill her. I told her over and over again. Did she listen to me? Of course not. Well, this is what she gets."

Again, Carol's callousness toward her own daughter was jarring. Pocketing her phone, Josie asked, "How did Mira know Seth?"

Carol laughed humorlessly. "Oh, she didn't tell you? Of

course she didn't. They're a couple. He's had his hooks in her since she was eighteen years old. In fact, she took off with him for almost four years when they first met. Didn't hear from her once. Then she came back for a while. It's always been an on-and-off thing between them. Mira always goes back. Doesn't matter whether he hits her or cheats on her. Doesn't matter what weird shit he wants her to do, like only eating food he grows himself in some special soil, or moving into a shed on some random person's property because it doesn't have electricity. You know, if you don't have electricity, the authorities can't hook up their cameras to spy on you." At this, her laugh turned deep and lasted several seconds. Ash fell from her cigarette as she held her stomach. Her expression hardened once she finished. Taking another drag, she said, "Let me tell you something about my daughter and her precious Seth. Whatever he's done to her? She deserved it."

Josie worked to keep the shock from her face. Gretchen busied herself getting out her pen and notepad and Josie knew she, too, was trying to control her reaction.

Carol missed nothing. She stubbed out her cigarette and leaned back into the couch. "I know what you're thinking. I'm a terrible mom. How could I say that about my own daughter? Let me tell you something. When Mira got to be a teenager, she made it her job to judge me for staying with her dad even though he beat me to holy hell every chance he got. She never understood the way things were. She made such a fuss about why didn't I leave? How come I never called the police? She wasn't worldly enough to understand how those things work. He always controlled all the money. Never let me work. I couldn't just go out into the world and get a job and a house. With what skills? With what money? I called the police a few times when she was a baby, but I had nowhere to go but here. How could I press charges? He told me he'd kill me if I kept doing it. Every time I called, he'd break a bone. He wasn't afraid of the damn police."

She reached for the pack of cigarettes on the coffee table and shook one out. Stabbing it in the air, she continued, "He was in the army. Thought it made him a tough guy. There wasn't a man alive that could intimidate Gordon. Truth be told, he probably would have shot any police officer who came to our door to arrest him for beating me. I knew it. He'd kill anyone who tried to arrest him, and I'd be next. As sure as the sky is blue, one way or another he was gonna kill me and that was that."

"I'm sorry, Mrs. Summers," Gretchen said.

Carol found her lighter under a tabloid magazine and lit the cigarette, inhaling deeply. "Don't be. I'm here and he's not. Anyway, after four years with Seth, Mira came home with a black eye. I asked her, 'He do that to you?' She said no, but I could tell by her face that I was right. I told her, 'Well, that's the pot calling the kettle black, now, isn't it?' Then I asked her if she was going to leave him on account of him hitting her and she just burst into tears. She tried to tell me that it wasn't the same between those two as it was between me and her dad because Seth didn't mean to hit her and they were in love."

Carol said the word "love" like it was a punchline and then she laughed.

Gretchen jotted down some notes. "What did your husband think about Seth?"

"Gordon didn't like too many people, but he was okay with Seth, at first. He liked that Seth used to be in the army. Didn't give a shit if Seth hit Mira. That's what wives and girlfriends are for, right? But then Seth started acting funny. Kept saying that Gordon was in on some plan, that his old commanding officers in the army had to 'silence him,' and that Gordon was part of their little spy network. Well, that was that. Seth wasn't welcome here

anymore. Mira moved back out shortly after that. I think because
Seth insisted. She always did everything he told her. Everything.
No matter how ridiculous. But she'd move back in here from time
to time when they were on the outs or when he disappeared."

"Disappeared?" Josie said.

Carol sucked on her cigarette again, this time holding the
smoke in her lungs for a few seconds before exhaling. "Yeah.
He'd just take off. Not tell Mira where he was going—said it
'wasn't safe' for her to know. Could be months. Could be years.
Then one day he'd show back up and she'd take him right back."

Josie said, "Did Seth have children?"

"Hell, no," Carol coughed. "Can you imagine? No. Mira
wanted kids at some point, but he didn't. He thought if they
ever had kids, the government or the army would come take
them away."

Gretchen asked, "Do you know where Seth would go when
he 'disappeared'?"

"No. Who the hell knows with him?"

Josie stepped out of the way of another plume of smoke. It
was making her already irritated throat worse. "When is the last
time you saw him?"

"Not sure. It's been years. He didn't come to Gordon's
funeral even though Mira asked him, so probably before that."

Gretchen blinked several times. Josie could see her eyes
were getting red. Probably from the cloud of smoke enveloping
them. Would it be rude to ask Carol to open a window?

"Mrs. Summers," Gretchen said. "When officers responded
to the car accident that Mira was involved in, they found a
deceased passenger in her vehicle. Her name was April Carlson. Mira told us she didn't know her and had never seen her
before. You might have heard of her. She used to live in
Hillcrest—"

"Mira's half-sister, you mean?"

Josie exchanged a stunned look with Gretchen before turning back to Carol. "April Carlson was Mira's half-sister?"

"Yeah. The one whose rich family started whining about her going missing about a year ago." Carol rolled her eyes. More ash fell into her lap and she brushed it aside. "Heard all about it every place I went. People go missing around here all the time. Look at that police officer. They never did find him."

Gretchen flipped a page in her notebook. "How do you know April Carlson was Mira's half-sister?"

Carol sighed, as if she was becoming bored with the conversation. "My husband had a gal before me, but she was smart enough to get away from him just as soon as she got pregnant. She moved a town over, married a new fella. A good man with a good job. Treated her real sweet, but she never let that baby know who her real father was, which was smart. Guess when that baby grew up, she wanted the truth. Her mother told her finally. She showed up here one day asking around. Imagine her disappointment when she met my husband."

Carol laughed long and hard until a coughing fit seized her. She pounded on her chest with her free hand before resuming. "She never came around again, but her and Mira talked a couple of times after Gordon died. Mira never said, but I always thought that April got her that job at Hillcrest Elementary. That's around the time she stopped talking to me altogether. Guess that job didn't work out if she ended up around your way. Figures."

THIRTY-FOUR

April Carlson's family home was the opposite of Mira Summers's in every way. Ten times the size of Carol Summers's house, it towered over a generous four-acre lot of meticulously cut grass. Carefully trimmed bushes lined the long driveway and the front walk. They had called ahead and April's mother, Teresa Carlson, waited at the door, pushing it open to let them in before they could knock or ring the doorbell. Josie was struck at once by the resemblance between her and April—the April Josie had seen in photos, not the way she'd looked in death. Teresa's long hair was silver, but her bright eyes, high cheekbones, and wide mouth were identical to her daughter's, except for the tear stains that ran down her cheeks. She wore a fitted cashmere sweater and black slacks and carried herself regally as she waved them through the huge foyer into the back of the house.

The kitchen was twice the size of Carol Summers's entire house, with marble countertops and an island where Teresa motioned for them to sit. Stacks of flyers covered its surface, Officer Shane Foster's face staring at them again. Teresa quickly began moving them to the dinner table. "Sorry," she said. "I'm helping the Fosters get the word out. The three-year anniversary of Shane's disappearance is just around the corner. After what we went through with April, I felt like if I could help another family get through this, then it would give me some purpose." She paused to stare at Shane Foster's photo. "April went on a couple of dates with him, you know. Right before he disappeared."

"Heather told us," Josie said as she and Gretchen each sat on a stool. She was glad they wouldn't have to contend with smoke. She'd taken two more ibuprofen in the car on the way over but her throat—and nearly every other part of her body—still hurt. At least neither Carol nor Teresa had commented on the lingering rasp in her voice.

Teresa transferred the last of the flyers from the island to the table with a sigh. "April was so crushed. She took it really hard. I think she really liked him."

In the corner of the room a small table held a large, framed photo of April—the same one that had been used on her missing persons poster and on the news. It was surrounded by unlit candles. Teresa drifted toward it as if it was pulling her. She ran a finger over her daughter's face. The longing in the gesture made Josie's heart clench.

Gretchen said, "It's a beautiful photo of her."

Without looking away, Teresa said, "It's my favorite. It was taken on her thirty-fifth birthday. My mother gave her that bracelet—it had been hers. April was so moved. She wore it all the time until she lost it. She found it, thank God, but wouldn't wear it after that. It was too precious. Just like her."

The moment stretched on. Josie didn't feel as though they should interrupt Teresa's memories of April so they waited. Finally, Teresa used the heels of her hands to wipe at her cheeks. She turned back to them, managing a watery smile. "Anyway, can I get you officers anything? Water? Espresso?

Something to eat? My husband brought home some goodies from our local bakery yesterday."

"No, thank you, Mrs. Carlson," said Gretchen. "We don't want to take up any more of your time than absolutely necessary."

Teresa hugged herself. "When the county coroner showed up here to tell us..." She trailed off. More tears ran down her cheeks. A tissue appeared from the sleeve of her sweater, and she dabbed at them. "Sorry. It's just been nonstop waterworks ever since we found out. When April wasn't located after two weeks of searching, I knew that things weren't going to end well but of course, as a mother, you hold out hope. Heather—Detective Loughlin—has been wonderful. She stopped by after the death notification to talk us through everything she knows about the case. Now you've got a suspect. When you called the other night to tell me, and then I saw the photo of him, I felt... I don't know. I guess I expected to recognize him or something. It seems so strange to me that he targeted April randomly, but that's just me wanting her disappearance and death to make some kind of sense. It's like if he knew her and had some reason for doing what he did—however sick—then maybe it won't be so painful, but then I think if I had recognized him, and it wasn't random, then I would be beating myself up for not seeing any red flags that could have saved her. My therapist says that it doesn't matter whether it was random or not. It doesn't change the outcome."

She heaved a sigh and wiped at her face again. "I'm sorry. You didn't need to know all that."

Her grief was so raw and palpable that it broke Josie's heart, plunging her right back into that painful time in her own life after the deaths of people closest to her. It was months of performing endless mental gymnastics as a way to make sense of something senseless and to alleviate pain that was not meant to be alleviated. In her own time, Teresa Carlson would come to live with the fact that none of those emotional maneuvers changed the outcome—or mitigated the devastation. It was one of life's hardest truths. "I get it, Mrs. Carlson," Josie offered. "My therapist said the same thing to me after I lost my grandmother."

Teresa reached across the counter and patted Josie's hand. "Thank you."

Gretchen said, "We understand that this is an extremely difficult time for you and your family. The last thing we want to do is make things worse. We can come back another time."

Teresa smiled through her tears and waved a hand, dismissing the suggestion. "No. No. I've been trying to stay away from the news and social media, but my son told me that this man—Seth Lee—abducted someone else just yesterday. The woman who tried to save April. I want to help in any way that I can."

Gretchen folded her hands on the countertop. "We appreciate that."

"Also," Josie said, "we're not entirely sure that what happened to April was random." Given the fact that Seth had been dating Mira, and Mira and April were half-sisters, Josie knew it wasn't random at all. They now knew what connected the three of them, but they still didn't know why Seth had kidnapped and killed April—or where the child fit into all of it. Or who the child was. Josie took a deep breath and then plunged into their next line of inquiry. "In the course of our investigation, it has come to our attention that April's biological father was Gordon Summers."

What little color left in Teresa's face drained away. She swayed a bit and then grabbed the nearest stool, sinking into it. "God, I haven't heard his name since... since April demanded to know it. That was... ten years ago. Why are you asking me about Gordon? He's been dead for a long time now."

"Are you aware that April sought him out?" asked Josie.

Her hand flew to her chest. "No, no. That can't be right. She promised me she wouldn't. I told her the truth about him. She was old enough to hear it by then. I barely managed to escape him. The only reason he didn't sue me for custody of April was because he couldn't afford it. But he would have taken her from me if he'd had the chance. Not because he cared about her—he never did—but to hurt me. That's how Gordon was—spiteful and cruel. Once I married my husband—Bill—he had an attorney contact Gordon. It took months, but eventually he gave up his parental rights and Bill adopted her. That's why she's Carlson and not Summers. No one even knows that she's not Bill's except for us and our kids, and even the kids didn't know until they were adults and realized that Bill didn't show up in her baby pictures until she was almost two years old. Oh God—"

She swayed again as a realization hit her. "Mira Summers. She's Gordon's daughter, isn't she? My other children suggested it, but I told them it wasn't possible. Summers is a fairly common name. I thought it was just a coincidence. Oh no. No, no. Is it true?"

Gretchen grimaced. "I'm afraid so."

Teresa said nothing as she digested this fact.

Obviously, Teresa hadn't kept tabs on her ex or known that he'd had another daughter. Josie asked, "Gordon never contacted you again? After he gave up his parental rights?"

Teresa shook her head. "No. I think Bill's attorney intimidated him or he realized that he had lost control over me, and it just wasn't any fun anymore. God, I can't believe that April contacted him. I was honest with her about what he did to me. When he found out I was pregnant with her, he beat me so badly, I nearly lost her! I made her promise that she would never approach him. I don't think he would have been a threat to her at that point since she was an adult, but I just didn't think it was a good idea to poke that hornet's nest."

"I'm sorry," said Gretchen. "But it appears that she did, and from what Gordon's widow told us, meeting him once was enough to deter her from any further contact."

"I had no idea," Teresa whispered. "I remember seeing his obituary. That was years ago but I can't remember how long exactly. When did she..."

"We're not exactly sure," Josie said. "But he died five years ago so it had to be before that."

"I remember being so relieved when I saw his obituary because the temptation to contact him would no longer be there. And to think, I felt so guilty about not telling her he had died, but she'd already met him. I just can't believe this."

"When April disappeared and Detective Loughlin started her investigation, did you mention Gordon?" asked Gretchen.

"Why would I? Gordon had been dead for years by then and as far as I knew, April had kept her promise to never contact him. She must have met his other daughter when she reached out to him, but she never told me." Her entire frame shuddered. "Oh God. That poor child—enduring the fate I saved April from. I can't even imagine. I always hoped no other woman would be drawn in by him, but life is never that kind, especially not to women."

"All these years, you never knew he'd started a new family?" asked Gretchen. Her tone was curious, not accusatory. "The Summers don't live that far from here. Different town, but not a long drive."

"I truly had no idea. I didn't keep tabs on Gordon. I wanted to get away from him. There were a handful of times I'd see him in a store or at a gas station and I simply avoided him but other than that, our lives didn't intersect in any way. Thank God. Wait." She seemed to emerge from some pocket of the past into the present. "If Mira and April were in the same car when— They must have developed some sort of relationship after Gordon died and yet, she never said anything. Not one word.

To any of us. Not to her father—my husband—or her siblings. None of her friends ever mentioned it either, and Heather questioned all of us quite thoroughly."

Which meant that April had kept any relationship or contact she might have had with Mira a secret. If April had told anyone in her life, it might have gotten back to Teresa and Mira's last name would have been a red flag. As it was, Teresa's other kids had picked up on Mira's last name immediately even though she lived hours away in Denton.

"Why wouldn't she tell me?" Teresa murmured, almost to herself.

Teresa Carlson didn't seem like the type who would let her anger get the best of her. Josie thought it was far more likely that April kept Mira a secret because she didn't want Teresa to be disappointed that she'd broken a promise, especially one so important to her. Josie hadn't exactly had a traditional upbringing, but Lisette had been the closest thing she'd ever had to a real parent. She remembered how awful it felt to disappoint her. Josie would have taken Lisette's anger over her disappointment any day.

Gretchen pulled her notebook and pen from her pocket. "We don't know the nature of their relationship. It's possible that they hadn't grown close, or maybe they did and then there was some sort of falling-out that ended things."

Or April had met or found out about Seth and wisely decided to run screaming in the other direction. But that's not what she'd done at all. She'd moved to a town only a half hour drive from Denton. Closer to him. Closer to Mira. Yet, there was no evidence of contact between April and either of them the entire time she lived in Newsham.

Teresa continued, "Though I suppose if she was in touch with Gordon's daughter, it would have been easy to conceal. She moved out right after college and lived on her own after that. Though if she had developed some sort of friendship with

Gordon's daughter, wouldn't Heather have found evidence on her phone?"

Josie said, "The phone records Heather was able to get only go back two years. If April and Mira had had a falling-out or ceased to be in contact prior to that, then there wouldn't have been anything in April's phone records to find."

Teresa's brow furrowed. "You said you didn't think that April's abduction was random. What does that have to do with Mira?"

Josie cleared her throat. The painkillers were finally kicking back in, making it easier to speak. "Mrs. Summers told us that Mira was dating Seth Lee, for several years, apparently."

Teresa's eyes widened. "And if April became friendly with Mira then she would have had contact with Seth. This is some kind of domestic violence situation, isn't it? Seth and Mira. That was the example that poor girl grew up with, and then she fell in love with a man just like Gordon. Then my poor April got caught up in it."

"We're still trying to put all the pieces together," said Gretchen.

Thinking of the note that April had left for Mira on the Tranquil Trails brochure, Josie asked, "To your knowledge did April ever visit Denton or anywhere in that area?"

Teresa shook her head. "No, not that I'm aware of. We'd never even heard of Newsham, where she got that job. That's close to Denton, from what I understand."

"Did April have an interest in horseback riding?" Gretchen said, picking up on Josie's line of inquiry. "Or horses in general?"

"You're wondering because of those stables, aren't you? Heather told me about them but no, April never had an interest in anything like that. She loved animals but she was much more of a cat or dog sort of person." Teresa sighed. "I still don't understand why she didn't get a dog when she moved to

Newsham. Living in a strange new town all alone with no family nearby."

Josie took out her phone and found the child's drawing to show to Teresa. "Also, as I told you when we first spoke on the telephone—right before we released Seth's information to the press—we believe that there is a child involved somehow. This was found at the accident scene. Does this mean anything to you?"

Teresa found a pair of reading glasses on a nearby countertop and took Josie's phone into her hands. She shook her head slowly as she studied the drawing. "Is that an eye?"

"We're not sure," said Josie.

"I'm so sorry," Teresa said, handing the phone back. "I don't know what to make of it."

Gretchen jotted something down in her notebook. "I think that's all we have for you today. We really appreciate your taking the time to speak with us. As soon as we know anything more, we'll contact you. We've got to get to Hillcrest Elementary before the principal leaves for the day. We have some follow-up questions for her."

"Hillcrest Elementary," Teresa echoed. "My friend Hope is the principal there."

Which explained why Heather's investigation hadn't turned up the connection between April and Mira via the school. If they had made their connection known at work, the word would likely have gotten back to Teresa very quickly.

"She called me when that man's photo began circulating," Teresa added. "She said he looked so familiar to her, but she couldn't figure out where she might have seen him. She wanted to know if any of us recognized him but as I've told you, I didn't. Neither did my husband nor my other children."

The doorbell rang. Teresa glanced at the clock on the wall. "That will be my neighbor with candles and such for the vigil.

We're holding one for Shane Foster next week on the anniversary of his disappearance. If you'll excuse me."

Once she was out of the room, Gretchen tapped her pen against her notepad. Josie could see the diagram she'd drawn, complete with names and arrows.

Josie said, "You're thinking what I'm thinking."

"We can probably find out what we need to know by having the principal do one or two simple searches. Hillcrest Elementary is a public school, right?"

"Right," Josie said. "Public schools usually give us information without pushing for a warrant or anything."

"In our own jurisdiction, sure. We should get a records request letter together for Hillcrest just in case we need one."

Josie nodded. "That will take a little time, especially if Turner's doing it. The school day will be over soon."

"I'm so sorry," Teresa Carlson said, sailing back into the room.

"It's no problem at all," Gretchen replied smoothly. "We were wondering if you could do something for us before we go."

"Anything," said Teresa.

Josie said, "Would you mind calling the principal at Hillcrest and asking her to stay late to speak with us? Coming from you, it might help."

THIRTY-FIVE

As promised, Hope Bailey was waiting for them when they arrived at Hillcrest Elementary nearly an hour later. She stood outside the main entrance of the sprawling brick building beside a towering flagpole. Her posture was straight and tall. Blonde hair brushed her shoulders. Her simple white blouse and black slacks made her look official but also approachable. The last of the students ran to their parents' vehicles, waving goodbye to her. Josie and Gretchen's Denton PD polo shirts, and the pistols hanging from their waists, drew a few concerned looks, but Hope only smiled brightly at the stragglers as if to indicate there was nothing to see here. Once all the students were gone, she herded Josie and Gretchen inside the building. Josie adjusted her collar again to cover the bruises marring her throat. Then she focused on Hope, studying her as she led them down a long hallway that was wallpapered with children's art pieces. Hope was younger than Josie had expected. Teresa Carlson was over seventy whereas Hope looked about fifty.

Hope ushered them into a large office cheerily decorated with motivational posters. One colorful poster announced: *Today is a great day to learn something new!* How fitting. Carol

Summers had dropped quite the bombshell on them when she revealed that Mira and April were half-sisters. Josie hoped they would learn even more before they left Hillcrest, and that it would be something that helped them locate Seth Lee and the child.

Another woman sat behind the desk separating the door from the rest of the space. "I'll be in my office," Hope told her. "Not to be disturbed except for my daughter."

The secretary nodded, staring at Josie and Gretchen as they followed Hope around her desk and through a door marked *Principal*. Hope's inner sanctum was less chipper than the rest of the school with a simple desk, two guest chairs, a few filing cabinets, and bookshelves filled with tomes of academic texts. The posters on her walls were geared more toward adults. *Your poor planning does not constitute an emergency on my part*, read one of them. Another said: *Everything is hard before it is easy*.

Gretchen stopped in front of that one for a moment. Glancing back at Josie, she muttered under her breath, "No shit."

Josie suppressed a laugh. Once they were all seated, Josie and Gretchen presented their credentials. Hope gave them a cursory glance and then waved them off. "Teresa vouched for you. As I told you on the phone earlier, I just want to help in any way that I can. It's been difficult, as I'm sure you can imagine. When April was missing, we could be of use by searching and distributing flyers and posting on social media, but now... I don't know what to do."

Gretchen discreetly checked her phone and then looked at Josie, giving a quick shake of her head. Turner hadn't yet sent over the records request letter. What the hell was he doing?

While Gretchen tapped in a text message to Turner, Josie asked Hope, "How long have you and Teresa been friends?"

"Oh, going on twenty years now. We were on the board of the same nonprofit. We hit it off. Never looked back. But if you're asking me whether April got the job here because of that friendship, she did not. I hired her because she was the most qualified for the position."

Clearly, that question had been raised by people in the past if Hope felt the need to head it off at the pass. But it confirmed Josie's suspicion that if there was something April didn't want her mother to find out, she'd have to keep a lid on it in this environment.

"Of course," said Gretchen. She glanced again at her phone and Josie could tell by the set of her jaw that she was still waiting for the records request letter from Turner. "You spoke at length with Detective Heather Loughlin of the state police. We've read over that file, so we won't waste your time with questions she's already asked. I'm sure you're aware that we've got a suspect in April's abduction and murder."

"Yes, I saw it on the news. Teresa called to tell me before it came out." Hope lowered her voice even though they were the only ones in the room. "Teresa might have told you this already but that man looked familiar to me. I still can't figure out if I know him from somewhere or if maybe he just reminds me of someone."

They probably wouldn't even need the records request letter. Josie plunged ahead. "Is it possible he was the parent of a child enrolled here?"

Gretchen abandoned her phone for her trusty notepad. "You may have also seen on the news that we believe Seth Lee has a child with him."

"Yes, I did see." Hope pressed both hands over her heart. "I was horrified. Teresa told me what he did to April—the way he kept her... it makes me sick to think he has a child in his custody. To answer your question, I did search our database for his name. We've had quite a few families with the last name Lee over the years, but Seth Lee was not the parent of any student here."

Neither of them had expected it to be that easy. Josie

scooted forward to the edge of her seat. "Mrs. Bailey, could you check another name for us?"

Hope's fingers hovered over the keyboard. "Of course. The name of a parent?"

"Yes," Josie replied. "Mira Summers."

Hope's fingers lowered to the keys and then froze. Three lines appeared on her forehead. "Mira Summers? Wait. The woman involved in April's case? The one driving the car? The one who was just abducted?"

Gretchen tapped her pen against a blank page in her notebook. "Yes. That one. We also believe that she might have been an employee here for some time but right now, we'd like to know if she ever enrolled a child."

"An employee?" Hope muttered. "That can't be... but let me just... I'll check our student and parent database."

Josie's phone buzzed in her pocket. She took it out to see a message from Turner.

RR in your email. Tell Parker to get off my ass.

Was he trying to piss Gretchen off more than usual? Nudging Gretchen's elbow, Josie said softly, "I've got it."

Gretchen rolled her eyes. "All that, and we didn't even need it."

Hope wasn't paying attention to their conversation. Her hands stopped moving. A greenish hue overtook her complexion. Swallowing hard, she turned the laptop toward them. "Mira Summers enrolled her daughter, Rosie Summers, into kindergarten almost four years ago."

Rosie. Like the flower in the drawing.

THIRTY-SIX

There's no blood. I feel happy about that, but my heart feels weird and not right because when I touch her, she feels cold. There's a big bruise across her forehead and her arms are all wrapped up like a mummy. I try to wake her up, but she doesn't open her eyes.

"Leave her alone," he says.

"No," I say.

"Rosie, do what I say."

"I won't!"

He steps toward us and I throw myself over her. I am crying so hard that everything looks blurry. She still doesn't move.

His voice gets nice again. He tries to touch my shoulder, but I slap his hand away.

"It's going to be okay," he lies.

"No, it's not." It will never be okay again. Not ever. "You killed Mom!"

THIRTY-SEVEN

The student profile that filled the screen showed a school photo of Rosie Summers. Josie took a long moment to study the girl they'd been chasing for what felt like ages even though it had only been a few days. Six-year-old Rosie grinned at them, her bright blue eyes vibrant and intelligent. Brown curls tumbled to her shoulders. Josie could see the resemblance to both Seth and Mira.

Carol had said that Mira often went off with Seth for years at a time, cutting off all contact. It was entirely possible that Mira and Seth had had a baby together without anyone knowing. Josie wasn't surprised that Mira had never told her mother about Rosie. Carol Summers didn't strike Josie as grandmother material.

Gretchen tapped the screen with the cap of her pen. "Mira is the only parent listed here as a contact. There's no address listed in Rosie's record. Most districts are required to collect a host of documentation when enrolling students. You would have made a copy of Rosie's birth certificate at the very least, right?"

"Yes," Hope breathed. "Let me see if I can get that for you.

Seth Lee is her father, isn't he? That's why he looked familiar.
He's not listed here but he could have been outside the school.
Our kindergarten teacher would have only released Rosie to
Mira, since she is listed as guardian, but Seth could have picked
them both up."

"Yes," said Gretchen. "That's possible."

Josie said, "Rosie's kindergarten teacher didn't say anything
to you when the news broke about Seth Lee being a suspect in
April's abduction or murder? Or when Mira was taken? Her
photo has been on the news and on social media since last
night."

A frown crossed Hope's face as her fingers continued to
hammer the keys. "Mrs. Roman retired to Florida two years ago.
She probably hasn't even caught wind of this whole mess. It's
also possible that she did hear about it but just doesn't remember. We have a lot of students and a lot of parents come through
the school. We always have some that leave in the middle of the
year, and we never hear from them again. I'm not... I'm not
seeing anything. I'll try something else. Just give me a few more
minutes. This can't be right."

"No worries," Gretchen told Hope. She turned to Josie and
arched a brow. Lowering her voice, she said, "If Seth was Rosie's
father..."

Josie filled in, "It would be within his rights to take Rosie
anywhere he wanted. It would have been up to Mira to contact
the police if she believed that Rosie was in danger or to petition
the courts if she wanted full physical and legal custody of their
daughter."

Gretchen shook her head. "But she didn't do that."

"No, but she must have convinced Seth to let her enroll
Rosie in school. Maybe her working at the school to keep an eye
on Rosie was the condition."

"And April getting Mira the job there made it all possible,"
Gretchen finished.

"Detectives." Confusion deepened the lines of Hope's face. "We don't have a copy of the birth certificate. We don't have... anything."

Josie said, "How is that possible?"

"Could someone have deleted it?" Gretchen asked.

"No. It's not that." Hope clicked a few more times. "It's the McKinney–Vento Act. A federal law that applies to students experiencing homelessness. When I say homelessness, I don't mean they are necessarily on the street, just that they have no permanent address. Specifically, the act is in place to make sure that those students can still enroll in school and receive equal access to education."

"But you would still need to collect their information, right?" Gretchen pressed.

Hope sighed. "Not right away. Pennsylvania added another law to provide more rights to unhoused students in the same year that Rosie enrolled. It's called Act 1. Under that law, we have to enroll the student immediately, the very day they seek to be enrolled, regardless of whether they've provided any documentation."

Josie leaned in toward Gretchen, dropping back into a low tone that kept the conversation between them. "Seth would have wanted to avoid giving documentation relating to Rosie and his relationship to her at all costs."

"Right," Gretchen breathed. "He thought someone would take her if they found out. April would have known about these laws. She could have used them to help Mira get Rosie enrolled without alarming Seth, and it might not have been a stretch to prove Rosie was experiencing homelessness."

"True," Josie agreed.

Hope cleared her throat. "After the student is enrolled, we have to follow up and gather all the required documents from their parents as soon as possible. We have a faculty member who is designated—by law—as the McKinney–Vento liaison. They're responsible for identifying students experiencing homelessness, getting them enrolled, making sure they have access to all appropriate services to which they're entitled—"

"Who was your liaison at the time that Rosie enrolled?" asked Gretchen.

Hope said, "It's normally our school counselor. That's who most schools designate, but if I recall correctly, three and half years ago our counselor was in the middle of chemotherapy. Her cancer persisted for a couple of years before she finally went into remission. However, while she was in treatment, the more ill she became, the more of her responsibilities I tried to delegate to other staff members. Including the liaison designation."

"April became the McKinney–Vento liaison," Josie said.

Hope searched her laptop screen. "Yes, but she'd been doing it for well over a year by the time Rosie Summers enrolled. April was extremely conscientious. Detail-oriented. Well-organized. This... this is very unlike her."

"What's unlike her?" asked Josie.

"It looks like she never followed up on the documentation for Rosie Summers. We never received anything and then Rosie left."

Josie would bet her paycheck that Rosie hadn't "left" but that Seth had removed her from school. The question was what had happened to precipitate that.

"How long was Rosie enrolled?" asked Josie.

"Five months."

Gretchen said, "If there is a birthday listed for Rosie, we might be able to subpoena a copy of her birth certificate from the Division of Vital Records."

"Yes, there is." A printer behind Hope's desk whirred to life. "I'll print all of this out for you."

"If you could email us a digital copy of Rosie Summers's

photo," Josie said, "that would be great. We'd like to get it out to the press as soon as possible."

The picture was four years old, but it was better than nothing.

"Yes, of course."

Gretchen scribbled her email address on a notebook page, tore it out, and handed it to Hope.

Josie whispered, "Send that photo to Amber, not to Douchebag."

"No shit."

Hope's fingers trembled as she typed the email address into an outgoing message. "We have so many students. Year after year after year. It's difficult to remember them all, but I think I might have seen this girl in April's classroom sometimes in the mornings, before school started. I just can't be sure. I don't understand. If Rosie is Seth Lee and Mira Summers's daughter, how did April become involved?"

It wasn't their place to disclose the fact that April and Mira had been half-sisters, so Josie said, "We're still trying to piece everything together. As Detective Palmer mentioned before, we believe that Mira Summers worked here at one time. It was likely during the same time period that Rosie was enrolled. Can you check that for us?"

Hope's skin was turning greenish again. "No. That can't be right. I would remember if Mira Summers had worked here. I would definitely have recalled that when I saw her photo on the news. One of our teachers would have remembered!"

"We don't think she was a teacher," said Gretchen. "Maybe on the cafeteria or custodial staff? It's our understanding that April got her the job."

Hope started tapping away at the laptop again, murmuring as she searched the employee database. "I'll check, but that just can't be. I suppose it's possible that April talked to me about hiring her—she still would have had to go through the application process, getting clearances and all that—but given all that's happened the last few days, I'm sure seeing her face would have jogged those memories. I—"

She broke off, shock blanketing her features.

Her voice was shaky when she continued. "You're right. She worked in the cafeteria. Maybe I don't remember because that was almost four years ago, and Mira Summers only worked here for roughly five months. The exact same time frame that Rosie was enrolled here."

THIRTY-EIGHT

Hope turned the laptop screen toward them so they could see the photo of Mira that had been taken for her staff ID. She looked thinner and paler. Dark circles smudged the skin beneath her eyes. Her smile seemed stiff, but did anyone give a genuine smile for any type of ID photo?

Behind Josie and Gretchen, the door swung open. They turned to see a teenage girl wearing sweats stride in, a backpack slung over one shoulder. She carried a soccer ball under one arm and a set of keys in her hand. Her blonde hair sat atop her head in a messy bun. She pulled up short when she noticed that Hope had guests, but quickly managed a smile for them. Her features were a near-perfect facsimile of Hope's face. "Shit," she said. "I mean, you didn't hear that. Excuse me. I didn't know anyone was in here."

Hope laughed but there was a bit of uneasiness to it. She still looked as though she might be sick. "It's fine. Detectives, this is my daughter, Teryn Bailey."

Josie felt a prickle along the back of her neck. Teryn. Her name was so similar to one of the people Josie had been on the ill-fated retreat with last year. She couldn't help but bristle at the reminder of her own failure, especially while she was working a case in which she'd had physical contact with the suspect and had gotten her ass kicked so badly, she couldn't arrest him. Of course, if Turner had been inside the house... She choked out a hello for Teryn and quickly pushed all of those thoughts and memories back inside her mental vault.

Teryn gave a stiff wave in response and went to her mother's desk, handing the keys over. "I filled the tank. I'll be—" Her words died as she caught sight of Mira Summers's photo.

Hope didn't seem to notice. She took the keys. "Thank you. I'll be working for another hour after I finish here. You'll be on the field, practicing, I know. I wish you'd put some of that focus toward your Spanish homework."

Teryn smiled weakly, tearing her eyes from Mira's photo and taking a closer look at Josie and Gretchen. Her gaze zeroed in on the pistol visible on Josie's waist. "Mom, please," she said, but there was no fight in her voice. To Josie, she said, "Are you here about April?"

"Teryn," said Hope, a note of warning in her voice.

"I'm just curious, Mom. Everyone knows she was murdered. Everyone knows that creepy guy on the news took her. Did you catch him yet?"

"Not yet," Gretchen answered.

"Teryn," Hope said, this time as a reprimand.

The teenager was undeterred. She pointed at the computer screen. "That's the lady who was just abducted by April's killer, isn't it?"

Hope gestured toward the door. "Really, Teryn, that's enough. This is a topic for adults only. Now, please, go. We'll talk later."

Fury flashed across Teryn's features, but she didn't argue with her mother. With one last glance at Mira's photo, Teryn said, "Yeah, sorry. Nice to meet you."

The door clicked closed behind her. Hope sighed. "I'm

sorry about that. She's sixteen and to put it bluntly, extremely nosy. Well, I suppose she always has been. Lately she's been obsessed with true crime, which I'm not sure is appropriate for her age. On the other hand, she's old enough to learn that there are those out there who harm innocent people."

Josie said, "Was she a student here when she was younger?"

"Yes. We go from kindergarten through fourth grade on one side of the building and then fifth and sixth grade on the other. After that, the kids are sent to a nearby middle school for seventh and eighth grades."

"While April was a teacher?" asked Gretchen.

"Oh yes. April was Teryn's fourth grade teacher, but they knew each other outside of school as well since April's mother and I are friends. Teryn adored April. Even when she was no longer in April's class, she would find excuses to be near her. She was quite devastated when April left for her new job even though she'd moved out of April's class by then. Teryn helped a lot with the search for April, especially with the social media aspect. These kids are so savvy now with technology." Hope's eyes misted over. She took a deep breath. "I'm sorry. I'm on a tangent. I'm just... this is such a shock. I still don't understand how April got caught up in all this."

Gretchen used her pen to point at the laptop. "Can you tell us the circumstances under which Mira left?"

"Do you mean whether she was fired or left on her own?" Hope said, turning the laptop back toward her and skimming Mira's file. "She resigned from her position."

In the span of a few hours, they'd gone from not knowing what connected April Carlson, Mira Summers, and Seth Lee, to finding out that April and Mira had been half-sisters; Mira and Seth had been a couple; Mira had had a daughter—and Josie was certain the birth certificate would confirm that Seth was the father—and that Mira, with April's help, had enrolled Rosie at Hillcrest and also gotten a job here. Then, five months later, both Mira and Rosie stopped showing up at school.

It was a treasure trove of information and yet, it still didn't tell them what the hell happened that ultimately led to the police finding Mira and April stabbed inside Mira's car three years later.

"Are there any staff who might have worked with Mira while she was here?" asked Josie.

Hope looked puzzled but answered, "I don't know. The cafeteria supervisor for sure. I can ask around, but it will have to wait until tomorrow as everyone's gone for the day. Does it matter? Now that you know that the child they've been talking about on the news belongs to Mira Summers and that—that killer? That's what you were trying to find out, right? The identity of the little girl? There will be an Amber Alert now?"

Gretchen closed her notebook. "Yes, an Amber Alert will go out as soon as possible."

"It was some sort of custody dispute, wasn't it?"

"I'm very sorry, but we can't say at this juncture." Josie took out a business card and slid it across Hope's desk. "We appreciate your time, Mrs. Bailey. You've been extremely helpful. If you could ask any members of your staff who do remember Mira to contact us, we'd appreciate it."

For a beat, it seemed as though Hope might push the issue but she still looked quite nauseated. "Of course."

Outside the school, the parking lot was empty save for a handful of vehicles. Instead of going toward theirs, Josie and Gretchen began walking around the side of the building in silent agreement. Once out of sight of the front entrance, Gretchen said, "You saw what I saw in there."

It wasn't a question.

Josie nodded anyway. "Let's find that soccer field."

THIRTY-NINE

The soccer field was along the side of the building, sandwiched between a playground and a softball field. Teryn Bailey was the only person in sight. Since she was not a suspect in any crime, they didn't need Hope Bailey's permission to speak with her, even though she was a minor. They didn't even need to notify Hope that they were going to do so, which was a good thing because it was clear that Hope did not want her daughter involved in the investigation now that it was so much bigger than a missing persons case.

As they drew closer, Josie saw a line of small orange cones spread out in the center of the field. Teryn skillfully weaved through them, dribbling the soccer ball. Josie and Gretchen stopped about ten feet from the first cone and waited for her to turn back toward them. She halted for a moment when she noticed them. Then she bent her head toward her feet, a look of steely determination hardening her face as she zigzagged back.

"Does my mom know you're here?" she asked, resting one foot on top of the ball.

"No," said Gretchen. "We're not required to tell her under these circumstances."

Teryn used the sleeve of her hoodie to wipe the sweat from her brow. "Good. We probably have about a half hour before she comes looking for me. I know she said an hour but trust me, she'll be finished with her paperwork and calls before that, and don't worry, her office window isn't on this side of the building."

"We're not worried," Josie said. "But thanks."

Teryn gave a half-hearted shrug and rolled the ball back and forth under her foot. "What's wrong with your voice?"

"Laryngitis," Josie lied.

Teryn gave a quick scan of their surroundings but no one else was there. "I was right, wasn't I? About the photo my mom showed you in there. That's the woman who was just abducted by the guy who killed April. I saw her picture on social media yesterday and I knew it was the same Miss Summers who used to work here. I mean, the same hair! I thought about asking Mom to check the school employee records but she's nuts lately. Ever since April's body was found, it's like she doesn't want me even talking about it. Like she thinks that if I know the details, somehow I'll be in danger."

Knowing what she did about April's condition at the time of her death, Josie suspected Hope was just trying to spare her daughter the pain of knowing what April's last year and final moments were like. If Josie's mental vault didn't work so well, the image of April's gaunt face would drive her mad.

Gretchen said, "She's protective of you. That's a good thing."

Another shrug, feigning nonchalance. "Whatever. What do you want to know?"

Josie said, "You remember Mira Summers? She only worked here for five months."

Teryn tapped a finger against her bun. "The burgundy hair. Teachers and staff were never allowed to dye their hair different colors, you know, other than the standard stuff. Every kid was fascinated with her because of that, although keep in mind, we were all young and pretty stupid. I mean, now if I saw someone with burgundy hair, it wouldn't even register. It's not even a cool color."

"How well did you know Miss Summers?" Gretchen asked.

"Nobody *knew* her. She was just... weird. A little mean sometimes."

"In what way?" Josie asked.

"Like she was supposed to give food out in the cafeteria. We had free lunches back then. Now you have to pay, but anyway, that was literally her job, to give us food, and there were certain kids she would withhold food from. Like not put it on their trays and stuff. One time, she actually came out from behind the counter, right up to a table, and took food from a kid's plate."

Josie's heart fluttered briefly before resuming its natural pace. What had Rebecca said about Seth? *I can't have him thinking that the food we're eating has been tampered with or that our water supply has been poisoned.*

Carol Summers had said something similar about Mira always going back to Seth. *Doesn't matter what weird new shit he wants her to do, like only eating food he grows himself in some special soil...*

Mira hadn't just taken the job at Hillcrest Elementary so that her daughter could attend school, she'd been carrying out Seth's instructions, based on his delusions.

"Her boss or coworkers didn't have an issue with this?" asked Gretchen.

"No one on the staff saw it. That was the thing."

"Which kids?" Josie said.

"I don't know. I don't remember. I just know she did it. No one would tell on her."

"Was it multiple children?" Josie pressed. "Or only one?"

Teryn gave her a strange look. "I told you. I don't know. I just know it happened. I mean, I guess it could have just been one kid. I heard about it from a bunch of people. Some of them said 'kid' and some of them said 'kids.'"

"Your mother was the principal," Gretchen pointed out. "You didn't tell her?"

Teryn rolled her eyes. "I was like twelve years old."

"Seventh grade?" Josie asked. "I thought the seventh graders were in a different school."

"Sixth grade," Teryn said. "I didn't fail or anything. I'm a year older than most of the kids in my grade because my birthday came after the cutoff for my mom to enroll me in kindergarten. You had to be six by, like, September first or whatever to start school and I didn't turn six till September sixth, so I had to wait a whole year. Anyway, why do you care so much about my age?"

"We care about your memories of the time that Miss Summers worked here," Josie said, "and how accurate they are."

Teryn rolled the soccer ball under her foot again. "They're accurate, okay? And no, I didn't tell my mom because it was weird. I didn't know what to do. Besides, April caught Miss Summers doing it."

"You mean Miss Carlson?" said Josie.

Teryn glared, her tone becoming defensive. "She was April to me and to my whole family."

"Fair enough," said Josie.

"We heard that April was the one who got Miss Summers the job in the cafeteria," said Gretchen.

"I don't know about that. I just know that April saw her taking food away from a little girl one day and it did not go over well."

"What happened?" asked Josie.

"Nothing at first. I didn't even realize that April had seen it until I went to her classroom after school to work on an art project. She always let me come to her room after school while I was waiting for my mom. We used to have desk picnics. She would bring snacks and juice and a funny plastic tablecloth and put it over her desk, and we'd pretend to have a picnic while I did whatever work I needed to do. Although most of the time she just let me talk to her about stuff." Tears shone in Teryn's eyes. She reached down and picked up the soccer ball, tucking it under her arm. "I was there doing my project when Miss Summers knocked. It was weird. I didn't even know they were friends, but she was all 'Hi, are you coming out tonight?' And April got all quiet and angry and said something like, 'We need to talk.' Then they went into the supply closet in April's room."

"Did you hear anything they said?" Josie asked.

"Not much. Only parts of it. I was kind of far away from the closet and the door was closed. They were like, whisper-shouting at each other at first. I did hear the word 'food' a few times and something like, 'she's just a little girl,' and that's when I realized that April must have seen what Miss Summers was doing."

"What else?" Gretchen said. "Keep in mind, we're not going to be upset if we find out you eavesdropped."

Teryn exhaled loudly. "I'm not proud of it, okay? I was a kid. I was curious."

"What did you hear?" Josie pressed.

"I got closer to the door. I still couldn't really hear everything. I don't even remember all of it now, but April was like, 'you can't do that' and 'I got you this job because I thought you needed it.' She said something after that I didn't hear. Something about her career—April's career. Then she kept saying the word 'mandatory' over and over again."

"In what context?" asked Gretchen.

"I don't know. Maybe that lunch was mandatory? Because it is! Then Miss Summers started crying. Like ugly crying. It was so loud. I couldn't even make out what April was saying after that but Miss Summers kept saying, 'please don't' and 'I'm begging you' and then 'you have no idea what will happen,' or something like that. She said a bunch of other stuff, too, but I don't really remember it now."

"But you remember that exchange," Gretchen said. "From almost four years ago between April and a woman who worked in the cafeteria for a few months."

Teryn's head reared back. "Damn. Fine. Don't believe me. I don't have to talk to you."

She turned away from them and threw the ball back onto the ground.

"Wait," Josie said. Pain seared her throat. She lowered her voice before going on. "We're not saying we don't believe you. We're just trying to get a clear picture of what happened. My nephew is seven and he doesn't even remember all the names of all the kids on his Little League team."

Teryn looked over her shoulder. "I was really close to April, okay? If you don't believe me, then look." She ran over to the fence where her backpack rested and rifled through it until she came up with her phone. Her fingers swiped and scrolled against the screen as she walked back over. "These are of me and April. Disregard the shitty quality. I had a horrible phone back then. My mom would only get me the kind you paid monthly. That way if I pissed her off, she could just cancel it."

She wedged herself between them so that they could both see the screen. The first photo was a selfie of a younger Teryn cheek to cheek with April. Josie's stomach turned at April's luminous smile. Soft brown locks cascaded over her shoulders. Happiness radiated from her. It was such a far cry from the shell of a woman they had found in Mira Summers's car.

Teryn swiped through a few more, many of them selfies. One of a tabletop, showing only their hands as they worked on some glittery art project. Another was April alone, sitting in a chair made for one of the children, holding her palms up for the camera. Blue glitter covered them, winking at the camera like tiny sequins. Some had gotten onto her nose. Her eyes crossed as she tried to look at them. "She was so much fun," Teryn said so quietly that Josie could barely hear her. She resisted the urge to hug the girl.

Next was another selfie but angled so the camera was looking down at them. Teryn said, "This was the day she got a selfie stick. Remember those?"

She didn't wait for an answer, swiping again. A photo of April pinning different drawings to the display wall behind her desk flashed across the screen. In the next picture, she was facing the camera, smiling widely and extending a hand as if to present the drawing just above it. "That's mine," Teryn said. She pinched her thumb and forefinger on the screen and then zoomed in. "I wasn't even in her class then but she still hung it up. See? My initials are on the bottom. T.B."

Teryn sighed as she zoomed back out. "I remember the day that April argued with Miss Summers because it was the only time I ever saw her mad. Really, truly furious. It was the only time I ever heard her raise her voice in anger."

As Teryn went to close out the gallery app, Josie held out her hand. "Would you mind if I had another look at those?"

"Sure." Teryn handed her the phone.

Gretchen said, "I'm sorry. I didn't mean what I said to come out the way it did. Detective Quinn is right. We're just trying to get the details straight here. It could be important. What happened next?"

Teryn slowly rotated her body back to face them. "April screamed at her. Really screamed at her. She said something like, 'enough is enough' and 'I don't care.' That something was 'unacceptable' and she 'didn't want to be a part of it anymore.' I'm pretty sure she said 'mandatory' a couple more times. She kept saying something about her family. 'My family, too,' she said. Miss Summers was crying and crying but April told her to get out. Then she pushed the door open so hard it hit the wall and she kind of pushed Miss Summers out."

Josie looked up from the first photo that Teryn had shown them. "April physically pushed her out of the closet?"

"Yeah, sort of. I mean, not hard but she touched her. On her back. I don't even think Miss Summers noticed me. She just ran out of the room."

Josie swiped to the next photo and then the next, her eyes drawn to the background of each one. Something had flashed past when Teryn showed them the photos, but it had been too quick for Josie's brain to fully register.

"Did April say anything to you?" Gretchen asked.

"She said she was sorry I had to hear that, and I asked her, 'Is this because she withholds food at lunchtime?' and she kind of looked at me, like she was surprised I knew, and she said, 'That won't be an issue anymore.' Sure enough, Miss Summers didn't come back. That was that."

"You never told your mother about this?" said Gretchen.

"Why would I? April took care of it."

"A year ago, after April went missing, a detective from the state police was here to talk to your mother and the other faculty members. Did you talk to her?"

"The blonde one? Yeah, I talked to her."

Josie found one of the photos that showed the wall of drawings behind April's desk and zoomed in.

Gretchen kept the interview going. "Did you tell her about the incident between April and Mira Summers?"

Teryn returned to the soccer ball and nudged it back and forth between her feet. "No. Why would I? It happened like four years ago and Miss Summers never came back. Then April moved away. Besides, it was about food in the cafeteria. What would some woman withholding food in the cafeteria four years ago have to do with April going missing from Newsham?"

Absolutely nothing. On the surface. Because no one knew they were half-sisters. No one could have predicted that four years later, in a city two hours away, the two of them would be found stabbed in a car together.

Josie found another photo with the wall of drawings in the background and zoomed in once more. When she found what she was looking for, it felt like a bucket of cold water being poured down the back of her neck. "Gretchen," she said.

Both Gretchen and Teryn looked at her.

Teryn said, "You okay?"

Josie handed the phone to Gretchen zoomed in on a drawing of a flat-roofed red building with a flagpole near its front door and in front of that, two flowers—one a straight stem with pink blobs along its length and the other a rose.

Gretchen stared at it, stone-faced. "There's that flower again. Rosie Summers drew this."

"Who's Rosie Summers?" asked Teryn.

Josie pointed at the screen. "The rose is her signature. Like her initials. It represents her."

Abandoning her ball, Teryn walked around and crowded in between them, squinting at the image. "I had a friend whose actual first name was Princess. In third grade? She used to sign all her art with a tiny princess crown."

Gretchen said, "What about the other flower?"

"It looks like a sweet pea. It's the same as April's tattoo," Josie said.

Teryn frowned. "Hey, you're right. That does look like April's tattoo. Well, sort of. If a kindergartner drew it, maybe."

A kindergartner had drawn it. Rosie's artistic skills hadn't changed much in four years, probably given the fact that she'd been forced into Seth's nomadic life, but someone had worked with her on reading and writing, at least. Enough for her to make a plea for help.

Teryn added, "So if the rose represents the girl who drew this, does that flower represent April?"

"I think so." Josie reached over and used her index finger to shift the zoomed-in portion of the photo so that the building and flagpole were visible. "What is this?"

Gretchen opened her mouth to speak but Teryn said, "Duh, it's the school. You didn't see that ginormous flagpole out front? Like they couldn't find any other place to put it? It doesn't exactly fit the Hillcrest aesthetic, if you haven't noticed."

Gretchen looked at the girl and laughed. "All right, kid, put it all together. What's this drawing trying to tell us?"

Teryn arched a brow and looked from Gretchen to Josie and back. "You're kidding right? Are cops really this dense? It's not trying to tell you anything. It's just this kid, Rosie, and April, and they're together here at school."

Gretchen looked over Teryn's head and locked eyes with Josie. They'd worked together long enough to communicate a whole lot of things in utter silence.

In answer to Gretchen's unspoken question, Josie said, "That's right. The drawing from the scene isn't an eye that sees flowers. Rosie was trying to show someone—probably Mira— where she and April were being held. The drawing is a map. It's a damn map."

FORTY

While Gretchen drove them back to Denton, Josie pulled up the photo of the drawing they'd found in April Carlson's hand at the accident scene and studied it again, this time from a completely different perspective. What did the rings represent? Some kind of hole? A silo, maybe? Rebecca had said that Seth sometimes took work on farms. There were plenty in and around Denton. But if it had been a silo, wouldn't Rosie have just drawn that?

"I didn't think that kid was going to let us leave," Gretchen remarked. "Teryn."

"She's curious," Josie replied. "And damn smart."

What were the brown lines? Dirt?

"Josie."

"Yeah."

What were the small brown circles?

"Maybe if we figure out how things got from Hillcrest to there"—she reached over and tapped Josie's phone screen—"we might have a better chance of figuring out where 'there' is."

With a sigh, Josie dropped the phone into her lap. It felt like she was going to lose her voice soon but she needed to talk things out with Gretchen. "Assuming Rosie is still in this place. Seth might have moved her by now."

"Or he's holding Mira there now. Let's focus."

Josie's phone buzzed. "That's a text from Noah."

She read it off to Gretchen, leaving out the "I love you" and heart emojis at the end. "'No luck finding the florist that delivered flowers to Mira Summers's house, but I found a botanist to look at those clumps of fibers found on April Carlson's clothes. He's a professor at the university. Dr. Hensley Brooks. He's in California at a conference right now but should be back in town within the next day or two. I sent his assistant some photos. She'll set up a meeting with him as soon as he gets back.'"

"That's something, I guess," Gretchen said.

Josie typed in a thank you followed by some mushy stuff and even mushier emojis. Massaging her shoulder, she said, "Let's get back to what you were saying. Getting from Hillcrest to the point we're at now. Seth agrees to let Mira put Rosie into school like a normal child as long as she is also there to keep an eye on things and, evidently, monitor Rosie's food intake."

"Right," Gretchen said. "God knows what else. April finds out what Mira's doing. Monitoring Rosie's food intake on Seth's behalf and tailoring it to his specifications. Taking food away from her at lunchtime in front of the rest of the children. Depriving her of nutrition based on delusions."

Josie watched the lights of Hillcrest disappear. Soon, they were pulling onto the interstate. "As a teacher, April would have had an obligation to report her concerns about Rosie's health and well-being under the care of her parents to the Department of Human Services. She was a mandatory reporter. That was why April kept using the word 'mandatory' repeatedly in the argument with Mira."

Gretchen said, "April wasn't saying lunch was mandatory. She was saying it was mandatory that she report Mira and Seth to DHS."

No wonder Mira had begged April, "please don't." She must have known that Seth would pull Rosie out of school immediately at the slightest hint that DHS might get involved.

Josie said, "Would the school have a record of it if April made a complaint to DHS?"

Gretchen shook her head. "I don't think so. We dealt with this stuff a lot when I was with Philly PD. Schools don't keep records of any reports made by faculty to DHS. Teachers aren't even required to tell their superiors if they've contacted DHS. Those reports are anonymous unless the teacher chooses to give their information. A few times I caught cases where I wish the teachers had given their names because when cases went to trial, we could have used their testimony, but most of the time teachers don't go on record for fear of retaliation from angry parents or other family members."

"If Seth found out that a complaint had been made to DHS against him and Mira, he would have immediately blamed April, don't you think?"

Gretchen said, "That's what I'm thinking, but more importantly, he would have taken Rosie and left."

Josie tipped her head back against the headrest. The overpowering exhaustion of the case was back, making her limbs feel heavy. "Rosie stopped attending Hillcrest Elementary right before Mira moved from here to Denton. Mira wasn't following her man, she was looking for her daughter."

FORTY-ONE

"You're telling me these two broads are sisters?" Turner used his feet to push his chair back from his desk before launching his tiny basketball toward the tiny net. It missed, as usual.

"No one says 'broad' anymore, jackass," Gretchen complained, shooting him a look of disgust.

Josie leaned her hip against her own desk and watched the morning news play out on WYEP. Almost the entire half hour was now devoted to the scandalous Carlson–Summers–Lee case. It was press gold, always delivering more. Now little Rosie Summers's six-year-old school photo joined the carousel of faces connected to the case. Josie had called Amber late the previous evening while Gretchen drove them back to Denton to make sure they could get Rosie's face on the eleven o'clock news. Rosie was still the top story this morning. As soon as they'd arrived back at the station the night before, Gretchen had contacted the state police to make sure an Amber Alert went out right away.

Josie had gotten little sleep, spending most of the night studying Rosie's map and trying to make sense of it. She still couldn't figure it out. Noah had tried to help, without success.

When Josie arrived at work in the morning, Gretchen stood in front of the corkboard, also attempting to pinpoint the location before giving up. Turner had taken one glance at it after hearing Josie's theory that it was a map and dismissed it. "That's a shitty-ass map," he had told her. "Work some real leads."

Real leads. Now Josie lifted her latte to her lips and watched him toss his ball again. This time, it missed and bounced onto the floor. "Don't be so sensitive, Parker."

"It's Palmer," Josie said flatly. She was in less pain today, still with the aid of ibuprofen, and her voice was a little stronger.

Turner disappeared beneath his desk in search of the ball.

Gretchen shook her head and waved her hand at Josie, as if to say it's not even worth correcting him anymore. Josie shrugged in response. Keeping her voice low enough for Gretchen's ears only, she said, "At least Parker is close. All I get is 'honey' and 'sweetheart.'"

There was a bang and then a muffled "ouch".

"Serves you right," Gretchen groused.

"I heard that. Also, stay on topic, would you? Carlson and Summers are half-sisters and Summers has a secret kid with this lunatic?"

Gretchen said, "Seth Lee has a legitimate mental illness, but yeah. We got a copy of Rosie's birth certificate this morning confirming that he's her father."

Turner's voice still sounded like it was coming from far away. "Dude is still looney toons, Parker. I mean, a secret kid! What in the hell was this Summers chick thinking? Her mom didn't know about this kid? There's not one goddamn thing in her house about this kid. Nothing on her phone. Her email. Her socials. Where the hell has this kid been all this time? Camping in the woods with Murder Dad?"

Josie walked around to where she could see the soles of his

loafers and his ass sticking out. "Can we have this conversation with your face and not with your ass?"

Gretchen said, "There's no difference. Just answer him."

"I heard that, Parker."

Josie shook her head. "Mira was in an abusive relationship with Seth. She told her mother she was in love. For years, she did whatever Seth told her to do. I am sure I don't need to tell you how difficult it is for women to leave their abusers, no matter how dangerous the situation becomes."

Turner's body shifted but still, the only parts of him visible were his feet and ass. His tone, however, turned serious, his words quieter. There wasn't even any vitality to his "sweetheart" when he said, "No, sweetheart, you don't have to tell me. I watched my mom go through it with my dad."

"Huh," Gretchen said. "He might be human, after all."

"Heard that, Parker. Keep going, sweetheart. I wanna hear this theory of yours."

Josie took another sip of her latte. WYEP now had photos of Seth, Mira, and Rosie laid out like a family tree. Only April's picture floated to the side, disconnected. The chyron read: *Missing Child at Center of Apparent Custody Dispute that Ended in Murder*. It was a little wordy. Also, Josie wasn't sure it was a custody dispute. She wasn't sure what it was—yet. "By the time Mira had Rosie, I think she was so deep into the relationship, and the dynamic between her and Seth was so firmly cemented, that it was just more of the same except now with a child."

Gretchen said, "We don't think Mira ever physically had custody of Rosie. We think that Seth was too paranoid to leave Rosie with Mira. He had to have control of her. In his mind, he was protecting her. He believed that some type of 'authorities' were going to take her away from him. The one consistent thing that we've heard from just about every person we talked to about Seth was that he tends to disappear for long periods of time. That's probably what he did with Rosie. Every time his delusions got the best of him, he'd take Rosie and leave. He probably kept Mira in constant fear that she'd never see her daughter again."

"I doubt that Mira even knew where he went when he left," Josie said. "She just had to wait for him to return—and hope that he would. Rebecca said there was never a way to reach Seth. They just had to wait for him to show up. Mira was probably so afraid that she'd never see Rosie again or that he would hurt her that she didn't want to take the chance of suing him for custody and opening that can of worms."

"Yeah," came Turner's mumble. "Can't close that can once it's opened. I've seen cases where the parents take the kids and poof! they're never seen again. Or you find them living in some other state twenty years later, all grown up."

Josie looked back at the television. WYEP flashed Rosie's photo again. By now it was nearly four years old. She'd be ten. How much had she changed? With a sigh, Josie turned her attention back to Turner's ass. "Mira probably hoped that getting Rosie enrolled into a school where she was employed would give Seth a reason to keep her in one place. Settle down. Mira must have used her connection to April—as sisters—to try to put Seth at ease with the whole thing."

"Until April turned on him," Gretchen added.

"You mean until she realized what a certifiable nutcase he really was and decided to report him to DHS for starving his fucking kid?" Turner called. "Where in the hell is this ball? It's like a dimensional vortex under here. I think I just saw the back entrance to Narnia, for godssake."

Suddenly, Gretchen startled. Her chair creaked as she leaned forward, plucking something from the floor. With a triumphant grin, she held up the tiny foam basketball.

Turner's desk jerked as he banged his head. "Son of a bitch. That hurt. Hold on, I think I see it." His feet extended back, toward Josie, as he lowered himself to his stomach. "Okay so the sister—April—reports this guy and then he takes little Rosie and rolls. Did DHS even do any investigating?'

"I talked with someone in their office this morning," Gretchen said. "They claim they couldn't find Seth or Mira at the time the call was made."

"Convenient," Turner said in a strained voice. "We're assuming he brought her up this way since his brother's here. Next thing anyone knows, Mira Summers is living here too, and going to his brother's stables every week. If she didn't know where he was taking Rosie, how'd she know to go to Tranquil Trails?"

He's here. We have to tell.

"April told her. She figured it out somehow. It wouldn't have taken much. A background check on Seth using a paid service probably would have shown Jon Lee as his brother."

Gretchen squeezed the ball tightly in her hand, crushing it until it was the size of a marble. Then she opened her palm and let it expand again. "I can't quite figure out the sequence of events, but I don't think that April moving to Newsham a year after Seth disappeared with Rosie, and Mira moved to Denton, is a coincidence."

"You think April was looking for the kid?" Turner said, voice muffled again. "On her own?"

"Rosie was April's niece," Josie said. "During the argument that Teryn Bailey overheard between April and Mira, April used the phrase, 'my family too.' Rosie wasn't just some student, she was April's family."

"Somehow, Seth figured out that April tried to follow him," Gretchen said. "I have no idea how but he found out she was in Newsham. He started vandalizing her house. The 'stay away' message was from him. He wanted her to stay away from Rosie, specifically."

Why hadn't April gone to the police once she had some idea

where he might be? Josie could see why Mira might not have gone to the authorities to report that Seth had taken their daughter to parts unknown and might be starving her. After decades of being indoctrinated by Seth and trained to shape her life around his delusions, turning Seth in to the authorities was the last thing that Mira would do.

But why wouldn't April? In addition, why had she bothered to report him breaking into her Newsham home and vandalizing it but not told the police that Seth was behind it?

They were still missing something.

"So then what?" Turner said, drawing up onto his knees again. "This guy just decides he's going to kidnap April and keep her for a year? What in the hell does that accomplish? I'm telling you: looney tunes."

WYEP cut to their new star reporter, Dallas Jones, standing in front of Mira's town house, interviewing neighbors. Josie was surprised he hadn't set up shop in front of Tranquil Trails. Then again, there wasn't anyone to interview all the way out there, and Josie knew neither Rebecca nor Jon was going to speak with the press. As it was, the revelation that Seth and Mira had a child had rendered Rebecca speechless for almost a full five minutes. As a courtesy, and to stay on their good side in case she needed their help later, Josie had called the Lees late the night before to give them a heads-up before Rosie's face got splashed all over the internet.

Josie took another long sip of her latte. Gretchen was still peering at the basketball as if trying to decide what to do with it.

Finally, Turner wiggled backward and out from under the desk. His curls tumbled down over his forehead. A cobweb wrapped across the back of his head. From his knees, he looked across the desks at Gretchen. The ball had disappeared. He brushed dust from the shoulders of his suit jacket. He always dressed like he was testifying in court, no matter what. He reached out a hand to Josie. "Help me up, sweetheart." It was a demand, not a request.

Josie put her latte down on his desk and folded her arms across her chest. "What's my name?"

He looked at her as if he'd never seen her before. "Are you kidding me? You wanna know why my knee hurts, Paper Airplane?"

He didn't get to do one thing and then be excused from his irritating behavior ever after. She still wasn't over him flirting with Bobbi Thomas while she got strangled by Seth Lee. "What's my name?"

His head swiveled in Gretchen's direction. "Is she serious with this?"

"If you ever want to see your precious basketball again, you'll answer her question," Gretchen challenged.

Turner's chin sank to his chest. Josie heard a distinct chuckle before he put one hand on the edge of his desk and hefted himself up.

Josie shook her head. "So stubborn. When will you learn, champ?"

He rose to his full height and looked down his nose at her. When she didn't blink or step back, he did, his thighs bumping against the desk. He cleared his throat. "Learn what?"

"Manners."

He smoothed his hands over his lapels. "You don't need manners when you look this good."

Behind him, Josie saw Gretchen roll her eyes. "I'm throwing this stupid ball away."

"Don't you want to hear what I've got?" Turner asked, spinning to face Gretchen.

Josie sauntered back to her seat. "So you did do some work while we were gone."

He brushed off his pants. "Hey, when I wasn't working on your warrant last night, I responded to a half dozen bogus 'sightings' of Seth Lee. Apparently, now every time someone sees a damn food wrapper in the woods, they think he's been camping there."

From everything they'd gathered, Josie was certain that Seth Lee would never eat packaged food but that wasn't something they were going to share with the general public.

Turner went on. "We got a tip. From all the news coverage. This lady, Deirdre Velis, called. She owns an antique furniture store somewhere around here. Said she knows Seth Lee. Well."

Deirdre, like the name of the woman Seth had brought to his brother's wedding decades ago.

Turner plopped into his chair and held his hand out for Gretchen to throw him the basketball. When she didn't, he started drumming his fingers against his desk. "Said she might have information to help us find him."

"Like what?" asked Josie.

"She wouldn't tell me over the phone but as soon as we hung up, I looked her up. She's got an old conviction for passing bad checks from almost twenty years ago, but she's been on the straight and narrow ever since. I also checked into her shop. Furnished Finds. It's got two box trucks registered to it and one of them has a license plate ending in a 7. Already put out the BOLO. Oh, and ole Deirdre should be arriving downstairs in the next half hour. I drove out to her store last night right after she called so I could interview her, but the place was closed up. Dark. No sign of the truck, or anything at all, really. The place is in the middle of damn nowhere."

"Which is maybe a good place to keep certain someones you've kidnapped?" Gretchen suggested.

Turner raised both palms. "Already thought of that, Parker, but it's not like I could look inside without being invited or having a warrant."

That much was true, Josie had to concede.

"Of course, that didn't stop me from walking into the open

truck bay and hollering to high heaven to see if anyone answered," he added.

"Turner!" Josie said. "That's—"

"Against procedure. I know, sweetheart, but there's a kid missing. Also, I didn't actually cross the threshold into the showroom so technically, I was still outside."

But even if he had gone against procedure and stepped inside the building—hell, even if he'd searched the entire place —who would know? Especially since he'd gone there alone.

"Relax," Turner told them. "I promise, I didn't do anything that would fuck up this case later, and I called this Deirdre chick as soon as I got back here. She said she was at the grocery store when I stopped by."

Gretchen raised a brow. "Did you go back out there?"

"Nah. She said she'd be there if I wanted to but it was late and we got another Seth Lee 'sighting,' so I made her an appointment for this morning and checked out the tip instead. It was another dead end, by the way. In case you didn't notice."

Josie downed the rest of her latte and glanced at the TV again where Seth Lee's photo appeared once more. The bullet point list was back, too, except this time the words 'may have a child with him' had been replaced with, 'has 10-year-old Rosie Summers in his custody.'"

"We noticed," Josie muttered.

Turner held out his hand to Gretchen again. This time she threw him the basketball. If Josie didn't know better, it would seem like a peace offering.

FORTY-TWO

I stay on top of her the whole night so he doesn't touch her. I think I'm dreaming when she moves under me and groans. Did I die, too? Am I in heaven? Does heaven look the same as the forever-est place but with my mom in it? Do promises still count in heaven?

"Mom," I whisper.

She groans. Then her eyes open. When she sees me, she bursts into tears. Do moms cry in heaven?

"Rosie." Her voice sounds like a frog's croak. Mummy arms wrap around my body. Now she feels warm, so warm. I put my face in her neck like I always do. She smells like flowers, and I don't ever want to let her go.

"Are we dead?" I whisper.

I feel her head shake. "No, sweetie. We're not dead."

"Can we leave now?"

His shadow blocks out all the light around us. Before she can answer, he reaches down and drags me away from her. "Neither of you are going anywhere."

FORTY-THREE

Deirdre Velis sat at the head of Denton police station's conference room table, smiling at Josie and Turner. She was easily five or more years older than Seth. Her long silver hair was pulled back into a ponytail that sat low against the nape of her neck. Fine lines gathered at the corners of her brown eyes and around her lips. Her large cloth purse looked hand-sewn. The cream-colored sweater she wore over a simple white cotton shirt was worn with age. A smell of wood polish floated around her.

Josie had made the introductions while she and Turner sat in the two seats to Deirdre's right. Turner had already spoken with Deirdre by phone, so Josie let him take the lead.

He flashed a smile. "Thanks for coming all the way down here."

Deirdre returned his smile, although with no teeth showing. She folded her hands on the tabletop and took a deep, bracing breath. "I'm sorry I missed you last night. Thank you for speaking with me. I don't watch the news, but I do listen to the radio and when I heard Seth's name, I knew I had to call. We go way back. He was still in high school when we met."

Turner's fingers drummed against the arm of his chair. "No kidding. Guess those high school girls couldn't compete with a sophisticated woman like yourself."

Josie wondered if that was supposed to be a compliment, or if it was Turner's backhanded way of asking if Deirdre had entered into a sexual relationship with Seth while he was still a minor. Either way, Deirdre kept her tight smile in place. "He worked summers on my uncle's farm down in Fairfield. Nothing happened until he was old enough but yes, we fell deeply in love. We were together for many years. I wanted to get married. Settle down and have children. But Seth refused. He thought... well, he's always had some problems." She tapped a finger against her temple. "Here. He says it was from the service, but the truth is that he was starting to have some pretty strange thoughts before he went in."

"Delusions," Josie said.

Deirdre nodded. "Yes. The older he got, the more... entrenched they became. Now, don't get me wrong, he isn't some kind of monster. He's not unhinged."

Josie had a sudden flash of spittle raining down on her face while Seth tried to strangle the life out of her. The words 'monster' and 'unhinged' definitely came to mind, and yet, Josie wondered if there was something else at work that had caused him to escalate from his abuse of Mira to kidnapping and torturing her sister for the span of a year. Josie still felt they were missing something important. Rebecca had said something similar to what Deirdre was telling them.

Seth presents quite normally most of the time. He's quiet, polite, pleasant. He's not a monster.

Turner said, "You sure this guy isn't a monster, because—"

Under the table, Josie kicked her leg to the side, making contact with his ankle. He glared at her.

Deirdre said, "I guess I should rephrase that. The Seth Lee that I met and fell in love with decades ago was not a monster.

Even when his... issues were at their worst, he was still the man I loved."

"Did he hit you?" Turner asked pointedly.

Deirdre swallowed, looking down at her folded hands. "Yes. Sometimes. When he was extremely agitated, wrapped up in his... thoughts. When he got that way, there was no reasoning with him. Many times, I tried to make him get help, but he would never agree. I suppose I pushed too hard, because he left."

"He left you?" Turner said. "As in broke up with you. When was that?"

"About ten years ago now, I think."

Which meant that their relationship had overlapped with his and Mira's. Josie said, "Did you know that Seth was seeing Mira Summers?"

Deirdre's mouth pressed into a thin line. Anger flared in her eyes, but she kept her composure. When she spoke, her words were carefully controlled but Josie felt the undertone of fury. "I suspected. Seth would disappear for months, sometimes even years at a time. I had no way of knowing if he'd been faithful. Whenever I asked, he lied and said there was no one but me."

"But he left you. At that point, he didn't tell you about Mira Summers?" Turner asked. "Or their secret kid?"

"No. Never."

By now Rosie would be ten. The end of Deirdre and Seth's relationship had coincided with Rosie's birth. Coincidence? Or was she too embarrassed to admit that she'd known? It was one thing to find out your man was cheating on you. It was quite another to find out he'd had a baby with another woman, especially when you had wanted to have children with him at one point and he had refused. "When is the last time you saw Seth?" Josie asked.

"Oh, just a couple of weeks ago," Deirdre replied. "That's

why I'm here. We have been broken up for the last ten years but there have been times that Seth has come to me, desperate for money. His own brother won't help him, or so he says. I felt badly for him so when he needs work, I let him do deliveries for my store."

"Furniture delivery," Josie said. "In a box truck."

Deirdre smoothed her hair behind her ears even though no strands had come loose. "Yes. I pay him in cash. That is all he will accept. He doesn't even have a credit card or a bank account anymore. I give him a list of items and the addresses they're meant to go to and then he loads them into one of my trucks and delivers them. There aren't a lot. I sell antique and vintage furniture. There's not a high demand, but enough to keep my store open and to be honest, as I get older, it's a lot harder for me to do that kind of lifting."

"Does he ever help you with furniture repair?" Josie asked.

"Sometimes."

The awl. It was used in upholstery repair. Woodworking. Things that might be necessary in a store that sold vintage furniture. She looked over at Turner to see if he'd made the connection as well, but he had slipped his phone out from his pocket and was holding it in his lap, looking at something surreptitiously. Was he serious? Dared she hope it was work-related?

"Did you ever see him with Rosie Summers?" asked Josie. She got her phone out and pulled up Rosie's photo. She turned it toward Deirdre.

A flash of something crossed Deirdre's face. Resentment, hostility, maybe. Or... was that bitterness? Because she had met Seth first and wanted to bear his children, but he'd rebuffed her and then had a child with another woman? She shook her head. "He's always alone when he comes to my shop. Like I said, I had no idea that he and this other woman had had a child together."

"How about April Carlson?" Josie pressed. "You never saw him with her?"

"I told you, he's always alone, so no."

"Do you have any idea where he might have kept her? Where he might keep Rosie?"

"I wish I did," said Deirdre. "No. Seth never stayed in one place very long. If he's got hideouts, I was never privy to them."

Dead end after dead end. Turner was still engrossed in whatever was on his phone. His thumbs tapped against the screen.

Josie swiped from Rosie's school photo to the drawing they'd found at the accident scene. "Does this look like any place that you've seen before or are familiar with?"

Deirdre peered at the drawing. Her brow furrowed. She gave a little chuckle. "A place? Detective, that looks more like... an eye to me."

Josie pocketed her phone. "Does Seth stay with you? At your home, or at your store? Maybe during the winter months?"

Seth's whereabouts during cold weather had been nagging at Josie's brain from the beginning.

"My home is connected to the store but no, he doesn't stay with me. Not anymore. It's just not a good idea, given our history. Besides, he doesn't trust... being indoors. He thinks there are cameras hidden to spy on him. I've told him thousands of times there aren't, but he'll never believe me."

"How often does he deliver for you?" asked Josie. "Several times a year? Weekly?"

"It's very sporadic," Deirdre said. "Some months there are no deliveries and other months there are a half dozen a week. If Seth happens to stop by—I have no way to reach him—then I let him do it."

Turner nudged Josie with his elbow and whispered, "We got a tip."

"You let him take one of your trucks, but you have no way to reach him?" Josie said. "How do you know he'll come back?"

Deirdre laughed. "Because he needs money. I pay for the gas in the truck. I give him cash for... whatever he needs to spend it on. It's not much, but clearly, he needs it. Listen, I came here today because he's got my truck. I thought if I gave you the license plate number, maybe you'd be able to find him faster."

She reached into her purse and pulled out a copy of a registration for a box truck. Pushing it toward Josie, she said, "Unfortunately, it doesn't have GPS. It's pretty old. No bells or whistles."

"This will help," said Josie. "Ms. Velis, do you know where he lives? Where he stays?"

"I've never known," she sighed. "He always said he just went from campground to campground. If he had some sort of steady work gig, he'd stay with a coworker. That's what he always told me. But now I know he's had another woman all these years. Had a baby with her. Maybe that's where he was when he wasn't with me. Maybe he's got some other woman on the hook right now and she's hiding him."

There was no mistaking the bitterness in her tone.

Turner looked up from his phone and peered at Deirdre. "You know this guy is a loon. Now you know he kidnapped a couple of women. Stabbed both of them. Killed one of them. In fact, he almost got this one the other night." He elbowed Josie in the arm.

Deirdre gave her an appraising look. Josie was glad she'd taken the time that morning to use concealer on the bruises dotting her throat.

"Turner," she said, her tone a warning.

Naturally, he just kept going. "He didn't even balk at coming after a lady with a gun. Tell me, Deirdre. Aren't you even a little bit scared of this guy? What happens when he shows back up at your store with the truck, this time knowing he's wanted for murder and a whole bunch of other bad shit? This guy is seriously off the rails."

"Detective." Deirdre unfurled her fingers and placed her palms on the table. "I know how to handle Seth. I've had thirty years of practice. If he shows up at the store, I'll call the police and he won't have any idea I've done it until you've arrived."

FORTY-FOUR

A sheen of sweat formed on Josie's forehead and upper lip. She didn't ever remember May being this hot in Denton. It was still early in the day, and they'd be in the sun for at least an hour— more, if this tip that Turner had gotten panned out. She strapped on her bulletproof vest over her Denton PD polo shirt and watched him scroll on his phone like he didn't have a care in the world. He stood at the edge of the Tranquil Trails driveway where the gravel gave way to the asphalt of Prout Road. He had removed his suit jacket in favor of his own vest, but he was still in long sleeves. How was he not sweating?

Directly across from him on the other side of Prout Road stood Officer Brennan, guarding the riding trail that led to where Seth Lee had been spotted. By the time Josie and Turner arrived, he and three other officers had done a cursory search and found nothing but an item of clothing they believed belonged to Seth. The rest of those officers had remained in the area where the clothing was located to make sure the scene was not disturbed.

"Turner," Josie called as a line of cruisers approached.

Without even looking up from his phone, he stepped out of the way so the cars could pull into the driveway.

"You sure this is necessary, honey? I hoofed it through a half dozen campsites and other wilderness spots yesterday chasing these tips, and didn't find a damn thing. Just me and a couple of other guys. How many cops does it take to find nothing? Our guys already checked this one out. You sure you don't just want to call SERT?"

SERT was the state police's Special Emergency Response Team. They were specially trained to respond to high-risk situations. Comprised of a tactical unit and a negotiations unit, SERT filled in for police departments across Pennsylvania that didn't have their own SWAT units.

Josie fanned herself, wishing there were some trees to stand under. She couldn't tell if he was mocking her or not when he asked about SERT, but she answered the question as if he'd seriously meant it. "None of those tips were here, on Seth's brother's property. I'm sure that Seth feels some degree of comfort and familiarity here. It's not a stretch that he's returned here, even temporarily, and no, I don't want to call SERT. It's already been what? Two hours since dispatch got the initial call that someone thought they saw him? Since the first officers arrived on-scene? He could be long gone by now and it might take SERT another hour to arrive and set up. I'd much rather set up perimeters with our own people and start searching immediately."

The uniformed officers poured out of their vehicles and walked over, forming a loose circle near the mouth of the driveway. From the direction of the house, Rebecca Lee appeared, striding toward them, her face set in angry lines.

Turner sidled up to Josie, phone still in hand, and nudged her shoulder. "This is gonna be fun, isn't it?"

Rebecca didn't stop or even greet them. Instead, she walked right through the group of them and started to cross Prout Road, heading straight for Brennan, who stood unmoving, his eyes hidden by sunglasses. When she realized no one was following her, she paused and called over her shoulder, "Let's go. I'll take you to the other officers."

Turner, Josie, and some of the uniformed officers jogged to catch up. Turner said, "You can't be out here with us. It's not safe. We can find them ourselves."

Rebecca glared up at him. "Bullshit. This is my land."

He looked back at Josie, as if for help. "Mrs. Lee," Josie said. "Can we talk for a minute? Privately?"

Rebecca hesitated, looking toward Brennan who was still unmoving, an impenetrable barrier between her and the trail. Finally, she relented. She scowled at Turner as she followed Josie back to the driveway. Josie led her away from the group of officers. As she did, Turner walked over to Brennan. They conferred for a moment and then she heard Turner shouting out instructions for a wide perimeter around the place that Seth Lee was last seen.

Josie turned her attention back to Rebecca. "My colleague is right, Mrs. Lee. It's not safe for you to accompany us on the search."

Rebecca gestured around them. "No one knows this place better than I do! None of you have any experience with my brother-in-law. I don't think he would be violent toward me. I could talk to him. If he's even still here!"

Josie didn't mention her own experience with Seth. "I'm sure you're right, Mrs. Lee," she said. "But I still can't let you join us."

Rebecca's hands fisted at her sides. Her voice shook with rage. "This is bullshit. He's putting my clients in danger by being here, not to mention what he's doing to my livelihood. I help people here. My therapeutic riding program is meant to help people who have experienced trauma—not to cause it. He's

ruining everything, and my husband keeps defending him
and—"

She broke off, chest heaving.

Josie wiped more sweat from her brow. She and Rebecca
had one thing in common. They dealt with stress best if they
had something to do, if they could take some kind of action.
"You want to help us?"

Rebecca slowed her breathing. "Of course I want to help."

"Then you'll let us do our jobs—"

Rebecca opened her mouth to protest but Josie stopped her
with a raised palm. "And while we do, I need you to look into
something for me."

"Anything."

"You're not going to like it. I can get a warrant for the information, but it will take some time—"

"I don't want to waste more time. What is it, Detective?"

"How does Seth survive during the winter months? When
it snows or the temperatures drop well below freezing?" Josie
asked.

Rebecca shook her head slowly. "I told you, I don't know."

Something Rebecca had said to her husband at the outset of
their investigation had bothered Josie, taking up residence in the
very back of her mind, content to wait in the shadows of the
larger pieces of the investigation until Josie could tend to it.
"You said that your husband once rented an apartment for Seth
behind your back."

Rebecca sucked in a sharp breath, the agitation on her face
softening. "Yes. He did it for years without me knowing but I
put a stop to it. That was a long time ago. I see everything that
goes in and out now that we've taken over this place. I would
know if—"

She broke off, mouth hanging open as a thought struck her.
She didn't share it.

Josie didn't think she needed any more prodding, but she

said it anyway. "Is it possible that Jon was using an account that you don't review often? Or that he wasn't paying any landlord or property management company directly, but instead taking out cash to pay for Seth to have a place to stay when the weather is bad? Maybe you can check all your accounts for cash withdrawals made by Jon at regular intervals?"

Rebecca licked her lips and nodded. "Yes. I can check."

"Great," said Josie. "Now, my team is going to head down the trail where Seth was last seen."

FORTY-FIVE

Josie, Turner and four uniformed officers left Brennan standing sentry along Prout Road, across from the Tranquil Trails driveway, and waded into a meadow that sloped downward, covered in knee-high grass. A trail meandered through it, the width of a single horse. Where the ground turned to mud, Josie saw a smattering of hoofprints. Flies hovered lazily over large piles of excrement.

Turner waved a hand in front of his nose. "You've got to be kidding me."

Josie sidestepped a particularly robust heap. "Those fancy loafers of yours are not going to survive this."

They continued down the trail for half a mile where the grass became trees, plunging them into shade finally. Josie pulled her collar away from her neck and used the edge of it to wipe at the perspiration on her face. Turner rolled up his shirtsleeves one by one. "Where did you say this trail leads?"

"Did you even look at the map?" Josie said. The rush of water growing louder with each step made it obvious where they were. "The river."

Moments later, they emerged from the trees onto the bank

of the Susquehanna River and fanned out along its bank. Water swirled and rushed past their feet, sliding over rocks. Where sticks, leaves, and fallen trees jammed along the bank, a yellowish foam swirled.

"What the hell is that?" Turner stepped up beside her. "Are those suds? Did this guy do his laundry down here, or what?"

Josie shook her head. "It's river foam."

"*River* foam? Rivers have foam now?"

"Yes, it's just from debris that breaks down naturally. Leaves, sticks, organic matter."

Ignoring her explanation, Turner wrinkled his nose. "It stinks down here, by the way. Like horseshit and I don't know, something else."

The water was brown and shallow until it reached halfway across to the other bank, where the deeper water was a greenish-blue. Opposite them, the bank was shorter and steeper, reaching up to meet a narrow two-lane road. Beyond that was a tall rock face that made up the base of the next mountain.

Turner swatted a mosquito away. "You're telling me some horseback rider was on this trail and thought they saw Seth down here? How in the hell would he get down here? I don't see a box truck, or anywhere to park one."

"He could have abandoned that," Josie pointed out. "That would be the smart move, and he could have come from any direction on foot."

Turner pointed to the opposite bank. "Does that road connect to Prout Road at any point?"

"No," Josie said. "They run parallel. You'd have to take that into the city, cross the South Bridge, weave your way back through most of the city and then get onto Prout Road."

"I don't see anything," Turner said. He nudged a stone with his toe, sending it tumbling into the water with a splash.

Josie scanned the river, thinking how good it would feel to jump in. The air was warm but the river would be cold this time of year. Instead, she picked her way along the bank, toward a line of three Denton PD officers who stood sentry near the tree line. The other uniformed officers walked with her.

The riverbank would be a smart place to camp, assuming Seth didn't believe the water was poisoned. This particular area was pretty remote. To the north, heading away from the city, all Josie could see was water until it curved out of view. Southward, the water rushed toward the city. A few miles in that direction, there was another bend in the river where a tree-covered portion of the opposite bank extended well into the water. A blunted peninsula. Beyond that, no more of the Susquehanna was visible.

She heard Turner kick another stone into the water. "This is a waste of time."

"You have more pressing matters?"

He caught up to the rest of them easily, jockeying for position next to her. "I have to stay close to you, honey. Make sure you don't get your ass handed to you again."

He was like a splinter that broke off when you tried to remove it and then caused an infection. The kind that gave you pus.

"Will you just shut up?" Josie said wearily. Officer Conlen greeted the group of them with a nod and pointed toward the trees, away from the riverbank.

Between two large ash trees was an opening large enough for two people to walk side by side. Just beyond was a small clearing. The ground was mud and grass. A dead oak had fallen on its side, making a natural bench—or a shelter, depending on what you needed. On the ground under it a threadbare flannel shirt lay crumpled. It was faded red and white and from what Josie could see, missing at least one of its sleeves.

"A shirt," Turner said. "That could be from anyone."

"No," Josie said. "It's his. He was wearing that when he attacked me in Mira's house."

"That doesn't really help us," said Turner. "He knew someone saw him. Now we got half the force out here looking for him. Sweetheart, he's gone."

"Our K-9 unit might still be able to find him," Josie said, pulling out her phone.

FORTY-SIX

Josie stood once again at the edge of the Tranquil Trails driveway, sweating, as she and Turner waited for Luke Creighton to arrive. Turner peeled off his vest and tossed it into the back seat of Josie's SUV. She was gratified to see a long V of sweat along the back of his dress shirt that went almost to his waist. He started loosening his tie. "I thought we didn't have a K-9 unit."

"We don't, officially," Josie said. "It's never been in the budget. The Chief found a nonprofit organization that lends search-and-rescue dogs and their handlers out to police departments in need at little to no expense to the department. Our handler serves a number of departments in this area."

Turner threw his tie into the back seat and unbuttoned the top three buttons of his shirt. The collar of his undershirt was soaked. "This handler? He any good?"

Josie turned away from him, feeling that old familiar mix of emotions whenever she talked or thought about Luke Creighton. Once upon a time, they'd been engaged. He was the first guy she was serious about after her first husband, Ray, died. He'd been a state trooper. A rule-follower through and through until one day Josie asked him to bend a rule and got him shot almost to death for his trouble. He'd lost his spleen.

"Yeah," she said. "He's the best."

Turner was so close to her that his arm brushed hers. "You sure? You don't look convinced."

Josie had spent eighteen months nursing Luke back to health and back to work and then he'd lied to her, betrayed her, and cheated on her. He'd gotten caught up in a bad situation that he only made worse when he covered up a shooting. A complicated, ugly series of events led to him being kidnapped by bad men with mafia ties. They'd tortured him, leaving lasting and permanent damage.

"I'm sure," Josie said. "Besides, it's all about the dog, and Luke's dog is definitely the best."

"You really are a dog person," Turner said, staring down at her. "That why you didn't want me to shoot Kiki the Menace?"

Josie shaded her eyes as she looked up at him. "Would you really have shot her?"

He smirked. "What do you think?"

"I don't know what to think about you, Turner. Just do me a favor. When Luke gets here, don't... say anything about his hands, okay? Try not to react."

Both of Luke's hands and all of his fingers had been shattered during his ordeal. They were covered in silver scars. The tip of his pinky finger on his left hand was turned outward and the index and middle fingers on his right hand were flattened. That was after multiple surgeries. He said he was used to it and that people's reactions to his hands didn't bother him, but it bothered Josie.

Luke had paid for every one of his mistakes, losing his job, his career, and spending time in prison. He'd gotten his bloodhound, Blue, to help with the crippling anxiety he had as a result of what he'd been through, but found that Blue could also help him redeem himself by still finding a way to serve others.

Their record was nearly perfect, and Blue had saved Josie's life. It was one of those debts she could never repay.

"Hey." Turner bumped her arm gently. "You're really asking me for something, aren't you?"

"Luke is important to me."

He grinned. "Is it hard? Asking me for something?"

She elbowed him sharply, hitting ribs. "What do you think?"

"I think you smell like sweat and horseshit."

A dirt-covered white pickup truck appeared in the distance, climbing Prout Road. Josie stepped away from Turner to wave Luke into the driveway. "You're pretty ripe yourself."

Moments later, Blue was at Josie's feet, receiving ear scratches and words of praise while Luke introduced himself to Turner. Josie felt actual shock when Turner gave no visible reaction at all to Luke's mangled hands. She wasn't sure if it was because she'd asked him not to react or because he was so fixated on Luke's size. He was at least an inch taller than Turner with broader shoulders and a lot more muscle. A gentle giant. He'd long ago given up his buzzed state trooper haircut and let his brown hair grow out. It was a longer, shaggier look, but it suited him better.

As they made their way down the trail toward the water, Josie briefed Luke on the situation.

"I've been following the news," Luke said. "I was wondering if I'd get a call. I sure would like to be looking for that little girl instead of this bastard."

Turner clapped him on the shoulder. "You find this bastard and we'll get him to tell us where to find the girl."

Josie wasn't so sure but she kept quiet. Once they reached the clearing, Luke put Blue's harness on, his indication that it was time to work. He gave him the same soft instructions that he did with every search and let him scent Seth's shirt. Then he was off.

As usual, Josie had to run to keep up. Behind her, Turner crashed gracelessly through the forest, complaining whenever he managed to catch his breath. Blue headed south, toward the city, keeping to the trees rather than the river. They passed through an open meadow. Without the shade to cool her off, sweat poured down Josie's face, burning her eyes when she didn't wipe it away fast enough. Next to her, Turner's breathing was labored but his long strides still made him hard to keep up with.

Why had Seth come this way? It was risky, returning to a populated area where nearly every person knew your face and that you were wanted for murder and kidnapping. Did that mean that Seth was keeping Rosie and Mira near the city? In the city somewhere? Josie still couldn't figure out where he'd managed to hold April for an entire year, and the map little Rosie had drawn still made no sense to her. Seth could have found remote wooded places to keep April in the warm weather, but the winter was another story. Even if Rebecca found that Jon had been renting an apartment for Seth, would it be a place that he could imprison a grown woman without anyone noticing or growing suspicious? It seemed as though Deirdre Velis's truck was his primary mode of transportation. Is that where he'd kept April for most of the time? That would certainly account for the lack of sunlight she'd endured.

Blue darted to the left. A moment later they were on the riverbank. He sniffed the rocks and dirt on the edge of the water and then lifted his nose to scent the air. Josie scanned the river, trying to determine how far they'd traveled. Now that the bend in the river where the peninsula had formed was behind them, Josie had a better view of the opposite bank where it meandered toward Central Denton. Most of it was just more trees or rocky shoals. In one area what looked like an old garden shed now lay in a heap of wood and debris. The trees around it had been cut down. Someone was likely planning to build there.

Blue stopped sniffing and looked up at Luke. There was no active alert—a bark—and no passive alert—sitting or lying down. He'd lost the scent. It was extremely unusual for him.

Turner huffed behind Josie. "I didn't think this job would involve so much running. What's going on?"

Luke frowned. "He must have gone into the water. This is as far as Blue could follow the scent. I'm sorry."

"Don't be," Josie said.

"Can't dogs search in water, too?" Turner said. Suddenly he was an expert on search-and-rescue dogs.

Luke laughed. "You have a boat handy? Kidding. What you're thinking of are dogs that can find a body immersed in water. Unless this guy is dead, I think that would be a waste of a lot of resources."

"But just in case," Josie said. "Have some patrols drive up and down the road on the other side of the river and see if they can spot anything."

Turner used his radio to make the request while Josie squatted down to pet Blue. Luke gave him some water which he lapped up enthusiastically. A few minutes later, they were headed back toward Tranquil Trails, trudging along a lot slower this time and keeping the river in view so they didn't get lost. Josie was grateful when they entered the shade of the trees again, but she was beginning to think that Turner was right. She did smell like horseshit and sweat.

"Blue?" Luke stopped walking.

Josie looked around but didn't see the dog. Turner hunched over, putting his hands on his knees. "He have to take a leak?"

"I don't know." Luke walked back into the trees, searching for him.

Josie's heart slammed into overdrive. She hadn't even seen Blue leave the group. "Luke?"

He kept walking. "He just ran off. It's not like him. He—"

Luke pulled up short and Josie bumped into his back.

Edging around him, she saw Blue lying beside a haphazard pile of rocks.

Turner finally caught up. "Oh hell. He needs a nap?"

"No," Josie said, eyes fixed on the dog. "That's his passive alert—"

"—for a cadaver find," Luke finished.

FORTY-SEVEN

The dirt wasn't freshly turned. That's what Josie kept telling herself again and again as the hours passed. The dirt wasn't freshly turned. The grave wasn't new. It couldn't be Mira or Rosie. It probably wasn't even related to their case. Dr. Feist and the ERT were still working when the sun sank to the horizon and it would be hours more, maybe even morning, by the time they were able to transport the remains to the morgue. Josie and Turner waited outside the perimeter that the ERT had cordoned off, sitting side by side on another downed tree. Someone had brought them water. Josie drank her entire bottle without stopping to breathe while Turner poured his over his head.

"You don't have to stay," she said, throat aching after so much exertion.

He'd been fidgety as always. Drumming his fingers. Pacing. Skimming stones into the river. But he'd stayed off his phone almost the entire time. She wondered if he was having some kind of medical event.

"Neither do you."

"I just want to know—"

"Yeah, me too," he said, cutting her off.

They got their answer moments later when Dr. Feist exited the scene. Her camera hung from her neck. Tugging off her skull cap, she walked over to them. "It's not Mira or Rosie Summers. The decedent has been in the ground for some time. Years."

"How many years?" asked Turner.

"I can't say until I get them on the table."

"Homicide?" Turner pressed.

"Detective Turner," said Dr. Feist. "I won't know anything until I've had a chance to properly examine these remains, but in my experience, people who die of natural causes don't usually bury themselves."

Josie was too tired to laugh at Turner's expense. An uncomfortable relief settled in her chest. She was glad it wasn't Mira or Rosie, but she was never happy to know that a person had lost their life—especially to violence.

Oblivious to the bite in Anya's tone, Turner stood up and flashed her a smile. It was the same one he'd used on Bobbi Ann Thomas, which meant... wait, was he trying to be charming? Was he going to try to flirt with Anya? Josie's stomach acids roiled. "Turner," she said.

He gave her a quizzical look. She patted the seat on the log that he'd just vacated. "Sit back down. Dr. Feist might have something unofficial for us."

"That's what I was—" he began.

Anya cut him off. "Sit. If you want to hear what I have to say."

He put his hands up in surrender and returned to his place beside Josie.

Anya lifted her camera from her chest and clicked a few buttons until the digital display came on. She turned so that Josie and Turner could see the images she had captured as she flipped through them. Bones, darkened with age and decay, flashed across the tiny screen. "My initial impression, given the size of the femurs and the pelvic bone, is that the deceased is male."

"Really," said Turner.

Anya looked up from the camera long enough to pin him with a stern look. "Initial impression. You'll have to wait for my report for confirmation."

"Understood, Doc, understood."

Anya stopped on a photo of some sort of object. "The deceased was wearing clothing but it's badly degraded and there's nothing I can tell you about it at this point. No wallet or anything like that. However, we did find two items that may be of interest. They'll have to be taken into evidence and cleaned up for us to properly identify them. Here's one."

She held the screen out toward them. Next to what looked like part of the body's mandible was a dirt-crusted object that curled almost into an S-shape. "Is that a piece of chain?" asked Turner. "Or beads or something?"

"We believe it's metallic," Anya answered. "But from how long it's been in the ground and how dirty and degraded it is, I can't tell you precisely what it is."

Josie's heart gave a strange flutter. A precursor to something. She stared at the object until Dr. Feist swiped to the next photo. Her body was reacting. Some part of her knew what it was and why it was significant. She just needed her mind to catch up.

Turner nudged her with an elbow. "You okay there, sweetheart? You gonna be sick or something? I know this isn't your first dead body."

"It's not that."

"What's that, Doc?" Turner's attention had already left her, now focused on the next photo. Again, the object was so caked with dirt its surface was barely visible, but unlike the first item, this was round and roughly the size of a silver dollar, given the ruler that Anya had placed next to it when she took the photo.

"A coin," said Anya, zooming in on it. There were places where the dirt and grime weren't so thick. Josie was pretty sure she could see some color peeking through.

Not a silver dollar.

Turner was strangely silent. Josie's heartbeat went from a rapid flutter to a gallop, rattling her rib cage.

"I think I see a letter or two here," Anya said, zooming out and back in again, trying to capture the area she wanted to show them. "Here. See? That's definitely an H and the next letter looks like an I but I won't know for sure until we get it cleaned up. Anyway, I didn't know if it would be helpful or not, but I figured I would let you have a look."

Anya turned the camera off and let it hang from her neck again. She used the sleeve of her suit to push sweaty locks of her hair away from her forehead. "What's wrong with you two?"

Josie turned her head. Even seated, Turner towered over her. His curly mop hung down almost to his eyebrows. Those piercing eyes regarded her with curiosity. "You thinking what I'm thinking?" he asked.

Josie didn't know whether to be encouraged or disturbed that they might be on the same page for once. "It's a challenge coin."

He nodded slowly, not taking his eyes off her. Challenge coins were just that: coins or sometimes medallions with the insignia or emblem of a particular organization. They were carried by military service members and law enforcement. The coins were a symbol of membership in a particular unit or department and the bonds that formed therein. Sometimes they denoted a special achievement or were given in recognition of outstanding accomplishments. Service members and law enforcement officers often exchanged them as signs of respect or as a way to honor one another. Denton PD had their own. Josie knew for a fact that Turner hadn't earned one yet.

Turner said, "Could be military. Could be one of us. You got any officers who haven't shown up for work in a few years?"

Josie's blood roared in her ears. Her brain worked frantically to click the pieces of this puzzle into place. The first object wasn't a piece of chain or beads of some kind. It was a scarab bracelet. April Carlson's scarab bracelet.

He's here. We have to tell.

"He" wasn't Seth Lee.

"Quinn?" Turner said.

It was always so jarring now when he used her actual name. "Denton PD doesn't have any missing officers, but Hillcrest PD does—the guy April Carlson dated before he disappeared three years ago. Officer Shane Foster."

FORTY-EIGHT

I have to wait until the alone times to talk to her. If I don't, I get in trouble. I want to stay with her and hug her forever, but he tied her up, and so all I can do is curl up against her like a cat. When I was a normal girl, I got to pet and play with her cat all the time. She said it could be mine. I want her to tell me about all the things we were going to do together when she takes me again. She's told me a ton of times, but I never get tired of hearing it. I can eat anything I want. She said she won't have to 'restrict' my food like Dad used to make her do. I'll have a room. We'll go to restaurants and parks. We'll go shopping. I can watch TV. I might even have friends. I can go back to school even though, as she always reminds me, I have a lot to catch up on. I know I'm not like normal girls, but maybe I can be if I live with her again.

I feel her breath on top of my head.

"I thought you were going to come get me," I say.

"I was, honey. I was. But something bad happened."

My breath feels funny in my chest like there's not enough air. "Something bad happened to Aunt April?"

"I'm so sorry, sweetie."

His voice is mean and scary. "Don't call her that. She wasn't an aunt."

"She was!" I yell. "I loved her!"

His fingers wrap around my upper arm, squeezing until the pain makes my eyes water. Mom shrieks, "Leave her alone!"

It's too late. He drags me away. I try to fight but he's so much bigger than me and when he's angry, no one can stop him. "I told you to stay away from her." He throws me down so hard my entire back hurts. Leaning down until his face almost touches mine, his spit lands on my cheek. "If you go near her again—"

We both freeze. I hear footsteps. He does, too. His whole face changes and I know he's going to fake being nice again. Before he walks away, he finishes his sentence in a whisper. "I'll kill her."

FORTY-NINE

Josie and Turner trudged up the trail as night fell. He walked in front, using the flashlight app on his phone to make sure they didn't step in any excrement. Not that it mattered. Josie was pretty sure that neither of them could smell worse than they already did. Josie's phone chirped with a message from Detective Heather Loughlin. Josie had called her before they'd left the scene.

I'll get Foster's dental records to Dr. Feist ASAP.

Josie tapped in a quick thank you and focused on Turner's back. Her body ached everywhere—again—and she was starving. "Slow down," she told him.

For once, he didn't give her any shit, slowing his pace until he was beside her. The trail was narrow, though, and his arm brushed and bumped against her sore shoulder. She made him switch sides.

"What do you think?" Turner asked as he swung his phone's flashlight back and forth in front of them. "Seth Lee thought or knew that April called DHS on him while Rosie was in school, and then he found out she was dating a police officer and figured she was going to tell him about the weird food restrictions he had with his little girl and so he killed the guy?"

Josie sidestepped a pile of shit. "Something like that. Seth has had delusions that some type of authorities have been after him for years. I'm sure that played into it as well. But I think April was also involved."

Turner kept his eyes on the flashlight beam. "Because of the bracelet? How can you be sure it's hers?"

"I can't be sure," Josie said. "But it makes the most sense. April told her mother that she lost the bracelet. She was extremely upset. So much so that when she supposedly found it, she never wore it again. Teresa Carlson also said that April was crushed when Shane Foster went missing, even though they had only been on a couple of dates. Heather interviewed April about Foster and also had the impression that April was devastated by his disappearance."

"But she was actually devastated because she lost her bracelet while she helped Seth Lee bury him," Turner said. "She never wore it again because she didn't have it. Why would she help him cover up the murder of a police officer?"

Josie stumbled, her boot slipping in mud. At least, she hoped it was mud. Turner offered a hand, but she didn't take it. "I don't know that she would unless she had some part in it."

Turner scoffed. "This guy got Mira Summers to do some crazy shit for him over the years, but I can't see him manipulating April Carlson into killing a police officer, especially one she was dating. She called DHS the second that she thought little Rosie was going hungry. She wasn't afraid of Seth."

"But if she knew he'd murdered someone, that was her chance to get him out of Mira and Rosie's lives forever. A custody dispute or even intervention by DHS would have only resulted in him taking Rosie and vanishing. She helped Seth cover it up because she had a part in it. Maybe it was accidental,

I don't know, but once she made the choice not to tell, she and Seth achieved assured mutual destruction."

"She couldn't turn him in without implicating herself." The flashlight beam bobbed as Turner swatted at a mosquito. "Where does Mira fit into all of this? She got that note from April saying he's here—which April would only know if she helped bury this guy—and saying 'we have to tell.' Obviously, Mira knew they killed Shane Foster. Hell, maybe she was involved, too."

"I think she wanted to get Rosie away from Seth before anything about Shane Foster's death came out. April gave her the brochure. She moved to Denton, got a job, a place, and started coming here. Maybe the meetings with Seth at the produce stand were like visitations—maybe that's when she got to see Rosie. A year later, April moves out this way, to Newsham."

"Looking for them," Turner said. "Any of them. Seth, Rosie, Mira. Somehow Seth found out she was nearby and started harassing her, trying to get her to go away. Why didn't she just tell then? Walk into a police station and say, 'Hey, me and this nutjob my sister's been dating killed a cop and buried him at a horse farm.'"

"Maybe she knew that she would be implicated in Shane Foster's death—especially if she thought she'd accidentally buried her bracelet with him—but maybe she didn't think she could prove Seth's involvement. Or maybe she wanted to make sure Rosie was safe first. April knew what he was capable of. I don't think she could stomach the thought of him having Rosie. Given what happened between her and Mira at the school, I don't think she trusted Mira to do the right thing for Rosie."

"But why even report the vandalism?" Turner asked. "If she knew who was doing it and had no intention of turning him in?"

That was one of the things that Josie simply couldn't figure out. "No idea."

Turner huffed out a breath as the trail grew steeper. "So April is in Newsham for almost a year, poking around in Seth's business, and he kidnaps her. Then, instead of killing her right away and neutralizing that threat, he instead keeps her alive until that day at the produce stand. Do you think that Mira knew the whole time that he had April?"

Josie thought about the wounds on Mira's arms. "No. Unless Seth was using April as leverage to keep Mira under his thumb. To make sure that she didn't get any ideas about taking Rosie away from him."

Once they reached the road, Turner stopped to catch his breath. "These are some fucked-up people, Quinn."

There were three times as many police vehicles this time and one ambulance to carry the remains to the morgue. They crossed Prout Road. Beyond the lights of the police vehicles, the driveway was cloaked in blackness, but as Josie went to get inside her SUV, a beam of light bobbed, headed toward them. She could hear Rebecca and Jon's raised voices as they approached.

"I will not, Jon! I can't believe you would expect me to keep this a secret!"

"It's completely irrelevant! I'm telling you, Bec, I don't think he's ever set foot in the place!"

Turner was on the passenger's side. He tapped the roof and then pointed toward the Lees. Josie followed him. They met the couple where the first row of patrol cars sat, their beacon lights strobing. Rebecca looked even more furious than she had earlier. Jon looked like he hadn't slept in days. His clothes were dirty, his hair uncombed. He trailed behind his wife, hands outstretched in supplication. "Please, Bec."

Turner folded his arms over his chest, peering down at Jon like he was a rodent. "We just heard that whole thing, so we know Mrs. Lee's got something to spill. You can stop begging now."

Jon cursed under his breath and turned his back on them. Rebecca pointed her flashlight beam at his head. "Really? You're here. You should be the one to tell them."

When Jon said nothing, she swung her torch toward the ground. "You were right. My husband has been renting Seth a room at a boardinghouse for the last ten years. Behind my back."

FIFTY

"Let me help you with that, sweetheart." Turner came up behind Josie and started to adjust the shoulder straps on her bulletproof vest.

She shrugged him off. "It's fine. I can do it."

"Yeah," he goaded. "You can do everything. Except hop fences."

Josie ignored his quiet laughter. She wasn't getting sucked in. Not today. She scanned the parking lot of a local dentist that Denton PD and the Alcott County Sheriff's Office had chosen to meet up at before converging on the boardinghouse where Jon Lee had been renting his brother a room for the past ten years. It was located in Bellewood, which fell under the jurisdiction of the Alcott County Sheriff. Three days ago, after Rebecca told them about the boardinghouse and then got Jon to give them the address, they had contacted the sheriff's office to advise that they intended to arrest Seth Lee—if he was there. First, they put the house under surveillance. They didn't want to converge on it with a huge police presence only to find out he wasn't there. By trying to execute the warrant without confirming that he was on the premises they risked the other residents warning him off—making any future attempts futile.

As much as Josie hated waiting, especially with Rosie and Mira at risk, if Seth was there, she didn't want to blow their best chance at arresting him by moving too quickly and without enough intelligence. The white box truck registered to Deirdre Velis's Furnished Finds was in the rear parking lot, which had sent a buzz of excitement through the investigative team but then, after three days without any sightings of Seth Lee, Chief Chitwood had concluded that he'd likely dumped the truck there and moved on. He'd instructed them to go in using a less aggressive approach, which meant trying to get a key to Seth's room from someone on-site, if possible, rather than breaking down his door. The truck could be impounded afterward. They'd brought enough manpower to put a perimeter around the entire premises in addition to the officers who would secure the inside of the building. Right now, everyone milled about, checking their equipment. Noah moved among them, giving out instructions.

Behind her, Turner perched on the hood of his car, sucking down one of his energy drinks. In his other hand was his cell phone. He used his thumb to scroll. Without looking up, he said, "This is taking forever."

Ignore, ignore, ignore, said the voice in her head. Another Alcott County Sheriff cruiser pulled into the parking lot. A few minutes later, Noah gathered all the officers together and went over the plan a final time.

A surge of adrenaline rushed through Josie's veins as they got into their vehicles. The boardinghouse was only two blocks away on a residential street. The three-story building with blue siding towered over the neighboring houses. A driveway ran alongside it, the asphalt cracked in multiple places, forming a web connecting over a dozen potholes. There and around the front porch, weeds sprang up from every opening. In moments they had the entire place surrounded.

The sagging wooden planks of the porch creaked beneath their feet as Josie, Turner and two other officers approached the front door. Additional teams waited out front. A cluster of metal mailboxes were affixed to the wall beside the door. Only some of them bore names. She didn't see one for Seth Lee. The front door was locked. Someone had handwritten the word *Office* in marker below the single doorbell. Josie pressed the button and was rewarded with a muffled ding from somewhere deep inside the building.

A moment later, the door swung open. A man appeared. A black ballcap was pulled low over his forehead but his eyes darted from Josie to Turner and then the large police presence behind them. Frozen in place, his lips parted as if to speak, and then clamped shut. He was young. Maybe eighteen or nineteen. His black T-shirt, jeans, and tan work boots looked old and worn. His forearms were tan and corded with muscle.

"I'm Detective Josie Quinn from the Denton Police Department," she said, producing the arrest warrant. "We're looking for Seth Lee."

His eyes darted to Turner again, the officers gathered behind him, then back to Josie. He was unnaturally still.

"Do you work in the office?" Josie asked.

He relaxed slightly. "Yeah, I help out the landlord and she takes some off my rent. Uh, Mr. Lee has a room here. Third floor, number 12. But no one sees him. He's never around. I don't even think he sleeps here."

"We're still going to have to check out his room," Josie said. "It would go more smoothly if you could provide us with a key."

He tugged at the brim of his ballcap. "Uh, yeah, I guess I could do that."

Turner stepped forward, his large body filling the doorframe. "You got a name, kid?"

"Ryan."

Turner smirked. "Ryan? That's it? Like Cher or Shakira?"

"Who?"

"You got a last name, Ryan?" Turner said. He turned back to Josie but hooked a thumb toward Ryan. "Is this for real? These kids don't even know who Shakira is?"

"Tramel," said Ryan. "Are you here to arrest Mr. Lee? Because of the stuff on the news?"

Ignoring his question, Josie said, "If you're not able to provide a key to Mr. Lee's room, I'll have to ask you to step aside." She turned her body so that he had a better view of the police cars crowded around the front of the house. Noah stood next to one of the SUVs, overseeing everything. He stared at Ryan. "You can wait over there with my colleague, Lieutenant Fraley."

"Come on, kid," Turner urged. "Find us an extra key. I'll tell you all about Shakira."

With one last glance at Josie, Ryan backed up and gestured for them to follow him through the foyer and down a hallway. "I have a key. Come on, I'll get it for you."

Two teams of officers poured in behind them. Their feet pounded up the steps, one team moving to the third floor and the other to the second floor to ensure there were no surprises or ambushes. Ryan led Josie, Turner, and the two uniformed officers with them to a door marked with a sign that read: *Office*. He jiggled the knob several times and then lifted it up, pushing at the same time to get it to swing open.

The interior was dim, lit only by a small sliding sash window high along the exterior wall. It smelled of dust, chalk, and wood polish. An old oak desk that looked like it had been pilfered from a principal's office circa 1950 took up most of the room. The copy machine alongside it didn't look much more modern. Along the far wall was one blue metal filing cabinet with a matching metal table next to it. Both were dented, their sharp corners rusted. Ryan bypassed the desk and went for the table which held a Keurig, two chipped mugs, a selection of coffee pods, sugar packets, Coffee Mate, and a handful of plastic spoons. "Want some coffee?"

"Just the key, kid," said Turner.

"Sure, sure." Ryan walked behind the desk and bent to rifle through one of the drawers.

Josie could hear the rapid tap of Turner's fingers on his thigh. He groaned softly.

Ryan moved on to another drawer, his hands moving faster. "I'm sorry," he mumbled. "I swear it's here somewhere."

This time, Turner growled, patience lost. "Listen, kid. I don't have time for this I-Spy bullshit. I was trying to be courteous, but we can smash in the door, no problem. You stay here. My colleague has some questions."

Ryan's head whipped up, his mouth hanging open. He started to speak but Turner was already gone, taking the uniformed officers with him. Looking to Josie, he said, "I'm sorry. It's here. I can find it if you just give me a minute."

"Forget it," said Josie.

Ryan shrugged. "Okay, but the landlord's not going to be happy about the property damage."

Ignoring his comment, Josie asked, "When is the last time you saw Mr. Lee?"

"I've never seen him here." Ryan abandoned the desk for the Keurig. He pressed a pod into the top of it and then placed a mug beneath the brew base. He tapped a couple of buttons until the machine started making gurgling noises. Coffee streamed into the mug. "That's what I was trying to tell you out there. He doesn't come here."

"He doesn't come here, or *you've* never seen him?"

The Keurig emitted a long buzz and then went silent. Ryan lifted the lid to get to the pod and then disposed of it in a small trash bin near his feet.

"Ryan?" Josie backed up until she was on the threshold. From there she could see inside the office, but she could also see up and down the hall. Other officers were moving from room to room, checking the common areas.

"I've never seen him." He dumped three sugar packets and six Coffee Mate creamers into his cup and stirred them in with a plastic spoon.

A slow series of creaks came from overhead. More footsteps on the stairs. Someone calling for a prybar. "His truck is parked out back," Josie pointed out.

Ryan pulled a napkin from his pocket and folded it in half. Then he tucked the plastic spoon inside. Leaving it on the table, he picked up his mug and swiveled in her direction. He took a long swig before his gaze settled pointedly on her pistol. "That's his truck? How do you know?"

"We know, Ryan. How long has it been out there?"

"I'm not sure. Maybe some of the other guys might know." Ryan slugged down the rest of his coffee and returned the mug to the table. "Maybe one of them saw him but I doubt they'll admit it if they have. The people who live here don't much trust cops."

Josie had not seen any cameras on the exterior of the house, but she asked anyway. "Are there cameras out back?"

His hands hung loosely at his sides. His fingers flexed once. "Does this look like the kind of place that has cameras?"

Josie heard the rapid-fire sound of shoes on steps. Just from the frenetic pace, she was certain it was Turner. Moments later, she felt his breath ruffle the hair on the top of her head.

"He's not here, but come on up and have a look at the room. LT is arranging for the truck to be impounded."

FIFTY-ONE

One look around room 12 and Josie could not imagine Seth Lee keeping anyone there. It just wasn't big enough. A neatly made bed took up eighty percent of the space. Standing near the window that overlooked the driveway, she could hear the residents from both adjacent rooms complaining to officers about the intrusion. Every resident of the building was being questioned to see if any of them had seen Seth Lee here recently—or Mira, Rosie, and even April Carlson in the past year. Even if someone had seen something, Josie doubted they'd admit it. This was definitely the kind of place where people minded their own business.

"Closet's empty." Turner brushed by her and rounded the bed. He used a gloved hand to open the top dresser drawer. "We got some shirts. Flannel. Must be his favorite. Coupla pairs of jeans, socks and underwear. I don't see any shoes anywhere."

Josie sighed. "Maybe he uses it as a place to keep a few extra things? Every person we talked to said he doesn't like to stay indoors. I think he just used this place to dump the truck. He abandoned it out back where no one except other residents would see it. None of them would report it. At least not right away. Maybe the landlord would have called to have it towed if it sat too long. If Rebecca hadn't found Jon's cash withdrawals, we wouldn't even know about this place."

Turner opened the next drawer and stared at its contents. "Store a few extra things, huh?"

Josie walked over as Turner pulled out the remaining drawers. They were packed with food. Prepackaged food. Granola bars. Protein bars. Pouches of oatmeal. Cups of microwaveable macaroni and cheese. Cans of soup. Chocolate bars. Peanut butter cookies. Several different types of crackers.

"What in the hell is up with this guy?" Turner said. "I thought he had a thing about food being tampered with. Isn't that why he's eating from his brother's produce stand? But he's stocking food here? You think he comes here and eats it and then goes back to whatever hole he's got his kid living in and makes her eat mud?"

The thought was deeply disturbing. "Maybe his brother left it here for him?" she suggested. "I can call Jon Lee and find out."

Turner slowly closed the drawers and peeled his gloves off. "Back to square one. Let's get the hell out of here."

Turner left the boardinghouse before anyone else. Apparently a more pressing matter had come up. Josie and Noah stayed until all the residents had been interviewed and then they returned to the stationhouse. The press had caught wind of what they were now calling the "raid" on the boardinghouse in Bellewood. Several reporters crowded the municipal entrance at the back of the station, shouting questions as Josie and Noah pushed past them and into the building.

"How did you track Lee to that boardinghouse?"

"How long was he staying there?"

"Did he know you were going to try to arrest him there? Did someone at the house tip him off?"

"Where do you go from here?"

Josie was relieved when the door closed behind them, cutting off the voices. Even after spending an hour at her desk in the great room, that last question haunted her. Where *did* they go from here? Before she worked on her reports, she had called the Lees to find out from Jon whether he stocked food and clothes in the room he rented for Seth. He claimed that he had never actually been inside the room, nor did he have a key, but Josie wasn't sure whether to trust him or not. The one thing Jon Lee had proven consistently was that he was willing to lie on behalf of his brother.

While Noah made phone calls, Josie stood up and went back to the corkboard. It had grown in scope. Things were starting to overlap. There was the aerial view of Tranquil Trails with pins to mark the produce stand, the place on Prout Road where Mira had stopped for twenty-two minutes after the stabbing, and now the approximate location of Shane Foster's body. By now, most of the map was covered with printouts of other things related to the investigation. There were photos of the four people who comprised the drama they had all been swept up in: Seth Lee, Rosie Summers, Mira Summers, and April Carlson. There was the Post-it note that April had given Mira, telling her where to find the body of Shane Foster. Someone had hung up a page with all the information pertaining to the truck that Seth had been driving, including a copy of the registration that Deirdre Velis had provided. There was also now a copy of a crime scene photo that showed the strange fibers found on April Carlson's body. Whoever hung it up had drawn a thick black question mark next to it. Then there was the drawing that Rosie had made, the supposed map, and her message on the back, pleading for help.

The stairwell door opened, sending a blast of air through

the room. The pages on the board fluttered. Turner sauntered in. His vest had been replaced with his suit jacket. An energy drink peeked from one of the pockets. As always, he held his phone in one hand, thumb scrolling endlessly. He glanced at Josie.

"You still obsessed with that stupid drawing?"

"You have anything better for us to follow up on?" she asked pointedly.

Turner sank into his chair, trading his phone for his foam basketball. "Where's Parker?"

"Palmer," Josie said, turning her back to the corkboard.

Noah hung up his desk phone. "She's off today. That was Anya—Dr. Feist—with apologies for taking so long to get us her full report on the body Blue found on the Tranquil Trails property."

Turner tossed his ball at the net and, predictably, missed. "She matched the dental records days ago. We know it was that Hillcrest officer, Foster."

Noah's cell phone buzzed with a message. While he checked it, he spoke. "Right. Hummel took what was left of the clothing and shoes found with his remains into evidence and sent them out to the state lab to see if any DNA can be pulled that might link Seth Lee or anyone else to the body. She also cleaned up the challenge coin and the bracelet. The coin was from Hillcrest PD, as expected. The bracelet was a scarab bracelet. She was able to send Teresa Carlson photos. As far as she can tell, it's a match to April's, but she's going to gather as many photos of it as she can so they can do a more detailed and comprehensive comparison."

Which would tell them what Josie already knew. It was definitely April's bracelet. "What about cause of death?"

"Undetermined," Noah said.

"He was in the dirt too long," Turner said. "He could have

been stabbed, smothered, beaten to death, but soft tissue and organ injuries don't show up on a skeleton."

"What about blunt force injuries?" Josie asked. "Broken bones? Skull fracture?"

Noah looked up from his cell phone. "Both of his femurs were broken, as was his pelvic bone. Several rib fractures as well. Anya thinks the injuries might be consistent with a long fall or being struck by something, like a car, though she can't say for sure. The fractures wouldn't have caused his death but if he'd sustained injuries severe enough to do that much damage, then he likely had internal injuries that did lead to his death."

Josie's money was on some sort of injury by motor vehicle. Possibly accidental. It supported her theory that April hadn't been a willing or enthusiastic participant in Shane Foster's demise.

Turner popped the tab on his energy drink. "Assured mutual destruction. What else do you have, LT? 'Cause we're running low on leads, and your little wifey over there is about to go cross-eyed staring at that drawing."

"Turner!" Noah and Josie snapped at the same time.

Unfazed, he sucked down the entire can of Turbo Powr, crumpled the can, and belched. He tossed the can at his trash bin and missed.

Noah waited until he picked it up and threw it away before answering his question. "The botanist I told you about is downstairs. Sergeant Lamay is bringing him up. Dr. Hensley Brooks from Denton University. He says he can shed some light on the fibers found on April Carlson's clothes."

"That's what you've got?" Turner said incredulously. "A botanist? Come on, LT. This guy is running circles around us and all we've got to show for it is another dead body and enough overtime to give the Chief a damn heart attack. By the way, I can't get the smell of horseshit off my shoes."

Josie folded her arms across her chest. Turner wasn't

entirely wrong, but they had to work with the evidence they had and right now, that evidence was plant-based. "If you've got a better suggestion, let's hear it."

Noah stood up as the stairwell door swished open again. Sergeant Lamay shuffled in, followed by a tall, distinguished black man in a navy suit. Glasses perched on his nose, and tucked under his arm was a manila envelope. He greeted them with an infectious smile, moving around the room to shake each of their hands and introduce himself. For a college professor, he was unexpectedly relaxed and informal, insisting that they call him Hensley. Noticing the photo of the fibers in question on the corkboard, he walked right over, standing at an angle as if he were in front of a lecture hall. "I brought my own photos and such." He pulled the envelope from under his arm and handed it to Josie since she was closest. "But this is a good start."

Josie walked over to where Noah stood near his desk. Turner joined them, watching as she pulled out a sheaf of papers. It was a report, complete with color photos and diagrams. She flipped through a few pages. Turner said, "Hey, Doc? I'm a slow reader. You think you could give me the bullet points?"

Hensley laughed and pointed to the photo on the cork-board. "I just want to start by reminding you that I wasn't able to examine the physical specimen since it is in the custody of your lab. However, I'm ninety-nine percent sure that this is from a plant called American burnweed. It's sometimes called fireweed, among other things. It's part of the daisy family."

Josie flipped back to the front page where the words *Erechtites hieraciifolius* were emblazoned over the top of a photo of a plant that looked very similar to a dandelion except much taller, fuller, and leafier. From the main stem, smaller networks of stems and leaves spread, each one heavy with multiple buds.

Turner said, "It's a giant weed."

Hensley laughed again. "It is technically an herb, but I can see why you would say that. It's extremely fast-growing. Some people will tell you it appears overnight. It will grow as tall as eight to ten feet at times and can spread quite rapidly. Most people don't find it attractive. It's an annual but in some places, it has a short life and can be a perennial. Its flower is not really what people typically think of as a flower at all but a collection of what you have right here in your, uh, crime scene photo. If you look on page four, you'll see several photos of the plant when it's flowering."

Josie flipped to page four. Here the photos of the plant—or herb—showed them in full bloom, except instead of petals, the flowers were made of thick white fluff. Dozens and dozens of them.

"I won't bore you with the scientific terminology but basically those clusters of white hairs held together by seeds? The flowers? They take flight, much the same way that dandelion seeds behave. They get everywhere."

Turner's fingers beat out an impatient rhythm against the edge of Noah's desk. "Doc, this is fascinating, but you might have noticed that we're trying to find a killer. He's got his girlfriend and kid with him. It's a pretty dangerous situation. How does any of this help us with that?"

To his credit, Hensley's enthusiasm was not dulled in the least. He clapped his hands together. "Lieutenant Fraley told me that these flowers were found on the body of a victim—the teacher would be my guess from having watched the news—and that before her murder she was being held somewhere. You don't know where, is that correct?"

"Yes," Josie said.

"I can't tell you if she picked up the flowers where she was being held or in transport or both, but what I can tell you is that American burnweed usually grows in open areas that have recently been disturbed. Roadsides, pastures, meadows. Land recently devastated by fire or where a great deal of trees have been cut down. It blooms in the summer but with how hot the weather has been this month, I wouldn't be surprised to see these flowering now."

Noah said, "You're saying that we should be looking at these kinds of areas if we want to find the place where April Carlson was kept?"

Hensley nodded. "Yes, that would be my recommendation."

Turner said, "No disrespect, but that could be anywhere."

Josie tried to remember if she'd seen any of these plants during her treks around the Tranquil Trails property. Even if she had, that didn't mean that Seth had been keeping April there. Surely one of the Lees' clients would have found them.

Noah and Josie thanked Hensley. Turner remained stone-faced and unimpressed. Once the botanist was gone, he said, "That narrows it down to almost the entire city. What else do we have?"

Josie said, "Even though April Carlson had these on her clothes and mud and grass in her stomach, for the majority of the year that Seth Lee had her, she was kept in the dark. She didn't get sunlight. She didn't have ligature marks, so he hadn't tied her up. She had to have been indoors. Locked away. If he had kept her outside, surely at some point she would have tried to escape or at least drawn the attention of other people."

"The truck," Turner said. "He kept her in the back of the truck."

"Too risky," Noah said. "Someone somewhere could have heard her. I think Josie's right. She was indoors for most of her captivity. He transported her in the truck to the produce stand. Wherever he was keeping her, that's where Mira and Rosie are now."

He didn't say it but he didn't have to—they all heard the unspoken part of that statement: if they're still alive.

Turner let out a long, frustrated sigh. "So this botanist is full of shit, then."

"No," said Noah. "There is one place, out of the way, on the outskirts of the city, surrounded by forest, that Seth has regular access to whether he chooses to sleep under the roof or not."

Josie said, "Furnished Finds. Turner, when you drove out there, did you notice any areas where there'd been fires? Building sites where the land was disturbed? Recent tree work?"

The fingers of both hands thrummed against his thighs. "I don't think so, unless you count the gravel pit around the back of the place where that Deirdre broad was clearly burning furniture. But we can't get a search warrant for her place. The flowers from some weed, a bonfire in the back of the store... even with her admitting that Seth had her truck, it's not enough. Assuming she lied about, well, everything, we can't prove that to a judge."

Noah picked up his car keys. "But we can talk to her. We can swing by to let her know that her truck was just impounded and what she needs to do to get it back."

Turner grinned. "I see where you're going with this, LT. Maybe we get her to admit to something that gives us enough probable cause for a search warrant."

Josie tossed Hensley's report onto Noah's desk. "Let's go."

FIFTY-TWO

Turner took his own vehicle while Noah and Josie followed in his SUV. Noah had clearly looked into Furnished Finds once they received the information about the truck from Deirdre, but Josie hadn't looked it up, too busy chasing other leads. Now she used her internet browser to see what she could find out about it.

"This place barely exists," she said. "If we hadn't spoken with Deirdre and seen the truck, I'm not sure I would believe it was real. Google says it's an antique furniture store, but it's got no website. There are no photos of it. Nothing. There's a phone number. That's it."

Noah said, "There's an aerial view of it on Google Maps. No street view though."

The dense residential areas of the city thinned out as they turned onto a narrow two-lane road that snaked up into the mountains. The GPS indicated they had fifteen miles before they reached the store. It was more populous than Prout Road, where Tranquil Trails was located, with residences spaced every quarter mile or so. Still, this far out from the city, Josie didn't see how Furnished Finds was able to support its business, unless it was a niche market or they had a dedicated client base. Josie had lived in Denton her entire life and grown more familiar with it once she joined the police department, yet she'd never heard of Furnished Finds.

She spent the rest of the ride studying the overhead view but it offered nothing illuminating. Surrounded by trees on every side—even across the road—the sprawling one-story building that housed Furnished Finds sat on a lot of gravel and weeds—none American burnweed though. Its exterior was painted a dull, fading blue. An eave extended from the roof over the tall glass storefront. On it the name of the store had been hand-painted in black.

Noah parked near the door, next to Turner's car, and they got out.

"Looks abandoned, doesn't it?" Turner said.

Some of the windows were covered with newspaper from the inside. The others offered a view deep into the cavernous store where dozens of desks, chairs, armoires, credenzas, kitchen sets and couches crowded together. It was less a show-room and more an overfull storage area. Josie thought she saw a sales desk near the center of the disarray, but no Deirdre or anyone else.

"Doesn't look like they move much product," said Noah. He tried the door handle, but it was locked.

"You're not getting in that way, LT," said Turner. "Let's walk around the back."

There were no windows along the side of the building. They followed Turner, but when they rounded the back, Josie and Noah stopped. A pile of furniture almost as tall as the building took up an immense amount of space in the expansive back lot. Recliners, tables, couches, bookshelves. Some of the pieces were broken. The upholstered furniture was torn and faded. Scorch marks marred the ground around it. Nearby were piles of ash. No burnweed.

Over his shoulder, Turner said, "That's one way to get rid of your unwanted inventory, huh?"

A white box truck identical to the one they'd impounded from Seth Lee's boardinghouse was backed up to a loading dock that extended from the rear of the building. Just like the other one, there was no writing on it, nothing to indicate that it was connected to any business. "Come on," Turner said. "The bay door is probably open."

When they reached the truck, Josie stretched upward and felt along the grill and hood. Cold. It hadn't been driven recently.

Noah said, "Slow down, Turner."

"Relax, LT. I've got this. Hello?" Turner bellowed. "Deirdre Velis? Hello?"

Through the narrow opening where the back of the truck met the dock, Josie could see that the bay door was open, just as Turner predicted. The cargo door of the truck was shut and latched. "Miss Velis?" she called, matching Turner's volume. "Denton Police Department. We just need to talk to you for a few minutes."

Turner squeezed behind the truck and hoisted himself into the bay. "Deirdre Velis?" he called again. "Denton PD. You have a minute?"

He squatted down and extended a hand to Josie. She stared at it. Turner laughed. "The great Josie Quinn doesn't need help? Come on, sweetheart. I'm trying to help you up, not grope you. You think I'd try something with your husband staring right at me?"

"Turner," Noah said, pointing toward the bay door. "Focus."

Turner shrugged and stood up, turning away from them. Josie hoisted herself onto the ledge with little effort. Noah followed. They walked along the concrete slab and then paused at an archway that separated the loading dock from the back of the showroom, the three of them calling out for Deirdre and identifying themselves. Tightly packed rows of furniture spread out before them. Along one wall was a large sales desk. Next to that was a hall. Deirdre Velis emerged from it, a metal baseball bat raised over her shoulder.

"Stop right there," she called.

FIFTY-THREE

Turner threw his palms up. "Slow down there, slugger."

Noah took out his credentials as an offering even though she was too far away to see them. "Miss Velis, Denton PD. You remember my colleagues, right? We just came to talk."

Lowering the bat to her side, she slowly walked toward them, the suspicion in her face dissipating as she drew closer. Eyeing Turner, she said, "I remember you, now. And you." She offered Josie a smile. "Sorry. As you can see, I'm all alone out here and now this business with Seth..."

For a woman who claimed to know how to handle Seth Lee, she was quick to pick up a bat at the sound of people approaching.

Noah gave her one of his dazzling smiles. "We understand. You can never be too careful. May we come in?"

"Yes, yes, of course." She waved them across the threshold, down the ramp, and into the store. As they followed her to the sales desk, she added, "Sit anywhere," and laughed. There had to be dozens of different types of chairs in the place.

As if taking her invitation seriously, Turner drifted off to the nearest cluster of furniture, six couches all tucked up next to one another. Deirdre moved behind the sales desk, which formed a square with a small opening on the side nearest the hall. She set the bat down on the countertop. Josie and Noah took up position on the other side of it.

"Have you caught him?" Deirdre asked. "They said you were still looking for him on the radio but since you came all the way out here, I thought maybe you had news."

"I'm afraid not," said Noah. "But we did locate your truck. We had to impound it..."

While Noah talked to her about the impound process, including when and how she could get her property back, Josie noticed that Deirdre's gaze was locked on Turner, following his every movement. He meandered further away from them, running a finger over the surface of a dining room table.

Josie surveyed the clutter behind the desk. It was what you'd expect to find behind the desk of a furniture store that specialized in antiques, minus some modern technology like a computer. Piles of receipts. A cordless phone in its base. A ledger book. Several hardback books about pricing and repairing furniture. Notepads. Pens. A bowl with a set of keys inside it. A coffee mug. Candy bar wrappers. A bottle of WD-40. Several different woodworking tools that Josie couldn't identify by name.

"I can get by with one truck for now," Deirdre said, eyes still on Turner. "Do you have any leads? Any idea where Seth has gone now that he's on foot?"

Noah frowned. "We were hoping to get some insight from you. Other than Seth's brother, you've known him the longest."

Josie's gaze snagged on something on the other side of the desk. It was the whisper of an instinct that told her it was important, but she couldn't say why.

Deirdre's eyes flared with annoyance as Turner abandoned

the dining room table and moved toward a small grouping of desks. "I already told these other detectives that I have no idea where Seth could be. If I knew, I would have already told you."

"Hey, Quinn, look at these." Startled by the use of her actual name, Josie looked over to see Turner trying to fit his long frame into a child's school desk. The seat and the desktop were pine. Wrought iron piping connected them at the base. Somehow, Turner managed to squeeze into it. "This is what you call rustic. Hey, Deirdre. What is this from? The fifties?"

Noah hid it well but Josie could tell that he was more than annoyed with Turner's antics.

With a stiff smile, Deirdre answered, "The thirties."

Turner lifted the desk's flip-top and peered into the storage compartment.

Deirdre started for the opening that led from behind the counter to the show floor. "Would you mind not touching things?"

But Turner was already on his feet, wandering toward a large armoire an aisle over. Deirdre slowly returned to her spot behind the sales counter, rolling the bat back and forth nervously. "As I was saying, I can't help you find Seth. Yes, I've known him a long time but we're no longer close."

Changing tack, Noah said, "You also have a Chevrolet Cavalier registered to you personally. Where is that?"

"In the shop."

"What shop?" Turner called.

Momentarily caught off-guard, Deirdre looked back and forth between Noah and Turner. "I have a friend who owns a shop in the city."

Josie eyed the items on the countertop again. "What's the name of the shop?"

Deirdre's fingers trembled slightly as she rolled the bat again. "Oh my, I don't remember the name of it. Isn't that silly?

This is what happens when you get older. I just think of it as my friend's shop. It's the one on Aymar Avenue. You know, near Campbell Street?"

"Oh yeah," Noah said easily. "I think I know the one."

There was no auto repair shop anywhere on Aymar Avenue. Or Campbell Street. Deirdre was lying.

Josie said, "Do you have other employees or subcontractors besides Seth?"

Deirdre's eyes seized on Turner again as he appeared behind Josie and Noah. "No. It's just me."

Turner's breath ruffled Josie's hair. "Hey, I gotta hit the head. Deirdre, honey, you got a restroom in this place or what?"

Deirdre's fingers flexed along the handle of the bat. "It's not a public restroom."

Turner smiled and winked at her. "I'm not the public, Deirdre. I'm here to serve the good citizens of Denton, including you. If you haven't noticed, we're about a million miles from civilization. I'll never make it back to Denton proper in time and these two"—he clapped a hand on each of their shoulders—"they sure get mad when I make a mess in the car."

Even though they had come in separate vehicles, Noah smiled and went along with the joke. "He doesn't like it when we make him walk."

"I could go out back, but I'm not entirely sure I won't see a bear out there. I know you don't want me to get mauled by a bear."

Deirdre, her pleasant facade slipping, looked like that was exactly what she wanted but relented, gesturing toward the hallway. "Last door on the left. Hurry, and I would appreciate it if you didn't touch anything."

"Not even to flush?"

Before Deirdre could respond, he was gone, laughter trailing behind him, his long strides eating up the distance to the hall in a heartbeat. Once he turned the corner, they could no longer see him from where they stood.

"I'm sorry," Noah said. "We'll be out of your hair soon. Just a few more questions. When you and Seth were dating, did you live together?"

"What?" Deirdre said. "I don't see how that is relevant to—to what's going on now."

The sound of a door creaking floated from the dim recesses of the hallway.

"Standard questions," Noah said.

"No, I don't think so. These don't seem standard to me." Deirdre pushed away from the counter and turned in the direction of the hall. Her expression hardened. "Where is your friend? What's taking him so long?"

Josie knew Turner was up to something, probably doing a plain-view search of whatever he could see along the hall. He wouldn't be able to open any doors or otherwise nose around, but anything that was in plain sight was fair game in terms of them being able to act on it. It was the same strategy Josie had employed the first time she'd been inside the Lees' house.

Except the Lees hadn't looked downright homicidal when Josie emerged from the bathroom.

Josie circled the desk, putting herself between Deirdre and the mouth of the hallway. "If you needed to get in touch with Seth, urgently, how would you do it?"

"I wouldn't. I told you—"

A loud crash, followed by another, swallowed up the rest of her words. Next came a grunt, another crash. Wood splintered. Then Turner's voice, "Stop right there. Get on your fucking knees—"

Josie and Noah unsnapped their holsters at the same time and drew their weapons. A shot rang out from the hall, the boom echoing through the cavernous showroom. Deirdre picked up the bat and drew it back, pinning Josie with a murderous glare. The concussive noise of the gunshot faded enough for Josie to make out the sounds of a struggle in the hallway. Noah aimed his pistol at Deirdre. "Put the bat down," he said calmly. Then, to Josie, "Go."

FIFTY-FOUR

Josie sprinted into the hallway but pulled up short when she saw Turner locked in battle with Seth Lee. His pistol lay on the floor on the other side of their fused bodies. They were still on their feet, each man trying to gain control of the other. Seth pinned a forearm against Turner's throat, holding him against the wall. She started to call out commands for Seth to stop, but Turner kneed him and then the two of them spun, crashing into the other wall. The plaster gave way but not even the groin shot was able to slow Seth down long enough for Turner to gain control of the fight. Josie couldn't get a clear shot. They were moving too quickly. Behind her, she heard Noah shouting commands at Deirdre. Once he had her cuffed, he would call for backup.

Seth headbutted Turner. The crunch of bone went right through her. Blood spurted from Turner's nose. He stumbled and Seth drove him backward, into a wooden door. Josie holstered her pistol, ready to join the fight. If she couldn't shoot Seth without potentially injuring or killing Turner, she wasn't going to stand around and watch Seth beat him senseless. But then the door groaned and cracked. Turner's hands reached for

Seth's throat. Before he could grab flesh, Seth fisted a handful of Turner's hair and slammed the back of his head into the door. Josie charged down the hallway, aiming her shoulder at Seth's hip. He took the impact of her body against his with a grunt, all of his focus still on Turner.

Noah was behind them now, reaching past Josie for one of Seth's arms. It slipped out of his reach. Josie reset herself, pivoting to the other side of his body. Between her and Noah, they would be able to subdue him.

But before they could take hold of him, Seth rammed Turner's head into the door again and it splintered right off its frame, buckling inward. The men tumbled over a concrete landing and down a set of stairs into darkness below. Josie heard the thuds of their bodies making contact with the steps, punctuated by grunts. Only a small portion of the door was still attached to the frame. Jagged edges poked out from its ruined remains.

Noah stepped past it onto the landing, pistol drawn. "Turner?"

Josie scanned the inside of the doorway. No light switches. No dangling cord or bulb over the landing. She followed Noah as he started down the steps. Her throat felt like it was closing up. She hated dark, enclosed spaces. Another remnant from her horrific childhood. She'd braved them before, but they always sent her to the edge of panic. Even now, she could barely hear, barely concentrate over the thundering of her own heartbeat.

To make sure she could still form words, she, too, called, "Turner?"

"Down here!"

She focused on Noah's back as her body automatically dropped into box breathing. There was a brief flash of light from the base of the steps which seemed a thousand miles away. Turner's phone screen. Not enough to illuminate anything, although he was pointing it away from the stairs.

"I need help," Turner said. "It's my knee. I can't see him. He's somewhere down here."

Keeping his eyes forward and pistol ready, Noah used one hand to pull his phone out of his back pocket. He shook it and Josie took it from him, quickly turning on the flashlight app and handing it to him so that he could light the way down. She did the same with her own phone, ignoring the vibration of terror in her hands as they descended deeper into inky darkness. To their right was a stone wall and to the left was a railing.

Turner found the flashlight app on his own phone and flicked it on, aiming the light to his left. Josie's eyes started to adjust to their lights, and every last bit of illumination felt like the air she needed to breathe as she and Noah reached the bottom. The unmistakable odor of human waste filled her nostrils. Under any other circumstances she might revel in the idea that perhaps Turner had lost control of his bodily functions, but every single cell in her body was screaming that something terrifying had happened in the bowels of this building.

Did the basement extend beneath the entire building?

The foul smell grew stronger, coating Josie's tongue and burning her eyes. She heard rustling. Turner's torch bobbed wildly. Her heart stopped for two beats before thundering back to life at a speed that was surely not tenable. She leaned to the side just far enough to see around Noah. Turner was on one knee. Just like the day at the stationhouse after he'd searched for his basketball under Mett's desk. His desk. Except now his face and shirt were covered in blood.

Noah said, "Can you get up?"

"I can't. I need someone to hold onto. Keep your eyes over there, LT." He nodded in the direction of his flashlight beam. There was only a dirt floor and then darkness. Seth Lee lurked somewhere beyond the reach of their lights, unless there was an alternate exit. "Quinn, you help me up."

Noah kept his gun trained on the dark area of the cellar,

panning with his flashlight. One of Turner's large hands
gripped Josie's hip. His weight tugged her downward, but she
maintained her balance. It took her a second to realize that he'd
used her belt to pull himself to standing. "Get ready," he said
softly. "Lights in three, two, one."

Josie was vaguely aware of the sound of a cord being pulled
and then a dull yellow glow filled the space. It took seconds for
her mind to work out that they were standing in a small room
that likely joined the rest of the basement via a door near the
back of the staircase. A door that was padlocked shut. Her eyes
followed the path of Noah's pistol, aimed at Seth Lee in the
farthest corner. He was on his knees, his back turned toward
them.

What was he doing?

Noah advanced on him. "Seth Lee. Stand up, put your
hands where I can see them, and turn around."

Seth stood, extending his hands up and over his shoulders
so they could see that they were empty.

Josie's eyes raked over the rest of the tableau in less than a
second. A five-gallon bucket, its sides streaked with something
dark. A pile of something congealed on the floor a few feet away
from it. Unidentifiable stains everywhere else. Vomit threatened
to rise to the back of Josie's throat, but she swallowed it down.
Clenching her jaw, she found the drawer in her mental vault
filled with things that tested her faith in humanity and shoved
the sights and scents of this dungeon deep inside, narrowing her
focus to Seth.

"That's good," Noah told him. "Turn around slowly."

Seth did as he was instructed. As Josie and Noah drew
closer, she saw that his eyes were filled with tears. Dirt covered
his palms. Had he been burying something or unearthing
something?

Noah said, "Turn around, nice and slow, and lace your
fingers behind your head."

"I'm sorry." His voice was surprisingly husky. "I never wanted her to get hurt. I didn't want this for her."

Noah repeated the instructions and this time Seth complied. She and Noah reached him at the same time, drawing his arms down behind his back and securing his wrists with zip ties. Josie recited his Miranda rights, but even after he verbally indicated that he understood them, he continued to talk, his voice strained and filled with what sounded like remorse. "I didn't want this to happen. I didn't want this to happen. I never wanted her to suffer. I didn't know when she was here... I didn't know."

He began to sob as Turner limped over and helped Noah guide him back up the steps. Josie holstered her pistol and walked along the edge of the room until she could see what had concerned Seth so much on the other side of the bucket. Something had been gouged into the floor and by the looks of it, Seth had been trying to erase it.

She took out her phone again and quickly found the flashlight app, aiming the beam at the floor. Josie felt a piece of her heart crack at exactly the same time that a swell of admiration filled her chest. Admiration and respect for the woman who had made sure to leave her mark on this black hellhole so indelibly that it could not be erased.

April Carlson had carved her name into the floor.

From the top of the steps, Seth howled, "I'm sorry!"

FIFTY-FIVE

I wait until we're all alone again and then I sneak back to her, mostly because I'm afraid maybe he did kill her. But she's still alive and I rub her back and stroke her hair like she always did to me.

"Rosie," she says. "You can't be here."

"No one else is here," I say. "It's okay. Are you hungry? I can find something. Everything here tastes bad, but I don't want you to look the same as Aunt April when Dad brought her here."

"Oh God." Tears spill from her eyes, and I wonder if I did something wrong. Then she says, "I'm so sorry you had to see her like that, honey. I didn't know. As soon as I found out, I told your father he needed to bring her to me, and he did, but then—"

I put my hand on top of her head and make a "shhh" noise like she used to do to me when I cried.

"Everything went wrong," she says, and she sounds like a squeaky toy.

I do the "shhh" thing again until she seems calmer.

"Rosie, listen to me." Her eyes are super serious. "This is

very important. I need you to really listen and do what I say. If you have a chance to leave here, I want you to do it. Get away. Run. Go to the police. They're not the people your dad thinks they are. They *will* help you. I *promise* that they will. You need to tell them everything you know, no matter what."

I nod and nod even though the things she's saying are making my heart feel like it's going too fast.

"Do you understand me?" she keeps going.

"Y-yes."

"And this is really important, too. If you have to, leave me here. It doesn't matter what happens to me, as long as you get away."

"No, I can't—"

We are looking at each other so hard and talking about so many important things that neither of us hears him. This time, he pulls my hair.

"What did I tell you would happen if you went near her again?"

FIFTY-SIX

Josie stood at the edge of the lot in front of Furnished Finds, right where it met the road. The toes of her boots rested on the yellow line. She'd been out here for almost three hours now and still couldn't get enough fresh air. Behind her, multiple emergency vehicles littered the gravel. Cruisers, Hummel's mobile ERT unit, an ambulance, and Gretchen's unmarked car. She had come as soon as she got word and was currently inside the building with Noah. Turner sat in the back of one of the ambulances, a large ice pack over his knee and gauze stuffed into both his nostrils.

The additional officers who had been called in had searched the entire building quickly and thoroughly before the ERT began to process the dank cell where April had spent the last year of her life.

Mira and Rosie Summers were not there.

A light breeze caressed Josie's face. She closed her eyes momentarily, breathing it in.

"Hey." Noah appeared behind her, resting a hand on her lower back. She resisted the very strong urge to melt against him. "Deirdre and Seth are being transported to holding cells.

We couldn't get anything out of either of them. Deirdre demanded an attorney pretty much from the moment I put the zip ties on her."

"Not surprising," Josie said. "She's a lot shrewder than we gave her credit for. I think maybe..."

Noah's hazel eyes appraised her. Gently, he tucked a stray strand of hair behind her ear. "You think what?"

"The things Seth said in the basement. He didn't want this to happen, he didn't know... he didn't want April to suffer. He wasn't the one who starved and tortured her. It was Deirdre."

Noah said, "When we brought Seth out, we walked him past her. She gave him this look and he—he was afraid. You could see it in him. Right after that, he asked for an attorney as well."

Josie massaged her sore shoulder. "Deirdre is calling the shots. I bet all the times he 'disappeared' over the years, from Mira, from his brother, he was here. She has some kind of hold on him. I don't think they ever really broke up. Maybe he's tried to escape her influence over the years. That's how he ended up with Mira."

"But Deirdre didn't want to let him go," Noah said. "He was hers first. You said that Deirdre wanted children, but Seth wouldn't give them to her."

"Yes. Then he went and had a child with another woman. I think Deirdre knew about Rosie all along. She was angry and hurt. She lost him to someone else. Maybe he never really wanted to stay with her, but he didn't feel like he could cut ties completely. Seth was just a kid when they met. He could have been impressionable and easily manipulated by her to the point where he felt trapped or obligated to her somehow. I'm sure his delusions didn't help matters. Oh shit."

Josie paused as another thought struck her. Seth kept coming back to Deirdre. A different person would have left her and never looked back once he felt the relationship no longer served him. Most people would. Breakups happened all the time.

"What is it?" asked Noah.

"What if Deirdre's been using Seth's own delusions to control him? All she would need to do is play into them. Amplify his fears. What better way to manipulate him? Noah, what if she weaponized his disorder and she's been wielding it against him and everyone he loves all this time?"

The strain on Noah's face told her that he thought her theory had some merit. "I think you need to see what we found inside."

Josie followed Noah back inside the store, through the showroom, past the sales desk to the hallway, which had been photographed. From the doorway that led to the basement, harsh bright light flared. The ERT had set up halogen lights down there to better document and process the scene. Josie suppressed a shiver. Not even the light from a thousand suns could drive away the darkness that stained that room. Near the back of the hall, Gretchen stood outside of a doorway. She stepped aside to let Josie pass.

Josie's heart did a double tap.

"What the hell is this?"

The room was closer to the back of the building. A row of clerestory windows ran along the top of the back wall, making the large room seem even bigger and airier than it already was. Unlike the depressing browns and whites of the rest of Furnished Finds, this room was painted an array of bright colors. It was like a giant classroom. A desk sat before a dry erase board. Behind it was a carpet bearing the alphabet. A bookshelf teemed with children's books.

Gretchen pointed to a standing partition at the far end. "On the other side of that is a bed. The comforter has pink unicorns on it."

Baskets of toys and stuffed animals dotted the room. A corkboard stood near a small table filled with all kinds of crafting supplies. It was lined with a child's drawings. Each one had a set of initials drawn in the bottom right-hand corner.

R.L.

Rosie Lee. Not Summers. In the house of Deirdre, the girl would use Seth's last name. How Deirdre must have resented Mira. What better way to get back at her and claim the family she had always wanted with Seth than to make a home here for Rosie? Josie wondered if, every time Seth seemed to drift back to Mira, taking Rosie with him, Deirdre manipulated him into returning so that she could keep the child she always wanted.

The child who was still out there somewhere with her real mother. Were they still alive?

Josie turned back toward Gretchen and Noah. Now Turner stood behind them. "Pretty creepy, huh, sweetheart?"

"We have to find them," Josie said.

FIFTY-SEVEN

For what felt like the hundredth time, Josie stood in front of the corkboard in the great room, staring at Rosie Summers's drawing. Behind her, Noah, Gretchen, and Turner sat quietly at their desks. Even Turner was still for once. No tapping fingers, no missed baskets. They were waiting for her to come up with some brilliant idea.

So was she.

Turner's voice was nasally from the broken nose Seth Lee had given him. He had at least gone home to change into a fresh suit. "If that's a map, it's not a map of that creepy furniture place."

Maybe she had been too focused on the idea that Rosie and April had always been in the same place. She had just assumed that wherever Seth went, so did April and Rosie, that he'd been carting April around like a piece of cargo.

Gretchen said, "Noah, did you get in touch with the attorney for Seth and Deirdre?"

"Yep. The DA talked to him as well. Offered them both the possibility of lesser charges for what they did to April if they told us where to find Rosie and Mira. Their lawyer strongly advised them to do it, but they're not talking."

Josie heard Turner shift the ice pack on his knee. "The kid is ten years old. What a couple of garbage humans."

Josie stepped forward and took down the photos of Seth and April as well as the registration document for the box truck, uncovering the pin marking the produce stand. If Josie was right, Mira Summers had been meeting Seth there so she could visit with Rosie. Mira's prints were all over the drawing that Rosie had made. The girl had given her mother a map. Not to find April—the sweet pea was nowhere on the drawing—but to find her. If Rosie was being kept at Furnished Finds, she could have just told Mira that.

Gretchen said, "There are a lot of garbage humans out there, Turner."

"Whoa, did you just call me Turner instead of jackass?"

Gretchen's chair creaked. "Don't get used to it, jackass."

Josie took down the photos of Mira and Rosie. She had their faces memorized.

If Rosie wasn't staying at Furnished Finds, that meant she was always with Seth—outdoors. If he was telling the truth about not knowing the full extent of April's condition because he had left her with Deirdre, was it possible that he had discovered how badly Deirdre had been treating April and then took her from there? Had he taken her to wherever he was keeping Rosie outdoors? Was that why she'd had mud and grass in her stomach at the time of her death? That had to be the reason she was covered in American burnweed flowers.

Josie removed the photo of the Post-it note April had given Mira and then the picture of the American burnweed fluff. Now only the drawing and the large map of Tranquil Trails remained. She took a few steps back, her eye catching on the pin marking where Mira had stopped after the stabbings.

Why did she stop for twenty-two minutes?

Josie traced a line from the pin—where she had pulled onto the side of the road—into the meadow and across until the map stopped at the riverbank. Shane Foster's body had been found about a mile upriver. Even if he'd been buried right on the side of the road, he couldn't possibly be the reason she stopped. Not for so long after she and April had both just been stabbed. Josie's finger trailed along the river toward the pin that marked the location of his remains.

She stopped halfway.

Her heart started hammering. She glanced from her finger to the drawing. The river. The drawing. She unpinned the drawing and brought it to the other side of the board, spinning it so it stood vertically.

Noah was beside her. "What do you see?"

Josie shook her head. "It was right here the entire time."

Gretchen's chair creaked and then she was on Josie's other side. Turner wheeled up behind them in his chair, balancing the bag of ice on his swollen knee. Noah stepped to the side so he could see the corkboard. Josie pointed to a place along the river bank opposite the Tranquil Trails property. "The river bends sharply here. Look at the bank."

It was a wide, flat area filled with trees. A small black square peeked out from the canopy. No bigger than a garden shed.

"This is all gone now," Josie said. "This shed is demolished. These trees are gone. I saw it from across the river when we were following Luke and Blue." She tapped the small light brown circles on the drawing. "These are the tree stumps. This weird gray thing that looks like a square teardrop? That's this shed."

"Holy shit," said Gretchen.

Noah touched the area on the map. "Plenty of room here for someone to park a truck. When the trees were still there, they probably hid it nicely."

Turner said, "I was there with you, Quinn. That whole area

is open. There's no way Mira and Rosie are just sitting over there."

"Not there," Josie said. She trailed her finger from the small black square representing the demolished shed, over the bank, and across a wide portion of water to an island in the middle of the river. It was one of those small rocky areas that rose up from the river in many places throughout the year. Most ended up submerged whenever the water levels rose. "Here. When we were out with Luke and Blue, I thought this was part of the bank where the shed is—that it was all one piece of land, sort of like a big peninsula reaching halfway across the water. Because of the bend in the river and where I was standing when I looked at it, I couldn't see that it wasn't part of the bank at all. It's actually an island in the middle of the river and it's directly across from the part of the bank with the destroyed shed and tree stumps."

With Rosie's drawing lined up next to the aerial view, it looked like a perfect match.

"Are you crazy, sweetheart?"

"But those islands aren't permanent," Noah said. "The majority of them aren't. They're subject to the water level, and a good deal of the time they're underwater."

Gretchen tapped her finger against the Google Maps view of the island. It was much smaller than what Josie had seen the other day. Then again, the Google Maps view was at least a year old. "That's exactly why it's the perfect place to hide. Plus, we're talking about Seth Lee here. It doesn't have to be permanent. It just has to be outdoors. Bonus if it's so close to his brother's place and somewhere he can keep an eye on the police officer he buried there."

Josie looked down at Turner. "Remember the river foam? We couldn't differentiate it from the other smells—"

"You mean the horseshit."

"But it has a distinct odor. I smelled it on April at the accident scene and again on Seth right before he attacked me in Mira's house. They're here. They're on the river but in a place no one would ever think to look."

Turner got closer, wedging himself between Josie and Noah. "How do they get onto it? They swim?"

Josie pointed at the drawing where the gray line connected the black and brown rings, which Josie was certain represented the island, and the area with the light brown circles. "They have something. They must have a boat or something—at least to get April over there—but maybe Seth had some kind of line rigged up so they could just pull themselves across. The point is I think this is where they are. Mira stopped here." Josie tapped the pin and then drew an imaginary line from it to the island. "Which lines up almost perfectly with the island. I think Rosie was still there. I don't think she was with Seth the day of the stabbing, but Mira had a map. She might have checked it out before, maybe waiting for her chance to get over there and get Rosie."

Noah said, "But she was losing blood and April was dying."

"And she had no way to cross the river," Gretchen added. "So she went back to the car."

"We know the rest," Turner said impatiently. "Let's get everyone we can find and get them out of there!"

FIFTY-EIGHT

Despite Turner's enthusiasm, he stayed behind at the stationhouse, nursing his leg, while Josie, Noah, and Gretchen headed out toward the riverbank with two ambulances just in case Rosie and Mira were injured. The police department didn't have its own Marine Unit, but the city's Emergency Services Department, well-equipped for carrying out flood rescues, had everything they needed. Within an hour, a city truck towing an inflatable rescue boat pulled onto the bank, skirting the demolished shed and tree stumps and jostling the eight-foot burnweed plants hard enough to send tufts of white flowers airborne all around them. For several minutes, it looked as if it was snowing. The clumps stuck to everyone's hair and clothes.

The emergency services crew set up on the bank, distributing life jackets to Josie, Noah and Gretchen. Josie had kept a careful eye on the island, hoping to glimpse Mira or Rosie or any movement, but there was nothing. A cold dread crept up her spine. Seth might have been an unwilling participant in some of Deirdre's crimes, but he had still shown himself capable of violence. Had he killed them and then hidden himself away at Furnished Finds?

"This won't take long," said Mitch Brownlow, tapping the side of his boat to indicate that they could get in. He was one of the city's longest-tenured and most experienced swiftwater rescue experts. His personality left something to be desired, but there was nowhere safer on the river than with him.

Josie didn't know the other guy working with Mitch, but he helped each one of them on board, starting with Noah. Josie went next, followed by Gretchen. Mitch smirked at her. "You're the one who turns green, aren't you?"

Gretchen tightened the straps of her life jacket as she settled in. "I promise to vomit over the side."

Moments later, the motor revved to life and Josie's body bounced against the side of the boat as Mitch steered them toward the small island. There was no time for Gretchen to get sick. The island was close enough that they probably could have swum across, if not for the current and the fact that they had to rescue two people whose conditions were unknown.

"We'll wait here," Mitch said as they hopped out.

They left their life jackets with him and picked their way across the rock-strewn ground. When they reached the tree line, Josie turned and looked at the riverbank. Now she had a wider view of it. There were their police vehicles; the Emergency Services Department vehicle; and the two ambulances. The remnants of the shed. The grove of tree stumps. Then a wall of burnweed and beyond that a cluster of tall, healthy trees, undisturbed by the clear-cutting and demolition. Among them, Josie spotted something metallic and blue. A car.

Gretchen walked past her and stumbled, the rocks under her feet shifting. Josie's hand shot out, grabbing her arm and keeping her upright. "Wait."

Noah and Gretchen turned. Josie pointed at the car.

Shading her eyes with one hand, Gretchen said, "Is that a Chevy Cavalier?"

Noah took a few steps to the side, trying to get a better angle. "This must be the 'auto repair shop' owned by Deirdre Velis's 'friend.'"

"Is Deirdre's Cavalier blue?"

A prickle of unease rippled across Josie's skin. "That's what the registration said."

Gretchen said, "Maybe Mira's not a victim. Maybe she's in on all of it. Unless Seth drove it here and left it, but that's a pretty long hike from here to Furnished Finds."

"No," Josie said. "I don't think Mira..." She trailed off. Again, there was that something fighting to break through the shadows in the back of her mind. What was it?

Noah picked his way back to her. "You don't think Mira what?"

Josie couldn't make the thoughts break through. "Never mind."

"Come on," Gretchen said.

Hand on her holster, Josie turned away from the bank and followed Gretchen into the trees. Noah took up the rear. The foliage was dense but the island itself wasn't very big. Even on this side, they could see slivers of the water and riverbank on the other side.

"Rosie? Mira?" Gretchen called.

Closer to the center of the island, the treetops formed a canopy, making the area feel dark and closed in. A flash of color to Josie's left stopped her in her tracks, but it was just a small jon boat.

"There's your way on and off the island," said Noah.

Except if it was here, that meant that whoever had come on it was still here. But it couldn't be Mira. Josie's gut told her that Mira was in just as much danger as April had been in, just as much as Rosie was in now.

But how was that possible?

"Rosie? Mira?" Gretchen called again. "Denton Police. We've come to get you out of here."

Over the rush of the current all around the island, Josie thought she heard a high-pitched sound, almost like a squeal, but it was muffled. The three of them froze, trying to figure out from which direction it had come. There was nothing around them but tall, narrow tree trunks and leafy branches.

Noah gave a signal for them to spread apart so they could cover more ground and have a better chance of spotting any potential threats.

"Rosie?" Josie called. "Mira? You're safe now. We're going to take you home."

The squeal came again and then a figure came crashing through the trees from Gretchen's side. Before she could think rationally, Josie's hand unsnapped her holster and drew her weapon. She swung it toward the sound of labored breath and pounding feet just as a girl flew into the open and right into Gretchen's arms. Staggering backward, Gretchen nearly fell. The rocks beneath her feet shifted as she worked to get her balance with Rosie Summers wrapped around her body. Noah quickly moved past Josie, tapping lightly against her elbow, indicating she should holster her weapon. Gretchen was still flailing with Rosie clinging to her like a barnacle. Noah gripped Gretchen's shoulders and held on until she had her footing.

The girl was taller than Josie had expected and, thank God, at a healthy weight. Her brown curls hung down her back, tangled and dotted with leaves and sticks. Purple leggings, striped with dirt, hugged her legs, and the back of her gray T-shirt showed a few small holes near the bottom.

Josie holstered her pistol but the relief she expected to overwhelm her didn't come. Something was off. What was she missing? Her mind worked backward through the case: the long days, the endless dead ends and leads, the small details that her

brain had logged even though they seemed completely mean-
ingless.

Noah took a few steps in the direction that Rosie had come,
peering through the trees. Gretchen gripped Rosie's shoulders
and pushed gently, making space between them so that they
could see her face. Her skin was cleaner than her clothes, but
her eyes were wide with wonderment and fear. "You came!" she
whispered.

Something about the sales desk at Furnished Finds. The
initials on the drawings in the freaky romper room—R.L. Josie
went back further. Mira's house. The roses. SORRY. The two
coffee mugs. Mira had had coffee with someone and then left,
only to be abducted by Seth in the white truck moments later.
But then he had come back.

But had he come *back*?

Gretchen smiled down at Rosie. "Yes, we came. I'm Detective Gretchen Palmer, that's Lieutenant Fraley, and this is
Detective Josie Quinn. We're going to get you out of here."

Josie's mind went back to the roses. SORRY. The two coffee
mugs. A napkin next to one of them with a spoon tucked inside
it. The napkin. The spoon. The roses. The sales desk at
Furnished Finds. R.L.

Rosie looked over her shoulder, where Noah was about to
disappear between two tree trunks. "Don't go that way!" she
said. "Take me the way you came from. We have to hurry. It's
not safe."

Josie's eyes searched all around them but saw nothing. Her
mind was still working at breakneck speed. There had been an
empty coffee mug along the back portion of the sales desk at
Furnished Finds and next to it, a napkin with a spoon folded
inside of it. All those drawings in the creepy room signed R.L.
Some of them old and faded, the skill level much more
advanced than Rosie. No drawings of roses. Josie hadn't given it
any thought at the time.

Noah stopped walking and turned back toward them, smiling. "You're safe now, Rosie. It's okay."

Gretchen gave her shoulders a light squeeze. "You and your mom are both safe. We're here to take her back, too. Can you take us to her?"

A teenage boy had brought Mira roses. They hadn't found the florist he worked for because he didn't work for a florist. You could buy a dozen roses at a supermarket. He had delivered them and stayed for coffee. He was driving the truck. That was how Seth was able to abduct Mira and then return so quickly to search her house. Because Seth hadn't been there earlier.

It was the boy.

Rosie's bottom lip quivered. She dropped into a whisper again. "I can't. It's not safe. She told me to save myself."

Noah's brow furrowed. He took a couple of steps back toward Gretchen and Rosie. "You don't need to save yourself. We're here for both of you."

It was the boy.

That's how the truck ended up behind the boardinghouse with the room never used by Seth but stocked with prepackaged food. So uncharacteristic of Seth. Because it was the boy. In the office of the boardinghouse, Ryan Tramel had stirred his drink with a spoon and then placed it between the folds of a napkin.

Not Ryan Tramel.

R.L.

Not Rosie Lee.

Ryan Lee.

Rosie pulled away from Gretchen but kept hold of her hand. "Come on. Please. There's a boat. I'll show you."

Carol Summers had told them that Mira disappeared for four years after meeting Seth when she was just eighteen. More than enough time to bring a pregnancy to term and give birth. Enough time to care for a baby until he was a toddler. Then one day his father disappeared with him. The cycle began. Mira stayed with Seth long enough to have Rosie because she was already tethered to him by Ryan. Always waiting for her child's return, always searching for him, always hoping that one day she could be the mother she wanted to be, never knowing that Seth had turned that privilege over to Deirdre Velis.

Gretchen said, "Rosie, we have our own boat. We need to get your mother."

Mira had been so young. Only eighteen or nineteen. She had truly been at Seth's mercy—or rather, Deirdre's, by proxy. Ryan must have grown up largely separated from her, bonding more with Seth and Deirdre. He probably spent almost all of his time with Seth. Was he there the day of the stabbing?

Rosie pulled on Gretchen's wrist with all her might. "Please. We have to go now. He'll kill her and you!"

If Seth had removed April from the Furnished Finds cellar and brought her to the produce stand where he knew he was going to meet Mira, had he intended to free her? To turn her over to Mira? But why give her up after a year? It made no sense. Why the sudden change of heart? Why suddenly risk both Mira and April turning him in? Unless...

What had Seth said when they'd arrested him? *I didn't want this for her. I didn't know.*

He didn't know she was there. At least, not right away. When Seth left Hillcrest after April's call to DHS, he had wanted to get away from her and protect Rosie. He already had the death of Shane Foster to hold over April's head, to keep her in check.

Gretchen said, "Rosie, no one is going to hurt you or your mother."

I never wanted this to happen. I never wanted her to suffer. But April was still looking for him and Rosie. Seth may have thought that their assured mutual destruction status meant she wasn't a threat but Deirdre or Ryan—or both—may have felt otherwise. Mira had been ineffectual as a girlfriend to Seth and a mother to Ryan and Rosie. Neither Deirdre nor Ryan need concern themselves with her, but April could blow up all their lives.

"He's going to kill everyone!" Rosie keened.

It was Ryan who had harassed April and vandalized her home in Newsham. He was the one telling her to stay away. That's why she'd reported it to the police. She had told them it was a case of mistaken identity. Maybe Mira had never told April about Ryan.

It was Ryan who took April, whether of his own volition or at Deirdre's direction, and then Seth found out later. Mira convinced him to free her. They'd met at the produce stand.

Noah said, "Rosie, no one is going to be killed."

Josie tried to imagine Mira's distress when she saw how badly April's health had deteriorated. It wasn't a simple matter of nursing her back to health. Had Mira and Seth argued? But if Seth hadn't meant for April to be harmed and had intended to return her to Mira, why would he stab her and then Mira when she came to her defense?

Josie felt that uncomfortable ripple across her skin again. Trepidation. From the beginning she had wondered why Seth would let Mira and April drive away from the scene of the attack without finishing what he started. But there was that unknown set of fingerprints on the awl. Although the tool had certainly come from Furnished Finds, the unknown prints didn't belong to Deirdre. She had a conviction for passing bad checks. She would have shown up in AFIS.

But Ryan Lee's prints wouldn't be on record anywhere.

"Rosie, we have your father in custody now," said Noah. "He's in jail. He won't get out for a very long time. He can't hurt anyone now."

Seth let Mira drive away with April because he was more worried about getting Ryan out of there. Protecting his son. He didn't want the authorities to take his children away.

Rosie looked up at Noah as if he'd grown two heads. "Not my dad. My brother."

Josie rushed toward them, stumbling over more rocks. "It's Ryan," she said. "The teenager from the boardinghouse. Gretchen wasn't there that day but—"

Before she could finish, a soul-rending scream ripped through the air.

FIFTY-NINE

Rosie began to scream. Another scream from elsewhere on the island joined in until it sounded like they were standing in some kind of echo chamber of terror. Over the din, Noah shouted to Gretchen, "Get her back to the boat and off this island. Now."

Gretchen didn't hesitate. She squeezed Rosie's hand tightly and dragged her away.

As her shrieks receded, Josie and Noah drew their weapons, holding them in compressed ready positions so that they could better thread their way through the densely packed tree trunks. They spread apart and let their steps be guided by the melee. Those howls could only be coming from Mira Summers, and as long as she was screeching loudly enough to raise the hairs on Josie's arms, she was still alive.

No sooner was the thought alive in Josie's mind, Mira's voice cut off, leaving them in silence. They froze, listening. Something up ahead was moving. Noah caught Josie's gaze and signaled for them to keep moving. From her periphery, Josie saw something flying toward Noah. She opened her mouth to warn him, but it was too late. A large rock sailed through the air and straight at his face. Noah feinted and pivoted. The rock grazed his shoulder. Then came another. He dodged that one as well. Josie kept moving, circling around to where the barrage came from.

Noah called out, "Ryan, I know it's you! Come out with your hands up. We've got your dad and Deirdre in custody. It's over."

Another rock streaked past Josie's face this time, the breeze in its wake brushing her cheek.

"Why is this kid throwing rocks?" Noah grumbled.

"He's desperate."

Josie had met many souls at their most desperate. They were often wild and irrational. It never ended well. In this case, Ryan was cornered. There was nowhere for him to go unless he intended to jump in the river.

"Ryan!" she shouted. "We don't want anyone else to get hurt. Stop throwing rocks and show yourself. Hands up."

With the stones focused on Josie now, Noah moved more quickly, trying to gain ground. Josie could sense his progress, but she kept her focus on the trees ahead, trying to catch a glimpse of Ryan.

"We just want to talk, kid," Noah yelled.

They were getting closer. The sound of Mira's voice, so close but just a rasp, begging Ryan to stop, sent a surge of both hope and fear through Josie's veins. She picked up her pace. Then a rock smashed into her ankle, sending her flying sideways into a tree. She managed to stay upright, pushing off the thin tree trunk and back into pursuit. Pain bloomed in her ankle, but she ignored it, catching up with Noah just as they emerged into a muddy clearing. Josie's brain registered the details in a heartbeat. Four tents. Rusted outdoor chairs. Camping equipment. A ring of stones filled with ash.

Ryan stood about twenty feet away. He held Mira pinned against him, one arm wrapped across her chest while he pressed a knife into her throat. Her wrists were bound with nylon rope, but her fingers dug into his forearm as she struggled to stay upright. More rope was wrapped tightly around her ankles. In addition to the large bruise that stretched across her forehead, a long gash split her cheek. "Sss—top," she begged.

Josie found herself standing directly in front of them. "Drop the knife. Let her go and put your hands up."

Ryan's gaze darted from her to Noah and back. "No. No. Where's my dad? What did you do to him?"

There was no way that Josie could take a shot at Ryan without hitting Mira, not from her position. She was a good shot, but it was too risky. From the corner of her eye, she saw Noah moving toward Ryan's knife side, angling himself so that he could see as much of Ryan's body as possible.

"Please, please," Mira gasped. Her body sagged. Ryan's arm tightened around her.

"Shut up," he told her.

Josie's heart thudded in her chest. She dropped her pistol into a low ready position, resting her forearms against her hips with the barrel pointed toward the ground, at an angle. It would be easy enough to raise it again should she need to take a shot, but it would also make her seem less threatening to Ryan. She hoped. To keep his attention on her and not Noah, who now had his gun aimed at the kid's rib cage, she said, "Your dad is fine. He's in our custody but he hasn't been harmed in any way."

She didn't mention the scuffle with Turner, especially since Turner had gotten the worst of it.

"He didn't do anything wrong," Ryan blurted. "Let him go and I won't kill her."

Mira tried to yank down on his arm, but he was stronger than her and he hadn't been stabbed, injured in a car accident, and abducted all in the last week. "Ryan, please. Stop this. It's enough. Your dad needs help and so do you."

The knife scraped against her throat as he hoisted her up,

trying to hold her nearly dead weight. "He doesn't need help," Ryan spat. "He needs someone to look out for him. That's what I do. We were fine until you and that bitch April started nosing into things. You ruined everything."

"Ryan," Josie said, voice firm and loud. "We cannot bring your father here to you but I'm sure that we can arrange for you to see him. We can show you that he's fine, but you need to let Mira go. Drop the knife. Put your hands up."

"I was trying to do the right thing," Mira said. "You deserved better. You and Rosie. I'm sorry I failed you when you were a baby. I was your age back then! I had no idea what I was doing, and then he took you—"

Ryan's knife hand dropped slightly, putting space between the blade and Mira's skin. "You're not my mother. You were never my mother. Dee is my mother. You gave me up and she took me in."

"I never wanted that!" Mira cried. As her body sagged again, the knife fell to her collarbone. If she fell or if he dropped her, Josie would have a shot at his center mass. It would still be risky. "I didn't even know you were with her until you were Rosie's age! He took you away! He always took you away! If I had known where to look, I would have come for you."

"Bullshit." Ryan's voice was thick with emotion. His eyes grew glassy with unshed tears.

Josie softened her tone. "Ryan, let Mira go. Nobody here wants your dad to be harmed. We're all here because we care about Rosie and about you. We can talk about everything, but not here, not like this. Drop the knife."

Noah's pistol was still aimed at Ryan's rib cage. From where he stood, Josie could see that he didn't have a clear shot at Ryan's shoulder, which might loosen his grip on the knife and get him to drop it. He might have a shot at Ryan's armpit, but it would likely nick his heart and he would bleed out in minutes, if not seconds. It was how Mettner had died.

Josie pushed that thought deep down.

But they had to do everything they could to protect Mira in this situation. Josie hoped that wouldn't mean one of them shooting an eighteen-year-old kid. She knew Noah was keeping quiet so as not to draw attention to himself. Ideally, Josie could talk the kid down and no one would get hurt.

Ryan lowered his mouth to Mira's ear. "You did find out though. You found out about Dee, and you never came. You only cared about Rosie. You were going to take her from us. We were a family until you and that bitch, April, started screwing everything up."

"N-not true," Mira huffed as the arm crossing her chest crushed her against his body. "Dee is not your family, Ryan. She's crazy. What she did to April—"

He needled the skin of her throat with the point of the knife. "April was going to take Rosie and then send Dad to prison. We had to do something. We had to protect him."

A drop of blood slid down Mira's neck. "Dee was never trying to protect your father, or you. She just wanted to be in control. She wanted the family I gave him for herself. Couldn't you see what she did to your father? How she twisted everything in his mind? How she got him so worked up and so panicked that he did everything she said? He was so much worse with her."

"You're wrong. She told me how you stole Dad from her, how you tried year after year to keep him—and me—away from her. When it didn't work, you got your sister involved. You're nothing but a selfish bitch." Sensing a shift in Ryan's tone, from a frightened little boy to a vengeful man, Josie shouted at him again. "Put the knife down now."

Mira squeaked, "I'm sorry."

"Drop the knife, Ryan!" Josie hollered again.

Ryan wasn't listening to her. He pressed the knife's blade across Mira's throat. Her skin was already raw and pink from the constant jostling of his body and more blood leaked from where he'd pierced the skin earlier. Mira's eyes bulged. Josie yelled for him to stop.

A gunshot boomed. Noah.

Ryan's body bucked, the round hitting him in the side, near the bottom of his rib cage. He stumbled backward. The arm holding the blade dropped, the knife falling to the mud near his feet. Mira gave another tug at the arm that held her against him. It gave way, and she sank to the ground, her bound hands reaching for her throat. As Josie rushed forward, holstering her gun, she was relieved to see that the blood wasn't gushing through Mira's fingers. Ryan went down, legs crumpling. Noah was already at his side, making sure the knife was well out of reach. Holstering his weapon, he stripped off his polo shirt and pressed it to Ryan's side, trying to stem the flow.

Josie radioed for help as she joined Noah on the other side of Ryan's body.

On her knees, Mira tried to lurch toward them, but it was impossible with her feet tied. She fell forward, her dirt-covered, gauze-wrapped forearms taking the brunt. A shriek of pain ripped from her body.

Ryan's face was sickeningly pale, his lips leached of all color. He tried to speak.

"Don't try to talk, kid," Noah said. "Your lung is probably punctured. We've got ambulances on the shore. They'll be here soon and then we'll get you off this island and to a hospital."

Whether they would attempt to transfer him by boat or have to call in Life Flight was another story. If the paramedics could stabilize him long enough, he could be airlifted.

Noah met Josie's eyes briefly. In them, she saw everything. His cool, calm demeanor and, behind that, what it cost him to have to shoot someone. He said, "Get Mira out of here."

Josie got to her feet and spun in Mira's direction. Gently, she turned Mira onto her back. The wound on her throat was superficial. Josie started at Mira's ankles, working at the rope until she had it untied. Then she moved to Mira's wrists.

From the trees, Josie heard shouting, followed by footsteps moving swiftly toward them. Relief coursed through her. Chancing a glance at Noah and Ryan, she saw that the kid was hanging on, Noah bent to his face, speaking softly and rapidly.

Mira's wrists came loose, and her upper body sprang up. Her eyes were wide and hopeful. "Rosie?"

"She's safe."

Mira threw her arms around Josie, her entire body shaking with sobs. "Thank you," she said, again and again. "Thank you."

SIXTY

Josie threw her forearm up over her eyes as the Life Flight helicopter kicked up dirt, leaves, and American burnweed fluff. Debris whirled around them as it took off from the edge of the island, carrying Ryan to Geisinger Medical Center in Danville. It was too soon to tell whether or not he would survive. She watched as, across the river, Noah emerged from the trees. His white T-shirt and pants were covered in Ryan's blood. He looked haggard as he hopped into Mitch Brownlow's boat for the short ride back to the bank.

As the noise of the copter's rotors faded, Josie could hear Mira speaking to Rosie. The two of them were huddled in the back of one of the ambulances, waiting to be transported to Denton Memorial to be checked out.

"I don't want you to leave," Rosie cried.

"I'm so sorry, honey. I don't want to leave either, but I will have to. I've done some bad things and now I have to be held accountable."

Josie turned and studied them. Mira was sitting upright on the gurney. Somehow, Rosie had managed to fit her body onto the bed as well. Rosie gazed up at her mother with adoration and fear. "What does that mean? Accountable?"

Mira stroked her hair out of her face. "It means that when you do something bad, like break a law, you have to face the consequences—the things that happen when you break laws."

Rosie whispered, "Like go to prison?"

A tear rolled down Mira's face. "Yes, honey. I'm so sorry. But you will be safe. I promise. There is someone I have in mind to take care of you, and you'll love her."

Rosie clutched at Mira's waist. "No. I don't want someone else. I want you."

Mira squeezed the girl and stroked her hair until Rosie fell asleep, the events of the day too much for her.

Josie walked over and stood at the back doors. "We're going to get you out of here soon."

Mira nodded. "Will you call Rebecca? See if she'll speak with me? With both me and Seth in prison, she's the closest family. I don't want my mother involved in Rosie's life. Not that she would agree to it."

Josie had a feeling that in spite of Rebecca's strong negative feelings toward Seth, she wouldn't hesitate to take in Rosie. "Of course."

She started to walk away. Noah was almost to the bank.

Mira said, "I'm sorry for all this. You probably want to know—"

Turning, Josie held up a hand. "Mira, we're going to need to talk to you at some point to close out our investigation, but it doesn't have to be now."

"But I—"

"I'll need to read your Miranda rights," Josie said.

Although Mira was a victim, Josie was guessing that the District Attorney would want to press charges against her for not telling the police about Seth right away. Then there was the Shane Foster matter, but that was out of Josie's jurisdiction.

Mira squeezed Rosie more tightly against her body, like she might never get a chance to hold her again. "Go ahead."

Josie recited her Miranda rights. When she asked Mira if she understood them, Mira answered yes. Then she sighed. "Everything I said back there was true. I was practically a baby when I met Seth. I fell hard for him. By the time I got pregnant with Ryan, I started noticing that he would act strangely sometimes, become fixated on odd things. I went along with it because I loved him. I loved him so much, and we were having this baby. But his suspicions got so much worse. He was convinced that some authorities somewhere were tracking him, and they were going to take Ryan."

"Those were delusions," Josie said. "From what I understand."

Mira nodded. "I didn't understand at the time. I honestly thought we could have a real family life. Maybe we could have. I always wanted the opposite of what my parents had, and we might have been able to do it except that then he disappeared with Ryan. I saw him again when he was about five years old but then I didn't see him again until he was ten years old. By that time, I had Rosie and I was so afraid he'd take her from me, too. Permanently."

"You didn't talk with police?" asked Josie. "Try to petition for custody?"

Tears streamed down Mira's battered face. "I wanted to but I was broke and terrified. I had no support system. My parents were horrible. Once, I went to the police station and talked to the officer at the front desk, trying to explain to him that Seth had taken my son and I couldn't find them. He never even wrote anything down. Said it was a matter for the courts, not the police, because we were both on Ryan's birth certificate and there was no custody order in effect for the police to enforce."

Sadly, Josie knew this was true. Technically, Seth hadn't done anything wrong by leaving with Ryan. Had Mira sued him for custody later, the fact that he had disappeared and kept Ryan from her would have counted against him, but that would have been of no help to her when she was trying to locate them.

Mira sucked in a shaky breath and continued. "There was a time that I threatened to sue Seth for custody. I wasn't sure how I'd do it, but I thought I'd figure it out. The next time he came back without Ryan, I threatened him. That was the first time he ever laid a hand on me in anger. It was terrifying. He said I would never see Ryan or him again if I tried anything like that. Then he kept Ryan from me for five years. I was in so deep I couldn't see a way out. I was completely focused on just trying to keep Seth with me as much as possible and hope that he would let me see Ryan again. I never knew where he kept him. There were times I tried to follow him but eventually I'd lose him. Then one day he caught me. He beat me badly that time. Then he said that if I ever tried to follow him again, I wouldn't see my son for the rest of my life. Sometimes—" She broke off, stifling a sob. Rosie stirred in her arms but didn't wake. "Sometimes I worried he was dead."

"He was with Deirdre Velis," Josie said. "Here in Denton. Seth's ex-girlfriend."

"When I finally got to see Ryan again—when he was ten—he told me that I wasn't his mother. A woman he called Dee was his mother. Neither he nor Seth would tell me anything about her. All I knew was that her name was Dee. Seth swore they weren't in a romantic relationship but now, looking back, I think Deirdre and I were always in a battle for Seth, and for Ryan, without ever having met."

"Rosie never met her?" Josie asked. She took a quick glance over her shoulder. Noah was on the bank now, talking with Gretchen.

"If she did, she was too young to remember," Mira said. "Or she hasn't told me. I don't know. But Rosie is all mine." She looked down at Rosie's sleeping face and touched her cheek.

"Seth gave you access to Rosie?" asked Josie.

"I was with her almost all the time until she went to school. I couldn't believe that I got Seth to agree to put her in school. April helped with that, and I promised to make sure she only ate things he approved. He took her away a few times when she was a toddler but never for more than a few weeks. I lived in absolute terror that he would take her away completely like he did with Ryan."

Josie's ankle started to throb from standing on it so long. She knew it wasn't broken but it was going to take a week or two for it to stop hurting. "After April called DHS, that's what he did, didn't he?"

Mira sniffled. "Yes. In hindsight, she was right to call but I lost Rosie because of it. April stopped speaking to me altogether. I always knew she thought I was sad because of the way things were with Seth and Rosie, but we were starting to become friends. She fell in love with Rosie in a hot second. She only talked to me twice after Seth took Rosie."

"You never told her about Ryan?"

Mira looked at her feet. "No. I was too embarrassed. Besides, his whole life, I'd only seen him a couple of times. He was never really mine."

"When April spoke with you after Seth took Rosie from Hillcrest, it was about Shane Foster, wasn't it?" asked Josie. "Were you there the night he died?"

Mira shook her head, still not meeting Josie's gaze. "No. They told me afterward. Seth asked her to bring Shane to the park so she could prove to him that she hadn't ratted Seth out. Her dating a police officer? The worst possible thing, in Seth's mind. He thought if April just introduced him as her sister's boyfriend, they could have a beer on the lake and he could figure out what Shane knew. Things didn't go so well. Shane pretty much immediately knew that something was off. April was too scared, and she couldn't hide it. There was some kind of argument. Seth got into his truck to leave but instead, he tried to run both Shane and April down. She managed to get out of the way but Shane didn't."

"April was too frightened of Seth to tell," Josie filled in.

"Seth made her go with him to bury Shane. Right after it happened, she was in such shock that she wasn't thinking straight. Seth had just tried to kill her, too. She blacked out. She didn't even know where Seth had taken them. She said that one minute she was standing near the lake while Shane and Seth argued and the next, she was in the pitch-black woods helping Seth roll Shane's lifeless body into a grave. By the time they got back, she thought she was in too deep. She'd gone too far. She hadn't tried to get away from Seth at any point during the drive, even when they stopped for gas. Seth convinced her she'd go to prison, lose her teaching license, and worst of all, no one would ever see Rosie again. I heard the same story from them both, and I didn't tell either."

A truck roared to life nearby. Mitch leaving with his boat now that his work was done. Josie picked pieces of burnweed from her shirt. Mira's admission that she'd known about Shane Foster's fate and not told the authorities would most definitely result in charges.

As if reading Josie's mind, she said, "I confess. Whatever happens to me now, I don't care. Rosie is safe."

"You said you spoke to April twice after she called DHS."

Mira ran a hand up and down Rosie's arm. "The second time was when she came to me before I moved here and said she had paid for an online background check on Seth. It said he had a brother—Jon—and she thought if I came to Denton and talked to Jon, I'd be able to find Rosie."

"Was that when she gave you the brochure?"

Mira's eyes widened in surprise. "Um, no. Not then. But wait, you found that? Under the drawer?"

"Your cat wasn't exactly happy about us removing it from the cabinet, but yeah."

"That's why it was under there," Mira said. "My cat doesn't let anyone in that cabinet where I keep her food."

Josie shifted her weight again as the throb in her ankle worsened. "April approached you while you were still living in Hillcrest and told you that Seth's brother lived in Denton, but that's not when she gave you the brochure?"

"No. All I knew when I moved here was that Seth had a brother named Jon. I found Tranquil Trails and enrolled there. I didn't know what kind of relationship that Seth had with his brother, if any, and I didn't want Jon scaring Seth off by telling him I was there, so I didn't tell anyone I knew Seth. I just became a client and hoped I'd make contact with him at some point. It was the only lead I had to find Rosie."

"When did April give you the brochure?" Josie asked.

"Not for a long time. About a year after I moved here, she came to the insurance firm where I worked. I don't know how she found out I worked there but she showed up one day. Acted like she wanted to buy insurance. I pretended to do intake. She never purchased any plans. I had no idea she'd just moved to Newsham."

The visit to the insurance firm in Denton might have shown up on April's GPS when Heather conducted her investigation, but it wouldn't have sent up any red flags. Insurance was something most people bought, and since April hadn't bought any plans from that office, there would have been no reason to even look into it.

Mira sighed. "April was a mess."

"In what way?" asked Josie.

"She was consumed with guilt about Shane. She wanted to tell but she didn't want to go to prison. Also, she wasn't entirely sure where she and Seth had buried him. It was the middle of the night when they did it and like I said, she had kind of blacked out. But she was convinced it was somewhere on his brother's property. She wanted to confess everything to the police and tell them to search Tranquil Trails."

"But there was still the matter of Rosie," Josie pointed out.

Mira touched the crown of her daughter's head with a feather-light touch. "Yes. April still wanted to find Rosie, but she was afraid that Seth would kill her if he felt backed into a corner. Neither of us trusted the police to find them. No offense. At that point, I still hadn't made contact with Seth. I convinced April that us going to the police about Shane would only ruin our lives and any chance we had of finding Rosie. I told her that Seth had help from another woman but I didn't tell her about Ryan. I begged her to give it more time. We wanted to find a way to get Rosie away from Seth without both of us going to prison. We just didn't know how."

From her periphery, Josie saw that Noah and Gretchen had moved within earshot. "That's when she gave you the brochure with the note?"

"No. A few months later, she left that envelope for me at the firm. She was getting impatient. I think the guilt was eating her alive. It was her way of telling me she was sure that Shane was buried at Tranquil Trails and that we needed to just tell the authorities."

"She didn't want to try to find Rosie first anymore," Josie said.

"I don't know, but that's the impression I got. By that time, I had started having regular visits with Seth, Rosie, and Ryan at Tranquil Trails, trying to build trust with them. I was trying to figure out a way to get Rosie from Seth. I had saved money. I was going to sue for custody. I wasn't there the night Shane died so I was banking on the fact that Seth wouldn't play that card. But Ryan had become so angry. I was more afraid of him than Seth. Every time Seth would seem open to me taking Rosie off his hands, the next week he'd come back and have changed his mind. Like someone was talking him out of it. Ryan, or that other woman, I don't know. I tried looking April up so I could tell her my plan, but she'd already been abducted."

"You had no idea that Ryan had taken her?" Josie said.

"Not at first, but then I realized that I had once told Rosie that when I finally came for her, she could see Aunt April again, too, because she lived nearby. Apparently, Rosie let that slip but when I confronted Seth, he had no idea what I was talking about. I accused him of abducting her. He was mystified."

"Because Rosie didn't let it slip to Seth," Josie said. "She told Ryan."

A tear slid down Mira's face. "Yes. The next week, Rosie told me that she'd heard Seth and Ryan arguing about April. Seth kept saying Ryan did a bad thing and had to let her go. I confronted them both, right then and there. I told them I was going to turn Ryan in, call the police, and, well..." She looked away. "Ryan came after me. He wanted to kill me. He only ever cared about protecting his father. Seth got him to calm down, barely. I lied to them both and said if they returned April to me, only me, I wouldn't tell and that I had enough influence over her to convince her not to tell, either. I mean, she hadn't told about Shane. They bought it. But then when they brought her, and I saw the condition..."

A sob rose in Mira's throat. She pressed a hand to her mouth. Rosie shifted but still didn't wake.

Josie was aware of the EMTs approaching. "Ryan stabbed you both."

Mira nodded. "When I saw her, I—I wasn't prepared for it. I got so upset. I started screaming at Ryan. How could he have done this to her? Then I yelled at Seth. How could he have allowed this to happen? What kind of son did he raise? At that point, Ryan decided our deal was off. He wasn't giving April back. She must have heard him because she made a run for it. Well, she tried. She could barely walk. It must have used up everything in her to take those last steps. Ryan went after her. He was just in a rage. He had that thing in his hand. I tried to stop him. I mean, there was no way that April was a threat, but he just went nuts. Seth finally pulled him away but by then it was too late. He was more worried about getting Ryan out of there than about us."

"You put April in the car and then you stopped to try to get Rosie."

More tears streamed down her cheeks. "She'd drawn me the map a few weeks earlier. They hadn't been there long, but she'd explained to me as best she could where they were. I'd already checked it out. But when I pulled over, I was so dizzy and there was so much blood. I knew I couldn't go all the way down to the shore, swim there and swim back with Rosie. April was dying. Then there was the accident and... I'm sorry I lied to you."

"You knew where Rosie was when we spoke with you in the hospital," Josie pointed out. "We could have rescued her that day."

An EMT climbed into the bay and started checking Mira's vitals. Sawyer touched Josie's shoulder as he followed his colleague. They started discussing whether or not they should put Rosie in the other ambulance.

Mira's attention was still focused on Josie. She gave a bitter laugh. "Any other day in the history of knowing Seth, he would have immediately come back here, picked Rosie up, and left. I never thought, in a million years, he would stay here. I thought they had left. The next day, Ryan followed me from Bobbi's house to mine. Brought me flowers, as if that could make up for what he'd done. He's really sick. I think that woman twisted him up worse than she did Seth. He wasn't sorry. He just wanted to make sure I wasn't going to turn him in. He told me Seth and Rosie were gone and if I wanted to keep Rosie alive, I'd keep my mouth shut. I promised I would but I guess he didn't believe me because no sooner had I left my house, he came by with the truck and snatched me off the street."

"Leave the girl," Sawyer told his colleague. "Let's just go."

The other EMT began checking that both patients were secure on the gurney. Mira took one last look at Josie. "Thank you for saving my Rosie."

Josie nodded and stepped away from the back of the ambulance. Sawyer gave her a mock salute as he pulled the doors closed. "Until next time," he said.

No, she thought. Next time wasn't going to be like this. She'd get him to come to dinner instead. They were family, sort of.

As she watched the ambulance pull away, the weight of the case and its sheer horror pressed down on her. Then Noah's hand swept across her back, his touch an instant relief from the sadness and tension of the day. "Let's go home," he said.

SIXTY-ONE

Noah's voice floated from the laundry room into the kitchen. From where she stood at the stove, Josie could see his profile as he threw a load of wet clothes into the dryer. "Did you talk to your sister?" he called.

"Yes. Did you?"

Noah laughed. "Yes. She can't keep a secret."

Josie smiled to herself as she watched the potatoes boil. Trinity had been absolutely giddy when they spoke.

"She told you why your parents wanted to have this family dinner tonight?" Noah said. She heard him twisting dials on the dryer.

"Yeah." Trinity had, in fact, told Josie the moment she found out the big news. Their parents, Shannon and Christian Payne, were moving to Denton. If they were going to be grandparents—assuming Josie and Noah would be approved to adopt—they wanted to be nearby. Trinity said they were going to announce it at dinner that evening. The prospect filled Josie with joy and a strange sort of nervousness. What if they didn't get approved to adopt? What if they did, but didn't match? Or took years to match? Their home study had been rescheduled three weeks from now, but that didn't make Josie any less nervous.

"We have to act surprised," Josie called back.

She turned off the burner and carried the pot to the sink where she attempted to empty the water but leave the potatoes using the lid as only a partial cover. A searing pain slashed across the tops of her fingers. With a yelp, she dropped the pot of still boiling water into the sink. Wedges of soft potatoes tumbled out. The glass lid clattered into the basin as well. Sizzling liquid splashed upward. With another cry, Josie jumped back, grateful that none of it was able to reach her. Near the back door, Trout jumped to his feet and started barking. He frequently barked whenever Josie was agitated or hurt or startled. He didn't know what was happening, he just knew that something with her wasn't right.

Josie rested her burned fingers in the other palm, wincing at the pain that grew in intensity with every second. "It's okay, buddy," she told Trout, but he didn't believe her. He was still barking when Noah rushed into the kitchen, looking from Josie to Trout and back to Josie.

She held up her hand. "I burned myself."

"It's okay, Trout," he told the dog, who immediately went quiet. But he kept careful watch on Josie, his brown eyes capturing her every move and the points of his ears standing at attention. "Let me see."

Josie let Noah take her hand in his large palm. The skin across her index and middle fingers was hot pink. "It feels like they're on fire," she said through gritted teeth.

He led her back to the sink and turned on the cold water. The pot she'd dropped just seconds ago sizzled under its spray, releasing another cloud of steam. "Be careful," she said. "That's how I just did this."

He let the cold water run, holding her hand gently. "The boiling water splashed across your hand?"

"No. The steam. I was trying to empty the water out of the pot so I could mash the potatoes. I used the lid to try to keep the potatoes in while letting the water out, and I guess I wasn't holding it right? The steam... it just..." She let out a stream of expletives.

Noah guided her hand under the cold water. Immediately the unbearable sting abated. "Keep it there. At least twenty minutes."

"Twenty minutes?" Josie blurted.

She heard the slide of a drawer and the opening and closing of a cabinet and then Noah started fishing crumbling potatoes out of the sink with a spatula and depositing them into a bowl.

Josie sighed, keeping her fingers under the icy water. "I don't think we can salvage those."

Noah smiled at her. "Sure we can. The sink was clean. You didn't lose any skin in here. None that I can see, anyway."

She bumped her hip against his. He was trying to lighten the mood but the simple act of ruining what small part of dinner she had agreed to prepare and injuring herself in the process felt like a defeat for the ages. It had been two weeks since he shot Ryan Lee during their rescue of Mira and Rosie. Ryan had survived, barely, but Josie couldn't stop thinking about him, and for all of Noah's stoicism and equanimity, she knew he continued to replay the shooting in his head during the quiet moments of each day. Ryan survived, but he would spend the rest of his days in prison. Not that his upbringing excused April's murder or any of the other crimes he'd committed, but he'd never had a chance at a normal life.

Some cases hit harder than others and lingered long after they were solved.

The only good to come out of the entire thing was that Rebecca and Jon Lee had agreed to take in Rosie. While Josie wasn't crazy about Jon being one of her guardians, she trusted Rebecca to take good care of the girl. Rosie was lucky she'd have a live-in psychologist to help her wade through all the damage that had been done to her in her young life. Josie had visited Tranquil Trails just yesterday and found Rosie following Rebecca around, glowing with curiosity and her newfound freedom. She'd shown Josie her new room, new clothes, and told her all about the meals that Rebecca and Jon prepared for her in the short time she'd been with them. Then she'd prattled on about all the things that she was going to do in the future now that she lived with Rebecca and Jon.

"I'm so normal now," Rosie had told her giddily.

It made Josie happy and broke her heart all at the same time.

"Josie," Noah said. "What's going on?"

Her voice lowered. "God, Noah. I can't even handle a pot of boiling water. The only reason Trout didn't get hurt when I dropped it and it splashed everywhere was because he was over there and not under my feet where he usually is—"

Abandoning the potato rescue, Noah snaked a hand around the back of her neck and pulled her in for a hard kiss. Then he rested his forehead against hers. His free hand reached over and moved her fingers back under the falling water. "I was teasing you the other day," he whispered. "I've seen you handle things that would break most people. The pots will never win."

Josie laughed, long and hard, drawing her head back from his so she could look into his hazel eyes. It felt good to laugh after the days of digging through the wreckage Seth, Ryan, and Deirdre had left in their sizable wake. "The pots will never win?" she repeated.

A smile spread across his face. One of those heart-stoppers that he saved just for her. He let go of her neck and went back to salvaging the potatoes, adjusting her hand again so that her fingers remained under the icy spray. "They won't."

He dug around in the sink for what was left of the mushy

potatoes and then replaced her fingers under the spigot once more. "Only a few more minutes," he said.

Josie couldn't feel her hand at all. As promised, a few moments later, Noah gently moved it out of the stream. He wet a washcloth, squeezed the excess water from it, and wrapped it around Josie's fingers. Then he led her over to the kitchen table, pulling out a chair so she could sit.

Trout walked over to her, jumping up, his little paws pressing into her thigh. He sniffed at her lap and then nudged her elbow. She swore she could see worry in his brown eyes. With her good hand, she scratched behind his ears. "I'm fine, buddy. Really." The burn in her fingers was returning but the cool washcloth felt good.

"I thought you'd be happy that your parents were moving to Denton," said Noah.

"I am. I think. It's just that they're uprooting their entire lives for us and a baby we may never get."

"You're worried we'll disappoint them." It wasn't a question. "Josie, your dad told me years ago that they couldn't wait until they were able to retire so they could move here to be closer to you."

A wave of warmth washed over her. "Really?"

"Yes. Josie, they missed the first thirty years of your life. They just want to spend more time with you. If we give them their first grandchild, they'll be thrilled—and we'll be lucky to have more babysitters—but you could never disappoint them."

She looked down at Trout. He was still watching her intently. "I don't know about that. They haven't eaten my cooking yet."

Noah laughed as he unwrapped her hand, gazing at her fingers. The skin was an angry red. "No blisters," he said. "I think this is going to hurt like a bitch for a day or two, but you should be fine."

"Everything hurts like a bitch." She could still feel the

aches, pains, and bruises that lingered everywhere from the Seth Lee case, her ankle most of all. She leaned forward and kissed Noah softly. "But thank you."

"Always," he whispered.

She glanced at the abandoned bowl of boiled potatoes. "Should we just order out?"

Noah squeezed her knee. "No. We'll try again."

A LETTER FROM LISA

Thank you so much for choosing to read *Her Dying Secret*. If you enjoyed the book and want to keep up to date with all my latest releases, just sign up at the following link. Your email address will never be shared, and you can unsubscribe at any time.

www.bookouture.com/lisa-regan

This is the twentieth book in the Detective Josie Quinn series, and I can hardly believe it! It has been an incredible journey from the first book, *Vanishing Girls*, in which we met an angry, abrasive, bitter Josie who solved her problems with Wild Turkey, to the Josie you've just read about in this very book, who is a very different woman. It's been my pleasure and privilege to bring readers these stories and to watch Josie grow and change as a character. I am grateful to every single reader and reviewer who has given Josie a try, no matter where you joined her along her journey.

Speaking of journeys, Josie and Noah have started their quest to become parents. I did a great deal of research into the topic of adoption for this book. I learned so much, and have gained an even more profound respect for all the parties involved in the process including birth parents, adoptive families and the people who staff the agencies that bridge the two. My hope was to portray the process as accurately as possible. Any mistakes or inaccuracies in this portrayal are my own.

Please also note that in this book, two of the three towns mentioned in Bucks County—Hillcrest and Riddick—are fake. I made them up. They don't exist.

Again, thank you so much for reading. Watching this series grow and reach so many new fans has been immensely gratifying. I love hearing from readers, new and old. You can get in touch with me through my website or any of the social media outlets below, as well as my Goodreads page. Also, I'd really appreciate it if you'd leave a review and recommend *Her Dying Secret*, or perhaps other books in the series, to other readers. Reviews and word-of-mouth recommendations continue to be a huge factor in helping readers discover my books for the first time. Thank you so much for your loyalty and passion for this series. Josie and I remain ever grateful, and we hope to see you next time!

Thanks,

Lisa Regan

www.lisaregan.com

f facebook.com/LisaReganCrimeAuthor
X x.com/LisalRegan

ACKNOWLEDGMENTS

Amazing readers: We have reached such an extraordinary milestone together! Book 20 in this series! There aren't enough words in existence to express how grateful I am to each and every one of you! You are the very best readers in all of the world! Thank you so much for your steadfast loyalty to this series. Your commitment to Josie and her team humbles me. Your unending and relentless enthusiasm makes writing this series one of the greatest joys of my life. You are all so engaged. I love hearing all of your thoughts and I appreciate all of your messages, comments, emails, and DMs. Thank you to the members of my Reader Lounge. You continue to maintain an online space filled with kindness, good humor, encouragement, and respect all while celebrating your love of reading and all things Josie. I treasure that.

Thank you, as always, to my husband, Fred, for being there for absolutely anything I need. Sometimes it is help with research or plotting or coming up with devious clues (the spoon in the napkin was all him). Sometimes it's words of encouragement and support. Sometimes it's as simple as reminding me to sleep and making sure I eat! It's all part of making sure I feel as though I can write the best book possible. Thank you to my daughter, Morgan, for the brilliant idea to use a child's drawing as a clue. Thank you for giving up so much time with me and also being so incredibly supportive and always knowing exactly what to say to make me laugh and de-stress! You're perfect. Never change.

Thank you to my absolutely fabulous assistant, friend and first reader, Maureen Downey, for keeping so many plates spinning while I do what I need to do. You are a rock star and a superhero and I love you. Thank you to my first readers and friends: Katie Mettner, Dana Mason, Nancy S. Thompson, and Torese Hummel. Your insights are always vital to making the book shine! Thank you to Matty Dalrymple and Jane Kelly for being my plot first responders! I think our brainstorms could solve any plot problem!

Thank you to my grandmothers: Helen Conlen and Marilyn House; my parents: Donna House, Joyce Regan, the late Billy Regan, Rusty House, and Julie House; my brothers and sisters-in-law: Sean and Cassie House, Kevin and Christine Brock and Andy Brock; as well as my lovely sisters: Ava McKittrick and Melissia McKittrick. Thank you as well to all of the usual suspects for spreading the word—Debbie Tralies, Jean and Dennis Regan, Tracy Dauphin, Claire Pacell, Jeanne Cassidy, Susan Sole, the Regans, the Conlens, the Houses, the McDowells, the Kays, the Funks, the Bowmans, and the Bottingers! I am so thankful to all the incredible bloggers and reviewers who follow this series and take the time to read and review each and every book. I'm also very thankful to the bloggers and reviewers who have picked up this book as their first Josie Quinn story. Thank you for giving her a chance!

Thank you, as always, to Lt. Jason Jay for all your help and for answering each and every one of my questions, and my goodness, there were many! I can't thank you enough for your patience and for walking me through so many scenarios again and again with variations. You are the best. Thank you to Stephanie Kelley, my phenomenal law enforcement consultant, for all your help and for entertaining so many of my crazy questions and scenarios. Thank you to Michelle Mordan and Kevin Brock for answering my EMT questions! Thank you to Denene Lofland for all your help with blood typing and DNA analysis!

Thank you to Megan Rodriguez, Alicia Jay, and Melissia McKittrick for answering so many of my questions about policies and procedures when it comes to schools as well as educational law. Thank you to Meghann Chiappa and Alyssa Cole for your kindness, generosity, and patience in taking the time to answer so many of my questions about adoption. I truly appreciate it. Thank you as well to my cousin, Chris McAllister, for helping facilitate some of my research!

Thank you to Jessie Botterill (we're BACK, baby!) for your absolute brilliance in helping me to find the heart of this book and for getting me through all the intricacies to make everything work. Thank you for getting me so much extra time to make this the best book that I could! You are amazing and I adore you. Finally, thank you to Noelle Holten, Kim Nash, Liz Hatherell, and proofreader Jenny Page, as well as the entire team at Bookouture.

PUBLISHING TEAM

Turning a manuscript into a book requires the efforts of many people. The publishing team at Bookouture would like to acknowledge everyone who contributed to this publication.

Audio
Alba Proko
Sinead O'Connor
Melissa Tran

Commercial
Lauren Morrissette
Hannah Richmond
Imogen Allport

Cover design
The Brewster Project

Data and analysis
Mark Alder
Mohamed Bussuri

Editorial
Jessie Botterill
Jen Shannon

Made in United States
North Haven, CT
29 May 2024

53034309R00211